THE DANDELION FARMER

Mathew McCall

DEDICATION

For my Mum
Elizabeth McCall

This story would never have been written
without the love and inspiration of
Nikki Jackson

With thanks also for the help and
encouragement of

Nick Lambert
James Richardson-Brown
Ian Furey-King

Cover photo by
Grace Jackson Photography

Cover design by
Nick Lambert

Special thanks

Sir John Sydeian and James Sydeian remain
the copyright of
James Richardson-Brown.

The Melancholy Ballad of the Clockwork
Soldier,"

with special permission from
Holly Marks.

Contact the Author;
Email; **Doktormatas@gmail.com**
Website; doktormatas.weebly.com
Facebook; Mathew McCall, Author.

Proem.

Dear Reader,

After some years, if not decades, of careful consideration, and, admittedly, no little amount of procrastination on my part, I have finally arrived at the decision to publish my father's and grandfather's journals, especially those dealing with the proceedings now often spoken of as the Flammarion Incident.

As some of my fellows from the academic community and those interested minds drawn from the wider municipal will already know, I have amassed over the last few decades, either first-hand facsimiles or originals, of all the known letters, testimonials, log entries, diaries and journals of the various individuals involved.

Consequently, it has been possible for me, with the meticulous assistance of my darling wife, Andromeda, to correlate the various documents into a cohesive chronological narrative.

The content of which, especially those portions drawn from documents still residing in private hands, have never been published before.

As I feel that more than enough historical time has passed, I have not endeavoured to modify or censure the opinions and views expressed by the authors of these documents.

I would like to assure all those interested that I have included as much of the original texts from the primary sources as possible, along with any secondary sources, as they may help the reader to appreciate the unique situations and circumstances that guided the actions of my relatives and their companions.

The worlds we live in today are greatly transformed from that time, not least by the repercussions of those events my father and grandfather initiated, unwittingly or not.

It is my sincere hope the details of the events laid down in their own words will indeed finally silence those detractors who have, for so long, doubted the veracity of their story and decried their legacy.

Although the collected documents, letters, reports, journals, testimonials, etc. run, in total, to over thirty-five thousand pages and thus could not all be presented in entirety, the editing of these documents has been carried out with great care so as not to give any misleading impressions of individuals or events.

Captain James F. Ransom. Rtd.

London.

"Well, I dreamed I saw the silver
Space ships flying
In the yellow haze of the sun,
There were children crying
And colours flying
All around the chosen ones.
All in a dream, all in a dream
The loading had begun.
They were flying Mother Nature's
Silver seed to a new home in the Sun."

AFTER THE GOLD RUSH.
NEIL YOUNG.

PART ONE

THE DANDELION FARMER

"In one respect at least the Martians are a happy people,
They have no lawyers."

A PRINCESS OF MARS

EDGAR RICE BURROUGHS

CHAPTER ONE

<u>THE VISITOR</u>

To

Mrs Eleanor A. Ransom.

Locksley Hall.

Machen,

Tharsis.

September 21st M.Y. 26

My dearest Nelly.

It was so wonderful to have spent some time with you and the children again. I so enjoy our time together and oh how I wish you could come back and join me on the farm. But I understand, I do, and your Papa is correct, until circumstances are more settled it is not truly safe. It is just that my heart does miss you all so.

I must admit I could not resist but opened the letters and gifts from the children on the journey. Please forgive me! But I could not help myself! The watch is wonderful and please tell Tabitha and James that I love their drawings. We have such talented children, Nelly my love.

The journey from Tharsis to Alba was interminable – as always! But my train journey from Alba to Tremorfa was greatly enlivened by my chance meeting with an American gentleman. No less than a real life "Yankee"!

Well, a "Texan" really, he says, but I am not sure exactly what the difference is. Such a splendid chap, he is, with a great dry wit, gravelly rasp and a luxurious horseshoe moustache. He arrived here just before the UDI to make his fortune prospecting! What he doesn't know about mining probably is not worth knowing.

I would so like for you and your Papa to meet him, a fascinating fellow! We talked and shared a few cigars all the journey to Tremorfa station. He has such great affection for this extraordinary acreage, but he has never truly gotten used to the "darn cold!" I explained I could truly not envisage living in a place where the sun was ever as hot as he talked about!

But the news gets better! He is travelling to Tremorfa to become our new Constable!

We will have the proper rule of law in the county at last! After almost 5 months! He says he is well experienced in these things and determined to make it safe for decent people to live here. We talked at length about the situation since the death of our last Constable– although I thought it improper to burden him with our particular difficulties – however, he seems to already be well versed in local goings on, so to speak.

I am so excited! And much cheered! I almost leapt off the train and danced merrily on the platform! My spirits are so lightened! I pray soon things will be settled enough for you and the children to return home!

The ride home took longer than expected because I just had to stop and watch the sunset. It was indescribably spectacular this evening. I know this can be a harsh place, Nelly my love, but... oh, the beauty of it! I forget sometimes that all we have to do is look up and see how lucky we are to live here.

I am sitting on the veranda writing this to you in the dying light of that wonderful sunset. The sky is an artist's palette of greens, yellows and blues! I hope you too saw it this evening.

Karl and the chaps send their regards! And everyone is asking about you – but I have been quite despicable since I told them I must finish this letter before I tell them all the news. Minnie is cooking something that smells wonderful for a late supper and she tells me she has been baking all day!

Well, that's all My Love. I am now home safe and sound, and voraciously hungry! And so, a good meal and off to bed, then tomorrow I will see what has occurred while I was away!

Love to the children and give my regards to your Papa.

Your loving husband Edwin.

PS! An exciting mystery! Karl has just informed me a couple of the chaps believe someone is living in the old pump house ruins on the East Field. They have tried to spot him, but he has been elusive. However, they are absolutely sure someone is squatting out there! We will take a ride out in the morning and see if we can flush the bounder!

Love Edwin

PPS! Oh! I forgot to say; the new constable's name is Captain Everheart, Lucius Everheart. A most excellent fellow.

E x

Mathew McCall

To
Mrs Eleanor A. Ransom.
Locksley Hall.
Machen,
Tharsis.
September 22nd. M.Y. 26
Dear Nelly.

A truly interesting day. I so wish you could be here and have seen it all for yourself.

I ate well last night and slept the sleep of the exhausted. This morning I was up at the crack of dawn, wide awake and ready to take on the day. It is so good to be home. I know you miss it every bit as much as I miss you being here.

And today I could have really benefited with your guiding hand and wise head! I am afraid I sort of bumbled into things as usual! You would have at least reproached me for being foolhardy but, no worries, all is well! And I have exciting news!

We dispensed with most of the day's business over breakfast this morning. Karl, as always, is an excellent Overseer — I believe he gets more and more competent every time I go away. He keeps this place running like the watch you bought me for my birthday! Tick-tock, tick-tock...

There's a little problem with blockages in the overflow to the inferior maceration block, but I think we cannot do much else but to regularly unblock it manually until I can get back into Tremorfa to order a new valve and filter. Cost, cost, cost...! I may be an engineer at heart, but that is going to need some heavyweight blacksmithing! I was going to look to see if I could knock up something just to take the pressure off the filter, for now. However, time ran away with me so I will have to do it tomorrow.

So just after elevenses, we were preparing to ride out to see if we could beard this fellow lurking out in the old East Field pump house. When three rough looking strangers, rode up to the house and rudely demanded to speak to me.

At first, I had no idea who they were, though, by the look of them, I quickly surmised they were more of Eleuthère Du Maurier's men. Two thuggish types led by a weaselly fellow in a bowler hat and the scraggliest beard, I have ever seen – looked a little like when Philippa's King Charles had a bad attack of mange that time, and with the same protuberant eyes to boot. Not a well-looking fellow at all.

Although they introduced themselves respectfully enough, they nevertheless had a sneering about them that belied everything they said. And they were quite heavily armed!

I was awfully glad that, being we were on our way out, we too were able to display a show of strength which I do not think they were expecting.

Well, the weaselly fellow in the bowler said he had a letter for me from Du Maurier and that, "If yous know wot's good for yous, Yous should read it." I forced myself not to correct his grammar, but I took great umbrage at his tone. I must admit I grew quite outraged at his impertinence and told him that I could guess full well the extent of what was in the letter; another mixture of empty threats and pathetic briberies. None of which will change my mind or stand up in court. I told him this is my land, it belongs to my family and it will remain so. It is not for sale now and never will be.

I also informed this weasel I had met the new Constable, and that he would not be the kind of fellow who would allow for this kind of badgering and harassment of homesteaders and agriculturalists to continue.

I told him to tell Du Maurier to go to the devil!

Karl and the chaps, however, using rather more assertive language, disarmed the three of them and sent them packing. I assured them I would hand over their weapons to the Constable next time I go into Tremorfa.

They were mightily put off, but (I hope you will not think ill of me for this) it was a pleasure to see their discomfort. Hopefully, they will take that to their master.

Once we were assured we had run them off it took us a little while, and a stiff drink, to calm our nerves. So much so that we did not get out to the old East Field pump house until late afternoon. In light of the morning's visitors, I left most of the chaps at the house and just took Karl and two of the field hands with me. I suppose we were all still a little unnerved and jittery.

The ride out to the ruin was pleasant as it was a lovely day. It was good to be back in the saddle and Trago seemed to be relieved to be out of the paddock. The spectacle of the carpeted fields of Russian dandelions, their bright yellow heads bobbing in the breeze, I always find wondrous. Bright yellow and verdant green fields lying in a patchwork across the rugged russet soil under the harsh turquoise sky. Only a hundred years ago who would have dreamed this would one day be real? I marvel at these things every day. That I, that you, and our children were born here. So far from that cradle of humanity.

Forgive me, Nelly, for I digress.

When we reached the ruined pump house I instigated a search. Karl showed me where he thought the squatter was sheltering. I readily agreed that indeed someone had been sleeping there on the dirt floor. We found a few items hidden away; a moth-eaten old blanket, a broken knife, a battered enamelled bowl and a small brown leather-bound notebook, a diary possibly but not in a language I recognised. Though, no doubt, your Papa would have easily identified its origins.

We remounted to do a sweep of the area. As Karl said; if we could not catch him, then at least we could put him off returning. I agreed but my heart was growing heavy after the sight of the poor wretch's few possessions. Was it not uncharitable to drive him off if he was doing no harm?

I spoke of my intention to leave the provisions we had brought for the ride and forget all about it. However, Karl was adamantly against it. First, you allow just one to live in a ruin, then there will be two, then three.... Where would it stop?

I had no choice but, with a heavy heart, to agree with him. Squatters and vagabonds are not such a problem outside of the cities, but if we encourage them... well, who knows! Life out here is difficult enough without adding such problems.

We left his little stash of possessions piled neatly outside the remains of the pump house door. In hopes that he would understand it was a polite notice to move on. Karl would not have been so polite if he had had his way! He wanted to leave something more overt as a warning. I refused to allow it as we do not know this wretch's story or what has brought him to such a low ebb he should be forced to find shelter in such a place. 'There but for the grace of God,' and all that. I suppose it is hard for Karl to understand. I felt it was enough to ask our unwelcome guest to politely move along rather than drive him away with harsh threats.

Once done, we struck out for home.

However, as we rode away, I could not help but think of the squatter starving out there, alone in that ruin. I could not do it. Although I knew Karl was right, I could not just ride away. I resolved to pop back to leave my trail rations with the pile of possessions. I know you will not think badly of me, for I could not just leave it like that. The poor wretch must be destitute. I dread what would you think of me if we found out he was indeed starving?

I left Karl with the others, I must admit because I feared he would again challenge my resolve, and trotted back the few hundred yards to the ruin.

I had just dismounted with Minnie's sandwiches in my hand when suddenly I was eye to eye with the fellow! He was standing in the doorway with a look of utter shock on his face. I would think it was easily mirrored by my own! We stood there transfixed in the moment eying each other cautiously.

He is a biggish chap, well proportioned, of olive skin and dark hair. Obviously, given to attending to himself properly under better circumstances, his chin was almost clean shaven and his clothes, however, battered and grimy now, were once of good quality. He even carries a pocket watch in his waistcoat! But his face, oh Nelly, I wish I could send you a picturegraph of his face.

He is a mass of savage scars, the likes of which I have never seen — save for that fellow, the old soldier, who used to beg near the park in Alba. The marks lend his face a brutal aspect, however, totally belied by his dark eyes. I have never seen eyes like them; in the same instant, those dark eyes are intelligent and desperate, as if full of some great sorrow, and yet unafraid.

We stood there for what seemed like an age. He, as still as a statue, and me as if my wits had escaped me.

Finally, nudged by Trago into awareness (he had sensed the opportunity to make a play for the sandwiches), I did the only thing I could think of and offered the poor fellow the food!

Well, I must say I was totally surprised when he reached out to take the packet, and thanked me for my kindness in a most courteous manner. He apologised for imposing on me by using the ruins for shelter without permission. I was stunned and a little shamed by my earlier assumptions. As your Papa so rightly says; one should never "assume" anything. He was cordial and polite and appeared even unfazed when Karl and the others returned to check on me.

And so we sat there on the tumbled down walls, chatting and sharing sandwiches. I, the landowner, and him my newly discovered tenant, like friendly acquaintances meeting on a park bench.

We introduced ourselves. His name is Adam Franklin. He assured me he would no longer impose upon my hospitality and would be gone as soon as he could pack up his possessions. I asked where he was going? He did not seem to have any definite ideas. So I suggested Tremorfa, as only just over a good day's walk from here, for a stout fellow like himself.

I asked him where he had come from, but he grew guarded, changing the subject by saying he had been on the roads for several weeks — something I could not quite accept as his appearance suggested only a short time living in this rough way. However, I chose not to challenge him on it.

Then, curiously, he asked about our farm and why we grow all the dandelions and sunflowers? I must say I was amused that someone who, obvious from talking to him, was more than passably educated, would not know or understand where the fuels that drive our engines, generators, in fact, our whole world, come from. I found myself explaining the whole process; maceration, distillation, biological mass, the lot. As I had that day for the children at your sister's school! He listened as intently and quizzically as any of them did that day. Though he asked many a pertinent and insightful question he seemed to truly not know!

In my enthusiasm to explain the processes and the applications, I walked him into the field and we found ourselves examining the plants. I uprooted one example to show the root system and handed it to him. It was then I suddenly noticed his right hand.

I suppose up to then he had managed to keep me on his left, away from his right side. Now suddenly I saw it. It was metal. A metal hand. Not just that, but the finest wrought one I have ever seen! Not like Karl, all old copper plate and brass, but a high-quality gunmetal if ever I saw it, perfect in form and articulation. I just stared open-mouthed. Adam simply said; "Accident. An accident, a long time ago."

I know it was presumptuous of me to ask him if I might see it closer, but, true to his gentlemanly demeanour, he showed me not only his hand but his whole forearm. The workmanship is marvellous and so realistic it would be easy enough to pass a real hand when gloved even in the finest material.

I chose not to press him anymore on the matter. Instead invited him to the house for dinner. I know you may think it rash, but this is a most singular fellow, and I did not feel in any way concerned at inviting him. I was also desperate to know more about him. Nonetheless, of course, Karl will make sure all things are proper.

I will sign off now and finish this later before bed so I can tell you all I learn from this Adam Franklin.

Ah, Nelly! My love. My guest tonight is a strange one indeed!

He chose to make his own way to the house and arrived a little before six this evening. I offered him the use of the facilities to bathe and shave and he readily accepted. My clothes, however, are far too small for him, so Minnie managed to sort out cleaner attire from the laundry room. Possibly some of Philip's old things, but that is her concern and not mine.

Spruced up, Mr Franklin looks the model of a gentleman, though a battle scarred one, and his manners are impeccable. We had an excellent meal, although he does not drink wine, preferring to take only water and tea.

I must admit I did question the chap extensively. Granting he is an excellent guest, obviously well-read and educated, he seems genuinely to have some major gaps in his knowledge. I wondered at first if he was simply playing me along, however, I began to wonder if he has undergone some trauma and lost some part of his memory.

In the later evening, over tea, he relaxed a little and confided in me something which confirmed my suspicions. He admits he really does not remember how he came to be wandering; he can remember wandering for quite a while but not from whence he came. He only knows his name because it is written - in English - on the cover of the little journal we discovered in the pump house. I asked him if he could read the language in it. He says he cannot, however, he could easily read a page from one of my engineering books. Nonetheless, and here is something very intriguing, he says he knows it is his own handwriting, though cannot name the language or read it!

His intact memories span in total no more than a few days, though he does tell me that there are bits and pieces of memories which flash by in his mind's eye. His dreams are full of strange images.

•

The poor chap is deeply perplexed. Not least about his own right arm.

Oh, Nelly! I shall try to describe it in detail, but you must meet him and see this marvelous contraption. This is not like the clanking old mechanics like Karl — God bless him — but something entirely new to my eyes.

I was wrong about it being just his hand and forearm, he graciously showed me that the whole right arm has been replaced and anchored to the shoulder. The metal is the finest quality burnished red brass and the workmanship is exquisite. The whole contraption is elegant and perfectly symmetrical with his real left arm. Not only is the articulation perfect, the dexterity is beyond any automaton I have ever seen. An android built of such would make Karl appear no more than a suit of animated knight's armour. However, he has no memory of it happening, nor of the scars on his face and body — the accident story was one he made up on the spot.

I think my fascination with it has helped him a little, as he, at first, seemed a little reviled at the whole thing.

I understood he was becoming quite apprehensive at my questioning so I decided to change the subject. We spent quite a while (in fact far too long a while now I look at the time!) talking about the farm and my notions for sun-powered installations.

Yet it was an offhand remark he made just as we were preparing to retire which truly struck me. We were on the veranda to watch the sunset. He had just finished his tea when he sighed and said; "I never knew places like this existed in England."

I was shocked, so shocked, in fact, I blurted out my reply without thinking, "Adam, dear chap. You are not in England! This is Tharsis. This is Mars."

He laughed nervously saying; "Of course." Still, I could tell by his eyes he truly had no idea.

Well, counting the hour and how taken aback he appeared to be I have lodged him in the annex for the night. (And yes, before you start worrying, I have set Karl to oversee security.)

Well, off to bed for me. In all a very exciting day! I hope this finds you and the children well.

All my love, your loving husband Edwin.

E x.

Journal of Adam Franklin.

Today I met Lewis E. Ransom, although he prefers to be called Edwin, a lean young man, with a somewhat diffident manner and an intermittent stammer. He farms this land, sardonically describing himself as a 'Dandelion Farmer.' He is hugely passionate about everything to do with those frightful wildflowers. Evidently here they make fuel out of them, apparently to power all manner of engines and apparatuses.

Instead of running me off his land he has invited me to his home for dinner. Should I go?

Mars?

Mr Ransom tells me this is Mars. Which is ridiculous. He seems deeply earnest, but nevertheless, I am loath to accept such a fantastical conceit.

However, the sky we regarded this evening looked like no Earthly firmament, beset as it is with strangely shaped pieces of what must be a long since shattered moon.

Ransom has treated me well, welcomed me into his home, clothed and fed me with unstinting generosity. However, throughout he questioned me with great intensity. He wants to know from where I come and who I am. Alas, I can only tell him the truth; I do not know.

Maybe the answer lies in this journal yet I can't bring myself to read the words. Though as I write I write in the same language. In fact, it is all in my handwriting. 64 pages of it. I told my new friend that I cannot read the words in this journal – I found it distasteful lying to him - but for some reason it frightens me to even think to read it. What memories do those pages hold?

Now I rest here in a warm, clean bed. There is a guarding watch which reminds me of something... what, I cannot remember. There's a fear in my heart at the thought of a guard upon my door. Also, it is the machine manservant; Karl. Ransom called it an "android", an automaton. If it is an "android" what am I? Half human, half....? Machine?

And as for my face. Before our meal this evening I took the opportunity to attend to my ablutions. After scrubbing myself for some time in a steaming bath, I set about to shave, though upon casually wiping the condensation from the bathroom mirror, I was startlingly confronted with my own face. Surely this could not have been for the first time, but my mind reeled as if it were so, such is my horrific physiognomy.

I resemble some Gothic monstrosity or some wretched casualty of some appalling war.

What has happened to me? Who am I? I feel like I have awakened after a dreadful nightmare to find myself entrapped in someone else's body.

I fear to sleep and yet I fear tomorrow too.

To
Mrs Eleanor A. Ransom,
Locksley Hall,
Machen,
Tharsis.
September 23rd. M.Y. 26
Dear Nelly,

Our guest took breakfast with me. He seems much rested and in a lighter mood this morning.

Minnie has cleaned and repaired his clothes and he appears much more relaxed.

I apologised to him for my boorish behaviour last night and resolved not to continue questioning him. I admit I feel a little ashamed at my directness, nevertheless together we put it down to the port and a little over excitement on my part.

This morning I had a number of duties to attend to as well as a disheartening amount of paperwork. I left our guest to his own devices after breakfast to attend upon my tasks.

When I went to find him for elevenses he was in Grandfather's library intently reading Beresford's History of the Martian Colonies. Over tea, it was his turn to question me with equal intensity. I must say he really does not seem to have any knowledge of where he is or how all this came about. I tried to make some sense of it all for him by filling in the gaps in Beresford's narrative as best as I could.

The poor chap though, has obviously lost all recollection of his past, his professional calling and, by far the worst, his family.

Nelly, dearest, to lose the memories of one's loved ones would be beyond all endurance. If I lost you and the children I think it would be the death of me.

In some ways, however, explaining these things to Adam — he insists I use such familiarity — only encourages me to wonder at the miracle of it all. We talked about Babbage, Strange, Hamilton and the rest. The discovery of the Interloper's ship, the race for the Moon, the Martian Colonisation and the Wars of Independence. Of which he knows nothing!

If I didn't know better I would think he had just stepped off an Aethervolt Schooner from Earth.

We talked until luncheon, after which I used my duties as an excuse to provide Adam with a tour of our little fiefdom. He was most intrigued by the processes! He finds it incredulous that plant life should grow so vigorously in this apparently barren red regolith. I told him of the discoveries of the levels of topsoil fertility by the Arboriculturist Professor Driscoll.

Adam was even able to add a few useful observations as to the solution of our problem with the overflow to the inferior maceration block. He suggested rather than doubling up the existing filters we should insert two coarser graduated filters earlier on in the pipeline using a double breech system, much like a gun barrel, so we do not have to shut down the system simply to clear them. We may still have to replace the valve at some point, however, it will take the strain off the existing filters and the valve for now. Also, it will prolong the life of the replacements as well as being something we can cobble together here out of what we have, rather than buying in expensive parts.

It occurs to me we could rejig all the filters using breech access points throughout the whole maceration system? We talked and drew and theorised all afternoon. It would be costly, yet nevertheless easily offset against the number of days we lose to routine blockage removal. I will, of course, defer to your superior gift for accountancy, still, I roughly estimate we lose ten or eleven days a year on the Helianthus Diesel production alone which must run into a cost of hundreds if not thousands of guineas! If he had not had engineering training, then he certainly has a mind for it, he understands quite a bit about irrigation techniques as well. Even Karl was impressed!

Minnie seems quite taken with him too, she got out all mother's finest china in honour of his visit and served her splendid Martian Blue beef a la Russe. Which she knows is everyone's favourite.

Adam talked to me over dinner about his lack of memories – he says that he cannot account for it, but he feels the answer might lie in the journal he has. If only he could read it. He told me he is sure it is in his own hand. He fears something deep inside him is not allowing him to read those strange words. I asked him why. He replied, with no hint of mendacity, he feels such a strong foreboding it has stopped him from even trying – although he knows not why.

He also tells me he has strange dreams, not so much nightmares as simply bizarre. He was just about to illustrate what he meant when Karl burst into the drawing room to tell me there had been an incident.

Seeing the hour, I shall try to keep this brief; Michael, one of the new field workers (Joshua's youngest son) had been fishing near canal junction 5. He was walking back when someone shot at him! Luckily he has only a nasty gash across his right temple where he hit a rock as he dived for cover. He says whoever fired at him cracked off another two or three before making off on horseback. He thinks there were at least two horses.

I wanted to go out to search for the culprits, but Karl refused to allow me. Saying it was already too dark, also the blighters will be long gone by now. Or worse, it could be an ambush. Sometimes I both love and hate the pragmatism of Karl's worldview.

Instead, I went over to the field hand's bunkhouse to speak to Michael and Joshua. Who in Hell's name would take pot-shots at a young boy for fun? Or was it to frighten us all?

I fear I know who did this as well as why. Karl and the men are all of the same mind as well. Nevertheless, we have no proof. Du Maurier's thugs are too careful for that. Tonight I will sleep easier knowing you and the children are safe where you are.

Because of the turmoil the incident caused, I felt obliged to explain our situation to our guest. It is quite absurd when explained and reflected upon in simple terms. That a man as rich and powerful as Du Maurier would so desperately want our little piece of land that he would resort to such harassments, vandalism and outright intimidations.

Adam asked me what the motive for all this was. I had to be totally honest and say that other than greed fueled bloody-mindedness I know no other reasons. The man owns half the County. He is the largest producer of fuels in the whole region. Why he seems to need our tiny corner of it, I have no real idea.

I have resolved to go into Tremorfa tomorrow to speak to the new Constable. This intolerable harassment has to stop.

Ah, Nelly, the hour is late and I need to get some sleep.
All my love
Edwin.
E x

Journal of Adam Franklin.

Something strange is going on here, behind Mr Ransom's bonhomie, there seems to be something truly wrong. He tells me he has a wife and two children, but they live in the city of Tharsis with her father. I believe he moved them there for their safety. Though Ransom doesn't seem to understand what the level of menace truly is. This whole area has no constable, no one to keep the peace or enforce the law.

One of the young boys who work on his farm was shot at today. Ransom believes it was thugs working for Eleuthère Du Maurier, a rival landowner. Evidently, this Du Maurier has been using all sorts of tactics to drive Ransom and some others to sell their land to him. Ransom talks of "harassments" but the incident today was no simple bedevilment, it was an unadorned attempt at murdering a young boy.

I want to help, I know I can, but something tells me I must not get too involved. I fear my involvement may only make the situation worse.

Ransom is going into the local town tomorrow to report the incident to the man he says is the new Constable. I shall go with him. Ransom paints a picture of a very much frontier town, where, no doubt, few men are questioned about the circumstances leading to their arrival in such a place. I shall enquire around for work and accommodation – Ransom has kindly offered me some money to pay for lodgings if I want it. Nevertheless, I am concerned about Ransom's safety, he is almost childlike in his trusting manner. Which I have already seen the benefit of.

Regardless whether I am to stay here or in town I shall find out more about these men Du Maurier uses to terrorise people, for some reason it offends me greatly that men should do this kind of bidding. I owe Ransom for his kindness and generosity.

I had a worse than usual nightmare last night. I awoke stifling a scream. I can remember only snippets of it – none of which makes sense; Ransom, I and the automaton, Karl, were lost in a desert. We were fighting off waves of strange creatures, hundreds of monstrous beasts. Then Karl was "killed." Ransom and I tried to bring him back to life with simple machine tools.... But inside his metal shell, he was flesh and blood and far too injured to save. Karl, who knew he was dying, cleaved on to me crying; "Save me, brother. Save me brother... we cannot die!"

I have decided to force myself to read the earlier pages of this journal.

To, Mr L. Edwin Ransom.
Ransom's Farm.
Tremorfa.
September 23rd. M.Y. 26.
Dear sweet husband,
It was so joyous to spend the time with you on your birthday. I so miss you. We all miss you.

The children are well. James has finally thrown off that horrid sniffle. Tabitha is missing you terribly and has been pining for you. We were all so pleased that you like your new watch, you know what I am like at these things so it was James who actually chose it from the jeweller's collection. Papa said it was an excellent choice. We are all desperate to know if you have yet discovered its secret. I shall say no more.

Edwin, I do so wish we could all be together. Papa wants you to know that his offer still stands if you are tired of this whole business, then come back to the city and work for him. He said again, only last evening, he would really value you back here working with him again. We could all be together. Oh Edwin, have you no idea how your visits lift all our spirits, even Papa's. As soon as we had said our goodbyes, he retreated again into his study to paw over those dusty old books and maps of his. Some days, neither I nor the children see him. Mrs Carstairs tells me that he has even taken to locking the door.

I was so pleased to hear your journey was not all dull. This Constable Everheart sounds a frightfully interesting gentleman. I believe Texas is the largest state in the Wild West! No doubt he has many wondrous and thrilling tales to tell, but do you really think he is up to the task ahead of him? I hope so! Tremorfa has been too long without a proper Constable.

Today Papa was more his old self. After the Meeting we took the children to the park. We went to view the new Dreadnought aerostat that Papa's friend has built for the Fleet. There was such pomp and celebration. I do so love a brass band and all the ceremony. Even President Bradbury was there.

The children were so excited! It is the largest dirigible I have ever seen! Papa's friend, Mr Henry Giffard, was so kind as to offer to give Papa, myself and James a guided tour of the gondola, after the ceremony. Though Tabitha and Nanny had to stay on the ground as Tabitha was too afraid to climb the rope steps. Poor Nanny, she missed such a treat, the views across the city were worth all our exertions!

Mr Giffard says without Papa's inspiration the ship would have never been built. I was so proud for Papa. I would have so loved for you to have seen that moment with us.

It is such a vast fearsome machine. Mr Giffard believes that with a fleet of only six of these monsters on duty, all Tharsis will sleep soundly and safely in our beds.

We were not allowed to see the engine rooms – I know you would have been so disappointed - but Mr Giffard kindly showed us the gun deck, James was fascinated by those newfangled recoilless Gruson steam-powered turret guns and rotation guns. Papa was so impressed. However, I must say, such talk was a little alarming; one prays that no day will come when we have to unleash such ordnance against anyone. Mr Giffard says two or three of these Dreadnaughts alone would have ended the War of Secession – still, no one likes to call it that –of colonial independence in but a few short weeks.

However, Mr Giffard is a charming and agreeable gentleman. He is rather passionate when talking about the past. I do believe he was quite a revolutionary in his day. He forbade me to say too much about the details of the ship, however, he says it is the fastest, most powerful, dirigible ever built. They are going to properly name her tomorrow, but I believe she is to be called "The Daedalus," after the ancient Greek engineer.

Mr Giffard invited Papa and I to dine with him and some of the other notables at his club this evening. I tried to decline because I did not feel comfortable, nor proper, without your accompaniment, but Papa insisted he should escort me for the evening.

I will be quite late, so I will write to tell you all about it tomorrow.

I miss you, darling husband, with all my heart.

Be careful.

All my love

Your Nelly.

PS. I have enclosed another of Tabitha's drawings, she says it is Capt. Horatio Pug, from the story you were telling her, in one of Papa's top hats! She drew it especially for you.

P.P.S Elder MacAulay sends his regards!

To

Mrs Eleanor A. Ransom.
Locksley Hall.
Machen,
Tharsis.
September 24rd. M.Y. 26
Dearest Nelly.

Another eventful day! It has been a most exciting tumultuous day, but rest assured that, though shaken by the day's events, we are all safe and well. Though my hands are still a little shaky even now.

Firstly, though; your letter came quite early this morning — at least this new postal rider system works well. I was thrilled to read about your adventure! I would have so liked to have seen Mr Giffard's aerostat, it sounds everything your Papa said it would be. What a wonder! I would have so liked to have met Mr Giffard and to have had a peek at those engines!

I hope you enjoyed the dinner and were able to attend the naming ceremony, you must tell me all about it — spare no detail.

Give my thanks to Tabitha for the drawing, I shall treasure it! I have already pinned it up in my study. She has a true talent for art. Dare I say I shall have to work harder on the tales of the intrepid Capt. Pug?

This morning we arose early, as I had resolved to travel into Tremorfa to report to the Constable's office the attack upon Michael and the threatening manner of those three ruffians Du Maurier sent the day before yesterday.

Minnie saw us off with a hearty breakfast so we were soon on our way. We loaded the waggon with the weapons confiscated from Du Maurier's thugs and set off. Adam and I rode while Karl drove the waggon with Michael. I left the rest of the men with explicit instructions to concern themselves only with keeping the house and buildings safe.

It was a pleasant morning, the journey itself was uneventful so we made good time. Adam and I talked most of the way. He questioned me quite pointedly about the situation regarding Eleuthère du Maurier's claims upon our land.

I explained Du Maurier has been trying to buy out or ruin every independent fuel producer in the county for the last few years. Adam was at a loss to understand the motivation of such a man. I tried to assure him that it is simple greed, a hunger for power, but Adam honestly seems not to understand how such a man can be so driven by the craving for money. I tried not to illustrate what has been taking place too graphically, but Karl was not reticent in filling in the pieces that I so deliberately tried to leave out so as not to unduly alarm Adam. I do not wish for him to think of us as merely nothing but a collection of ruffians and uncouth rubes, trapped in some backwater, fighting it out over scraps of land.

Adam has a strong sense of decency and was very strident in his condemnation of Du Maurier. I might even go so far as to say he expressed great outrage.

By the time we reached the Toll Station the dust had blown up a little. Behind our filter masks, we had fallen into quiet introspection. I think that is why we immediately noticed something was wrong. The gate was down, but there was no sign of the Toll House Master or a

Collector on duty. If we had not had the waggon we could have simply circled around and been on our way.

I must admit I did not think much of it at the time, but Karl, ever the cautious one, insisted we stop immediately and go no further until we knew what was afoot.

Karl told us to wait where we were, taking his scattergun, he began to approach the toll gate. Adam, without a word of warning, reached over, drew my father's pistol from my belt and dismounted to follow Karl. They were just a few feet away from the gate when all Hell broke loose!

Please, Nelly, be sitting down at this news.

Three thugs, the same ones that came to the house yesterday in the employ of Du Maurier, suddenly burst forth from the Toll House firing wildly at Karl and Adam! I have no doubt they meant to kill them on the spot, leaving them free to do away with Michael and I.

I must admit, Nelly, as you know I am not a man of violence, I was quite useless. I panicked, the goggles of my filter apparatus steamed up and I had one of my coughing fits. It was all I could do to jump off Trago, grab Michael and hide behind the waggon like a coward. Michael had more sense than I, he had seized two of the confiscated rifles we had with us, but in my terror I could only fumble aimlessly with them.

There was a brutal exchange of gunfire, the likes of which I have never heard before. Karl was hit twice, but nothing severe. Adam received a nasty abrasion across his chest from a bullet. Regrettably, or not, Du Maurier's men were not so fortunate. Karl wounded one immediately and knocked the other's legs from under him with his second blast. Adam moving with incredible speed, dodged the hail of shots from the hand-cranked pom-pom gun of the bowler hat wearing thug, and shot him dead.

I do not wish to dwell upon it, but I have never seen such a display of marksmanship since the day we went to see that chap at the theatre in Alba.

As soon as the shooting stopped I left Michael behind the waggon to join Adam and Karl. I was about to enquire if they were injured when another of Du Maurier's thugs appeared in the Toll House doorway. He took a shot at me with a ray pistol! Fortunately, Adam saved my life by pushing me to the ground before firing back. At that point I did not know, but, although he had been caught by the blast, Adam killed that thug too!

The bullets had hardly dented Karl's chest plate under his coat. The ray had burnt more of Adam's waistcoat than it had of him and he seemed not concerned with the injury at all. I have never known a man so calm under such extreme circumstances.

We decided we had to establish what had happened to the staff of the Toll House. On searching the building and the outhouses, we found, in the stables, the Toll Master's body and that of his young son whom he was training up. We thought them both dead at first but upon checking, we discovered the boy was badly beaten, but thank God, still alive.

We took the boy back into the Toll House, where we tried to decide how to go about summoning help. I suggested I go on into Tremorfa to summon help rather than put the boy and the wounded thugs through an arduous journey.

That's when Adam surprised me again. He said that he believed he knew how to use the telephonograph equipment in the office to summon the Constable and a doctor. If the thugs had not cut the wires. As luck would have it, indeed they had not.

By the time Constable Everheart, along with the doctor in addition to several of the town's men, arrived, the Toll Master's son, Davey, was recovered enough to tell some of what had happened to him and his father at the hands of those murderers. Regardless of the protestations of innocence of the two surviving killers they were given short shrift by the Constable who told them, in no uncertain terms, they would hang for this.

I must admit, Nelly, I found myself standing in the midst of this bloody slaughter utterly inconsolable. Was this all my fault? Has my stubbornness led such a ruthless man as Du Maurier to this? Three men lay at my feet dead, an innocent man just doing his job, along with two evidently notorious criminals. A young boy, beaten almost to a pulp and now fatherless. My new friend wounded and my young employee terrified. Why? Because of one man's self-indulgence as much as the other's obdurate stupidity. Which of them, I am, I do not rightly know.

We accompanied the Constable into Tremorfa so as to give our witness statements as well as for me to make my complaint about the incidences of the previous few days. Which I must say seemed of little consequence in light of today's tragedy. Constable Everheart questioned me vigorously on the details and history of all our previous altercations with Du Maurier's minions. He questioned all of us, even Karl, as to what exactly happened at the Toll Station.

When we had finished, Constable Everheart confided in me that the Toll Master's son had given a statement that supported our version of the events. The murderers had arrived only a short time before we did. They attacked the Toll Master and his son, beat them and threw them into the stables. Dr York says the Toll Master died of his injuries from the savage beating.

The Constable has endeavoured to question the two surviving thugs, but they appear to have neither the wits nor the intelligence to be trusted with anything other than the simplest orders. They claim the rat-faced chap in the bowler hat, one Samuel Teece, hired them in Alba, but he gave them no information pertaining to whom he worked. I think the Constable's method of questioning – nevertheless a little forceful – was thorough enough to establish what they assert was, in fact, true.

Constable Everheart says he has no doubt they were in the pay of another and preparing to ambush us. Though he cannot prove it. Fortunately for us, but unfortunately for evidence sake, they had no time to truly organise themselves. And o it appears, to all intents and purposes, that we simply came upon a group of freelance robbers in the act. Thus the ensuing violence was unpremeditated!

Instead, he had to warn me of city ordinances regarding the arming of an automaton! I know it appears insane, and he was apologetic, but I suppose it is the price to pay for the rule of Law being re-established. He said he would not take me to task for this, but Karl must not carry a weapon outside the confines of our property.

He also questioned me comprehensively about Adam Franklin. I cautioned myself to adhere only to what I know as facts; what he had done in the heat of the moment he had done so courageously. We all stand witness to his bravery.

This evening the four of us have retired to a fairly pleasant guest house in town; Mrs Phillipott's - I believe it was the one that your sister stayed in when she visited a couple of years back. Where we are being treated with great courtesy and not a little celebrity! A reporter from the local newspaper has already presented himself at the door! Twice! However, we were counselled by Constable Everheart not to speak to such persons at least until his investigations are concluded.

It does appear, however, this Teece was a brigand of quite some notoriety with a sizable reward upon his head!

So, dear Nelly, as we settle in for the evening I will not be sorry to never see a day like this again! Fear not, we are completely safe. The Constable has placed an Officer on duty outside the guest house for our peace of mind.

Kiss the children for me!

Your loving husband Edwin.

E x

TREMORFA STATION. 08.17/24/09/0026

TEECE DEAD – (stop) - OTHERS DEAD + WOUNDED – (stop) - RANSOM ALIVE. - (Stop) – UNHARMED - (stop) - SITUATION UNDER CONTROL BUT PUBLIC - (stop) - VERY VOLATILE – (stop) - RANSOM HAS ASSISTANCE – (stop)-
WILL SEND COPY OF REPORT – (stop) -ADVISE RESTRAINT – (stop)-

E.

THARSIS BULGE TRANSMITTING STATION. 10.32/24/09/0026

NAKWAKEN – (stop)-
UTMOST CONFIDENCE - (stop)-

M.

Journal of Adam Franklin.

Today I killed two men. Although I am assured by Mr Ransom, and even by the Constable, that I did nothing immoral, yet I feel like a murderer. Why?

For the reason that it was so easy. They were impossibly slow, like marionettes in some children's puppet show (Why do I remember a puppet show?). I merely executed them – one shot each in their foreheads with as little effort as swatting a fly. They died instantly. I felt nothing. No panic or fear, no excitement or exhilaration. Nothing.

Who am I that I can kill so easily? I took Mr Ransom's gun from him without a thought as to whether I even knew how to use it, and use it I did, devoid of conscious cerebration.

Also, I was injured. I have a gash on my chest and another on my left shoulder, I was hardly aware of them. Now, regardless of the doctor's ministrations, I have discovered that they are most of the way to being healed. I am sure this is not normal.

Mr Ransom has explained to me who those men were. They were in the employ of a man called Du Maurier. This Du Maurier has designs upon the Ransom's family farm. He has broken several other farmers, driving them off their lands. Now he has got what he wanted, a bloodbath, but not the result he would have hoped for. I wonder if this will stop him.

The Constable questioned me at length as to my part and as to who I am. I could not help him, but made up something I reasoned would sound plausible enough; I was a friend of the family visiting from Tharsis (I believe that is the city where Ransom's wife is staying). I used to be a soldier. I was invalided out after the battle of Arabia Ponds (As luck would have it Ransom had told me this morning about his uncle who died in that battle – against whom? I have no idea). It appears to have been acceptable, as the Constable immediately changed the subject.

I have done as Ransom suggested keeping my right hand gloved at all times to avoid additional questions or piquing people's curiosity. Still, I have raised a few eyebrows of suspicion at the dinner table of this guest house Ransom has billeted us in. Even the automaton, Karl, is with us. Ransom indulges it, seeking its counsel as if it was a valued old human companion. I find this both strange and in some way charming – I have no idea why. I have not seen any other of these "androids" since we reached Tremorfa. Yet no one seems surprised to see this bronze machine man wearing clothes and a Stetson freely walking amongst them.

Here they have gas lights in the houses, there is a railway station, telephonograph lines and there are engine powered carriages in the streets – nevertheless, the horses outnumber them considerably. Ransom says those horseless carriages are powered by his crops, his and tens of thousands of other agronomists like him across the planet.

Tonight the lady who owns the guest house played music for us on a machine she called a "gramophone" while she and her daughter sang in accompaniment. Earnest though it was, my nerves were thankful when their caterwauling ceased.

I have not read any of the previous pages as yet. I tried for a few moments before I began this entry, but I have such a sense of foreboding that I cannot bring myself to do it.

To, Mr L. Edwin Ransom.
Ransom's Farm.
Tremorfa.
September 24rd. M.Y. 26.
Dearest Husband.

I received your letter this morning. Oh, my dear, you must be so careful of those men Du Maurier sends! He is a frightful, vulgar little man, and I believe totally ruthless! Please, Edwin, be careful. Promise me you will keep Karl with you at all times and not take risks.

It does not please me to tell you this, but I encountered Mr Du Maurier yesterday at Mr Giffard's dinner party.

It was a large reception in the library of Mr Giffard's club – The Phileas Society – there were so many important people there that I can only remember a few; Mr Giffard's lovely wife, Mildred, Colonel Carter Jahns (the Hero of the siege of Hellas), Dr Spender the famous archaeologist, as well as the explorer Mr Fontenelli and his Aresian wife (I have never actually met a real Aresian before – her skin is almost the same sandy red as the soil!) Some of the guests were quite outraged that Mr Fontenelli had brought her with him but she was most civilised, educated and spoke excellent English! I heard it rumoured she was once a Princess of her people! To me, she seemed most enchanting. The President of the Republic, Mr Bradbury, and his wife were the guests of honour, but Papa and I were treated almost as well.

Oh, Edwin, Papa is so highly regarded! The President himself shook his hand, thanking him especially for his work on the Damocles project – it seems Papa was involved far more than he is allowed to say.

The Dean of Tharsis University, Professor Lambertini, spoke at length with him about going back to teach at the School of Martian Sciences. Oh, how I wish he would, it would get him out of his dusty old study and back into the academic world he so loves. Now that Mother has been gone for over a year it is high time he started living again. I know that's what she would want. But while Papa was busy talking to the Professor during the welcoming drinks I decided to be so bold as to try to speak to Mr Fontenelli's wife, or at least get close enough to listen to her speak, when suddenly I was accosted!

My elbow was seized by a vile little man with a van Dyke beard, wearing ridiculous spectacles, who reeked of garlic and Macassar oil. Far too close for decency's sake and with his greasy face gleaming up at me, he said (and I shall write it down exactly as he did say it); "I am Du Maurier. Your husband should know I will not give up. Up to now, I have been patient, I have offered a reasonable settlement. If you value his life over that piece of land, then I suggest you tell him to take it."

At which point Colonel Jahns stepped in, a true gentleman, to ask if this man was bothering me? I thanked the Colonel for his concern, but Du Maurier vanished as suddenly as he appeared.

Edwin, Du Maurier is a truly horrid man. I could see it in his beady little eyes, there was such intensity, more dangerous than simple threats. I believe he means to do you, to do us, terrible harm if he does not get his way. This separation is dreadful enough, but, if something should happen to you, what would I and the children do? I could not go on living without you. Please, please believe me, I know your father's vision means so much to you, but is it worth all this distress? With the money he is offering we could return to Tharsis to start again, even build a house of our own. You know Papa would love you to work with him again and there are now so many wonderful opportunities.

But I shall not pester you about this anymore, I have said my piece enough for you to understand my feelings. I am your wife, I trust in you to make the right decision for all of our benefit.

Your loving wife

The meal was pleasant, but I would have exchanged it for a good plate of dear Minnie's Blue Beef any day! I sat between Papa and Mrs Giffard. Mr Giffard is a witty speaker, very enlightening, he mentioned Papa several times in his address to the whole room. Papa was asked to stand to receive an ovation! The President spoke at some lengths, though not as entertaining as Mr Giffard, about the triumph of Tharsis over our rivals and how the Damocles Project, Daedalus along with its sister ships, will ensure our freedom to face the future untroubled by outside threats. The President even mentioned Papa! It would seem that Papa had a major hand in the design of something important to all these new aerostat dreadnaughts.

I would have so liked to have stayed for the whole evening, but I felt it was not seemly. Papa seemed restless, so we took our carriage quite early to return home. Colonel Jahns fearing I might still be distressed by Du Maurier's behaviour, insisted on sending four of the younger Officers to escort us home.

This morning after breakfast Papa, the children and I went to the official naming of the Daedalus. Which was a grand affair. The President's wife and grandchildren christened the ship with champagne. James so loved seeing all the soldiers in their finest uniforms. I was thrilled to meet Colonel Jahns again, who is such a gallant man. There were several Ambassadors from the other Republics – even Ausonul – but no one from Utopia, nonetheless Colonel Jahns and Mr Giffard both agreed that Utopia's eyes would be watching. (I think they meant; spies in the crowd.)

It was astounding to see such a titanic armoured leviathan, its belly sheathed in flashes of lightning, rise majestically into the sky above our great city! Oh, Edwin how I wish you had seen it. What a wonder! Both awe-inspiring and terrifying at the same time. If there were Thylian or Utopian spies in the crowds, then their hearts must have sunk to the very ground beneath their feet. Even more so when President Bradbury announced two more dreadnaughts would be ready for service within the month, and by the end of the year, all six would be ready for any eventuality. Men and boys threw their hats into the air. We all cheered and shouted, "God Save the Republic!"

Papa had been asked to attend a meeting with the President. He seems so happy today, much like his old self, so off he went clutching a huge bundle of papers from his study. I do hope it is more of this nature of work because – whatever it is he has done for the Government – it seems to have brought him out of his reverie. While Papa was at his meeting, the children and I took tea in that lovely little Corner House overlooking the park. With Mrs Giffard, Mrs Jahns also Miss Spender, the daughter of the great archaeologist Octavius Spender, who is a delightful young lady, so charming and well-read, though utterly unconventional. She regaled us with some truly outlandish stories of her father's exploits out beyond the Red Seas. She wears men's breeches and constantly smokes horrid little cigarillos without a holder! She even claims she can even race one of those Aresian sandflyers single-handed! I am not sure I should believe a word of it, but she is so amusing.

My dear Husband, please take all precautions to keep safe. Keep Karl close.
The children send their love.
Your loving wife,
Nelly.

PS. I will be fascinated to hear more of this Mr Franklin. How could he not know where he is? Very peculiar. I wonder if he has suffered a fugue or a blow to the head. Such things – I am told – can bring on an amnesia in which one can forget even one's own name. But an automated arm, how extraordinary, perhaps he once was a soldier.
You have always been a fine judge of character but please be careful as Mr Franklin does sound a little bit of an unknown quantity – even to himself.
All my love.
N.
PPS. Papa has just told me that we are having a small dinner party here tomorrow night for selected guests – whoever they may be! He seems so chirpy. I wish you could be here!
N.

*"First thing every morning before you arise
say out loud, 'I believe,' three times."*

OVID

CHAPTER TWO

<u>SOLO NOBLE</u>

*The Diary of Dr James Athanasius Flammarion.
24th Sept. 26th.*

At last today I had my chance to present my findings to the Cabinet. Although they gave me little notice to prepare. They made me have to spell out every point as if I were talking to my grandchildren. All this backslapping bonhomie is for show, but at least because of my bivariating dynamic pyromagnetic displacement apparatus finally making powering their damnable new war machines possible (Forgive me, dear God, forgive me.). But, as I hoped, they felt obliged to give me a hearing. Probably more to humour me than to seriously consider the evidence, but even so that old curmudgeon, Bradbury, finally had to concede that I am right; Muhe Ca is not "folklore." It must be out there.

At least Johns supported my contentions. I swear he knows more than he will say. They will not contribute a red penny, but at least they will not hinder me.

I have decided that tomorrow I shall invite a few trusted friends for dinner. I shall put it to them. In fact, I shall invite Fontenelli and his wife so I can put my questions to her directly.

I suspect things that are even too incredible to place into words on these pages, for fear I may read them myself at some later date and think myself truly insane.

To

Mrs Eleanor A. Ransom.

Locksley Hall.

Machen,

Tharsis.

September 25rd. M.Y. 26.

Dearest Nelly.

Again, what a day! I missed reading your letter this morning as no doubt it went to the farm. I pray all things are well with you, the children and your Papa.

I hope you enjoyed the reception soirée, was there anyone of interest? Did you get to see the naming ceremony?

I am afraid events here are not so fine. We were visited early this morning by Constable Everheart. He informed us that a person has come forward to claim they were an 'independent witness' to yesterday's events at the Toll House. Unfortunately, rather than corroborating our version of events this individual has described a completely different sequence! In fact, this 'witness' asserts that Adam and I caught the brigands unaware and all but murdered them in cold blood!

I strenuously protested, but the Constable explained that, even though he does not personally believe this new witness' statement makes any sense, and though the Toll Master's son's statement supports ours, he must follow the Rule of Law in this case. Until the situation is clarified, he has placed both Adam and myself under house arrest. We cannot leave the precincts of the guest house. He has even placed an armed guard at the front door. Karl is also to remain in the guest house with us, only Michael can freely come and go.

Everheart was quite firm; we should not speak to anyone about the events and that we should seek legal advice. I did not see the point as this man's statement is obviously a tissue of lies, but Karl and Adam insisted I engage the services of a solicitor.

Everheart had suggested a chap named Docket, of whom I've never heard, but, as I know of no other in Tremorfa, I sent Michael to fetch Mr Docket as soon as Everheart left.

Eubulus P. Docket arrived in an open-sided steam driven Buckboard Flyer (not one of those air flyers) in the early afternoon. A small, thin man in an overly large fur coat and a pre-war filter mask which covered his entire head like some sort of medieval helmet. Divested of his outer apparel, he wore an expensive colonial style suit and, though bald, sported the most outlandish ginger Dundreary cheek curtains I have ever seen. He was quite a personable fellow; he took tea with us and discussed the weather and county cricket – while we were in such difficulties yesterday Tremorfa County roundly defeated Alba on the last day of the test match. We all would have so loved to have seen that! We talked about the news from Tharsis city. He mentioned the new aerostat Dreadnoughts. I told him some of what you wrote about your visit and he was most impressed.

Finally, at Adam's insistence, we got down to the business of his visit. I, with Adam and Karl's interjections, explained the whole unfortunate incident. Docket listened, carefully making occasional entries in his little notebook. When we had finished, he asked a few questions, mostly about Adam and Karl.

His advice to us was that we must remain under house arrest until the Constable has completed his investigations to determine the veracity of this new witness. Any attempt to leave would exasperate the circumstances and would not look at all favourable to our situation. Such actions could force the Constable to formally arrest us. Docket explained, though we all held to the same sequence of events and maintain there was no other witness, there was no other truly independent witness to refute this man's claims. Not even the Toll Master's son. Only a proper investigation by the Constable will verify whether the witness was indeed at the Toll Station. If so, it would be up to a Court of Law to decide whether the witness' statement was believable or not.

Of course, the man is flat out lying, so the Constable is certain to see through such deception quickly enough, but proving a negative is often a time-consuming activity — especially in legal terms. Adam inquired how long such an investigation could take? Docket replied that he could not guarantee, but he has known these things to take weeks if not longer.

I took the news as stoically as I could, but I cannot be away from the farm for 'weeks.' If we are held here more than a few days I might as well give up and sell out to that cad Du Maurier. I impressed this upon Mr Docket. He promised he would inform the Constable that I have engaged his services to represent Adam and myself so as to pursue as speedier solution to this situation as possible. I asked him if he could request that our 'house arrest' be at least transferred to my home so I might be able to continue to supervise the work which needs doing. Docket suspected it would not be allowed, but he would request it.

Adam inquired about the law regarding Karl, as he is an android and thus a machine? Docket replied that automata are different. If said automaton was suspected in the commissioning of a capital crime, it would be treated as a murder weapon, thus would be impounded by the authorities and — if the prosecution led to conviction of the owner or the belief the automaton had gone 'rogue' — as he put it — then it would be crushed or dismantled and the miscellanies auctioned off piecemeal to help meet expenses! Docket's advice is that Karl stays here with us.

This was not good news, but Docket assured us this was only the worst of cases and, by far, the least likely of many possible outcomes. He believed us wholly and, 'through the grapevine' as he put it, believes most of the town's people and the Constable are sure of our innocence also. All we have to do is sit tight and wait a few days for this to be resolved.

He left us promising he would pay a visit to the Constable on his way back to his office to request further details of the charges and the nature of this house arrest.

After that, Docket went chugging off into the dusty late afternoon sun — there must have been a sandstorm out beyond the Mare Cimmerium, with both Phobos and Deimos riding high in the sky, it was a magnificent skyscape, but my heart was too low to truly appreciate it.

Over some tea, the three of us settled down to discuss the situation ourselves. Adam says he does not trust our new Constable — although I could not see why and he can only express his worries in terms of vague feelings. Karl suggested we allow Docket speak to the Constable and put forward my request. He is a reasonable man who intimated strongly that he does not believe this so-called new 'witness.' He surely will allow us to return home. I had no concerns about Constable Everheart's abilities, I understood he must follow correct procedure, so I found myself agreeing with Karl; it would be better to remain here and let Mr Docket represent our concerns to the Constable.

The landlady, Mrs Phillipott, was most accommodating and dinner was quite a feast. We were settling down to distract ourselves with a few hands of whist, when there came an urgent rapping on the front door.

Upon investigation, Karl discovered, curiously, our police sentry was no longer present outside the guest house. The journalist who had been trying to get to speak to me yesterday was now freely hammering, with evident urgency, upon the knocker. In light of the situation and the man's obvious fluster I bid Karl let him enter.

The chap proffered a card which carried the legend; "Freelance Journalist & Inquiry Agent." To my complete astonishment, dressed in men's attire, under a long duster with a fur hat pulled down almost over her eyes, it was, in fact, a robust young red headed woman by the name of Miss Charity Bryant-Drake.

She brusquely disdained taking tea with us preferring to plunge on into the matter of her intrusion. I suspected it would be about the unfortunate incident yesterday or our subsequent house arrest but, instead, she stated flatly that she had evidence Samuel Teece had been in the regular employ of a millionaire fuel industrialist called Eleuthère Du Maurier. Not wishing to give her too much information I told her if that be the case she should present the evidence to the Constable as such confirmation would go a long way towards pursuing a criminal case against Du Maurier. It was then that she asked me a question which chilled my bones. Was I aware the new Constable, Lucius Everheart, was, for several years, in the employ of Du Maurier as (what she termed) a "Gunman," an armed enforcer, on his extensive estates and plantations? Everheart had been charged, but never prosecuted, with the death of at least one 'Puddler,' who was trying to organise a strike amongst the refinery workers.

I sat in astounded muteness as Adam questioned her as to how she had gained this information. She said she has had an interest in Du Maurier for some time because of his other concerns. When he inquired what those 'other concerns' were was she would only say that Du Maurier was an extremely curious man, absolutely ruthless in his pursuit of whatever he desires. She claims evidence of other acts of violence, even murder, against those who obstruct his desires.

At that, she seemed to shudder, slump and requested that cup of tea we had offered. My impression of her changed almost as instantly; from a brusque, tough young woman to a rather – dare I say – vulnerable girl. With disconcerting earnestness, she fixed my gaze and told me with certainty there is no 'other witness.' Everheart had fabricated the whole thing.

I said we must inform our Solicitor immediately so as to put an end to this whole charade.

At that Miss Bryant-Drake produced several headed letters to various people from Eubulus P. Docket & Sons, Land Conveyancing Specialists, and informed me Docket was not a criminal case Solicitor. He has never even set foot in Tremorfa's Assizes, he is little more than a clerk. His specialty these days is 'representing' those who wish to sell out their holdings to Du Maurier.

Nelly, I fear we have been duped. Miss Bryant-Drake fears all our lives are in great danger.

When Adam argued it was nonsense to set out to murder men over a patch of weed-covered land. Miss Bryant-Drake said she did not believe it was simply over the land. In her opinion for him to go to such lengths, there must be more to it, much more.

I said I have no idea what she could mean? What, other than my plantation, could he desire enough to go to these extremes to obtain?

We sat for some time wracking our minds for some possible other motivation. Could it be the land itself, water or mineral rights? No. I had the land surveyed after my father's death, it is only really good for growing dandelions and sunflowers. Adam suggested maybe I was just 'in the way' of something, a new railway line or canal perhaps? But then again, unless there was planning for some major endeavour out beyond Tremorfa's boundaries, I have not heard of any such thing. I pointed out there was nothing beyond my land, but red dust and rocks. There is nothing special or different about the land

I own. Then could it be personal? Had I upset or crossed Du Maurier in some way as to create a personal grudge? No, most definitely not. I have never even met the man. Was it the processes I have been working on? No, Du Maurier's works are much more efficient and on a far larger industrialised scale. Was it my ideas for other uses for the by-products of the fuel processes? Or my concepts of harnessing the sun's power to create photovoltaic energy? I do not think so, I know of at least three other inventors working on similar concepts. What about my father, had he encountered Du Maurier? I do not believe so. I do have his journals and all his records. There is no mention of Du Maurier whatsoever. I was sure Karl would know if there had been some issue, as my father brought him just after the UDI. He had always worked with him closely by his side. Karl could only confirm there had never been any mention of a Du Maurier in all the time he knew my father.

Miss Bryant-Drake asked Karl if he had ever noticed anything at all unusual about the plantation land, anything at all?

He knew of only one thing that could remotely be thought of as a little odd. When he first came to our farm, my father was showing him the whole of the estate. Near the end of their patrol they came upon a patch of land on the edge of the west field boundary, a few yards from the hedges, there my father told Karl was an old water well that had become 'dangerously contaminated.' It had been filled in and sealed off. His orders were that it was never to be re-opened.

Contaminated with what? I asked. Karl assured us my father never visited the subject again. I admitted it was curious as no such thing was mentioned by the surveyors I employed. That, Karl explained, could be because he never took them out to there. They never asked so he did not see a reason to tell them about it.

On contemplation, the surveyors took lots of tests; soils, water and air, but never mentioned any indications of any kind of 'contamination' anywhere on my land. Surely a bore well 'dangerously contaminated' would have shown up on some test results at some point? I began to become concerned for our whole livelihood.

Adam asked how it had been sealed off. Karl said there was a large flat hexagonal stone over the whole thing, but now it has been buried by the winds as well as grown over.

At the mention of the stone, Miss Bryant-Drake became very excitable. She questioned Karl as to its appearance, its size, shape and whether it had any 'markings' on it. Karl was not able to elucidate further, only able to add that the stone was pale with a faint bluish tinge, as he only saw it from several yards away. I asked Miss Bryant-Drake what this was all about. She replied maybe that was indeed the thing Du Maurier is truly interested in. When I asked; why? She explained; Du Maurier is a strange man with numerous interests beyond simply making money. He is also a collector of various things; beautiful young women, fine art, corrupt civil servants, and, most interestingly, Aresian artefacts.

Naively, I asked; "So why would he be interested in an old well on my land?"

"It's not a well," said she and Adam in unison.

"Mr Ransom, it's a tomb, an Aresian Royal tomb." She continued, "And if the hexagonal capstone is still in place and undamaged, it might just be an undisturbed tomb. If so it could be incredibly important. Far more valuable than all your land and its production put together."

I asked how she could be so certain. She explained that her step-father is a xeno-anthropologist with a special interest in Aresian culture, he had once been approached by Du Maurier's people to help catalogue his collection.

"Did he?" I asked. No, she said tersely, her step-father considers such private 'collections' as little more than looting so he refused. Although it caused him a great deal of difficulties with the Museum authorities who were hoping to garner substantial endowments from Du Maurier. That, coupled with a malicious letter, did great harm to her step-father's career and the cause of Aresian anthropological study for years.

She seemed most upset so I apologised for my insensitivity. She told me that solely because her stepfather said no to him Du Maurier set out to not only ruin his career but destroy their whole family. There is much more to her story, but I would rather you weren't distressed by the information, suffice to say; she has made it her life's aim to learn everything there is to know about the wretched fellow. "He is a most ruthless man, capable of anything, including murder, to get want he wants."

We sat for a while whilst she regained her composure, then we discussed our situation. I feel we should return home and write directly to the Provincial Governor of

Tremorfa, to alert him of our situation. Adam and Karl insist we should leave for Alba straight away to place ourselves in the hands of Mr Bogdanov, the High Sheriff. At least we know we can trust him. Miss Bryant-Drake agrees it will be the best cause of action. But I am unsure of how to act.

I have standing in this community, responsibilities, I cannot go running off. And so I have resolved to speak directly to the Constable tomorrow. Constable Everheart seems such an upright chap, it is hard to believe he would be in cahoots with Du Maurier let alone murderous thugs. What I have heard tonight, however compelling, is only one young lady's interpretation of events. If tomorrow our suspicions are confirmed, we shall have no other recourse but to travel to Alba to present ourselves to Mr Bogdanov.

Oh, Nelly, my love, how I wish you were able to guide me in this. What would your advice be?

I shall try to sleep on it.

Please do not worry. I am sure this sounds all far worse than it will turn out to be.

Your loving husband,

Edwin.

PS. I will have Michael drop this letter into the telepost room tonight. Hopefully, it should be with you in the morning.

I love you.

E x

Journal of Adam Franklin.

Men came to kill us tonight. Several men entered the boarding house under the assumption that we were all in our beds. Fortunately, I was still awake reading Mrs Phillipott's copy of Beresford's History of the Martian Colonies, which her late husband profusely annotated in the margins. She has generously donated to me. Karl was with me playing Solo Noble, an odd little board game (I have no idea why an automaton so much enjoys playing games). We were sitting quietly in the drawing room with just one small oil lamp between us. I suppose the intruders must have assumed no one was awake.

Karl alerted me to an unfamiliar sound. When we went to investigate we encountered a group of armed thugs coming out of the scullery. They, we discovered later, had gained entry by forcing the back door.

Fearing for the lives of all those in the house, we armed ourselves crudely with what was to hand in the kitchen and laid into the intruders. I discovered that a good sized cast iron cooking pot makes a fine weapon in a rough brawl. Karl weighed in with a heavy rolling pin and a meat cleaver. Luckily we had stolen their element of surprise. In the darkness – I have discovered I have excellent vision, even in a kitchen lit only by the embers of a stove, so we had them at a crucial disadvantage.

I am still fairly shocked about how all this violence comes so easy to me. Regardless of them outnumbering us, being far better armed, they stood not a chance. I beat down the one in the lead, a huge man almost as wide as he was tall, with two strokes of the cooking pot, and disarmed him. With the addition of the club I had taken from the first, I battered the next man, one toting a scattergun, to a bloody pulp. Karl hacked the hand off of one gun waving thug. He cracked the rolling pin down on another's head so hard it sounded like an egg being hit with a hammer. In the blackness, as others piled in, it all dissolved into a frantic melee. I have no idea how many we wounded, but we stood our ground until Ransom, Michael and Mrs Phillipott joined us and we routed them.

Leaving Mrs Phillipott with Michael, we pursued the rest of the intruders out of the house. They made their escape on foot across the fields behind the barn. Karl wanted to give chase, but Ransom was adamant that it would be too dangerous, even for him.

In clearing up the kitchen, we discovered ourselves inheritors of three guns, several cudgels, three long knives, four hats and a breathing mask. Karl with true mortuary humour held up the hand he had struck from one intruder bemoaning it was a left hand and thus would be of no use to me. I did my best to take it in good part suggesting he might like to try it for the fit. Although Mrs Phillipott did not share our black wit, she did point out that with so large an amount of blood left around the kitchen and scullery, some of those fellows probably would not survive to make it back to wherever they were mustered.

Ransom was inconsolable. I fear the man does not know what he should do for the best. His almost blind faith in Everheart has finally been ripped asunder. I feel he is becoming paralysed by indecision.

He could not accept what the young lady journalist told us this evening no matter how we tried to impress it upon him the danger he is now in. Mrs Phillipott is quite a redoubtable woman, I think it was she who finally helped us convince Ransom there is no other course of action than to leave here immediately to travel to Alba to seek help. There is a High Sheriff in Alba (some kind of Chief of Policemen) whom it seems is a trusted friend of Ransom's father-in-Law.

Mrs Phillipott has furnished us with provisions and a sketchily drawn map of the back lanes she asserts will get us a good half the way before dawn. She says there is a postal station along with a water tower at a place called Alba Kirk Crossing and we can get the train from there.

I pray she is right.

I have no idea what I have gotten myself into. Though I am distracted, my own needs and fears are taking a back seat, it feels so much better than to be sitting contemplating my own woes as I have done for as long as I remember. Which I tally at roughly nine days.

I have still not read the preceding pages of this journal. A little pusillanimity, I think.

Now, as we pick our way through the back lanes of Tremorfa, I am scribbling this by the half-light of a spluttering lantern, in the back of Ransom's covered wagon, wondering if I am running away from some great danger and towards something far worse.

TREMORFA STATION. 10.32/25/09/0026

I ADVISED RESTRAINT –(stop)- YOUR MEN FAILED AGAIN –(stop)- R FLED –(stop)- TIPPED OFF –(stop)- C BD HERE –(stop)- WILL FIX C BD ISSUE –(stop)- RAISING POSSE –(stop)- IN PURSUIT –(stop)- DO NOT INVOLVE SELF FURTHER –(stop)- NALATIG –(stop)-

E

To, Mr L. Edwin Ransom.
Care of Mrs P. Phillipott.
Mrs Phillipott's Guest House for Gentlepersons.
Heinlein's Avenue.
Tremorfa.
September 25rd. M.Y. 26.
My dearest Edwin.

I thought it best to address this to you at Mrs Phillipott's Guest House for Gentlepersons. I hope it reaches you, but I trust Mrs Phillipott will be so kind as to forward it if it misses you.

Your letter arrived before breakfast this morning. I was glad to have Papa's company when I read it. Thank the Good Lord himself that you and the others are safe! Thank God also for Karl and your new friend Mr Franklin, who seems to be a very brave man indeed. I am sure Constable Everheart will spare no means in prosecuting these murderous men to the fullest extent of the Law.

Edwin, you must come home. I know that I need not remind you, but your responsibilities are to us your family. Nevertheless, I so understand your need to honour your dear father's vision, I feel it is too dangerous. I know he would never have wanted to see you in such peril. That man Du Maurier is a vicious cad. You and everyone out there are in mortal danger. Papa has said he will talk to his friends in the Government about Du Maurier. It is high time someone took him down a peg or two.

Come home, Edwin. Bring Karl, Minnie, Mr Franklin along with any of the workers you think will want to come to the city – Papa promises will find them work (The Lord knows this house needs enough work on it to keep all of them busy for several months). Come home. Please. We all beg you.

Today's events seem trivial in the light of your dreadful shock, but as you insist I recant to you every day's events I shall tell you about today's activities. I only hope it will bring you some distraction from your terrible concerns.

Lenora called upon us this morning. It was so good to see her. She told me - in confidence, of course – that there is a rather dashing young man who has just joined her faculty, a teacher of

"Geographical Sciences" no less, of whom she is rather enamoured. Though she has not had the courage to tip her hat in his direction. He sounds such a perfectly suitable young man for her. Papa would surely approve of him being an educated man with good career prospects. However, a House Master's stipend might be a little parsimonious to start a family with. We chatted all afternoon. She sends her regards and thanks you again for your wonderful lecture as well as the practical demonstrations. She says you have a natural gift for teaching and the children so enjoyed the experience.

I was hoping she would stay for Papa's dinner party, but she was only in the city to procure some supplies for the school, unfortunately, she had already purchased her Airtrain ticket back to Xanthe. So I had Carstairs drive us to the mooring station so I could see her off.

There was quite a kerfuffle outside the Airtrain Station with police officers and several soldiers involved. When we inquired, the porter told us he had heard they were after a Utopian spy! Can you imagine it! We did see the officers roughly hustling a rather dishevelled young man away, but he did not look particularly Utopian or dangerous for that matter.

After seeing Lenora off, I stopped in the city to do a little shopping as a diversion. Carstairs was very patient with me, carrying everything, but shopping is not enjoyable on your own. Though I did order you a new winter coat from Harringay's as that old thing you are wearing is about to fall to pieces.

The children had been out with Nanny all day. She took them to the zoo to draw the animals. They so enjoyed it. They have a whole sheaf of pictures for you. Nanny is so good with them. They have learnt so much. They even saw a baby Aresian Man-o'-War. James says its body was only a couple of inches long, but its tails were nearly three yards long! He says they can grow more than 160 feet! Can you imagine something like that flying about? Thank God we do not have them here in Tharsis. James is so excited he wants to take you to see it as soon as you can spare the time.

Mrs Carstairs did such a fabulous job of laying on the dinner party this evening. It was so lovely to see the house all lit up and full of people again. This is the first party we have held since Momma passed away and, although it brought back memories for all of us, at least we did not dwell upon them. Although Momma would have loved to have seen it.

Papa had invited the courageous Colonel Jahns, Dr Spender and his daughter, Parthena, of whom I wrote about yesterday, Professor G.P. Serviss, the Anthropologist, Mr Fontenelli and his beautiful Aresian wife, Aelita. Along with a man who I have never seen before, or heard Papa mention; Sir John Sydeian, by reputation an adventurer and big game hunter.

Although it was a little strange to take what was Momma's role in the proceedings, I must say I enjoyed the reception. The meal was delightful – Mrs Carstairs had hired in additional help in the kitchen including a rather wonderful young pastry chef from one of the pâtisseries in the city.

Parthena was as enchanting as usual, always very endearing. Her father and Professor Serviss seemed to know each other well. Old chums, I believe. Mr Fontenelli and Sir Sydeian too seemed to know each other well, but were far less genial, in fact, I could often sense a degree of standoffishness between them. While Sir Sydeian is a charismatic gentleman, quite self-deprecating, Mr Fontenelli is quite bombastic, being often quite flamboyant in his mannerisms, all bushy beard and wild gesticulations. A bit of a windy-wallet as Momma would say. Madam Fontenelli, however, is a revelation.

Her skin is a dusky red, as red as the Martian sands themselves, with the largest, most compelling eyes I have ever seen. The irises are a rainbow of colours, almost kaleidoscopic, and she fixes you with utter attentiveness. Her hair, fashionably kept in a Psyche knot, is the blackest black, and she wore the simplest of pale gowns. I must say that the gentlemen, not even Papa, could keep their eyes off of her. If this is what the Aresian women were like then I dare say they could have conquered you men with the force of their beauty alone.

Resourcefully I took my chance to dispense with formality and had my place set next to hers. I thought she might be a little shy but if anything, it was she who spoke to me first. Although we were only able to exchange some small talk before Papa steered the conversation to more important matters. For all of her exotic alien-ness she is an utter delight; softly spoken, charming, intelligent besides being exceptionally well mannered.

Oh Edwin, did we truly make war upon such people?

Due to my unconventional seating arrangements, I was in the position to notice that Sir Sydeian, although trying hard not to be observed doing so, watched Madam Fontenelli's every movement and gesture with absolute assiduity. I know how you tease me about such things, but my intuition coupled with Mr Fontenelli's attitude towards Sir Sydeian, suggests to me there may have been more than a just gentlemanly professional rivalry between them.

We were all about to enjoy the lovely desserts the young man from the pâtisserie had prepared for us when Papa tapped his dessert spoon against his glass to gain our attention. I have never seen his face so resolute, apparently, he had something truly momentous to say and, Edwin, he did indeed.

Papa explained he had called everyone together because he wanted to share with us all the evidence he had yesterday presented to the President himself. Papa says he has proof the Aresians are still here on Mars! They did not simply "disappear" nor did they withdraw from the planet completely after the battle of Tyrrhena Mons.

Dr Spender and Professor Serviss wanted to know where they could possibly be?

No one has set eyes on an Aresian – present company excepted – in twenty-five years.

Papa said he believes there are still Aresian cities, undiscovered out beyond the Red Seas, cities mentioned in texts but never seen by human eyes, out there beyond our reach, hidden somehow, but still inhabited.

Sir Sydeian asked what evidence there could possibly be to support such a wild hypothesis.

Papa told us some of the evidence is highly secret, but he could divulge that numerous reports have been made by Aethervolt Navy officers of sightings of unidentified aethervolt ships entering and leaving the high atmosphere as well as in deep space. When Papa gathered all these disparate reports together, he discovered there is a regularity to them. There is even a possible origin; right here on Mars.

I did notice that Colonel Jahns sat completely impassive throughout the whole of Papa's revelation. Only to finally speak up to ask a question of Madam Fontenelli.

"Madam," he asked. "I know this may be difficult for you, but forgive me, I must ask; do you know anything about this? Have you any information we should know or any knowledge you can share with us?"

I thought Mr Fontenelli was going to explode with outrage (Sir Sydeian was almost as livid) but she placed her hand firmly upon her husband's wrist, and he calmed down instantly. In a soft, level tone, she explained to the Colonel, and the hushed guests, that when the battle of Tyrrhena Mons occurred, she was only a very small child resident in the Catholic orphanage run by Japanese nuns, St. Kakure Kirishitan's, on the slopes of Olympus Mons. Except for a few fragmentary recollections, she can barely remember her parents. She has always understood they lived here in the Old Citadel in Tharsis City as part of an Ambassadorial delegation from the Kings of the Peerrohs Aresians. They were seized and thrown into prison after independence was declared. They died of disease by the time she was three. She had a brother, Gethen, who was with her in the orphanage, but he died of consumption when she was five. In truth, she said, most of what she knows of Aresian culture, she has learnt from books and her husband. In fact, there were probably men at the table, like Dr Spender or Professor Serviss, who knew far more of her people than she would ever know. I thought how awful that must be for her, poor soul.

At that point Sir Sydeian protested on her behalf. The Colonel, affected by her story as much as the rest of us, apologised unreservedly for his manner.

Appreciating this possibly might be all too upsetting for Madam Fontenelli, I suggested we ladies retire to the morning room to let the gentlemen continue their discussion over brandy and cigars in the drawing room.

So, unfortunately, I did not hear the rest of Papa's ideas, but I will talk to him in the morning about it. Madam Fontenelli was most gracious. Parthena was a treasure, distracting us with more of her wild stories and self-deprecating humour. She even tried to get us to smoke one of those horrid cigarillos she partakes of. I declined, but Madam Fontenelli decided – against my advice – to try one. I thought she would just die coughing! We did our best to talk about almost anything other than the topic of our dinner conversation. I showed them Mother's orangery and the atrium. They were both greatly impressed by the whole collection. Aelita, as Madam Fontenelli wishes us to call her, told a humorous tale of how she first encountered her future husband in St. Mary's Cathedral when he was on his hands and knees trying to copy the inscription on an ancient Aresian tomb. She, being only a young girl of thirteen years, rushing to Evensong, tripped over him and went sprawling across the nave. She was only sixteen when she married Mr Fontenelli. She made such a joke of it, saying it was either him or the Convent! Although he is much older than her, she does seem to adore him.

They were such good company I think I got lost in telling them about you and your dandelions, we simply forgot the time. The men were ready to leave before we even knew it.

I have retired to our room to write to you before preparing for bed. It has been quite an eventful day. Papa, the Colonel and Sir Sydeian are still in Papa's study, but the door is locked so I will not disturb them.

I hope this letter will be of some small distraction to your worries.

I will not reiterate my fears again, because I know how much it upsets you, but please Edwin, for myself and the children's sake. Please come home. We need you safe here with us.

Your devoted wife.

Nelly.

The Diary of Dr James Athanasius Flammarion.
25th Sept. 26th

Things went better than I expected! The Fontenelli woman's memories were of no real value, other than to remind us all how alien they are, but my observations were well received. I cannot believe, Madam Fontenelli remembers nothing. My own mother died when I was 5 years old, but I can still remember her face, the sound of her voice, the touch of her hand. I believe Madam Fontenelli remembers far more than she is either telling us or, possibly, knows herself. Once people no longer see the garishly coloured skin of an Aresian, they listen to her talk in genteel words, they forget that inside she is as alien to us as any of those extraordinary monsters out there in the sands of the Red Seas. Spender and Serviss agree the Aresian texts point to there being a far larger network of major conurbations than we ever became fully aware of. The numbers of the warriors, along with the size of the fleets of aerobarges they could field, would need far larger populations to support. The reckoning of it all simply does not make sense unless there were (at my calculation) at least another ten or twelve major population centers. Serviss openly admitted to me he had been researching the fabled Muhe Ca himself for years. He has promised to share with me all his findings. Spender admitted he has never accepted the premise they simply "went away." He was a young subaltern in the Tharsis Military Intelligence Service at Tyrrhena Mons, he was one of the few who actually witnessed the Aresian fleet massing for the final assault. He also mentioned an observation made to his own commanding officer at the time; he did not recognise most of the banners those Aresian aerobarges were flying. He has never accepted the official account they had just "run away." He feels, as I do, we did not in any way defeat them, their culture was too advanced. They had access to technological resources we have never even imagined. At Tyrrhena Mons they could have easily wiped our forces off the face of Mars. It is his estimation that Aresian civilisations date back to at least 150 to 200 thousand years. Far older than anything on Earth. He and Serviss agree the Aresians have been capable of travelling the aether between worlds for at least 80 thousand years, maybe even between the stars. Fontenelli – ever the demonstrous Italian– was still furious with me and the Colonel for questioning his wife, however, he too had to admit that his own conclusions concur with mine. They are still out there beyond the Red Seas. The abandoned derelict metropolises are simply what the Colonel calls a "Burnt Earth Strategy," a tactic they undoubtedly learnt from us.

Sir Sydeian (who probably knows those lands beyond the pale of our city-states better than any of us, including Fontenelli and Spender) has seen the evidence with his own two eyes. He pointed out to us a location where last year he came across an abandoned Aresian aerobarge he feels could not have been more than a few weeks old. In a later private conversation, the Colonel finally shared some of the information that I suspected the Government holds back from us; eight years ago five Kitreenoh Aresian warriors were killed in a failed ambush of a detachment of our soldiers on reconnaissance north of Argyre. It was officially hushed up, attributed on a Thylian incursion. The "unofficial" official explanation puts it down to an isolated incident with a small group of desperate Aresians stragglers, left behind after the withdrawal. In truth, the Colonel says they were well armed, well equipped and disciplined. The survivors, of which there were several, showed our boys a set of clean heels. What they were doing there is unknown to this day. I asked if that was all there was? The Colonel, with classic military candour, said if there was not, he would say, but if there was then he could not say. Nevertheless, he did add that the Tharsis Aethervolt Navy and Aerostat Air Arm has standing orders not to engage any Aresian craft... an order that was made five years ago... twenty years after Tyrrhena Mons. They are out there and our Governments damn well know it.

Emboldened by their acceptance of the facts, I unveiled my plan to make contact with the Aresians. Sir Sydeian, as I expected, was first to agree to come along on such an expedition. The Colonel himself said he would be delighted, but, though semi-retired, he would have to come along in a non-official capacity. He claims the Army owes him half a lifetime of leave. Spender is also up for it so long as he can bring along his daughter as his assistant. Unfortunately, Serviss feels such an expedition might be too much exertion for his heart ailment, besides he cannot leave his wife alone too long as she has a nervous condition. I invited Fontenelli and his wife directly, his geographical knowledge will be useful, but Madam Fontenelli will be invaluable to helping us in our first contact. Fontenelli was reticent, however, I think he did not want to be outdone by Sir Sydeian, so he agreed to join us. The Colonel, I and Sir Sydeian spent some time after the others had left discussing other aspects of these Aresians.

I wanted to know what they made of the more exotic claims made by the earliest explorers. Such as Hamilton and Stranger's claim that the yellow-skinned Aresians could communicate words and pictures into each other's thoughts and could move objects without touching them. The Colonel pointed out that Stranger was not the shrewdest of men, recovering from exposure, half-starved of decent air and faced with mind-numbing wonders, he most simply mistook Aresian technology for magic. Sir Sydeian, like myself, was not so convinced, but had to admit Hamilton never mentioned directly witnessing such abilities. Though the Colonel's question, "If they had had mesmeric mind powers, why did they not use them in the wars?" was indeed a valid one. I have deliberated about in some detail. Perhaps they did. I believe Serviss thinks so too, but he scuttled off too early for my liking.

My illustrious companions have agreed to meet me again at Covingdome Aerofield on Thursday morning. I have something to show them.

Notes to self. **25/9/26**

Submitted piece to Assignment Editor. Hate using telephonograph! Why no Grey's harmonics out here I have NO idea. Too backwards looking!

D. Maurier is going to be well poked up about it, the murderous munz'er.

Got back to Hotel to find lock had been forced and papers scattered. Have no idea what is missing. Bullet left on my pillow.

Hotelier claims not to know anything – looked utterly frightened.

Overheard gossip in the bar - men who attacked Ransom escaped from jail! Everheart barely pretending now.

Little squiffy -too much of the bath water- however, decided must go back to warn Ransom. Almost crashed the Hemmings and burnt my thigh on the engine!

Bloody cold out here at night. Don't know how they can stand it. Had to wear two coats.

These damn masks hardly filter the dust. Will be coughing up red mucus for days.

Got there too late. Ransom and others were gone. Mrs Phillipott distressed – gang of men attacked the house. Hell of a fight!

Mrs Phillipott thinks they came to kill Ransom. I think me next. Thank God I brought Daddy's old Eliminator pistol and my stenowriter.

Eventually convinced her to tell me where they have gone. Decided to follow the story. Had to borrow extra fuel from Mrs Phillipott.

I should easily catch up with them on the monowheel. Tally oh!

Journal of Adam Franklin.

Alba Kirk Crossing.

We arrived not long after dawn.

If I have seen lonelier, more desolate places I am grateful I do not remember.

The road from Tremorfa to Newell crosses the tracks here. There's a postal drop, a water tower, a corral for wagons and horses, about six yards of raised platform, and that is it. Ransom assures us we can request the train to stop by hoisting a red signal by the Ramsey gibbet. The hand crank on the signal was too stiff for him to manage as dust had choked the mechanism, so I wound it up as high as I could.

Out here the wind blows ice cold and straight through you. "A lazy wind," Ransom calls it. "The Tremorfa Breeze," he joked. It steals your body heat and forces you to wear a filter mask all the time. Nevertheless, nothing seems to keep out the really fine dust as it gets into everything. Even with their masks on Ransom and Michael spend a lot of time coughing. I do not have such a problem, nor so much with the cold, but it irritates my eyes terribly.

When I enquired if it was a problem for Karl, he told me he was built to withstand these conditions. He was created here on Mars, at a munitions manufactory, Rosumovi Univerzální Android, in Abiathar, an industrial metropolis in the heart of Ophyr. After the wars ended, he was decommissioned to be sold off as surplus. I asked if that meant he had been a soldier. He said they took his program cards so he cannot remember anything before he was retired from service, so now he was just like any other automaton. Which he is most definitely not.

It was strange, but he almost seemed sad, if such a machine man can be sad. Unexpectedly, I felt he and I had much more in common than I could ever have imagined; the machine man had had his memories stripped out of him whilst I have no idea who or what I am. At least he has the solace of knowing who, when and why. I have nothing, only a little leather-bound notebook that probably holds the secrets of my past, secrets I am too frightened to explore.

We had been growing bored waiting for over an hour when Karl spotted a dust plume in the distance. It was coming from the direction we had travelled. Not knowing who or what was following us we took up arms and scattered, leaving Karl standing alone by the wagon.

Something fast, a powered vehicle, was approaching at high speed in a zig-zag pattern as if avoiding hidden obstacles. From my position, crouched beside the Ramsey gibbet, I tried to make out what the vehicle was dodging. Plumes of dust were sprouting close to it. The dust plumes I thought the machine was throwing up at first, but were, in fact, explosions from the ground as if something was impacting around it.

Suddenly, as understanding dawned on me; I shouted a warning to the others as the thing giving chase burst through the dust cloud into sight.

A small, ugly looking, dirigible with sparking toroidal engines thrust out each side on gantries was bearing down on the fleeing vehicle. Guns mounted either side of the gondola's fuselage, spat destruction into the path of its fleeing quarry. Instantly the silence was shattered by the deafening cacophony of engines and gunfire.

Instinctively, I broke cover and ran towards the oncoming vehicle. It was a monowheel like the young lady reporter had left the Guest House on last night. Stopping clear of everyone else I stood stock still, took careful aim with the lever-action rifle Karl had issued me, and fired off all seven rounds in quick succession straight at the gondola of the dirigible. Whether they found their mark or not I had no idea. My concentration was only broken by the thunderclap of Karl's scattergun going off beside me. The dirigible banked steeply veering off to the right with one engine spluttering and discharging like a ball of lightning on a stick. We must have struck something.

I have no idea why I react in such a way to danger.

The monowheel roared to a halt in front of us. It was indeed the young lady reporter, Miss Bryant-Drake, she was wildly distressed however seemingly unhurt. We tried to calm her, but before she could speak coherently Edwin began shouting to us.

I thought he was cautioning us that the dirigible was returning, but instead, he was alerting us of the imminent arrival of the train. There was no time for genteel niceties; I scooped the young lady up, threw her over my shoulder. Karl hoisted her monowheel and we ran for the safety of the arriving locomotive.

The Asterion, a gigantic behemoth of a machine, arrived in a cloud of choking dust, belching thick black exhaust. Its massive hunched bulk, deliberately, no doubt, reminiscent of some great black iron bull, growling and sighing from its labours as it came to rest beside the platform. It was a colossal locomotive, easily 30 feet high, surmounted by an enormous towering stack billowing fumes and sparks like some ancient volcanic fissure.

The packed passenger coaches were three decks high. The goods wagons were the size of warehouses. Even in the chaos of us clambering aboard, Edwin enthusiastically informed me how this great iron monster was fed by biomass from the very same dandelions he grew on his farm. I must admit to getting a little terse with him and ordering him onto the train. Thankfully, he did so quickly enough, for just as Michael was freeing the horses.

Karl called out that he had spotted riders approaching at a gallop. Edwin ordered them to leave the monowheel and horses and get aboard as quickly as possible.

We all stood staring out the third level windows for what must have been less than a minute, though it felt like an eternity, as we watched the horsemen charging across the plain towards us. Miss Bryant-Drake was sure it was Constable Everheart and a posse of men from Tremorfa, but we could not be certain at such a distance. I think I had not taken a breath for some time when suddenly the locomotive lurched into motion, we were off.

No horse, no matter how fast, will be able to catch us now.

To

Mrs Eleanor A. Ransom,

Locksley Hall,

Machen,

Tharsis.

Dearest Nelly

I do not know if this note will ever reach you. I have been such a FOOL. How can you forgive me for my obstinacy, my selfish narrow vision. I should have listened to you and your Papa. What an idiot I have been to bring this all down upon my head. Now I am a fugitive from my own home. I have put Karl, young Michael, even Adam's lives in jeopardy for what? A dead man's dream few thousand hectares of red dirt?

How could I have been so stupid to think I could withstand such a ruthless tyrant as Du Maurier? Me, I am nothing more than a foolish little dandelion farmer scraping a living out of the dust, what did I imagine I could do against such a martinet?

And as for Constable Everheart, what a deceiving scoundrel he has turned out to be. To solicit my trust in such a way with clear intent to betray me. I have come to believe Miss B-D is right, when she said he arranged to encounter me on the train journey home to gain my confidence knowing full well what dastardly scheme was afoot.

I fear Du Maurier has no soul. He sent men to murder us in our bed last night. Thank God for Karl and Adam, for without their bravery we would probably all be dead. Nelly, you know I am not a man of violence, but I swear if

Du Maurier was here now I would ~~take my father's pistol~~ ~~and shoot him dead on the spot!~~ knock his block off!

Even Miss D-B is not immune to Du Maurier's savage attentions. She came to the Guest House last night to warn us, but it was too late, so decided to follow us to Alba Kirk crossing only to find herself pursued by some murderous lunatic — no doubt another in the pay of Du Maurier — in a dirigible. If Adam had not acted so decisively I think she would have been gunned down in front of our very eyes!

Adam is so very resourceful, absolutely courageous. However, I still know really little about him, he has placed his life on the line for us all and saved my own life at least twice. This morning he saved Miss D-B's life through an act of utter heroism. He stood in the path of the machine pursuing her and, though it was wildly spraying gunfire, drove it off. Even Karl was impressed.

We have made it safely onto the train though we had to let Trago and the other horses go free. Mrs Phillipott, who lent us a fresh pair of dray horses for the waggon, assured us the old nags will always find their way home. I pray Trago follows them back.

I will try to send a message ahead to warn you of our arrival — I pray it reaches you speedily. Hopefully, we should reach Alba by this evening.

May the Lord bless you and keep you.

Kiss the children for me.

All my love,

Edwin.

Message Origin;   8.20/26/09/0026
TRANSMARS MOBILE ATMOGRAPHIC STATION TO
THARSIS B, RECEIVING STATION.
To Mrs Eleanor A. Ransom. Locksley Hall. Machen, Tharsis.
From Mr L. Edwin Ransom.
On route to Alba. Things taken a turn for the worse. Will need
legal advice. Do not inform anyone of whereabouts until spoken
to solicitor.
Do not trust anyone.
Edwin.

Message Origin;   8.50/26/09/0026
TRANSMARS MOBILE ATMOGRAPHIC STATION TO
TREMORFA RECEIVING STATION.
To Mrs Minerva Ransom. Ransom's Farm. Tremorfa.
From Mr L. Edwin Ransom.
Order the men to stand down. Pay off the casual workers, send
them home. Rest of you leave the farm immediately. I have
arranged for you to stay a night or two at Mrs Phillipott's Guest
House in Tremorfa before you get the train. She will find more
permanent lodgings for the others in town. Do not stay a moment
longer on the farm. Tell Joshua that Michael is with us safe and
sound. Nelly will be expecting you.
Edwin.

Charity Bryant-Drake.
Notes to self. 26/9/26
Still shaking.

I was chased for miles by some sort of military type configured dirigible. Very unusual engine mounting.

Disguised to appear like an aerostat privateer craft. Saw part of a Tharsis registration number painted over.

T – something – D -something- 18 H or K. (Will look it up!)

Must have been sent by D Maurier, as I got near Alba Kirk crossing it opened fire on me. No idea how it didn't kill me.

Ransom's friend Franklin saved my life. Never seen anyone so calm in such a situation.

I wonder what his story is.

We made the train, though only just in time. Everheart's posse was right behind us.

Ransom; withdrawn and anxious. He is worried about his people on the farm and family in Tharsis. He has taken to sitting scrunched up in the corner of the carriage drawing pictures in a sketchbook of an ugly little dog with a top hat on, he says it is for his daughter.

I feel like I am on the run with a band of reluctant outlaws. Heavily armed, frantic and not a little desperate.

This is going to go badly.

I am going to try to get a proper interview with Ransom down on record before we reach Tharsis.

Just watched Franklin strip down and clean the weapons in double time. Must be military trained. His face is a mass of scars – no machinery accident did that, an explosion perhaps.

Also noticed he keeps his right hand gloved at all times – even to eat. Intrigued.

After dinner, he left the dining car, to sit on the steps between the carriages reading from a notebook.

Journal of Adam Franklin.

I have begun reading my journal. Is this me?

"Sergeant Major Adam Franklin, DCM, Her Imperial Majesty's Royal Aethervolt Marine Corp."

It is insane.

"... I have written this down as I remember it. So I will remember it..."

"I awoke strapped to the operating table. It was some kind of hospital, I thought, though inside an old building. There was an infinite amount of strange apparatus hanging above me. Men, doctors I thought, were busying themselves around me. I called out, but they ignored my pleas. I begged for water, but no one seemed to hear me. Finally, another doctor came in, a woman, and gave me water. When I asked why I was here she only smiled, saying I should relax. I plead to be released from the straps, but she only said the Doctor would come soon. He would explain everything."

".... It was then I realised my right arm was missing..."

".... I could not feel my legs..."

"....they fed me through a straw..."

"....I awoke to find they had been using one of the strange contraptions on my head. There was blood in my eyes. I could not scream because there was something in my mouth..."

"....someone laughed."

"They talk in a language I do not know."

"...the pain was unbearable."

"The Doctor came to see me on what I think was the second day. He spoke softly almost compassionately."

"He asked me whether I remembered anything before I awoke here. I said, NO. He told me I had been wounded when my aerostat had been shot down by rebels. I had been badly injured. I wanted to know how badly injured?"

"He said I had been killed in the crash."

"...I could not stop the screaming... I did not know if it was me or someone else... "

"They kept me sedated. I would taste laudanum then it would all fade…"

"Today the Doctor came again. He asked me if I was ready to stand up. They unstrapped me and made me try to stand."

"I could not stand."

"I screamed… these were not my legs."

"I awoke to find they were fastening an apparatus to my right shoulder. They were drilling into the bones. I could feel the metal grinding into me. I tried to fight them, but I could not move…."

I ripped those pages out, allowing the wind to snatch them. I could not read anymore.

P.E.S. Seren Bore.   **10.32/26/09/26**

Ship's scrap log (excerpts from) Captain R. K. Llewellyn.

Ship ready for First Mate Mister Charles' inspection by 8 am. All well.

Staff meeting 8.15am.

Chief Engineer reports; all maintenance completed. Signed off 8.20am.

Purser's report; fully supplied and in readiness. 8.30am.

Prof. Flammarion and his party arrived at 10 am.

Prof. James Flammarion, Sir John Sydeian, Colonel Carter Jahns, Dr Octavius Spender, Miss Parthena Spender, Dr and Mrs Fontenelli.

Greetings, formal welcome and drinks in the wardroom.

I gave a short introduction to the history of the Seren Bore and handed over to the Professor.

The Professor explained that he had purchased the Seren Bore two years ago from the Miller Consortium then re-appointed myself as Captain. Since then we have spent considerable time and a great deal of the Professor's money on readying the ship for this expedition.

The Professor explained in detail his plans to travel North beyond the plains of Elysium, beyond the Hourglass Sea, beyond even the Great Red Sea to Neath Regio, Triton's northern province then possibly onto the ice cap itself.

The Professor pointed out the ice would be at its most retreated and the weather most favourable in the run up to mid-October.

Dr Fontenelli exclaimed it was a journey of over eight thousand miles into one of the coldest most inhospitable places on Mars.

Colonel Jahns expressed concern as to the threat from Utopian forces active in that area. Since Independence, they have been contending with Triton and Amenthes over Neath's eastern borders which they believe is a natural part of their territory. There has not been a shooting war for some time, but Utopia's forces patrol that area of the Red Seas. They are heavily armed and extremely active.

Sir Sydeian pointed out that, the miners of Neath have never acceded to Utopia's demands. In fact, they are a pretty rugged, free thinking independent-spirited people. He voiced his only concerns being about any danger from the wildlife we may encounter.

With the Professor's permission, I pointed out the Seren Bore flies a flag of Private Enterprise. She is registered as such with all major national authorities, including Utopia. We are protected by the International Convention on Free Trade and Exploration.

Dr Fontenelli became almost hysterical accusing me and my crew of being Skypirates! I had to speak firmly to Mister Charles as he became quite outraged at the accusation.

Mrs Fontenelli, who is a Peerrohs Aresian, was able to calm her husband.

I informed the gentleman that I served in Her Britannic Majesty's Aethervolt Navy for 18 Earth years and another 15 years here in the Tharsis Aerostat Fleet, in which I achieved the rank of Commodore. I also held the rank of Wing Commander in the Tharsis Air Arm. I retired 10 years ago to take this post as Captain of the free merchant trader Seren Bore. I am not and have never been a Skypirate nor a Reaver, neither has any member of my crew.

In fact, I was the Commodore in charge of hunting down and destroying the pirate ship Queen Victoria's Revenge. It was my command that brought her notorious Captain, Léopold Trouvelot, to the gallows.

Dr Fontenelli regained himself enough to apologise though I felt it was a rather forced apology.

Miss Spender asked about dangers from Pirates or Reavers out over the Red Seas? I assured her the Seren Bore is fully equipped to defend herself adequately against any threat or danger, whether pirates or beasts. She has also recently been fitted with two

Cogswaine fulcrum mounted steam driven rotation guns on the fore and aft deck, under the Professor's instruction.

Sir Sydeian asked if I were indeed expecting to encounter "difficulties" on our journey to Neath. The Professor and I assured him we were not. Nevertheless, as both of us are careful men, responsible for this ship's passengers and the crew's safety, we have addressed any possible concerns. In fact erring decidedly upon the side of caution.

I left it to Mister Charles to give the guests the tour of the ship. While the Professor and I spoke alone. I informed him that the fitting of the transverse bivariating dynamic pyromagnetic displacement apparatus across the main engines has been a success and thoroughly tested. He was delighted to hear the engine's power output has at least doubled. Which will double our range. In flight tests, we also made over 70 knots. The Chief Engineer says we should be able to run them constantly at 40 knots for the entire journey if we wish.

Under the current long-term weather forecast, it should take less than 8 days to reach Neath if we can maintain a good 40 knots with no diversions or unscheduled stops. We have enough fuel and provisions to last a journey of a maximum of 20 days at a push without refuelling or resupplying. If, as we hope, we can resupply on the way, or fully at Neath, we should be able to extend our expedition for as long as the weather allows. Presupposing we can use one of Neath's aerodrome as a staging point for routine maintenance.

The contracted crew members are signed on until Christmas Day, but we cannot be above -60° North after early November.

We took the time to make a final double check the specialist equipment the Professor requested and to run through the course I have plotted.

The guests returned from their tour quite impressed. Even Dr Fontenelli had complimentary things to say about the ship. Although he made a disparaging remark regarding Jones and Jules (He claims his wife is "allergic" to animal fur). I assured him I shall have the Steward keep the cats away from all the passenger compartments.

Prof. Flammarion introduced the question of a departure date for the expedition. In view of the ship's readiness, he wished to set off as soon as possible. He proposed tomorrow morning before 8 bells, but none of his guests were ready enough for that, so it was agreed we will depart at 8 bells, morning watch, on the 30/9/26.

Prof. Flammarion and his guests left by 1.30 pm.

Senior crew members briefing. 2pm.

Extracts from
Beresford's History of the Martian Colonies.
3rd Edition. Milton and Dante.

Chapter 2. The First Settlers.

Of the strangest effects upon the Tellurian mind and body, the most interesting is the increase in life expectancy. The effect was observed firstly by Dr Brackett, who noted that although Stranger had been away from Earth for almost twenty years he seemed more like a man in his early fifties than in his early sixties (i). It was not until the first Imperial troops, British and German, garrisoned on Mars for long periods returned to Earth was it realised there had been a retardation in the normal ageing effects. Later studies amongst long-term settlers confirmed this, thus proving it to be a slowing of the ageing process rather than a simple extending of longevity.

Settlers on Mars were demonstrably living longer in addition to ageing slower. The specific cause of this is still a matter of considerable debate. It had been suggested the phenomena is a side effect of the lower gravity and thinner atmosphere. Although some learned minds believe it is the result of better diet as well as cleaner air. One early suggestion put forward by Dr del Rey was that the slowing of the ageing process is due to effects on the human body of travelling through the rabbit-hole spatial anomaly to Mars then back (ii). This was debunked by evidence of the slowed gestation and ageing of those first generation children born on Mars.

The last detailed study by Professors Kornbluth and Merril suggested the phenomena could be due to the effects of consumption of minerals, extremely rare on Earth, but common on Mars, in the soil, regolith and water supply. (iii) The current theory favoured by most reputable scientists suggests the effect is a correlation of a number of biological factors unique to the Martian environment.

This resonates with the evidence of those returning to Earth after prolonged sojourns on Mars suffer no serious ill effects.

Their bodies return to a normal ageing process after six to eight months.

The Martian day is extremely close to the Earth day to make it almost indistinguishable without resorting to higher mathematics, but the year, with attendant seasons, is almost twice as long, six hundred and sixty-seven days (in a non-leap year). The imposition by the colonial authorities of their Earth-centric calendrical systems made complete sense to the early colonial administrations, but rapidly began to cause myriad complications as it was completely out of step with the Martian year.

Attempts by astronomers and mathematicians to solve the issues were rebuffed by the colonial authorities often on the orders of the terrestrial Imperial Governments. Which led to the common Martian Secessionist accusation against the Earthbound authorities; Out of step, out of time.

Upon the Unilateral Declaration of Independence the new authorities almost unanimously agreed to adopt the calendrical system proposed by Professor Wells; a Martian Year of 667 days (668 each leap year) with a familiar division of twelve months and four seasons, using commonly accepted titles depending upon the culture.

The new Martian Year, taking 1899 as its Year Zero is roughly 1.8 standard Earth years.

The effect of the elongation of life expectancy, upon establishment of a Tellurian Martian culture has not yet been fully explored by scientific study. The ratio of the slowing has been suggested by a number of studies as being a factor between 1.75 and 2.10. (iv) But this has not had any particularly noticeable effect upon population numbers for as, to paraphrase Thomas Hobbes, life expectancy on Mars up to UDI and in the ensuing Aresian Wars, was indeed often; 'poor, nasty, brutish and short.' (v)

Page 149.

Notes
i.   Dr L. Brackett, (1858) Medical Examinations of Mr J. Stranger, Esq. The Lancet. Vol. 1.
ii. Dr L. del Rey. (1860) The Rabbit-hole Effect. Consequences of Space and Time Displacement on Human Physiology.

iii. Kornbluth and Merril. (Year1896) The Methuselah Syndrome. Longevity, a Review
of the Martian Question.
iv. Wells, et al. MY 1. Time and Tides. Calendrical Science on Mars. 1895.
v. Thomas Hobbes. Leviathan. Ch.12. 1651.

Miss. Lenora Flammarion.
Industrial Instructor.
The School for Ragged and Orphaned Children.
The Raikes.
Hydraotes Key.
Xanthe Province.
Tharsis.
September 26rd. M.Y. 26.

Dearest Lenora.
Forgive me for burdening you so with this, but I must tell someone. Papa is so preoccupied. I have no one else to turn to. Would you were here I could so rely upon you to help me through this anguish.

I am beside myself with disquiet. I fear Edwin is in such misfortune and I can do nothing to help!

This morning a letter arrived from him saying he is under house arrest! For the deaths of those bandits who tried to murder him at the Tremorfa Toll House. My Edwin, accused of murder! No one in their right frame of mind could possibly suspect my dear Edwin of such a horrendous thing. They have placed him under house arrest at Mrs Phillipott's Guest House for Gentlepersons, him and his friend; Mr Franklin. They are also holding Karl and little Michael, Joshua's youngest boy.

The new Constable, Mr Everheart, who seemed to be reasonably fair-minded, recommended a local solicitor to advise Edwin on what to do, but has since then Edwin has spoken to a journalist who came to the Guest House. It would appear it was all some terrible charade! Everheart, and the solicitor he recommended, are apparently in cahoots with Du Maurier; that evil tormentor I told you about. The very man who most probably sent those brutes to murder my husband!

Edwin signed off his letter saying he would confront Everheart this morning and if unsatisfied, he would endeavour appeal to Mr Bogdanov, the High Sheriff in Alba.

I showed the letter to Papa. He felt it was the right course of action. He promised to contact his friend Mr Bravett. Mr Bravett is a much-esteemed barrister in Alba. Papa assured me once Mr Bravett was on the case Edwin would be completely exonerated. Papa is also going to write to Mr Bogdanov, whom he went to the Military Academy with.

I was still so upset that I could not accompany Papa to meet his friends at Covingdome Aerofield to see the dirigible he has brought. Yes, Papa has brought an airship! I had no idea. What else has he been up to without our knowledge?

While Papa was out an urgent wireless telegram arrived from Edwin. He says, "Things have taken a turn for the worse." He is already on route to Alba. He asks me to trust no one!

Oh, Lenora, I dread to think what has happened. I can only suspect the worse!

That malevolent man Du Maurier seems intent on destroying my husband but for what? The journalist suggested it might be to do with an Aresian tomb buried on Edwin's farm. What could be so compelling in a pile of dusty old bones?

I do not know what to do. If I did not have the children to worry about I would be on the first railplane to Alba to meet him.

When Papa returns I will make sure he has contacted Mr Bravett, also I will ask him if he will send Carstairs to Alba to collect Edwin and the others and bring them home. At least here they will be safe.

Oh, Lenora. How I wish you were here.

Your devoted sister.

Eleanor.

The Diary of Dr James Athanasius Flammarion.

26th Sept. 26th.

Eleanor received a very disturbing letter from Edwin this morning. It would seem he has gotten himself mixed up in some unsavoury business. I have always liked the boy, but he should never have left the city to go play farmer in a dust bowl like Tremorfa. What he knows about geoponics could be written on the back of a postage stamp. Then to try to stand up to a ruthless petty autarch like Du Maurier on his own? Now the whole fiasco has turned to violent bloodshed. I must say Edwin does not lack for courageousness in his convictions, but it is utterly foolish. I am only relieved I managed to convince Eleanor that she and the children would be safer here than there, after the first incident last year.

I returned this afternoon to find out Edwin is now on the run from the authorities (in so much as what "Law" exists in that georgic chaparral) and Eleanor imploring me to act. It seems Edwin may well have questions to answer regarding the deaths of the two rogues who tried to ambush him and his companions. However, if the local constable is in the pay of Du Maurier, I think it is better he should place himself into the hands of Wilberforce Bravett, then to formally surrender himself to Alyaksandr Bogdanov, the High Sheriff in Alba. At least then he will be beyond the reach and corrupting influence of Du Maurier. I explained to Eleanor that I went to school, then the Academy, alongside both men. I know that, without need of asking for favour, I can rely unreservedly upon their integrity. She did spout some nonsense about taking off to Alba to rescue Edwin, but I strictly forbade such lunacy. Nonetheless, I have sent word to Edwin that I shall dispatch Carstairs to meet them from the train and see them safely accommodated in Alba. I shall have to have this situation dealt with with some alacrity as it must not be allowed to impinge upon my own schedule. As for that conniving poltroon Du Maurier; for all my father's teachings, I shall take a switch to the man if I ever lay eyes upon him. It would seem his interest in the Ransom family's farmland may be more about his obsession with Aresian artefacts than simply the application of merciless business expedience. I am also intrigued; if that tomb is undisturbed, then I wonder what secrets it might hold? If I were not so engaged with my own project I would relish such an opportunity, however, my business is with discovering living Aresians, not ancient dead ones. To that end, we met today at Covingdome so I could show my prospective team members around the ship. They expressed quite some high levels of appreciation. I must say, however I do not at all like that man Fontenelli; What with his affectation of his father's title (that he has no right to) he is purely a blustering popinjay who veers from abject cowardice to childish hysteria like a weather-vane in a storm (I must thank Sir Sydeian for such a spot-on metaphor). I find myself seriously questioning my own wisdom in including the man, but none the less I cannot chance losing the involvement of the only remaining Aresian in the whole of Tharsis.

The engine modifications are completed. Extra armaments have been tested and the crew drilled thoroughly. Llewellyn, as always, has done an excellent job. I do not think we could be better prepared. There was some nervous talk of the dangers from Utopian forces in the area around Neath which we allayed. Nonetheless, I feel our biggest threat in that quadrant may come from the filibusters of the Sea of Sands north of Triton and Utopia. I have it on good authority that, though Amenthes has done much to make the region safer, Utopia has never rescinded a single letter of marque in the last twenty years let alone executed a single sand or skypirate. Nonetheless, I am sure if those buccaneers decide to ignore our pennants of registry to chance their arm, then the Seren Bore and her Captain, are more than a match for anything they could throw at us. We have a departure date; 8 am on Sunday 30th. Less than four days to go. I must admit to being quite excited myself. This will be the culmination of over ten years of preparation in addition to five years hard work.

I truly believe the answers I seek are out there just beyond Neath shielded by the vast shield walls of ice. I believe I have convinced the others that at least the possibility is worth their effort. If we can be the first in twenty-five years to make peaceful contact with the Aresians then none of this will be in vain. I believe the Aresians were far more puissant than we ever suspected. It is self-evident they were not just travelling between our planets, they have interstellar travel and the key to the universe itself. I believe they also have other technologies we have never dreamed of, including mind manipulation powers. I believe it is they who hold the key to the whole of mankind's future on Mars, if not the whole of mankind's future. Without their help, I believe we are ultimately doomed to extinction.

I look forward to Monday morning.

Extracts from
Beresford's History of the Martian Colonies.
3rd Edition. Milton and Dante.

Chapter 3. A New Eden; the Flora and Fauna of Mars.

Human colonists soon became aware that, though physically similar to Earth humans, the Tellurians, there were marked differences between the races. There were, at least, three major distinct races of human or "hominid" Martians, plus other sub-races. At least one major non-human race.
Page 194.

The three major humanoid races were most commonly differentiated by the colonists citing skin colouration – as one might call a Negro "black" or an American Indian "red." The three major groups that presented themselves to early colonists were thus identified simply as; "Yellow, or Kitreenoh," "Green or Prahsino" and "Red or Peerrohs" Martians. Their skin colouration being much more manifest than the subtleties of diverse human skin colour pigmentation.
Page 195.

It was documented that there were three (possibly more) distinct types of communities within Martian culture. The first encountered were the "Heterogeneous Communities" where all Martian humanoid races were numerically represented to a greater or lesser extent. These were usually highly segregated or organised on rigid caste restrictions, often reflecting a similar pyramidal social power structure. The second type of community was the "Limited Community" where all members of the social structure, apart from the helot class, are drawn from one racial group. These were often communities dedicated to or dependent upon a single "product" or activity, i.e.; the mining community at Hellas was a rural society made up entirely of the Prahsino Martians. The third society type encountered were termed "Seclusive Communities," these were the hardest for Tellurians to

gain any opportunity to study due to their geographical isolation, reclusive nature and frequently extreme xenophobia. They were rumoured to range widely from internally rigid single gender based communities to freely racially intermixed (including other non-human races) and were often engaged upon one social aspect such as religious societies (orthodox or dissenting) or culturally anomalous activities.
Page 197.

Overall Martian social structures within their communities mirror similar societal constructs existing or have existed on Earth. The most obvious difference being their lack of apportioned gender-based cultural or social roles and their approaches to raising children.

One main difference observed was (ii) that apparent gender categorising into male and female social roles appeared unknown. The females only withdrawing from active participation during the late third trimester and often returning shortly after giving birth. Deviant sexual behaviour or proclivities have never been observed.

Professor Icke H. Elron in his thesis "Martian Parthenogenesis and the Semitic Gods," (iii) put forward his ludicrous theory that the Martians were an asexual humanoid race reproducing through parthenogenesis. This he linked with his heretical theories of the origin of Christ. Although thoroughly discredited his theory often resurfaces amongst the less well informed possibly due to the dearth of solid anthropological data it has been possible to obtain within the subject. Also the lack of any documented interracial Martian Tellurian pairings leading to procreation.

Along with a number of other aspects of their societies, the Martians have so far managed to completely obscure this major facet of their nature and cultures from academic study.
Page 198/9

Although by no means the absolute norm, there appears to be a prevalence within some Martian societies, especially the

Seclusive Communities, for children to be brought up in a form of communal residential crèche, somewhat like the Spartan agoge, but less rigorous. It has been suggested this could be due more to the demands of the socioeconomic role of the parents than any traditional social, cultural or religious imperative. It has been suggested this agoge system may also be used as a form of orphanage or worse; a method of unburdening individuals or families of illegitimate children.

The widely broadcasted claims of Dr Fidious Mountweazel (iv) that the existence of this agoge system substantiated his assertion Martians practised culturally sanctioned or ritualised panmixia remains highly implausible.

Page 201.

As recounted earlier the first Martians encountered by Hamilton and Stranger were the so-called Yellow or, as later designated, Kitreenoh Martians. These are a race of humans with faun coloured skin, amber coloured eyes, with caprine pupils and pale blond hair. The males and females were otherwise exceedingly Tellurian like, in height and build. In Heterogeneous Martian Communities, they dominated the professional and artisan classes.

The so-called Green or, as later designated, Prahsino, Martians were the physically shortest of the three races, often not growing taller than five feet two inches tall. Males and females are of a uniformly pyknic build. The greenish hue was originally attributed to poor iron uptake in their major food groups resulting in a form of hereditary chlorosis. Their hair was uniformly black and thick, naturally greying with age, and eye colour ranges across the green spectrum. They also shared the distinct caprine structure to their eyes. In Heterogeneous Martian Communities, they often gravitated to labour intensive roles in agriculture, construction or warfare.

The Red, later designated Peerrohs, Martians, are the most imposing of the three races. Often taller than the other races, some males were recorded at over six and three-quarter feet tall, lissome and physically powerful. Their skin colour, like the other races, can range across the hues, but their eye colour was exclusively black with black hair which does grey with age. Unaccountably, they do not share the caprine eye structure of the other two races, their eyes are most humanlike. In Martian Heterogeneous Communities, they most often formed the ruling noble and elite warrior castes. Generally, their Limited Communities were often aggressive, warlike and heavily slave labour based.

Interestingly, members of the Kitreenoh and Peerrohs equally formed the elite of the intelligentsia and political classes in Heterogeneous Communities.
Page 203.

Rumours of the existence of White and Blue humanoid Martian races, and even others, have never been fully confirmed let alone taxonomically described. The dearth of corroborated information or physical evidence supports that these may simply have been isolated instances of hybrids or atypical mutations rather than distinct races.
Page 205.

Messrs Golton and Derwin in their seminal work on the subject (iiv) suggested the new science of Eugenics could easily explain the distinct colouration in the skins of Martian Hominid races, being the result of natural occurring environmentally driven physical adaptations. These may have presented initially as anomalies within an originally wider group which somehow became integral to rigid social identification and caste selection. Much as those which appear in some lesser or uncivilised Tellurian societies.
Page 210.

Notes
ii. G. Le Rouge. 1886. Investigations in Socio-Gender Compartmentalisation in Aresian Societies.
iii. Professor I. H. Elron. 1886. Martian Parthenogenesis and the Semitic Gods.
iv. Dr F. Mountweazel 1884. Panmixia and Other Immoralities within Martian Culture.

Mathew McCall

iiv. F. Golton, C. Derwin et al. 1886. Inquiries into Xeno-Human Faculty and the Influence of Gemmules in Inherited Characteristics.

Chapter 4. The Birth of Identity; the First Human Martians.

The adoption of the term Aresian to denote the autochthon inhabitants of Mars came about due to the dichotomy presented by the birth of the first children amongst the colonists. The Colonial Authorities, while accepting these children were, in fact, colonial subjects, chose to require them to be registered as "Martian."

Page 276.

In 1862, the British Imperial Colonial Government was the first to see the political benefits of requiring those registering these children's nationality at birth as "Martian." Thus creating the firstborn human "Martians." Other Colonial Governments quickly followed suit. This met with both agreement and violent responses from various groups within the ranks of the colonists. Some felt this was a step towards being disenfranchised and stripped of their securities as citizens of their mother nations and Empires, while others delighted in what they believed was recognition they were no longer Tellurians, men of Earth, but Martians and thus with privileges congruent with such status. Regrettably, the colonial powers did not see it that way.

Page 279

The contradiction, of course, was that the autochthon inhabitants of the planet Mars were also referred to in both Tellurian common parlance and official documentation as "Martians." A term on Earth and in the Martian colonies synonymous with "alien."

The decision was made – originally by the British Governor General, Sir Oswald Carfax – in 1863 requiring all future documentation and official correspondence to refer to the aboriginal, or indigenous, (iii) peoples as "Aresians."

Ares was the Ancient Greek name for Mars, named after their God of War, and still in use in the Greek language today. Objections this would somehow demean the autochthon Martians were dismissed as it was considered they had no cultural investment in the name Martian or Mars. Their own languages, of which seven were known, had numerous names for themselves and their planet (listed in Appendix C, pages 2001 – 2010) however, most were virtually unpronounceable by Tellurian tongue, and there was no known use of the term in indigenous or aboriginal communications.

Also, it was argued that "Aresian," being derived from a more ancient term, was respectful as it denoted the autochthon people pre-dated Tellurian human colonisation.

Notes.

iii. Chapter One; Theories of Pre-Colonial Settlement Pattern; Indigenous vs. Aboriginal.
Page 280.

Railway termini are our gates to the glorious and the unknown.
Through them, we pass out into adventure

E. M. Forster

CHAPTER THREE

<u>ALBA STATION</u>

Interview notes (unedited)

Interviewee: Mr L. Edwin Ransom Esq. The owner of Ransom's Farm, Tremorfa.

Interviewer: Miss Charity Bryant-Drake.

Location: Train from Yuma District to Alba Central station.

Date: 26/9/26

Time: 10.30 AM.

Interview recorded using a PDT (phonetic diction transcribing) device.

B-D (intro/narration); Mr Ransom is a man of 35 years. Just under 6 feet tall and slim. His chin is clean-shaven (though he sports a heavy five o'clock shadow) with a fashionable Suvorov moustache. He has a pleasant open face, topped with a quite unruly mop of dark brown hair. He wears round wire-rimmed spectacles which he uses for reading and has expressive green eyes. He habitually wears an original Harris tweed sporting cap, which has obviously seen better days, and a heavy Chesterfield overcoat and old Army issue filter mask slung casually around his neck, the type with a visor and filter all in one unit (British I think – must check).

When agitated or overwrought Mr Ransom occasionally stammers over his words (?).

Mr Ransom holds a Batchelor of Sciences Degree in Biological Fuel Technologies from the University of Tharsis at

Olympia, and until the untimely death of his father was studying for his Master's Degree under Professor James Flammarion. His family has been in the business of growing and producing fuel stuffs for three generations. He has four current patents to his name and another five under submission. He often wryly refers to himself as a "Dandelion Farmer."

Mr Ransom sits almost curled up into the corner of the carriage. Apparently trying to get as far away from the window as possible. His manner is distressed and his motions jittery. Since we boarded the train he has been quite uncommunicative and had passed the time writing letters and scribbling drawings - of an ugly little dog in various costumes- in his journal.

He has agreed to allow me to interview him and record the interview.

B-D; Mr Ransom. Is it true you believe what has happened to you is due to the direct machinations of the industrialist Mr Eleuthère D Maurier?

ER; Yes. Since the death of my father, he has sent men to threaten and intimidate me, my workers and my family. Culminating in the recent two attempts to murder me, members of my workforce and my friend.

B-D; So you are fleeing in fear for your life?

ER: In truth? Yes.

B-D; And to where are you going?

ER; It is my intention, and that of my friend and companions, to seek justice by surrendering ourselves to the High Sheriff in Alba.

B-D; Why do you wish to do that? Why could you not surrender to the local Constable in Tremorfa?

ER; Because I believe the new Constable, Lucius Everheart, to be in the pay of Eleuthère D Maurier and so to be part of this conspiracy.

B-D; With all due respect Mr Ransom, talk of a conspiracy might sound a little paranoid to some readers. Could you explain further?

ER; My father, God rest his soul, died almost two years ago and left the farm to myself and Minerva, the wife of my late older brother, Philip. Philip was killed when I was studying for my degree. He died saving the lives of a group of iron miners from a plains strider attack. Unlike me, he was quite the heroic adventurer. My father was devastated when we lost Philip. He was the apple of my father's eye, while I was always the pedestrian one; the studious one. The person everyone, including my father, could rely upon. Please forgive me, I do not mean to sound disparaging about my father; he was a great man and he loved both of us dearly. It was just I could never be as interesting or live my life as flamboyantly or as courageously as Philip. I am just an academic turned dandelion farmer, little else. I was studying for my masters, under the tutelage of my now father-in-law Professor James Flammarion, in Tharsis city when my father died suddenly. It was his wish that I return and run the family farm as its continued existence provides work and support for thirty people, including my sister-in-law. Also, we are one of the last of the independent botanical fuel and combustible mass producers left in Tremorfa district. My father believed without us independent producers, major industrialists would one day have a complete stranglehold on Tharsis' access to fuel, and that would deliver our hard won freedoms, even our democracy, into the hands of megalomaniacs like D Maurier and his ilk. I returned with my family to Tremorfa and I began to implement some of the ideas for improvements to the production systems I had been working on since I was at University.

B-D; When did you first encounter Mr D Maurier?

ER; We had been at the farm for about six months when the first letters arrived.

B-D; Letters?

ER; D Maurier's solicitors sent me several letters offering to purchase my father's land. At first, they were polite and business like. The offer they contained was at first derisory, but they rapidly increased to what could only be considered as a grossly disproportionate amount. Each time I politely refused. The offers continued, but couched in quite threatening terms. They threatened court action over my water rights and rights of access, even going so far as to suggest D Maurier's Solicitors could contest the validity of my grandfather's original land claim. Each time these were supplemented with a financial offer for settlement. I refused.

B-D; And then?

ER; There were four incidents quite close together that truly alarmed me. The first was the death of Mr Hindecker, my elderly neighbour to the east and one of the only other independent botanical mass producers left North of Tremorfa Township. He was killed when he disturbed an intruder in his home. No one was ever apprehended. Hindecker was known to be as poor as a church mouse and his homestead is so remote that I have only been there twice in my lifetime. No robber would travel so far out simply to steal a few trinkets from an old gentleman. Then there was the incident where someone let a whole herd of Martian Blues onto my north-end field, days before harvest. I lost tens of thousands of guineas in revenue and almost lost my railway fuel contract. No one ever claimed them so we kept them. The third incident was the death of Constable Nielsen. He went missing without warning and was found several days later lying on the roadside out in the wilderness. He had been murdered. An officer of the High Sheriff at Alba came down to carry out the investigation, several local ruffians were arrested but no one was ever convicted. Constable Nielson's killer, like Mr Hindecker's killer, is still out there.

B-D; You must have been getting concerned for the safety of yourself and that of your family.

ER; I was. My wife, Eleanor, was becoming very distressed and was frightened to allow me to leave the house unescorted by Karl (Mr Ransom has an android, an automaton he refers to as Karl. I believe it is an ex-military model – built by R.U.A. -and certainly more than capable of protecting Mr Ransom's family). We took all possible precautions for our safety. I issued what arms we had to the tenant workers and Karl also took to patrolling the house and grounds at night, but it was not enough. One morning, when Eleanor and Minerva were getting the children up, my daughter, Tabitha (seven), told them she had awoken in the night to find a "funny man" standing at the bottom of her bed. She said he had a strange mask over his face. He shushed her and told her to go back to sleep. So, bless her heart, she just did what he said. We checked the nursery thoroughly, hoping against hope, it had just been a strange dream. It was not. We found the window had been forced and there were obvious, almost deliberate, footprints on the carpet at the end of both children's beds. Worse of all the intruder had taken the children's pet dog, Mr Pug. The children were inconsolable.

B-D; That is when you sent them back to Tharsis to stay with her father?

ER; Yes. It was. Tremorfa was without a Constable and we had been unable to even truly secure our home. There was nothing else for it. I prayed that when a new Constable was appointed law and order would be restored to Tremorfa.

B-D; And you feel D Maurier was somehow behind all this? Have you any evidence?

ER; I cannot directly accuse Mr D Maurier of the murders of Mr Hindecker and Constable Neilson or orchestrating either the intrusion into my home or the cattle invasion of my land. But D Maurier has benefited; he brought up all Hindecker's outstanding debts and forced foreclosure on the estate. Mr Hindecker's family received not a red penny. Mr D Maurier owns the only large cattle herd in this area and is the only one who could possibly afford to lose two hundred head of cattle and leave them unclaimed. He has the wealth and the ruthlessness to hire men with the dubious skills required to carry out such acts including; breaking and entering and murder.

B-D; So you feel he was behind the attack on the Toll Station and on Mrs Phillipott's Guest House?

ER; Yes. I am certain. Three of the men who tried to ambush us at the Toll House were the same men that had turned up at my farm the day before with another threatening letter from D Maurier. And most probably the same men who took shots at young Michael. They were in his pay. Nonetheless, we will never be able to prove this as they were handed over to Everheart for arresting. I believe the claims of the existence of another witness by Constable Everheart were lies, used to trap myself and my companions in Tremorfa so we would be helpless to defend ourselves against the attack which happened last night.

B-D; For the reader's understanding, could you please tell me what happened last night at Mrs Phillipott's Guest House.

ER; Several brutes, heavily armed and, I believe, intent upon murdering us all in our beds, broke into Mrs Phillipott's Guest House. Only through the bravery of my friend Mr Franklin and Karl were they held off long enough for the household to be rallied against them.

B-D; And you contend this too was – to use your word – orchestrated by D Maurier?

ER; And Everheart. Yes. I believe Everheart is in the pay of D Maurier. I have seen proof the advocate he suggested to help me is also in the pay of D Maurier and only the other day D Maurier himself threatened my wife at a reception in Tharsis.

B-D; One final question, Mr Ransom, if I might be so bold; What is it you think D Maurier wants so much he seems willing to go to such brutal lengths for?

ER: I believe it is just for my land. He is one of those ruthless minded men that have to control everything. I also believe, as my father did, that the aim of such men is to gain a stranglehold on all of us, whether through fuel or food or whatever resource. To make our free nations beholden to them. I believe that wholeheartedly and it frightens me because I believe it threatens all our freedoms.

B-D; Thank you, Mr Ransom.

End.

Charity Bryant-Drake.
Notes to self. 26/9/26
Ransom did brilliantly.
Will get this polished up and submitted ASAP.
I'm not sure as to mention his stammering when he gets excited in the article as it may be seen as a feebleness of mind by some.
That will put the cat firmly amongst the pigeons! Hope it is not going to be his epitaph.
As agreed he did not talk about the tomb. Will see if Franklin will answer some questions next.

Transcription of an intercepted conversation using a Meucci electromagnetic telephonic transmission and receiving device.

Interception on the authorisation of; TOP SECRET.

Time of call; 11.32 am. 26th September 26.

Origin of call; Private office of Mr Eleuthère Du Maurier. Industrialist. Tholus 661. Tholus City. Zephyria.

Caller; Unidentified. Believed to be Mr E. Du Maurier.

Location of receiver of call; The Mayflower Lounge Hotel Lobby. Drury St. Tharsis.

Receiver of call; (Suspect) Mr John Lloyd, under the alias of Mr Uri Knapp (Foreign National). As identified by witnesses and hotel records.

Translated from Zephyrian French.

Caller;   "It is me."

Receiver; "The package arrives at 3.10pm. Platform 3."

Caller;   "Good."

Receiver; "How do you want us to solve this problem?"

Caller;   "Special delivery, but do not make too much noise if possible."

Receiver; "We can handle it quietly, sir, but if the package... if it proves too difficult to handle quietly do you want us to..."

Caller;   "Yes. I'm sick of this problem. Do what I pay you for."

Receiver; "I might need some additional manpower."

Caller;   "Are you attempting to extort me for more money? Mister Knapp?"

Receiver;   "No. No, sir, it's just what the... American suggested that they might be some problems... with the collection. That is."

Caller;   (Shouting) "I pay you to do this! This is what I pay you for! No?"

Receiver;   (Reply inaudible)

Caller;   "Then do it. Imbecile!"

Receiver;   (Reply inaudible)

Caller;   (Shouting. First part unintelligible).... Shoot him down on the platform if you have to. I have enough of this dandelion farmer! Kill him! "

Receiver;   "We will get the job done. Sir."

Caller;   "You do better or I will have the American deal with you as well when he gets there. Understand?

Receiver;   "Yes, I understand."

Caller;   "Cretin!"

Conversation terminated by the Caller.

Diary of Aelita Fontenelli (Mrs).
Thursday, September, 26th. MY.26
Dear Diary,

I was quite giddy this morning, as in the excitement of last night's soirée and such a late return I forgot to take my medication. Strangely, I felt so much sprightlier today, and my tummy feels less butterfly filled. I take those odious little brown pills Dr Hammond prescribes solely to please Giovanni.

This morning he took me to see Professor Flammarion's airship. It was good to be out of the house on such a pleasant day and I truly enjoyed the visit. Professor Flammarion has invited Giovanni and I to accompany him and his associates on his quest to investigate what he believes are clues to where my mother's and father's people withdrew to.

Professor Flammarion is certain there are still cities full of Aresians, like me, out there somewhere. I pray he is right and he believes I may be able to be some aid in communicating his friendly intent if we should discover them.

I have no idea if I will be anything more than an anomalous curiosity to them or maybe worse. Maybe they too will greet me with the revulsion and hostility some people still do. However, I feel this is something I must do as an Aresian. If there is the slimmest of chances I could find even a few of my own kind out there then I must try.

Giovanni does not wish to go, and I think that is more to do with his fears for me than for himself. Also, the presence of Sir John has made him quite anxious.

Giovanni still harbours great enmity towards Sir John, no matter how I reassure him, Sir John was ever the gentleman and nothing untoward happened on that journey.

Unfortunately, Giovanni lost his temper again and made quite a tomnoddy of himself. I fear sometimes people see him as much of an outsider as they see me.

How do I fit in? Giovanni does his best to surround us with compassionate and enlightened people, but it still does not stop the comments whispered behind my back and the harsh voices that cry out in the street. This all brings back to me the dreadful memories of my first days at the orphanage, when I had been so driven by the bullying of the other children that Sister Maris Stella caught me trying to remove the colour from my skin with a scrubbing brush and carbolic soap.

The Good Lord taught that I must learn to forgive, but bearing the weight of their unreasoning abhorrence often leaves my heart exhausted.

Diary, I have decided if there is but the smallest chance Professor Flammarion is right; that he could indeed discover others of my kind still here on Mars, then I must be part of such an undertaking. Professor Flammarion talks passionately about this being mankind's last opportunity to proffer the hand of peace to the Aresians. I must also play my part. If there is the possibility my presence might help ensure the success of the endeavour; then I must go. It is my duty to all the peoples of Mars, to every Tellurian I have loved or cared for and for all my own kind.

Last night I dreamed of my father for the first time in years. He was, as he was, so tall and handsome, but I was not a child. For all I tried I could not understand his words, but I knew he loved me. And I know he would want me to do this.

This evening I will tell Giovanni I will go even if he forbids me to and refuses to accompany me.

Journal of Adam Franklin.
The lady journalist tried several times to get me to partake in some form of spontaneous consultation, I think she aims to interview me. I maintain a courteous refusal.

She tells me it will help support Edwin's position. I informed her I would make my statement to the official authorities in Alba, under oath, if need be. Anything else is, in my opinion, meaningless. And would only serve to stoke the flames of newspaper sensationalism.

She tried to question me about my background. I refused to answer her questions, but she is not a young lady for whom "No" is an answer easily accepted. Unfortunately, her insistence forced me to be quite impolite, almost rude. I did concede that I could and will confirm the details of all the events I have witnessed and participated in.

She finally let it lie and sat writing her "piece" as she calls it. We rode on in silence with only Michael making the occasional excited comments on things passing by the window of our carriage.

My thoughts were elsewhere, but from what I could focus my attention on, the vistas were breathtaking. Panoramas of an immense alien landscape, its all-encompassing crimson incongruously dotted with the green and blue splashes of farmlands, forests and lakes. Sheltering under an immeasurable icy blue sky, adorned with the pale reflections of two peculiarly formed moons. We crossed wide empty plains of cinnabar sand, strewn with rust coloured rocks and wrought iron bridges that spanned glassy, forest banked, canals wider than any canyon on Earth.

From a high embankment, Michael excitedly demanded we all come look down upon what appeared to me as nothing more than a bizarre jumble of pale crystals all of megalithic proportions scattered across the plain below. Edwin, in sombre tones, told us it was the abandoned Aresian city of Ananthor. It had been a major Kitreenoh (yellow-skinned) Aresian trading city that suffered terribly during the phthisis epidemic of '63 and never recovered its position. It was eventually sacked by the British Military and Colonial forces from Tharsis in '66 and the surviving population dispossessed.

Michael asked what "dispossessed" meant, and Miss Bryant-Drake commented it means those that were not massacred by the Colonial Brigades were driven out into the desert to die of exposure or starvation. Michael attempted more clarifying questions, but we were all in too reflective a mood to answer them.

What else should I expect from a world named after the God of War, that its history would be brutal and blood-soaked? It would seem Sergeant Major Adam Franklin, DCM, had probably played an active part in that bloody history. I wondered how many people he - I - have killed in active service of my masters? From the events of the last couple of days, I have learnt I truly have the abilities of a ruthless killer, but do I truly have the stomach or lack of conscience for it? This Sergeant Major Franklin is as alien to me as those strangely shaped moons hanging in the sky.

I attempted to read some more of my journal, but with Michael's interruptions coupled with my own trepidation, I soon gave up. I excused myself and went off to the water closet. In the cramped confines of the booth, I undertook the strangest of self-examinations, I ungloved my right hand for the first time since we left Ransom's farm, and examined it in detail, as if newly acquainted. I noticed when I rested it upon the porcelain of the sink I could feel the cold ceramic under my fingers. I examined my left hand as carefully. It was warm and fleshy to the touch, a normal hand, but then I noticed something odd; The tips of my fingers are completely smooth, none of those tiny whirls on the top of each finger, nothing, they are flat and clean. With my curiosity piqued by this discovery, I decided to try something of an experiment; I rapped the sink hard with my right knuckles. I felt the blow, but not as I would have expected, there was a level of discomfort but no pain. Then with my left, my real, hand and there it was; the same sensation; discomfort but no real pain. I struck it again upon the stoutest part of the sink with a blow which should have cracked a knuckle or two. Nothing, less discomfort in fact. It seemed the harder the blow, the less the sensation of injury. I unbuckled my breeches and closely examined my legs. Real enough looking to me ... a tad hirsute with a number of small scars on my knees, the kind one acquires through the rough misadventures of childhood. An idea struck me. I quickly refastened my clothes and walked down to the dining carriage. I was in luck, for not only were the places already set, but a sign beckoned me on to a further toilet facility with a shower cubical no less.

I filched a fork as I passed through and headed to the washroom facilities. Thankful for the greater space, I stripped off my clothes and set about my impromptu experiment with more suspicion and dispassionate interest than fear. I could feel the prongs of the fork against the skin of my outer thigh, real, hard and pointed. As I pushed hard there was indeed enough discomfort to be classed as pain, but when I, with gritted teeth, thrust the fork deep into the flesh there was little or no sensation at all, but about half an inch in the prongs grazed against what felt like metal. Amazed, I tried the other thigh to the same result; a little initial "hurt" and a few drops of blood and something solid underneath. I even tasted the blood, and blood it was indeed. Then, with gusto, I set about a thorough and somewhat bloody examination.

After finishing my inspection and showering, I went to return to our compartment, but upon discovering luncheon was being served I joined Edwin and the others at their table. We would have eaten almost in complete silence if it had not been for Miss Bryant-Drake, who had obtained a complimentary copy of the morning's newspaper, The Olympian Herald, and was regaling us with her comments on various events. I, however, was too lost in my own thoughts to be drawn into any conversation.

The results of my experiment had proven to me that the body I inhabit, in its entirety, is nothing more than a flesh covered machine. Beneath this "meat suit" is something hard and metallic, most probably exactly the same as my right arm. I found myself looking at Karl standing guard back by the dining carriage door. In his denim overalls, long riding coat and wide-brimmed hat, he stands almost nonchalantly nursing his scattergun like some savage babe. Are we the same he and I; sentient machines? But here I sit supping tea and nibbling tiffin like a gentleman, while he, my brass brother, stands watch. He does not eat or bleed or defecate and is plagued no more by nightmares than – to use Docket's words - a steam tractor. I, on the other hand, do. And, though I know not what kind of heart beats inside my chest, I have a pulse.

I resolved I could no longer avoid the truth. Tonight I will read the journal. I must have the answers even if it threatens my sanity to do so.

To
Mrs Eleanor A. Ransom.
Locksley Hall.
Machen,
Tharsis.
September 26st M.Y. 26
Dearest Nelly,

I shall try and be as brief as I can, as I will give these letters to Carstairs and he shall deliver them to you.

As to whatever you may have heard; be assured we are safe. Carstairs has ensconced us in a hotel under assumed names.

Although Carstairs will be able to fill in the details this is what happened upon our arrival at Alba Central Station.

We arrived a little early, five or ten minutes I think, and disembarked. Travelling light we had only the clothes we stood up in, a few provisions and our weapons (suitably secreted upon us as best as possible to not cause alarm amongst the other passengers). We had no idea Carstairs would be meeting us and so we made our way up those amazing Ames Revolving Stairways towards the Tharsis railplane terminal. Michael and Karl were so confounded when confronted with the bank of moving staircases they elected to take the normal steps instead. Leaving myself, Adam and Miss Bryant-Drake to ride the moving stairway to the top.

The three of us reached the top first, of course, and stopped to wait for Karl and Michael to clear themselves of the madding throng of passengers, porters and tourists. Miss Bryant-Drake was distracted by the grandeur of the great hall with its vast iron ribbed and vaulted glass ceiling. I too was distracted; confirming the time on the Frodsham half-hunter you gave me against the magnificent station clock. It was only Adam who, thankfully, was watchful enough to see danger coming.

Someone jostled me, and as I turned my head to apologise, I was seized from behind by two men. The other, a big man wearing an old industrial respirator, who had first bumped into me, suddenly struck me to the side of the head with something very hard. Luckily, however, my cap had slid sideways in the struggle and cushioned most of the blow. In my panic, I must have kicked out because my foot connected with the respirator-wearing attacker's private parts and he staggered away cursing loudly.

Instantly Adam dragged one of the attackers off of me and flung him off into the crowd. I managed to twist enough to get to grips with the other thug. We were grappling violently when Adam struck him with such a punch to the jaw that I saw his eyes instantly glaze and he fell like a log.

I was too dazed to react swiftly, but Adam grabbed my elbow and hurried me away towards the steps up to the railplane terminal. Miss Bryant-Drake seized my other arm and they ran me like we do in the park with little James.

We had almost reached the terminal steps when a tall man in an Inverness coat and bowler hat stepped out of the multitude in front of us and levelled a Lancenett beam pistol at me. Miss Bryant-Drake screamed, the crowd scattered, and I froze.

I shall remember that man's face for the rest of my life, the pale pockmarked skin, the thin moustache over a cruel tight-lipped mouth. One eye was covered by a bizarre monocular apparatus which seemed to be bolted into his face, from which a corposant glow emitted. The other eye was like an unblinking piece of jet. I thought I had been frightened before, but the expression on the fellow's face petrified me. We stood there frozen for what seemed eternity staring at each other, then he pulled the trigger.

Click!

It misfired. I will hear that empty sound in my nightmares. I know not how or why, but I thank God himself it did not fire for I would surely be dead.

Adam hauled me off to the side. The gunman cursed and aimed his pistol again. This time it made a heavy "thrump!" sound, and a blaze of green light lanced past my head by a whisker.

Suddenly there was a terrific shout from behind me, it was Karl. He levelled his scattergun and fired into the gunman's chest. The blast sent the fellow staggering backwards, but he did not go down! Instead, he instantly regained himself and, ignoring Karl, again took aim at me.

At that, Miss Bryant-Drake slammed her satchel into his face. It stunned him enough for us all to run for our lives. We had almost made it to the very bottom of the steps when a whistle rang out and two uniformed Constables came rushing down the steps from the railplane terminal. I was so relieved to see them that I unthinkingly paused to call to them.

As I did, the gunman pursuing us shot them both dead. The Lancenett's beam punching straight through them. Right there on the steps in front of us and hundreds of bystanders. People screamed, dropped their possessions and fled or tried to hide behind railings or luggage trolleys.

I saw a small child, little more than an infant, wandering, confused and alone in the midst of the mayhem. I could not leave him there. I dashed across, snatched him up into my arms and ran for the cover of the flower seller's cart by the steps.

That's when the shooting really started. I thrust the child into the arms of a young woman hiding behind the cart and then, – the Lord forgive me Nelly because I do not know what came over me, – I drew my father's pistol and turned back to the battle. For a battle is what it had become.

Adam was standing exchanging gunfire with the other attackers while Karl and the gunman were trading blows with each other like two bare-knuckle pugilists. How any man could stand up to Karl in a fist fight I have no idea.

Adam had paused as he discarded his empty pistol to take up his repeating rifle, when the respirator-wearing ruffian, the one whom had first attacked me, took the chance to try to rush him.

Nelly, I did not think, I simply acted to protect my friend. God forgive me, I am no soldier nor marksman, but as the man broke cover I shot him dead.

Another, brandishing a Miéville storming gun, took the chance to jump up and take a better shot but he too was too slow. Adam is so very, very fast.

Miss Bryant-Drake was, from behind one of the great cast iron pillars, firing an old Eliminator pistol wildly in the direction of the newspaper seller's stand (The one owned by that old pleasant Russian chap from whom I always stop at to buy the Fellow magazine on my journeys). Behind the kiosk, another two thugs were sheltering and sniping back at her. I could see most of one clearly and before he could react I shot him too. I must have only wounded the blighter as he fell, but struggled to fire back. Luckily, for me, that is, Adam finished the job with a single shot.

The other attacker was well covered behind the newspaper stand. And so Adam started walking towards the stand, like a determined madman, firing round after round into the structure. Miss Bryant-Drake also kept firing at it.

Without warning, as if his nerve had broken, the thug made a dash for it. His speed most probably driven by fear. We simply watched him run away, for to shoot a fleeing man in the back would be unconscionable.

He was almost clear away when an older man in a cap stepped out from a knot of cowering bystanders and struck him such a blow with his cane it felled him instantly. It was Carstairs!

I turned to see Karl finally knock the gunman down with a blow which should have shattered bone and would have killed a lesser man. I thought he would most certainly be dead, but as we ran toward the beckoning Carstairs, I glanced back to see the gunman dragging himself back to his feet!

As we reached Carstairs, more rifle shots rang out. People screamed and fearing they were no longer safe in their hiding places took flight again. Carstairs began to marshal us out of the great hall when I suddenly realised Michael was not with us. I shouted his name and cast about frantically. I would have gone back into the melee, if Carstairs had not restrained me and assured me Michael was safe.

We escaped the concourse, through the doors opposite Tidhar's Coffee House on the Peckinpaugh Road where Carstairs had your father's Emancipation waiting. I thanked God that at the wheel, running the engine, sat young Michael.

All of us bundled unceremoniously into the vehicle and were almost away when another attacker, a huge red-bearded fellow wearing a great fur coat and a big ushanka pulled down over his head, stepped out of the crowds of pedestrians and started firing a handheld Bira Gun at us. Thank God the weapon was bucking so uncontrollably, as he tried to crank and fire it, it simply sprayed bullets wildly.

Carstairs, who had replaced Michael in the driving seat, cursed loudly, the first time I have ever heard him do so, and drove straight at the man. There was a sickening crunch and the man flew several feet across the road like a tossed rag doll.

We fled into the chaos of the traffic of Alba's main roads and across the city to a hotel Carstairs had already procured for us. One where he assures me discretion is paramount.

We have taken quick stock of ourselves. Apart from a few minor abrasions, we are all pretty much unharmed. I have quite a lump on my left temple and an interesting area of singed hair down the right side of my head where the Lancenett beam came too close.

Miss Bryant-Drake has a rather nasty gash on her left arm and hand where a bullet ricocheted off of the pillar she was hiding behind. But she is quite a no-nonsense young lady and had to be convinced to allow Adam even to do an ad hoc field dressing. Miraculously Adam had a very near miss, a bullet passed through his trouser leg and grazed his calf.

Only Karl was actually hit by the gunfire and is quite proudly sporting two bullet impressions, one in his chest plate the other in his right shoulder plate. Nonetheless, his coat now looks as if some very large and aggressive moths have been at it.

Carstairs has laid in provisions for us and we are going to stay low until your father's barrister friend visits tomorrow.

Be assured we are safe and relatively unscathed. I take comfort from the fact there were plenty of witnesses to what happened at the station this afternoon. Du Maurier's men attacked us, terrified hundreds of bystanders, and killed two officers in cold blood. I pray they will swiftly be apprehended and will hang for their crimes along with their evil employer.

Kiss the children for me.

I will soon be with you.

All my love,

Edwin.

Charity Bryant-Drake.

Notes to self. 26/9/26

TITLE; GUNFIGHT AT ALBA CENTRAL STATION (EXCLAMATION) -STOP

TITLE; TWO POLICE OFFICERS RUTHLESSLY SLAIN (EXCLAMATION) -STOP

Late this afternoon a gunfight erupted in Alba Central Train Station -STOP

As yet unidentified heavily armed men ~~tried~~ attempted to murder Mr Ransom in the main concourse of the Station - STOP

Mr Ransom was attacked as he arrived at the concourse by three assailants who beat him mercilessly about the head - STOP

Mr Ransom fought courageously managed to escape their clutches - STOP

A running gun battle erupted between the assassins and Mr Ransom's companions - STOP

At least ~~two~~ three of the assassins murderous thugs were killed in the bloody exchange -STOP

Witnesses saw ~~noted~~ that under direct threat to his life Mr Ransom stopped to heroically rescue a young child caught in the midst of the battle -STOP

This reporter was witness to the horrific and deliberate and cold-blooded slaying of two of Tharsis' finest Police Officers by the assassins as they bravely rushed to Mr Ransom's aid - STOP

Concerned for their lives and those of the bystanders Mr Ransom and his companions had no other recourse than to flee the scene - STOP

They were pursued even into the streets where another assassin indiscriminately opened fire on them - STOP

Fearing for their lives Mr Ransom and his companions are now safely hidden in the bosom of our city and awaiting the opportunity for contact with the authorities - STOP

Mr Ransom is convinced these assassins are ~~in the pay~~ under the direct orders of Mr Eleuthère D Maurier the ruthless Zephyrian Millionaire Fuel Industrialist -STOP

For more on this story read my interview with Mr Ransom inside -STOP

Submitted 4.23pm.

That little Napoleon has outdone himself this time.

I cannot wait until this hits the streets on the front pages tomorrow morning. Along with the interview, it'll make a feature!

Got you! You murderous little Zephyrian French popinjay!

Journal of Adam Franklin.

I have been shot. I have not told Edwin or the others, but I have been shot in the chest and leg. In the chest about an inch to the left of my heart. If whatever pumps inside my chest is indeed a heart.

I went to the bathroom and dug the bullet out with the fork I took from the dining car. I hardly felt the impact and there was hardly any blood. No pain whatsoever. Ruined a good shirt though.

Another bullet had torn a path through my trousers and ricocheted off my leg. I had to laugh it off as a near miss, but it would have blown a man's leg clean from under him.

This is almost beyond my comprehension. I should be dead several times over.

And then there are those I killed today. I cannot even find it in me to regret killing them, in fact, I can hardly dwell on the emotions which assailed me after the deaths at the Tremorfa Toll Gate.

One man I punched with my right fist so hard in the head I know he will never get up again. It was so easy, which frightens me.

I killed the one Edwin wounded as easily as a man would squash a weevil.

And they were all so slow! The one shot me in the chest tried again; he stood up, levelled his rifle and just seemed to stand there waiting for me to kill him. And I did. I looked right into his eye and shot him through the other. And all I felt was the satisfaction of a well-placed shot.

Who am I? What kind of monster am I?

The journalist seems to be elated by the turn of events, she has already contacted her newspaper editor. I must admit she was brave today, but, I understand her step-father suffered at the hands of Du Maurier, she sees this as some way of exposing him for the swine he is. Still, I find her euphoria is somewhat distasteful.

I also ardently wish Edwin would stop apologising to me for "dragging me into this." I feel obliged to keep assuring him I am here of my own volition. After all, what was I doing apart from wandering the byroads of Tremorfa and hiding in barns and outhouses like a stray dog?

Maybe I should simply go and find this Du Maurier and deal with him myself. I doubt there is much he can place between him and me that, in this strange state of being, I could not easily surmount.

The chauffeur, Carstairs, who was sent by Edwin's father-in-law, has left now to return to Tharsis. Edwin insisted he should take Michael with him. He says a barrister is coming to see Edwin first thing in the morning. I pray we will all see the morning untroubled any further.

To

Mrs Eleanor A. Ransom.

Locksley Hall.

Machen,

Tharsis.

September 27th M.Y. 26

Dearest Nelly,

Augustus Wilberforce Bravett SC called on us as we breakfasted this morning. Although the man must be 80, if he is a day, he drives a Jeter, - one of those old horseless steam road carriages - by himself.

A gregarious bear of a man, he robustly greeted us with great humour like old friends. He heartily apologised on behalf of his beloved city for our terrible reception yesterday. He says even in the city of Alba, over the last five years, lawlessness in the less salubrious environs of the city has spiralled out of control. He has himself taken to carrying a fearsome looking orgone oscillation pistol with him wheresoever he goes, and not for show!

Only a year since he had shot two "mug-hunters" dead in the street of the old Iron Miner's quarter! A wildly lurid tale he regaled us with over breakfast. What with his huge walrus moustache, toothy smile, wild mane of ash grey hair and sonorous baritone, he is still quite the force of nature that your father described.

After breakfast and disdaining more tea, he ordered a bottle of Gin and some tonic water and set about it with gusto. Peering intensely over the top of his rimless spectacles, like Mr Bubo, the old Eagle Owl your mother used to keep. He bade us to tell our story of how events unfolded from the very start, the Toll House incident. He listened carefully, only pausing to question specifics, but sometimes in excruciating detail. Firstly me and then Adam, however, he would not speak directly to Karl at all.

When we had both finished, he had us clear the breakfast plates and realised the whole episode at the Toll House on the table using the cruet set and various place settings as representative of all those involved. Like some peculiar game of chess.

Once we had played out our movements to his satisfaction Mr Bravett sighed deeply and declared flatly that under the Law it was a clear case of self-defence. Thus, it leads to no charge to answer. I pointed out Constable Everheart asserted there was another witness who had claimed we were the aggressors.

Mr Bravett snorted loudly and replied even if this supposed witness's statement was correct, being there was no Officer of the Law as yet sworn in for Tremorfa; Everheart cannot have yet taken the Oath of Office. Apprehension of criminals discovered in the act of murder and robbery is every Law abiding citizen's duty. Even if it should result in the unintended death of the criminal.

Mr Bravett threw out some rhetorical questions such as who this supposed spectator was? What were they doing there? Why did they not come to the Toll Master's aid? How he, or she, was not only present, and unnoticed, but was able to see the whole incident without themselves being noticed let alone getting shot, injured or apprehended? His conclusion, with our accord, was obviously there was no such witness.

Adam asked about our fleeing the house arrest and whether Everheart had had the authority to keep us there for as long as he wished. Mr Bravett assured us that until Everheart is officially sworn in, on the first Sunday of the Month, he has no more authority to arrest or detain anyone than any other citizen, and then only if detained within the commissioning of a crime or a known wanted criminal. The "house arrest" should be thought of as little more than an informal request. It fell upon our own gracious recognizance if we had chosen to comply with the request, which we had done. Nonetheless, of course, after the attack on the Guest House, it was totally unreasonable to expect us to remain.

Mr Bravett was not the least bit interested in the details of the assault upon Mrs Phillipott's Guest House. He reassured us under Tharsis Law, any householder, resident or guest, has the right to defend, or aid in the defence of, their home and property. Even to the point of deadly force and, as all those ruffians escaped, there is no legal point to answer.

When Adam asked him how sure he was of that assertion, as the Law, in practice, is really only a matter of interpretation, and Du Maurier has enough wealth to buy the very best solicitors.

Bravett smiled knowingly, "My dear Sir. It would be truly difficult for any solicitor, let alone barrister, no matter how highly paid or gifted, to argue contrary to my construal of the Law in this matter. As it was I, as an eager young man, upon whom the onerous task befell to draft the Laws of the Defence of Self and Property, the Government of the Republic ratified after UDI. Our Laws are not based upon interpretation of precedent like the old Empire, but upon such written statutes. So, you will bear with me, as it is not a simple, professional conceit that I believe my interpretation is the one which will always carry the day."

He questioned the three of us, myself, Adam and Miss Bryant-Drake, about yesterday's "reception," as he termed it. Again he had us play out the whole episode on the table, but again he would not speak directly to Karl. Adam became irritated by this and quite forcefully inquired as to why?

Mr Bravett paused, produced a large calabash, loaded it, deftly struck a match with his thumb and puffed determinedly. I could see Adam's annoyance growing as he probed again. Mr Bravett turned to him and said; "My dear Sir, if a steam omnibus, out there in the street, crashed into a tram would you consider the culpability of the tram or the omnibus?"

He did not await any attempted answer to his rhetorical hypothesis. "Neither, because they are machines. You could consider the negligence of the drivers or the maintenance crew or some other human factor. An automaton is a machine, I can no more take a witness statement from it, than from the train you arrived upon."

Adam reacted with uncompromising indignation. I had no idea he was so passionate about the issue of automaton's status.

Mr Bravett stood up and theatrically paced about puffing furiously on his pipe until Adam had finished speaking. He stopped by the fireplace, his back to us, and we all fell silent. After a long pause, he spoke; "Karl, are you human?"

We all turned to Karl, who had been standing by the window all through this, "No, Sir."

"Karl, are you a machine?"

Karl paused, he looked at me then at Adam and answered. "Yes, Sir. I am a machine. I am an Android. I was designed by Professor Čapek and built by Mr Rosumovi of the R.U.A. For the Tharsis Bureau of Military Defence."

"Karl, what are your commands?"

"To protect Mr Ransom, his family and friends at all times. To defend and protect the Ransom's property and employees. To maintain..."

Mr Bravett interrupted. "Thank you, Karl. Who gave you your instructions?"

"After I was decommissioned from military service Mr Ransom senior set my initial commands. Mr Edwin Ransom has amended them as required."

"Karl, are you malfunctioning in any way which affects you carrying out your commands?"

"Not that I am aware of, Sir."

"Thank you, Karl." Mr Bravett turned back to the room. "Karl is a machine. Admittedly, one that passingly resembles a human being. He is an automaton, a mechanical android. He carries out functions commensurate with the instructions given to him. He is not a human or higher sentient life form, he is only an anthropomorphic apparatus, thus he has no rights. He cannot be guilty or innocent. He is property. A mechanised tool."

Adam asked; "Then he could not be held responsible for his actions?"

"In no way. No more than our hypothetical steam omnibus. If it is malfunctioning it can be fixed, if it is damaged it should be written off, but it cannot be prosecuted. You cannot arrest a train or an omnibus. You cannot put a tram on trial for murder!" He chuckled, "After all, this is not the Aerian Republic. We have not completely lost our minds as to the distinction between man and machine."

Miss Bryant-Drake interjected; "But they could be impounded or confiscated."

Mr Bravett exhaled a large cloud of smoke and laughed. "Yes, yes, my dear, they could. If the owner had used it in the commission of a crime. But as no crime has been committed by Mr Ransom, so there is nothing to fear."

Mr Bravett grinned widely. "Do you understand me now?"

We all agreed we did. Adam asked another question; "What if an automaton, an 'android' as you called it, committed a crime of its own? On its own?"

Mr Bravett's eyes narrowed under his bushy brows; "Under the law here in Tharsis, a machine cannot commit a crime. There is no 'mens rea'; no mind to be guilty. It can dangerously malfunction and it can break down, but its actions remain the responsibility of its owner or operator or individual who set its directives."

Adam's concerns seemed mollified.

Since we had wandered far off of the reason for our meeting, I asked Mr Bravett what it was that he advises us to do.

Bravett explained: The incident yesterday at the station is all over the front of the broadsheets. Miss Bryant-Drakes article is prominent amongst them." He drew a bundle of them from his satchel and dropped them on the table. "And there are hundreds of witnesses whose statements have already corroborated your version of events. Also, some are hailing you, Mr Ransom, as a hero. Three of the 'anarchists' - as some newspapers are already calling them – were taken at the scene and are of foreign origins which have led to some journalists speculating with the idea of Utopian insurgents. Some are even pointing the finger at Zephorite agent provocateurs.

"I have already spoken to the High Sheriff himself via the Meucci, he contacted me, and he is in agreement that you are not suspects but potential victims and material witnesses in this incident.

"Mr Ransom, may I say, you may have a powerful enemy in Mr Du Maurier but your friends, or should I say those of your father-in-law, are far more powerful. We are expected at 1 pm at the Offices of the High Sheriff himself. You will be required to make full witness statements under oath regarding both the incident at the Tremorfa Toll House and at Alba Central Station. You will also be asked to swear an affidavit regarding the conduct and activities of both Lucius Everheart and E. P. Docket."

"And then?" Adam asked.

"Mr Ransom may have to pay a small penalty for allowing his automaton to carry and discharge a firearm outside of his own property without the required licences. Twenty guineas, I believe, plus the cost of the licence; twenty-five in all. That is it. After which, you will be free to go. I suggest you do not go back to Tremorfa for a week or two as things there will get a little interesting once the arrest warrants are issued for Everheart and Docket and others in Tremorfa administration. I believe the High Sheriff's Office has had its eye on a few people there for quite a while. I would suggest you go to Tharsis and spend some time with your family."

I asked what will happen about Du Maurier. Will he be arrested too? Mr Bravett explained there is no current evidence against Du Maurier and nothing to link him directly with these crimes. "Until the gunmen from the station and Everheart and Docket are questioned thoroughly there is no case against Du Maurier. But mark me well on this; someone will crack under questioning, especially when those reprobates fall under the shadow of the hangman's noose. The penalty for being, or knowingly consorting with, an anarchist, a spy or insurgent, is death. Someone will talk. They always do."

I said I did not think they were any of those things. Mr Bravett laughed and told us, "Of course not! They are petty criminals and guns for hire, but they will find themselves in the position of having to prove they are not enemies of the State. And to do so, they will have to give over their paymaster. That is when we shall have Mr Du Maurier."

For the first time in days, I felt elated. Mr Bravett then left us with clear instructions as to where to meet him, in what is now an hour and a half's time, at the High Sheriff's Office. After which, dear Nelly, I am coming home!

I fear I shall probably miss the last air train this afternoon, and so I hope to be with you first thing in the morning. I shall race this communiqué to your presence!

I am so excited about coming home. Until I can do so myself, please thank your father again for all his assistance. His friend, Mr Bravett, has put all our minds at rest.

I am coming home, Nelly.

And I shall ask you to forgive me for being such a fool.

Your loving husband.

Edwin.

Ps. I have enclosed some more sketches of Capt. Pug's adventures for Tabitha's storybook. Tell James, I shall bring him a small gift as well.

E x

Journal of Adam Franklin.

The Solicitor Edwin's father-in-law sent arrived this morning. A great bombastic wag in a musk ox fur coat and flying goggles, nevertheless he at least knows what he is talking about. He forced us to recite everything that has happened in intricate detail, "a blow by blow account," as Charity put it.

In the end, he told us the Constable back in Tremorfa was exceeding his authority and we have not broken any Laws. We defended ourselves and each other which is our right.

We trooped off to the Court House this afternoon and had to repeat everything again and again, as sworn witness statements some of which were specific only to Everheart and that little weasel Docket.

Edwin and I also had a short meeting with Mr Bogdanov, the High Sheriff. Who was a short, stocky fellow of Russian extraction, dapper and urbane but intense. The air in his private office is thick with the fumes of the foul little cheroots he smokes constantly. He holds your gaze attentively and seemingly does not smile. I noticed he had the firm handshake of a man more used to holding a gun than a pen.

After various pleasantries, he assured Edwin all would be done to hunt down the surviving assassins. Edwin asked what would be done about Du Maurier. Mr Bogdanov said once those responsible had been rounded up and interrogated thoroughly for what happened yesterday, they will face prosecution as anarchists. Then they will talk. Anyone conspiring with them will face the full force of the Law. Regardless of who they are; in Tharsis anarchism is treason, and carries a capital punishment.

Charity told me on the journey to the Court House that Bogdanov has a reputation for being as relentless and pitiless as the criminals he pursues. I left his office with the exact same impression.

It was early evening by the time we returned to the hotel. I do not think I have truly rested since we began this strange journey fraught with so many dangers. Edwin continues to apologise at any opportunity, but in some way, I am glad for the distraction from my own personal concerns.

This morning I questioned the Solicitor, Bravett, about the legal standing of an automaton. I did so under the guise of outrage at his treatment of Karl - some of which was genuine – however, I was more interested in what the Law here dictates. It would seem in the Republic of Tharsis any automaton, is a machine, not a person and cannot be held criminally accountable for its actions. So what of me?

Under this meat suit, I too am nothing more than a clever contraption, howbeit of a different order than Karl. If I have no "owner" and follow no "commands" so would I be considered to be malfunctioning? Or do I have "commands" but I just simply am not aware of them? If I got up now from this chair and went out, found this Du Maurier chap and murdered him. Right there in front of all and sundry, which I believe I could, and after I reveal my true self to those that endeavour to apprehend me.... What then? Would I face a jury or summary condemnation to the municipal scrap heap? Can I be killed?

Edwin wishes to be on the first railplane to Tharsis City in the morning, he is taking Karl and Charity with him to stay at his father-in-law's home. I have not yet decided if I will join them. After dinner, I must compel myself to sit down in the quiet of my room and read the rest of the diary.

For there was something else today that prompted me; as we travelled across the city to the Court House. The driver of the growler had to divert from what he said was his usual route. The roads were up due to laying new tram lines and he did not want to risk the horses stumbling or injuring themselves on the broken ground. I spent some time boredly looking out the window at the street scenes as they passed by outside. Suddenly I knew that I knew those places we passed through. It was not that I recognised them as one normally recognises a place or a person; I simply knew that I knew those streets and back alleys. I could have gotten out of the cab and known exactly where I was but if you had asked me directions I could not have told you anything. I can only liken it to when something in the waking world "breaks your dream" and suddenly you remember, but the essence still remains elusive, intangible.

"The Old Garrison," Edwin called it. He said the whole area was once the British Army garrison, its ancillary buildings, the arsenal and the tenements for the soldier's families.

Did that mean something to me? He asked. I replied that I honestly did not know.

I believe tonight I shall read as much as I can endure of the diary of Sergeant Major Adam Franklin, DCM, and in the morning I shall decide what I am to do.

"I gazed into the looking-glass
And screamed to God on high.
A beast was staring back at me!
(Alas, that beast was I!)"

THE MELANCHOLY BALLAD OF THE CLOCKWORK
SOLDIER.

HOLLY MARKS.

CHAPTER FOUR

THE SERGEANT MAJOR

Journal of Adam Franklin.

'My Name is Adam Godwin Franklin, I was a Sergeant Major in Her Imperial Majesty's Royal Aethervolt Colonial Marine Regiment. I was born in Somers Town, in the Parish of St Pancras, London in 1840 and I died when my aerostat was shot down at the 2nd Battle of the Myrmidon's Trench, Mars, 1873.'

I knew everything would change once I truly read the diary, so I endured it, page after page until I had read every word. The characters of the peculiar Cyrillic style lettering now give up their meaning to my eye as plain as children's English. In that diary, I met a man I do not know. A man who died twenty-seven years ago. I read on and on as he tried to make sense of what was happening to him and I tried to comprehend the incomprehensible.

It was almost 3 in the morning when I finally closed the book. I had to get out of the hotel. I left Edwin a hastily scribbled note, grabbed my coat, hat and one of the handguns, a strange looking slide pistol we had taken from those who attacked Mrs Phillipott's, and took to the mist-shrouded streets. I just needed to walk and think.

My mind was lost in the turmoil of reconciling these disparate nightmares which now beset me; my reason besieged by horrific visions spawned by half-memories stirred from the dark corners of my mind.

While my mind whirled my feet took over, leading me through the swirling brume and gloomy thoroughfares of the city until the rays of the icy dawn flared across the building tops. Awareness found me on the edge of the Old Garrison Quarter, which I had passed through yesterday. An endless rabbit warren of crumbling tenements, cramped terraces and dusty drongs, bedecked with a spider's web of washing lines and cables and strewn with the flotsam of human squalor.

A few people scuttled along in the shadows, huddled forms wrapped against the chill, apparently shunning the cold dawn light. No one, but a gong farmer pushing his cart of night soil and horse dung, crossed my path and no one met my gaze. Following my own instincts, I picked my way along the narrow streets towards... I had no idea.

Further into the Garrison, where the overhanging tenement fronts narrowed the streets to the point that a man could reach out a window and touch the windowsill of the opposite house. Once or twice a voice invited me to tarry, an imploring hand reached out, but I passed on swiftly and quietly. Daylight seldom reached the pavements here and many lives were lived out in the permanent shadowy gloom.

I could half remember walking in these labyrinths, in good times and bad. At the end of a row, I came upon a burnt out building, an old soldier's gattering hole. I could see it in my mind's eye; the Stone, Wool and Craft. A Secessionist's bomb tore through it killing dozens. The lads took revenge without waiting for orders, discipline was already breaking down and junior officers were losing control. I know, the Sergeant Major was there. He too went across the city that night. He too came back with blood on his, my, hands.

I wandered further into the maze. I had lived here. From a young child to a grown man. This place had been my life. The tenements gave way to terraces of houses for the non-commissioned officers and their families, I passed a derelict house I knew I had lived in once, so long ago. The paint was peeling from the wooden door, stripped by the windblown sand, was a colour I chose from a pallet of three. I could remember she hated that shade of blue... She? My wife. A woman's face appeared fleetingly before me, then she was gone... a nameless face of someone I once loved. A voice shouted a challenge to the stranger on their doorstep. I pulled up my collar and walked on.

People were moving about now. A population waking from its slumbers. Drays pulling a cart full of night soil passed by, the stench unbearable. A knocker-upper goes about her duties rapping on windows with a long stick. Shabby people, hunched and hollow-eyed scurried past me, never daring anything but the most fleeting of glances. As I passed a doorway where two old women stood smoking. I heard one mumbled a speculation, "A 'tec in bona togs." I smiled, at least such an impression would keep people away from me.

Beyond the rooftops, I could now see the imposing defences of what I somehow knew was the garrison buildings themselves. The Citadel was a fortress, housing the barracks, stores, offices, hospital, the glasshouse and arsenal. I stepped around a corner and into the open space between the houses and the walls. I expected it to be lush and empty, parade grounds and mustering points, a great verdant tree edged swathe wrapped around the red curtain wall. Of course, it was no longer.

A shanty town had sprung up here. Amidst the debris, the middens and the piles of scrap, rough cabins had been constructed out of whatever came to hand, mainly wrinkly tin and scavenged timber. Hundreds and hundreds, thousands even, of hovels, back to back and piled upon each other. Tents, bivouacs, lean-tos and makeshift shelters of all kinds filled the whole space. The ruined bandstand had been absorbed into someone's shack, and beneath all of it I could still see the scars of battle. The trees were gone. Great shell holes had been torn into the ground, now full of stagnant water and piles of filth. The houses around the outer edge had mostly been destroyed, either by the defenders or attackers. The great curtain wall of the citadel, twenty feet thick of concrete and red ironstone, was scarred and broken. Smoke from numerous stinking campfires hung low in the morning air over the whole sordid mess, as if in some desperate attempt to shield this deprivation from the daylight.

Dirty people and even filthier children wandered like aimless phantoms amidst the squalor or crouched around the choking fires. Few even looked up as I passed, none spoke. One small grubby child, encrusted with muck and red dust, stood with its hand out silently begging, its huge eyes pleading to me to give it some small coin, but I had nothing to give. I felt such deep shame as I just shook my head and passed by.

Near the Great Gate, I came upon the ruined carcass of something I easily recognised; a Nutcracker, a huge mechanised fighting unit. A great walking steam-powered fighting vehicle, one of thirty the garrison could put into the field. This terrible engine lay discarded by a war that had long forgotten it. Stripped of its boiler, armour plate and weapons and scavenged down to little more than a rusting skeleton of twisted metal, what was left was a corroding frame for scarlet weeds.

Plastered upon the stone walls of the Great Gate was a vast senseless hotchpotch of handbills, posters and graffiti proclaiming the glorious 'Revoluution.' Proudly daubed all over were the blood red handprints of the Secessionist's fighters. I gazed back across the sea of degradation behind me and wondered how many of these people had fought for that revolution? How many of their parents and grandparents had suffered or died to bring about this glorious future for their children? A cesspit where the progeny of victors and victims had been left to marinate in their own filth?

I walked in through an entrance I had walked through a thousand times. Past the ruined gates and the shattered walls. Past the heaped rubbish and the small dunes of windblown red dust which seemed to coat everything. Past the demented collage screaming its jingoistic messages. Part of my mind was trying desperately to force memories into my conscious as another part tried desperately to resist. I was left with only fleeting images and splintered thoughts. Emotions, peculiar and unbidden, swelled up inside me, only to settle into a frightful dread.

The courtyard within the Bailey was a scene of absolute devastation. There had been a pitched battle here in the killing grounds, as the Secessionists had fought their way through into the heart of the Presidio. The massive Barbican gatehouse was a blasted ruin, smashed blocks of stone half the size of houses lay strewn where they had been flung by some mighty explosion. Every surface was pockmarked with bullet and shell holes. A Nutcracker, this one's metal skeleton torn in half, lay amongst the destruction. Parts of other war machines lay scattered amidst the debris. I knew the attackers must have brought up heavy ironclads or even field artillery, nothing less could have done this damage.

I followed a well-worn path through the rubble into the inner ward. The Great Yard with its training and exercise areas was no more, lost under another shanty town of wrinkly tin and scavenged wood. The edifices facing down onto the yard were torn and battered, but no truly heavy ordinance had been used here. Fire instead had rampaged through the buildings, and looting and vandalism had probably done the rest. Only the hospital and the glasshouse remained ungutted.

I stood transfixed by the sight of the hospital building and the looming wreck of the clock tower above it when someone touched my arm. I jumped away and almost stumbled on a jagged rock. Regaining my composure, I saw it was an old man dressed in little more than rags, his tangled dirty beard and hair stained with red dust.

"'Scuse me, Gov'nor. Didn't mean ta affraux yous so." He hawked and spat as if he had not used those vocal cords for some time. "Just wonderin' wot yous doin' 'ear? 'Snot a place for da likes of a bona fella...a gentlemen like yous." Beneath bushy eyebrows, bright green eyes searched me from head to toe weighing me up like some prospective victim.

I put my right hand on my hip, enough to clearly reveal the pistol in my belt. The look in his eyes changed as they moved quickly from the gun to my face. "No offence."

"None taken." I held his gaze until he turned away. "What happened here?"

He shrugged his bony shoulders, "War. Is wot war does." He started to relate to me how the fighting had torn through the Garrison. How the defenders had fought valiantly to the end. As he gabbled on, I grew a sense he was being careful not to sound too admiring of the British and Empire soldiers who died defending the Garrison. He told me that to finally defeat the defenders the Secessionists set fire to everything which would burn. I asked why the hospital and prison had not been burnt, but I could guess the reason immediately.

" 'Ad a lotta Red 'anders in both, would 'ave meant burnin' their own. So they didn't light it up." He suddenly looked me straight in the eyes. "A lot of good lads died that day. Wen da Arsenal went up, da lads, da defenders, 'ad no choice to chuck their hand in."

"I read the British here mutinied and handed over Collingwood to the Secessionists." I wanted to see his reaction to how I said it as much as what I said.

"Major General Collingwood," he corrected me instinctively. "And that's arseup'ards dat is. They 'ad to drag 'im outta here, not one of... da defenders 'ere never surrendered... it wos a massacre. Whoever told yous different is lying."

For a second I could see him, twenty-five or thirty years younger, in uniform. A bright-eyed, cocky little git with light fingers and a ready wit. I almost gagged. Sergeant Major Franklin knew him. I knew him.

"Wot's wrong with yous, Mister? You ol'right?"

"How did you survive then?" I blurted it out before I thought.

He stiffened and took a step back. "I ain't no soldier. They all died."

"Hood, Sapper John Hood, 'Robbin' Hood' they called you because you would steal anything not nailed down."

He looked like he was torn between attacking me or making a run for it. Instead, he froze in his confusion and mumbled. "They all died."

"Where were you, Hood? Where were you when those bastards massacred our lads? Where were you?" The voice coming out of my mouth was not mine, a snarling, angry guttural voice.

Hood appeared horrified. "I know you…"

I took a step towards him, "Where were you, Hood?"

He took a step backwards and stumbled. "I wos on a fizzer. So they stuck me in da Infirmary ta guard da bloody Red 'anders. I got banged on the 'ead by ah big lump ov stuff. I didn't wake up 'til it wos all over." His chin was quivering under his scraggly beard. "They got the Major General put a gun ta 'is 'ead an' forced 'im ta order us all ta jack it in."

I could not think of anything to say.

"I know you… don't I?" Emboldened by my silence he peered at me. "No. Yous can't be 'im… Yous ain't old enough." He swallowed hard, "Wot 'appened t' your face?"

I found the slide gun in my hand and the voice inside me growled again, "Shut it, Hood."

He looked terrified. "I didn't…"

"I said, shut up." He swallowed hard and fell silent. "The hospital, the Infirmary, who's been using it?" He seemed shocked at the question.

"Sand rats… jus' sand rats. Nasty things."

"You always were a bad liar, Hood," I told him to take me up there. Some mix of dread and need was compelling me to go into the Hospital block. He looked crestfallen, but complied and together we headed towards the building. The main entrance was blocked by rubble and a dune of red sand so he led me into the remains of the general stores, the Ambry, and in through a side entrance. All looked confusingly familiar and unfamiliar to me. We climbed stairs and finally entered the long tiled corridors of the Infirmary. Off of each corridor lay the long wards and the treatment rooms.

A small animal of some kind scuttled ahead of us. "See," Hood exclaimed. "It's jus' sand rats... No one com's 'ear." I ignored him and waved him on with my gun. We wandered through three floors of corridors, wards, offices and treatment rooms until we reached the end. "See, no one 'ere."

He was right, the whole place seemed almost completely untouched. Abandoned, stripped out at some point, but left undisturbed ever since. The lack of footprints amongst the animal droppings and tracks in the dust confirmed. "Why?" I asked Hood. "Why do they not come up here?"

Hood gave me a quizzical look, then answered matter-of-factly; "Ghosts." I snorted in derision, but he seemed deadly serious. "Peoples keep away 'cos they fear the ghosts in the place. Occasionally they might com' in here during the day to nick stuff, but no one stays 'ere at night."

I stood looking at him. Something in what he said made sense. There was a strange feeling about the place even with the cold morning light flooding through the smashed out windows. I could well believe there were ghosts here. Mars is full of them.

I felt tricked by my own mind, the half-memories and the diary entries had led me here, but it was not right. This was not the place.

"Wot is wrong with yous?" This time Hood almost sounded genuinely concerned.

"I need to find somewhere. I thought it was here. I was wrong." I shoved the pistol back in my belt and waved him away. "Go, go on."

Hood took a step or two, then dawdled. After a moment he turned back to me. "It is you Serge'nt Major, ain't it? It is you?" I could not answer him, I had no idea how to. "Serge'nt Major Franklin, sir?" I just looked at him blankly. "What 'appened ta you? How in God's name are you still alive?"

I was weak and bewildered and therefore I answered honestly, "I have no idea. I just need to find the place."

"Wot place?"

There seemed no point in lying. "A round room, stone-lined, an operating theatre, with a tall roof, I remember rafters going up into the darkness."

Hood regarded me quizzically. His expression changed as if something occurred to him. "Serge'nt Major, they threw us in a work camp hundreds of us. An old iron mine out in the sands near Hellas. Those they didn't work to death died o' starvation, they wouldn't even treat the wounds o' the injured. After the Spookers attacked Hellas the guards ran away, so who was left o' us escaped, I don't know how, maybe God was with us, but a handful o' us made it back to Tharsis. I came back here, I had nowhere else ta go." His chin was quivering again. "I couldn't go home not back to Earth, back to England. 'Ere is the only home I had left." He was crying openly now.

I had no idea what to say to him, so I simply asked a question, "Have you been here ever since?"

"I 'ave Serge'nt Major. I've carved m'self a niche 'ere. I've lived 'ere ever since, and I've seen all kinds of shenanigans goin' on. About a couple o' year ago there was somethin' goin' on in the old clock tower."

"Going on?"

"Lights, noise, comin's and goin's at night."

Abruptly something made sense. "Who?"

"I 'ave no idea, Serge'nt Major." He then added. "The only thin' a saw wos the lights and noises. I went up there a few days later... all sealed up tight."

I insisted he showed me how to get up there. He tried to put me off several times with excuses and prevarications about how difficult it was now, but in the end, I hit upon a lucky guess, or maybe a latent memory, and we found our way up to the stairwell of the clock tower. The door appeared impassably blocked with rubble, but on closer inspection and a little brute force, it was easily negotiated. Ignoring Hood's increasingly dire warnings about the dangers of collapsing masonry, I ploughed ahead. Thankfully the winding staircase up to the tower was noticeably clear of debris as we climbed in almost complete darkness, feeling our way with tentative steps and hands searching for the reassurance of the walls. After several circuits, the blackness was finally alleviated by a feeble light coming from above. We made it up to a landing where a smashed leaded window allowed the weak daylight to illuminate a small iron-bound door. Hood began babbling about it being locked fast and the dangers of the great cracks which ran from around its aperture up into the ceiling. I shushed him and concentrated. There was red dust everywhere, windblown, it had settled on the door and the landing, but clearly enough to read in the layers there had been footprints. Footprints came and went through the doorway recently enough to still be easily identified. It also occurred to me the dust itself was not the thickness of years, but a couple of months if that.

I looked back at Hood's face, but he said nothing. His eyes, however, were that of a naughty child caught out in a lie. I too said nothing, but turned back to the door and grasped the iron handle and turned. It rotated about half an inch and stopped. Locked. I shook the handle, but to no avail. I pounded on the door, but received only the sound of hollow booming beyond.

Hood started to explain how this validated what he had already been warning me about and that we should...

I drew the slide pistol and fired a round into the lock. Then another and another. In the confines of the stone tube of the stairwell, the noise was deafening. Hood grabbed his ears and started swearing loudly, but for me, the sensation was gone in seconds. I grasped the handle again and twisted it, this time it moved a little more and there was a clacking noise as if something was broken. I seized the doorknob with both hands and wrenched it around. Metal squealed and something in the door's mechanism loudly snapped.

The lock released, but the door held firm enough for me to have to shoulder it open to step through.

I stood open-mouthed. Frozen to the spot by a confused wave of deja vu, half recognition and horror flowed over me. I stood on the edge of a large round room, the stone walls about me rose to easily over twenty feet. I could see the corbels upon which rested the huge timbers supporting the vaulted wooden ceiling hidden above us in the darkness. Three small broken windows allowed light into the space.

It was the room that Adam Franklin, that I, had awoken in. Strapped to a table I had stared so long up at the wooden vaulting, I could recall the exact number of planks and beams. The table was gone, but there, in the floor, where the bolt holes which had once held it fast. Around the room, there were other marks where heavy equipment had been dragged or stood for a long time. I could remember the machines and contraptions.

Hood remarked that I looked as if I had seen a ghost.

I began to explain as I walked around the room. A mundaneum computing device, much like a Lovelace, but electrificated, stood here, and there was a mechanism which pumped blood in and out of me there, another terminal for the analytical engine stood there, and here; a vast array of surgical equipment and tools. And above the table like some huge cyclopean spider hung a bizarre contraption; a large rim lit lens with a dozen brass arms each terminating in some horrific looking instrument. All of which I gained an intimate knowledge of. I could make out the marks upon the lower rafters where the metal monster had been bolted to them. I felt dizzy; elated yet sickened, memories long repressed were now flooding back.

Suddenly something struck me hard across the back of my neck and shoulder. I was so confused for a second I could not even reconcile the impact with reality. Then again, something clanged off the back of my head. I staggered a step or two and turned.

Hood stood there aghast. He must have believed such a blow would have felled me instantly. In his hands a metal bar, something like an iron pin about a foot long, that he had struck me with. I hesitated in astonishment and he stepped forward and swung again. I knew he meant to kill me. I snatched the pin out of his hand, but he twisted and tried to grab for my pistol, I spun him around and flung him with all my strength away from me. He slammed into the wall with a sickening crunch and collapsed into a heap.

I was relieved that, although there was a lot of blood oozing from him, on examination he was still alive and conscious. I prodded him sharply with the pin until he seemed lucid and demanded to know why he had attacked me.

He began sobbing and whining that he was just following orders. I could feel Sergeant Major Franklin pushing me to make Hood answer the questions. The Sergeant Major knew exactly where and how to use the iron pin to inflict the most pain for the least injury. I knew he had done it before, many times. I thrust the head of the pin hard into his rib cage. I could feel the already broken bones grate under the pressure and Hood screamed. It took some time as he was more resilient than he appeared, or was it out of fear?

I rapped the iron pin harshly across his bare ankle joint. The fresh pain giving him the impetus I needed. Once he stopped screeching he gave me a name; Lanulos. A name I already knew from the diary, and another someone simply known as the Doctor. I knew both, but hearing them from another's mouth seemed to cement vague recollections and what I had read into solid memories. Another man, a foreigner, an American, working for them had paid Hood to keep scavengers out of the hospital and away from the clock tower. He had also told Hood to watch out for anyone snooping around asking questions, if they asked too many questions Hood would be paid more to do away with them. I asked him if he had indeed killed anyone for snooping around or asking such questions.

He said no one had ever shown much interest. I believed him.

He then started imploring me not to leave him there to die. It was pathetic as only a few moments before he had tried to smash my skull in and now he was begging for my mercy. I answered him honestly, if he did not tell me something I did not already know, I would indeed leave him there to die and be eaten by rats or whichever came first. Either was of no consequence to me.

Finally, he told me something worthwhile; A couple of years ago there had been activity here. There was a lot of coming and going up here in the clock tower and Hood followed two men down into the hospital boiler room where they were throwing bodies into the furnace. Bodies? I asked. Men, bits and pieces of men, he said.

  Suddenly I had to get out of there. I found myself halfway out the door when his cries brought me to my senses. He pleaded if I promised not to leave him here to die he would tell me something else; something important. I turned back to him and demanded what it was but he refused, insisting I give him my word as a gentleman. How quaint, I mused, that this murderous scoundrel, this thief and deserter, should still think to put a value upon a "gentleman's" word. Regrettably, I know I am no gentleman.

  I warned him if he was simply prevaricating, I would kill him. With our understanding reached he told me some of the equipment that had been in this room was now stored on the floor above. I dismissed the notion; there was no room on the floor above us to store anything. I had been up there once as a boy, the clock mechanism occupied the whole space. Hood said the machinery had gone, it had been stolen long ago. All that good quality British cast iron was stripped out to make guns for the Secessionists.

  I left him and walked over to a small door opposite the one we had entered. It was less substantial than the other, but without a handle or knob and firmly locked. Frustrated to the point of anger I pulled off my right glove and punched my fist through the wood. I hardly registered Hood's exclamations from behind me as I tore the lock out of the door.

  Behind the door, a narrow winding stairway led up to the room that housed the clock's once ticking heart, but no more. Hood was right, by the light coming through the broken glass of its face, I could see clearly all the mechanism was gone. But there was nothing stored up here, no boxes or equipment, other than a few bits of rubbish scattered about the room. It now had a new purpose as an ossuary.

  Three skeletons lay in neat order on the floor, coated with a fine layer of red dust. Tattered clothing clung to the frames. Flesh, dried to parchment brown, still adhered to the bones, though much had either rotted, been gnawed at by small creatures or blown away by the cold dry air gusting through the gaps in the glass. I examined the bodies closer.

Though I am no expert I could tell by the size and clothing they were three men, two laying on their backs and one on his front. The one face down had been a tall, powerfully build fellow in the rough clothing of a manual worker, his boots were older, probably army issue, but serviceable. His scalp still retained enough flesh to clearly tell he had had thick dark curly hair. I moved his skull just enough to see he had been heavily bearded, and though the ears had been eaten away there was a single gold earring in the dust next to his head. The type that sailors of both air and water still wear as an identifier and nod to tradition. The obvious cause of his death were two large penetrating holes burnt through his upper back. A Lancenett or some other kind of heat ray pistol.

The others were both of similar height and build and both wore, what had once been, taupe laboratory coats over the normal clothing of any man in the street. However, the one in the middle wore a good make of handmade shoes, by the stamp on the instep they had been imported from Italy. In his waistcoat pocket, he had a fob watch, I removed it and examined it closely. A fairly good quality looking half hunter in a finely tooled and hallmarked silver case. The inside of the back case was engraved with what I could guess was a dedication in what looked to me to be Italian or French. The watch and the shoes were far more expensive than one would have expected from a man dressed so averagely. I searched his pockets and found nothing other than his spectacles in his breast pocket and a fountain pen, both of superior quality. He wore a simple gold band on his ring finger, I removed it and discovered an inscription on the inside, again in either Italian or French. His exposed face was mostly gone, but I could see he once had a shock of grey hair and a Guillaume moustache.

I sat back on my haunches in disbelief. I could clearly remember this man; he was one of the doctors who had operated on me. He never spoke, none of them but the Doctor spoke, but I *remembered his coldly appraising gaze. There was a terrible sense of satisfaction in me that those eyes were gone now, rotted and chewed out, leaving just two gaping holes. There was a third hole, a large calibre bullet hole, almost perfectly placed in his forehead between his eyes, and most of the back of his skull was in shattered pieces beneath the back of his head. I pushed his head aside and checked the floor, as I suspected; no bullet hole in the wood. He had been murdered somewhere else and brought here.*

The last one appeared to be a much younger man; fair hair cut fashionably long, no moustache or nine o'clock stubble showed in the drawn dried skin over his chin. His hands were ring free and his clothes, yet modest, were cut in a more modern style. Well, modern to my eye. He wore a battered Garstin wristlet watch, I removed it and checked the back for an inscription; 'To dear Peter, in memory of his father, from his loving mother Alice.' Lower down was inscribed; 'Presented by the Tharsis Regiment of Aethervolt and Aerostat Engineers to Capt. G.S. Wansey on the occasion of his retirement. 1886.'

Upon searching Peter's clothes, I found nothing other than an empty silver cigarette case inscribed Capt. G. S. Wansey and a few coins. He had died from two shots to the chest from a large calibre gun. I noticed that he had a defensive injury to his left hand which would suggest he tried to fend off the attacker and both shots occurred in rapid succession. Either would have killed him instantly.

I stood up and took a step back. What had happened here? I surmised that at the least the big fellow had been used to haul the other bodies up here and then shot in the back, by whoever had killed the others or gave the orders to have them killed. But why? Removing witnesses, the dead are silent...well mostly. I caught and silenced a hysterical sounding giggle from escaping my mouth. I could remember the older man, the Italian as I had now come to think of him, but not the other two, the big fellow with a bushy beard would have been impressive enough in his day to have been more than noticeable, even by me in the delirious state

I was in, but young Peter Wansey could have been any of the dozen or so faceless assistants that scuttled about. Also, he would have barely been born when I and my lads crashed to our deaths in 1872 and the Italian would have been much younger than I remember him.

If this all, in its entirety, is not simply some fever inspired delusion but a concrete reality, then where did the time go? Not a mere matter of hours or a few days but years, decades to be precise? And how in Hell am I now like this? A walking machine with the face and memories of Adam Franklin?

Well, I was no further forward with those questions, so I opted to leave. I collected the items I had found on the victims and went to go, when I remembered I had not searched the big fellow's body. I hesitated for a moment I already felt like a pillager scavenging the dead. I had ordered such people shot in wartime, but I had no choice but to do it. So I silently undertook to see these personal effects returned to the families of the victims when they had yielded what little clues they held for my quest. They at least would get some relief from knowing what happened to their loved ones, even the family of the Italian.

I turned the body of the big fellow over with some effort, he had been sealed to the floor by a mix of his own dried bodily fluids and the red dust. I had to rip his clothes to turn him. His heavy fustian coat, its fibres weakened by time, tore open disgorging a few items; a Châtellerault knife, a couple of coins and a few rounds of .445 Webley ammunition. I had to rip open the rest of his coat to search his inner pockets. He wore a woollen waistcoat, but no pocket watch. I was about to give up when I felt something under the material. At first, I thought it was a breast pocket in his shirt, but it was not, there was a pocket on the inside of his waistcoat out of which I retrieved a pencil and a few folded pieces of heavily stained paper.

"(*Unreadable*)

7.45 am. I arrived

The Dr is really nervous today. Two of the Scientists have gone missing, Salgari and his assistant Wansey, no one has anything to say.

Indrid Lanulos was here this morning, early, grinning like a Cheshire cat. I'm sure that fixed face is some sort of mask or makeup. I have tried to get near enough to tell, but his henchmen keep everyone but the Dr at a distance. Something exceedingly strange about that man.

10.30 am. I followed Lanulos and his men out of the Garrison across town to some warehouse buildings on Walton Row, behind Clerval Street. Unfortunately, I lost them in the maze of back alleys.

(Unreadable)..... were ordered to dispose of more dissected corpses today. Three males rejected by the Dr as too badly damaged to be of any use. The Dr's experiments don't seem to be going to plan. I was told by Fritz that one of the poor wretches awoke and had to be put down last night but we didn't burn that one. The other is breathing, but hasn't awoken yet.

5pm. A delivery of mechanical parts. Spoke to the carman and he said (Unreadable) at the docks this afternoon. Pier 13.

6pm. Told by Fritz to wait around for the Resurrection Men to deliver tonight. Just going to be me and him. I have a bottle of Prusser's Tot, laced with laudanum, and once he is out I will have time to search for the poor wretch they put down last night and report it tomorrow.

6.45. Something is wrong. Lanulos is here. Fritz warned me. The Dr told him that Lanulos thinks there's a mouchard in the organisation. I have taken precautions as arranged."

There was no more. I searched him again, this time much more carefully, but found nothing. Nothing to identify him at all. Who was he? A journalist? A police officer? Spy? The thought occurred to me that I had noticed he wore old army issue boots. Boots! Damn it! I quickly pulled them off. Sickeningly, but not to my surprise, most of his feet came away with them, but as I removed the second boot, his left, a thin, mouldy and stained leather wallet fell out. I opened it and unfolded the contents carefully; a warrant card;

The Republic of Tharsis Bureau of State Internal Security,
This is to certify that
Percy Greg,
Officer 989AB
Holds the Rank of Inspector

In the
Detective Department

A Police Inspector. Tucked in the other side of the wallet was folded an old daguerreotype. A fresh-faced young man with a mop of curly hair and wearing a Police Constable's uniform looked back at me. His attempt at a stern gaze barely masking his pride. I folded the card and the picture back into the wallet and shoved it with the notepaper them into my pocket.

When I returned to the lower level Hood had dragged himself almost to the door. When he saw me he panicked and tried to scramble faster, but I seized him by his coat and hauled him back to the other side of the room. He left a bloody trail across the floor like some wounded slug.

I tried to question him about what I found upstairs. Did he know about the bodies? Did he know they had murdered a copper? But he was too weak and fast becoming delirious. After a few minutes, I gave up trying to get sense out of him and, in my anger, left him there.

As I walked away Hood cried after me, damning me as a welcher. I stopped, the Sergeant Major's voice ringing clear in my head, as clear as if he were shouting in my ear. Furiously I drew the pistol and returned back to where Hood lay. The insults froze in his mouth and he stared silently up at me. I stood over him with the urging of Sergeant Major Franklin's voice still ringing in my head.

Hood must have understood the turmoil going on in my mind because he stopped whimpering and blurted out; "They woz dead... no not dead, I mean...frozen stiff. They dug ah lot ov bodies outta tha ice at the bottom of tha Myrmidon's Trench. They brought them 'ere an experimented on them. I never saw who or what...I was just paid ta keep others away, an' let them know if anyone came sniffin' about. I know nothin' about murderin' no copper an' I never knew yous were one of them they dug up. Don't kill me, Sergeant Major, please, don't!"

I silenced the Sergeant's voice in my head and put away the pistol. Without any attempt at gentleness, I half lugged, half dragged Hood out of the room, down the dark winding staircase and finally out of the building. He was losing a lot of blood and lost consciousness a couple of times, but he was still alive when I left him outside the door of the Ambry. Before I departed I shoved the few coins I had found on the corpses into the hand of one of the ragged waifs wandering around the shanty town and bid him fetch a medician. I assured myself that was always what I was going to do anyway.

It took me a couple of hours to find Clerval Street, partly through trusting my senses and snippets of memories and partly through asking directions where I could. Clerval Street was actually a large square of grand houses which faced in on its own gated park. No ragamuffin's shanty town here, these houses had been built to home the rich and powerful and obviously still did. The materials were Martian, a deep reddish ochre-coloured sandstone, but the style mid-century English. Like the expensive trees in the park, imported as saplings from Earth, and the carefully manicured lawns. Those that still lived here, obviously maintained a level of genteel colonial reverence that belied their Secessionist politics. There were no Red Hands daubed on the walls here, and if there had once been, they had long since been thoroughly whitewashed over.

Nannies ushered along smartly dressed little children or pushed perambulators. Wealthy pedestrians dawdled along the pavement or strolled the dappled pathways of the park, taking the cold early afternoon air. Servants and footmen scurried about their work only pausing to nod or tip a hat in acknowledgement of each other. I noticed an automaton, dressed expensively in footman's attire, patiently exercising the tiniest dog I have ever seen, it was no bigger than a rat. Carriages and hackneys clattered by. Horse-drawn and steam-powered vehicles shared the road with cyclists and horse riders. I imagine it would have been much the same sight today in any of the wealthiest districts of England's great cities some thirty-five million miles away.

Instinctively, avoiding those in domestic service, I sort out one of the few working class men about; I passed a couple operating a steam-powered vacuum anti-defilement device mounted upon a wagon, its long tubes running up into one of the houses, the whole commotion making a spectacle for the gathered house's staff and onlookers. I passed a chimney sweep and his boy pushing their handcart up the street and a couple of road sweepers shovelling red dust and horse shit from the pavement. Eventually, I came upon a gardener tending the rose beds just inside the park railings. As I stopped I noticed that with a triumphant "Gotcha you bloody devil," he wrenched free from the red sandy soil a magnificent dandelion root, one Edwin would have been proud of. I think the smile on my face was enough to disarm the gardener to venture a comment. "Please don't you pay no mind to my language, Sir. Damn things get blown in and grow like…"

"Weeds?" I suggested and we both laughed. I had not laughed for as long as I could remember, it felt strange, euphoric, almost cathartic.

Once I had regained my composure, I inquired if he knew how to get through to Walton Row? He tutted and explained most of "the Row" had been bombed out during the last war, in fact, this whole area had taken a pounding, but no one had rebuilt the old Row. Lots of plans but no one owns enough of it to make a difference and the city Court of Aldermen will not stump up any money. Now it was nothing much more than ruins and a few burnt-out buildings. I asked him if it was truly abandoned. He hummed and hawed and finally confided there was word going around about a flash house back there in one of the old warehouses – selling potcheen and catering for a disreputable class of people. He went on to tell me the Police and the Assay Men had raided them several times earlier this year and all had been quiet since.

I assured him I was neither criminal nor Police only a man looking for an old friend of whom I had heard had fallen upon *hard times. I used Peter Wansey's name and showed him the pocket watch, saying I had recognised it in a pawnshop window, something that a young man only in the most desperate situation would part with. My intention was to return it to him. It was a good plausible story.*

The gardener commiserated with me, times had been hard for a lot of decent people. There were still some places in the Row where people could rent half a yard of rope to flop. Or if you were really desperate they could hold up in any of a dozen rookeries in there. He suggested a place to start my search and gave me directions on how to get there. I thanked him and set off to find the narrow alleyway he had indicated.

I found it easily, and it led me through to the maze of back alleys that formed the Row. At the end of the alleyway, I forced my way past a rickety old fence adorned with warning notices of the dire consequences of trespassing, and into another world. A world of charred timber, fire-ravaged buildings and broken glass, inhabited by fleeting ghosts and the familiar stench of human filth.

The gardener had been right; some great conflagration had reduced most of the buildings to sooty husks and blacken shells. Since the event of the fire, attempts at rebuilding had occurred, mainly using scavenged materials, which lent the whole place an air of crumbling decrepitude. I picked my way through the piles of refuse and the black mud that clogged the paths and deeper into the maze of ruins.

The atmosphere became thick with a haze of greasy smoke and the cramped crumbling buildings became more and more oppressive as I ventured onward. There were people here, ashen spectres that inhabited the miasma. From the shadows, suspicious eyes watched me intently. Outside it was broad daylight, but in here it was an eternal dusk of fumes and smoke. Some had used palings and sailcloth to cover the burnt roof timbers and so create passageways between the buildings. Here in the murky gloom, I encountered more people; grubby children and adults with dirty weary faces. No one spoke or looked me in the eye.

After a while, I came upon a sizable building that seemed fire damaged, but mostly intact, an abandoned warehouse or workshop. The front doors of the building had long gone and so, curiosity getting the better of me, I walked in. It had been a coach works or wainwright's once, there were still wrecked and fire damaged carts and equipment amidst the debris of human existence. A small boy shouted and scampered off into the darkness to raise an alarm at my intrusion into their world.

Quickly a group of several rough men coalesced out of the gloom, some armed with makeshift weapons and tools, all ready to defend their territory no doubt. A big burly man with a huge ginger beard and swinging a blacksmith's hammer spoke first. "Dis is no place for a gentleman, like you. Are you lost?" Innocuous words, but delivered as a clear threat.

I stepped towards him until we were almost eye to eye and I could smell his fetid breath. His sudden look of apprehension was enough for me to seize him by the throat and take his weapon in one swift movement. The others were too stunned to react in time to stop me taking the closest two of them down with a few hard taps from the hammer. The control of the confrontation was now mine, and I turned my attention back to their ginger bearded leader. I explained calmly I was looking for a man, tall, willowy, with black hair, well dressed, well spoken, and always smiling, like the Cheshire cat. As the words came out of my mouth, I was aware that I was describing a man I had consciously never seen.

I released the leader's throat, stepped back and pulled open my coat enough for them to see I was armed. Someone mumbled, "Rozzer," and I did nothing to disavow their conclusion. The big man rubbed his throat, choked a little and finally regained himself enough to speak. "Bloody hell mister! You almost broke me windpipe!" The other two swore and scurried away to lick their wounds.

I warned him I could do worse and would so if the man trying to sneak up on me from behind stupidly tried anything rash. Once I saw that I finally had their complete attention, I repeated the description of the man again. There were some glances amongst them before the ringleader answered. "The Grinning Man. Haven't seen him for a long time."

"How long?" I asked.

"Not for a year or so. Used to com' through here once a month or so with a group of blokes, right hard nuts. Had a gaff down near the old Union street, some kind of lock up in one of the warehouses. Storing stuff on the QT. Not the kind of blokes you'd want to get in the ways of."

Before I could ask one of the others added, "All that stuff's gone nows, Pete. I woz down there the other day and the place was as empty as the Bishop's heart. Cleared out."

I questioned what they had been keeping there, but no one admitted knowing. Nonetheless, they told me several times local people had been hired to help load and unload big crates, the size of coffins, but incredibly heavy. The Grinning Man was a good payer and the company he kept was pretty scary, so they just took the money and asked no questions. Scary in what way? I asked.

"Scary as in lots of muscle and shooters and not afraid to use either. Nasty types with more clobber than the Old Brigade," said the big one they called Pete.

Looking at them, I wondered how "nasty" someone had to be to scare these kind of men. I told them I would go and see for myself and they snorted and grinned. When I asked why, Pete replied, "That's the Union Street Boys territory, scuttlers they are, no offence, but a rozzer like you on your ownsome, no matter how handy, ain't going to be coming back from down there. They'll come at you mob handed."

I asked if these "Union Boys" were so dangerous how was it the Grinning Man and his people had no trouble with them? Pete shrugged his massive shoulders and pulled a face, "The Union Street Boys know enough not to mess with people like that anyways, and as I said, that ol' gigglemug was a good payer."

I thanked them for their candour and assured them I had no interest in them or their doings. These were, by nature, mistrustful men, but they let me leave the coach works without incident. However, as I expected, every step was observed carefully. I wandered a little making it plain I was not intimidated by them stalking me, but I had no idea which way to head for Union Street, which was in all probability as empty as they had claimed. Bored with the ensuing cat and mouse game, I ducked through an opening in a canvas wall, dashed through someone's makeshift living space, out through another doorway, ran a dozen yards, vaulted a small wall and slid into the shadows. For a few minutes there was the sound of running feet and raised voices, a few shouts of frustration, and then it all calmed down. I waited patiently for at least ten minutes before moving. Taking my bearings from the white ghosts of the moons hanging in the clear blue sky, I decided to head East as that seemed to make sense with how I envisioned the lay of the whole of Walton Row.

I had only moved a couple of yards when someone in the shadows spoke, "I know where the gent you're lookin' for lives." I stepped back in surprise, my hand on my pistol, but it was only a young girl.

"I know where's you can find him." No more than thirteen, probably less, dressed in soiled clothes of an older woman, but trying desperately to speak and move with the assurance of the profession she plied in these dirty back alleys. "The 'Grinning Man' they calls him."

I asked her name. She said it was Cora. I asked her how she knew the Grinning Man? She said everyone in the Row knew of him, but few had really seen him, not up close but she had. I asked how she had seen him 'up close'. Once Cora knew she had my interest her confidence grew. "I got taken up to his gaff, didn't I? A couple of us were regular comfort for them that were guarding that big house of his. Dead boring they said it was but worthwhile. Turned quite a few shillings I did." She said proudly, swinging her scrawny hips and trying to look coy. She asked if I had anything for her. I told her no. She looked disappointed and began to back away.

Thinking quickly I offered her the gold earring I had taken from Inspector Greg's body in exchange for what information she had for me. She came out of the shadows and eyed it keenly. She *was even younger than I had at first thought. A pallid grimy child, lice-ridden and painfully undernourished. Before she could snatch it, I palmed the earring and asked her again how she had seen the Grinning Man 'up close' and where was the house she had seen him in?*

The sight of the gold was enough to relax her tongue. She told me she had been visiting her punters at the house and when they were trying to sneak her out again they walked right into the Grinning Man. "He just sort of stood there with that stupid smole on his face, like he knew the answer to some joke that no one else knew. And he talks all kind of peculiar like, but there ain't nothing funny about him. They woz all scared of him. I thought I was a dead'en."

I asked her to tell me what he looked like. "Tall, thin, like a stack of bones, thick black hair greased back, no muttons nor nothing. Lots of teeth, big teeth and he had really weird eyes, great big dead eyes like a fish that's been on the monger's stall too long. And his face was all wrong."

I asked her what she meant and she tried to explain; "It was like his skin was too tight, like stretched out, like he was wearing someone else's face."

I asked Cora if the men called him by a name? She nodded and said; "Me and the girls just called him 'ol' Gigglemug,' but they said his name woz somethin' like 'Land-u-lass' or somethin'."

I was convinced enough by what Cora told me that she had indeed seen Lanulos at close hand so I questioned her on where she had seen him. She said it was in one of the houses on Clerval Street which backed on to the Row. I told Cora to show me which one then I would give her the earring and if it was the right place I would make sure she had a decent meal and a clean bed to sleep in for as long as she needed it. For a second there was a light in her eyes, but it was quickly clouded over by mistrust.

She took me deep into the Row and pointed out a massive, railing topped, rear garden wall of one of the great townhouses. There was a big tree, a willow, hanging over the wall from the garden side, and she told me the guards used to throw an old rope swing over the wall to help her and the other girls climb up.

I gave her the earring and told her again, if this was the right place I would make sure she had a chance to escape the Row. For a moment the light was there again, but then she just snatched the gold and scampered off into the maze of ruined buildings. I doubted I would ever see her again.

The wall was old and ill-kempt on the Row side so it was easy enough for me to scale it. I hauled myself up to the railings and, keeping to the cover of the willow branches and fronds. I took a careful look at what lay beyond. The garden stretched off about six or seven hundred yards towards the rear of the house in a series of immaculate lawns and flower beds. Below me, on the other side of the wall, was a large pond that the unwary might end up in if they clambered over the wall. True to what Cora had said there was indeed an old rope swing hanging from one of the branches and, if you were young and slightly built and with a little help, you could easily clamber down the tree and onto the knoll below it. It would be only a short hop across the water to the lawn. I am neither slightly built nor young, and so that route looked impossible for me.

I searched the area for signs of guards or dogs, but there was nothing. In fact, there were no signs of life or activity at all. Upon determining that all windows were shut; upstairs; curtains were drawn, downstairs; shutters were closed, I decided upon the bold approach. I stepped out onto the wall, climbed over the railings and, without thought of failure, launched myself with full vigour across the pond. I landed in the muddy edge of the water and gracelessly staggered on to the lawn.

There was no cry of alarm, no dogs, no evidence of anyone being aware of my intrusion. I straightened myself, wiped the muck off my boots on the long grass and walked purposefully towards the house. As I ventured forth I checked and reloaded the slide gun. I had no idea what awaited me in that house, but the fragmentary recollections stirred up by reading the journal of the Sergeant Major and my discoveries in the morning had left me in no doubt if this was the lair of Lanulos or the Doctor then I would need a loaded gun at the ready.

I reached the back of the house unchallenged. Partly, I felt relief but I also felt disappointment. Had I come all this way to find yet another series of loose ends? I chuckled as I remembered what my old Sunday school teacher taught us; a clue is a ball of string. And I had no idea how long this one was. Forsaking any pretence of care I made my way around the back of the building trying doors and windows. All were locked against me. Eventually, as frustration took hold, I found myself at the main French doors that opened onto a raised patio overlooking the gardens. I seized the heavy brass handles and wrenched them open. Wood splintered, glass cracked and metal screeched as the doors came apart. I stepped through and easily forced open the inner wooden shutters, shedding daylight into the large morning room. It was sparsely furnished with dust sheet-covered furniture that lurked like squat silent spectres.

I entered the room and drew the slide gun. No reaction to the noise, no sounds came from within the house at all. After a few minutes, I gave up waiting and opted to explore. My search revealed nothing more than an empty room after empty room of nothing more than few scattered pieces of dust sheet-covered furniture and the all-pervading smell of mothballs and decay. This was not a house closed up for a season, no one had lived here for a long time. It was opulently decorated and the rooms were of huge proportions. The main reception room alone was larger than half the ground floor of Edwin's farmhouse. I opened the shutters and paused to gaze out of the window onto the street and the park beyond. To gaze at the people going about their daily lives, children playing in the park, tradesmen and house staff coming and going, the android Footman still unwearyingly exercising the ridiculous little dog. All as oblivious to me, to my life, to my existence, as I was to theirs.

I turned back to the room and perused the lavish interior with its intricate lincrusta wallpaper, fine plaster cornices, the marble fireplaces with their great mirrors above them. The hanging works of art of nameless relatives and grim-faced notables entrapped in bulky gilt frames. I ran my fingers over the heavy embossing of the metal foil lincrusta and gazed at the gas-powered crystal chandeliers. What a life it would be to be able to own a home such as this? The cost of the imported rugs alone would have paid to have fed all those in the shanties of the Garrison for a week or more. I shuddered.

It was as I was reclosing the shutters that I heard a noise. I paused and listened intently. Footsteps above me. Without thinking I dashed out of the reception room into the hall, skidding wildly on the marble tiles and ran up the sweeping staircase to the first floor. I stopped momentarily on the landing to gain my orientation and caught the fleeting shadow of someone disappearing through a door at the end of the corridor. Abandoning caution I raced after the shadow and, gun held firmly in my hand, burst into the room.

"Hello, Adam." His voice froze me to the spot. Lanulos.

The room was a study bedecked with books and pictures, not some ostentatious collection for show, here books and papers were haphazardly piled everywhere. There was not a niche without a book or folio shoved into it, papers spilt across the desk and any available surface. Lanulos sat behind a huge dark writing desk. The grotesqueness of his features accentuated by the greenish glass shade of the oil lamp beside him. He looked like a grinning lime faced devil. Apart from the one lamp the room was in darkness, heavy drapes covered the windows and the gas wall lamps were not lit.

"We have been awaiting you. Expecting you." He spoke levelly and calmly in a strange nasal accent I remembered as soon as I heard it.

I pushed close the door behind me and cast a glance around the darkened room. There was someone in the shadows of the far corner. I waved them out into the light. It was Cora. Why was I not surprised?

"You will have to forgive my little deception, my ruse. Cora here is rather good, clever, at these things though."

The girl smirked at me in a truly disturbing manner and seemed to suppress a giggle.

I pointed the slide gun at him. "Who are you?"

Lanulos snorted and struck a match to light a cigar he plucked from his breast pocket. He puffed on it until it was a light and replied. "Come now, you know who I am. My name. You have been asking for me by name."

I was growing angry. The Sergeant Major's voice in my head was back and whispering that I should just kill him right now. "Who are you? What are you? Really?"

"There is no need for such hostility. Come sit, sit down and I shall explain. Enlighten you." His horrendous grin grew wider.

"I will kill you." To emphasise the fact, I fired a round into the finely tooled leather skiver of the desktop. The girl screamed in panic and fled back to the corner.

Lanulos did not flinch, he calmly tapped off the burnt end of the cigar into an ashtray on the desk and sighed. "My name is Indrid Lanulos. And I am your progenitor. Your father." He laughed, it was not pleasant nor was the sickening way his features distorted.

"I do not know what you are, but you are not my father." I fired again, this time into the stuffed leather headrest of the chair, only an inch from his ear.

There was a flicker of something in his eyes, then the smile widened. "Doing me murder may not be as easy, simple, as you may think."

"I have eight rounds left and if that does not suffice I will use my bare hands if I have to."

"Without me, you would not be here, would not be alive. I created you, I fathered you. You sprang from my mind, my thoughts. Like Zeus gave birth to Athena. You are my idea."

The Sergeant Major's voice was now so loud in my mind, I could barely resist his urging to kill. "I am not anyone's 'creation.' My name is Adam Franklin, Sergeant Major Adam Franklin of Her Imperial Majesty's Royal Aethervolt Marines. I was born in London, England. I had a wife and children and I am loyal to the Empress Queen. I have no idea what you have done to me or why."

"Fictions," Lanulos laughed again. "I created, I made, you." He picked up a wad of thin white punch cards, no bigger than calling cards, off of the desk and waved them at me. "Here you are. Here is Adam Franklin. Your memories. Everything you are. Here." He tossed them across the desktop, sending them cascading onto the floor. "Your program. Your soul." Lanulos laughed again. A bizarre hysterical guffaw. He looked like one of those weird laughing automata you might encounter at the fair or at the end of the promenade.

I put the first bullet in his forehead, splattering its contents over the chair back and the curtains, and then three more into his chest for good measure. Afterwards, I stood there for a moment, gathering my wits as the smoke cleared. Silence, even in my head. Silence, at last.

Lanulos was dead, but that damned grin was still plastered across his face. And I still had only questions and no answers. I should not have killed him, but I was so enraged I acted without thinking.

Ignoring the whimpering of Cora in the corner of the room, I walked around the desk and took a closer look at him, at that strange face. At least there was one question I could answer. Oblivious to Cora's cries, I drew the Châtellerault knife from my pocket and opened it.

I told Cora that she had best look away.

It was a messy task, Lanulos' blood and brain matter were everywhere, but I had to know. Seizing his face with one hand, I slit under the jaw line and up in front of the right ear. I dug my fingers in and pulled. Indeed, as I suspected, it was some kind of mask. As thick as pork rind, warm and textured as if living tissue, but a mask nonetheless. It came away with sickening ease. Underneath, smeared in bloody mucus and membrane, was another face. I wiped my hands on the handkerchief from his top pocket, and then threw open the curtains to let the daylight confirm what I had exposed.

I have to admit that I had expected metal. An automaton's faceplate, much as I imagined was beneath my own, but I was wrong. The face behind the mask was flesh. I took the small carafe of water from the desk, poured it over his face and used the kerchief to swab away some of the gore. The skin was smooth, hairless and unblemished, the features were angular and sharp, the mouth unnaturally wide. The amber coloured eyes were huge with goat-like pupils. The complexion was yellow, as yellow as one of Edwin's dandelion heads.

I stared at the face for a long time. A yellow-skinned Martian, a 'Kitreenoh Aresian' as they called them now. The Sergeant Major had another name for them; 'Yellow Spookers.' And these yellow-skinned blighters were the worst of them, ferocious, dogged and insanely fearless. I remember the Sergeant Major ordering the execution of dozens Yellow Spooker prisoners and wounded after the battle of Lasswitz Ridge. His voice filled my head with excuses about limited food and medical supplies, but these were my memories too, not the sum of a batch of punch cards, and I knew the truth. I knew the vicious detestation that drove him. I also remembered the strangely impassive mien in the prisoner's eyes as they were dragged to their waiting graves.

But everyone said the Spookers had been gone for twenty-five years or more. I ran my hand over the exposed flesh again as if trying to reassure myself that it was not just another mask. It was not.

I must have been so lost in the moment I did not notice that someone else had entered the room until he spoke; "They will hunt you down and destroy you for this."

Startled, I snatched up my gun and aimed it. The Doctor stood in the doorway, minus the lab coat he always wore, but just as I remember him from my memories and nightmares. A suave, lithe man with intense blue eyes behind narrow silver-framed spectacles. His thick grey hair was immaculately coiffured and his moustache carefully waxed. He raised his hands and spread his fine-boned long fingers. "I am no threat to you Adam, and I cannot stop you, I could not even if I tried, but I know you're not a cold-blooded killer."

"I would not wager upon that. I have just killed him, why should I not kill you?"

He elevated an eyebrow. "Because I will help you. If you will let me."

I must admit I was torn between absolute distrust and the urge to shoot him dead on the spot, but instead, I allowed him to pique my interest. "Go on."

"Adam. May I call you Adam? I feel I know you so well," He paused, but I did not react. "Adam, my name is Christian, Dr Christian Democritus. I was once a surgeon of encephalon and neurologia at the Freedom Hospital in Tharsis." He leant against the door frame nonchalantly. "Some time ago, driven by youthful imagination, I wrote a paper conjecturing the notion that it may be conceivable, given our foreseeable future advances in anthropomorphic automata, to preserve a human brain and nervous system within an androidic shell. An automatous automata, a pure marriage of man and machine. Think of all the lives we could save, all the lives we could extend and enrich!"

He seemed to be almost imploring me to understand. Instead, I stayed impassive.

"But at the time I had to admit it was pure speculation; a wild flight of fantasy. We had not the technical knowledge to create an automaton that was both fully autonomous and could house and sustain a human brain's consciousness, as well as allow it to interrelate with the machine to facilitate bodily functions, let alone to hear, see and speak. Yes, of course, there are those unwieldy bolt on contraptions some people sport. Replacement arms and legs grafted onto surviving muscle tissue and tendons, even some replacement eyes fashioned from photographic lenses, but all so crude and so limited. We just did not have the technology. I believed no one did." He bid me to excuse him while he lit a cigarillo, he took a long drag and blew smoke into the air.

"Then one day I was in my office at the Imperial, sorry the 'Freedom,' when this man turned up." He gestured towards the

body of Lanulos. "He said he represented a 'party' who was interested in backing my research into the collaborations of mechanical apparatus and the human brain's galvanic impulses. God forgive me, I was so focused upon the opportunity of refining my ideas I never questioned any of it until it was too late. He intimated to me that his backer, his 'Angel' as he called it, was in truth some element within the Tharsis Government itself. I had no reason to doubt him, I accepted that as fact. I left the Freedom, and Lanulos provided me everything; equipment, money, resources and materials it all seemed utterly above board. Within a scant few months, my ideas leapt from idle speculation to a tangible thesis backed up by the evidential outcomes from empirical experimentations.

"But he never seemed satisfied, always pushing on, demanding more, and then... and then..." He sighed and looked me in the eyes. "One day he brought me a piece of technology. He said it was top secret as it was captured from the Aresians. He said it was a contraption for the intercourse between the mind of an Aresian warrior and a weapon, a sensory apparatus. An instrument controlled through the neurological galvanic impulse transference, no less. I was so excited to have my hands on it that I never truly questioned where it came from. Slowly by introducing me to more and more alien technology, slowly he swallowed me up.

"He gave me support engineers and doctors versed in limb enhancement contrivances and the best automaton artificers. Within six months animal testing was over, no more damn Anemoi monkey men, and at Lanulos' constant urging, I needed to make the next logical step. We needed subjects; human subjects.

"At first we tried to use fresh corpses, stimulated by Galvinetic electromagnetism, but the results were worthless. My suggestion of obtaining volunteers who could not afford artificial limbs was instantly dismissed. I had no way to move forward... we had to find a source of human subjects. And apart from stealing them off the streets or out of the graves of Alba like some latter-day resurrectionists, we could not continue. That is when Lanulos

brought in Dr Salgari, who was an expert in anabiosis. The man was a genius. He had started as a lowly food scientist, but had done ground breaking work in not only freezing but unfreezing living material of lower order creatures. Salgari assured us if we could find anyone frozen at the point of death, he could bring them back. Though there would be a variable amount of damage to the higher functioning of the brain, the base nervous system would be intact. He assured me the subjects would be virtually dead, there would be no personality left, no memories, no soul, nothing more than a cerebral cortex and basic bodily functions. Ideal for what I needed for the next stage of the experiment.

"We were obsessed and without thought to moral considerations, we accepted it as a brilliant resolution to our nodus but where would we find such bodies? We are not Peerrohs Aresians, we do not bury our dead in the mountain snows. That was when Salgari told me of his plans. He had researched several locations where battles had happened in areas where temperatures fell well below freezing and where, due to inhospitable conditions or the fluctuations of war, numerous dead had been left where they fell in the snow. Salgari believed that he could make his name by retrieving and reviving one of those poor wretches, and restoring him to his family and friends. In fact, he admitted to succeeding in reanimating one such soldier, but the damage to the man's mind was far too extensive to be of use. And so..."

"And so; me," I interjected.

He nodded. "Yes. To cut a very long story short. Yes, and so you." He casually tossed the cigarillo butt away and lit another. "You and your men were the best possible discovery. Your airship crashed on one of the warmest days recorded in that part of the Myrmidon's Abyss. Straight into the icy slush you all went. The burning fuel and munitions causing an even higher localised temperature change just long enough for your bodies to be fully immersed. Your heavy equipment dragged you down into the anaerobic sludge and there within a few hours, you were all perfectly frozen. Impeccable specimens in icy aspic."

"How many?" I demanded.

He sighed. "They recovered thirty-one bodies. Mostly your regiment, but a couple of crew, including the co-pilot. Out of those, only fourteen were intact enough to be salvageable."

"What did you do with the others?" I knew the answer, but I wanted to hear it from his own mouth.

He paused as if realising that he had to be careful, but instead he spoke bluntly. "I will not lie to you, Adam. As with all medical waste; I had the remains incinerated. It had to be done. The other fourteen, of which you were one, were in exceptional condition."

"So there are others like me? Others of my men?"

He grimaced. "No. Only you. You were the only true success. But by then I had learnt what Lanulos really was, and who his 'Angels' really were."

"How?"

"A police officer had somehow infiltrated Lanulos' coterie of henchmen. He identified himself to me and told me he believed Lanulos to be a foreign agent and if I did not help him expose Lanulos and his people, I too would face the rope for treason. I tried to help but it was too late, somehow Lanulos knew. He killed the policeman, and Salgari because he suspected him of helping the police officer, and he threatened me."

I fought to keep my ire under control. "Threatened you? With what?"

"He killed my son-in-law, Peter, and took my wife and daughter hostage." His face tightened as if he was fighting back something. "And, when he was sure he had me where he wanted me, he revealed who he really was. What they really were."

"There are more of them?" I asked.

"I have seen several of them, but they all look the same to me."

"What do they want?"

"Lanulos told me I was to build an android that would pass for all intents and purposes for a human. It would be a chimaera of man and machine, but without self-will, so it could be set upon a purpose under their command."

"And so you did it."

He nodded. *"Yes. They had a gun at my family's heads, of course, I did what they wanted. But I did not succeed... of the fourteen there were only five that survived the transplanting procedures. Of them, only three were anything more than dribbling morons. One, upon awakening, went berserk and tore himself apart. One, the co-pilot, I forget his name, refused the programming completely and he too went insane so we had to refreeze him. And then there was you. You were the strongest from the moment we thawed you from the ice. Your heart was as strong as an ox and there was no discernible brain or neurological damage. After all the procedures were finished, and you had been programmed to obey their instructions, Lanulos was convinced we had achieved his aim. He returned my family to me and began preparations for whatever was the next step in his diabolical scheme."*

"And that was?"

"I have no idea. We were never to know. I can only speculate that he intended to build an army of such monstrosities, forgive my bluntness. I believe that when all was said and done, he would have all of us, myself and my colleagues, murdered. He was preparing to take you, I know not where, when the brain-altering paraphernalia must have failed. Your personality or memories must have resurfaced and asserted themselves. You attacked the orderlies, killed several people, wrecked a lot of machinery and fled. Lanulos was furious, but it was his work that failed not mine. That was six months ago. They have been searching for you ever since."

We stood in silence while I tried to digest all he had told me. Finally, when I had decided what I believed and what I did not, I asked, *"What are you doing here?"*

He flicked the butt onto the floor beside the other and crushed it into the carpet with the toe of his brogue. *"Lanulos never let us free. He moved the laboratory to another location and he has made us continue the work. He brought me along today because he thought I could reason with you. We were to spin you a web of* lies to convince you to come back with us. If not, then I was to lead you into a trap so that they can destroy you."

I levelled the slide gun. "That is not going to happen," I assured him.

He nodded. "You were not supposed to kill me. As far as I know, they do not have a secondary option planned. I suggest you run. Disappear again. Adam." He made to turn away from me and reached for the door handle.

"And if I do not?"

He turned. "Then we will find you. Destroy you."

I shot him. In the right eye, through his spectacle lens, exploding the side of his head across the door. Then twice in the heart before his corpse hit the floor. Why? At the time I did not really think, I just acted on instinct, though on reflection; it was not just that I was horrified by what he had done to me and my lads but that, at the end, he had started to speak like Lanulos. I knew there was something wrong. There was some terrible fundamental lie at the heart of his tale, obfuscated by actualities and half-truths. Maybe I should have taken my knife to him and found out if behind his urbane physiognomy there was another yellow face.

Without pausing, I fled the room and was halfway back down the main staircase when I remembered Cora. She was still in the corner of the study and she had heard everything. I swung around and raced back up the stairs. I had no idea what I would have to do to assure her silence, she was just a child, but I had to get her out of there.

The door of the study must have swung shut behind me so I flung it open and charged back in.

They were gone. No Cora. No corpse in the doorway, No dead yellow-skinned Aresian behind the desk. Nothing. The room was not even in the disarray I had discovered it. Bookshelves were empty. The stacks of papers were gone. The heavy curtains were drawn. There was no blood on the desk or on the carpet at my feet, nothing, not even the smell of gunpowder. I stood there dumbstruck. A mind trick? An illusion? I checked the slide gun in *my hand; it was still fully loaded. My hands and clothes were clean. There were no bullet holes in the overstuffed headrest of the chair, the door or the desktop. As I looked about me, my eyes fell upon the wad of carefully piled white punch cards that in my hallucination, if that was what it was, Lanulos had thrown towards me. They were the only physical part of the whole experience.*

I seized them and, I must admit, I ran as if all the hounds of Hell were after me. I broke the lock on the front door and fled into the comforting mundanity of the street.

It was only a narrowly missed incident with a portly fellow balancing precariously upon a steam-powered penny farthing that brought me to my senses. With his irate curses ringing in my ears, I found myself on the pavement a dozen yards away from the house with no idea of which direction I was heading.

"I say, old chap, are you alright?" One gentleman passing by inquired. I mumbled something and nodded, enough for him to accept, and with a whispered comment to his female companion, he hurried by. Probably taking me for a drunkard, or laudanum addict. I had no care for what people thought of me. The gardener I had spoken to earlier hailed and beckoned me towards the park gate.

"You look like you've taken a terrible turn, Sir. Would you like to sit down?"

I declined, but took up his offer of a nip from the hip flask he offered me. A damn good tot of gin and I needed it. I thanked him and pulled myself together. Pointing across the road, I asked him about the house I had fled; did he know who it belonged to? Had he ever seen anything unusual going on? He was reticent initially so I flashed him a quick look at Inspector Greg's warrant card.

"I knew it," he winked conspiratorially back at me. "I sure I have no idea these days who owns it. It's been shut up tight for at least five years. Rumour has it when the grand old dame that owned it, Mrs Beynon, or Benton, - Harris, died, she left it to some distant foreign nephew who was either too much of a dandy or already too rich to be much interested in it. Depends on what

story you believe of course. A bit of a pity, mind you to let a place like that stand empty. My old Dad used to tend their gardens back in the day. Nice enough people, but aloof, you know; very distant. Made their money in iron mining, I think. Never seen anything odd though."

There is nothing more I can add. I have no idea what to make of this whole situation. I am, of course, Sergeant Major Franklin, or what remains of him, and although vestiges of his memories remain, I have nothing in common with that man. If I am not a man, neither am I an automaton, then what am I? Was anything I experienced or learnt today, even real? Or just some strange, hallucinogenic episode? Had I been bamboozled with drugs or vapours or mesmerised somehow? I must have been. If it was true then what did happen in the house on Clerval Street? The gun I shot two people with and that had never left my hand had not been discharged. There were no signs whatsoever of anyone in that room.

It took me a couple of hours to walk back to the hotel and I arrived just before dinner. I was shocked to find Edwin and the others were still here awaiting my return. I felt somehow both deeply touched by their concern and exasperated that they had placed themselves in further danger by tarrying here in Alba instead of catching the railplane this morning. Edwin insisted that, as we were friends and, as he sees it, he owes me his life, he could not in clear conscience leave without me. I tried to disavow him of such a notion. It is I who am in his debt but he would not have a bean of it.

Being a gentleman Edwin did not question me about my exploits other than to simply to ask if I had found whatever I went seeking for. To assuage his concerns, I assured him that I had. Charity's questioning was much more forthright however, and so I placated her with a promise that when I could do so, when I know it fully myself, I would tell her my whole story. It is so strange to say this at this time and after such a day, but I am growing quite fond of Miss Bryant-Drake. Placing my initial irritation aside, I must confess I was gladdened to find her awaiting my return.

Barring the most unforeseen of circumstances, we shall all be on the railplane first thing in the morning. And I, for one, will not be sorry to leave Alba behind.

Now, as I sit in the comfortable surroundings of my hotel room writing this, I am forced to wonder if any of my escapades today ever really happened. I would not be totally surprised if it had not. Yet the things they told me made some horrifying sense or was it simply because I was in some induced state unable to tell truth from fantasy?

They used to say that Spookers had powers to turn a man's mind. To make a fellow see things that are not there and to drive him insane. I heard anecdotes, but I never met a man who could say it had happened to him. I wonder could they, or some other, have addled with my mind in such a way?

The stack of little white punch cards sit on the desk in front of me, but I have no way of knowing what secrets are held within their thousands upon thousands of tiny round holes and slots. Do I really want to know what is encoded in them? Or should I boldly throw them into the grate and be done with it?

"Trei did not stay to look out at the city, but went to find his
cousin.
He went smiling, and with a lightness to his step almost as
though he were flying,
for he felt at last that he had, indeed come home."

THE FLOATING ISLANDS

RACHEL NEUMEIER

CHAPTER FIVE

<u>THARSIS</u>

Message Origin;   8.05/28/09/0026
THE MIVART HOTEL ALBA ATMOGRAPHIC STATION
TO THARSIS B, RECEIVING STATION.
To Mrs Eleanor A. Ransom. Locksley Hall. Machen, Tharsis.
From Mr L. Edwin Ransom.
Bravett is a brilliant fellow. Unfortunately, we are delayed
unavoidably. Do not be alarmed by the broadsheets.
All is well. We are well. Will be with you tomorrow.
Thank your father for me. E.

Charity Bryant-Drake.
Notes to self. 28/9/26

All extremely concerned this morning when they awoke to discover Mr Franklin had disappeared.

He had left a note, but it was rather cryptic and elucidated little other than to cajole us not to await his return but to continue on to Tharsis without delay.

Mr Ransom resolutely refused to leave without his friend.

I and Mr Ransom's automaton counselled caution and we compromised upon staying one more day in Alba.

If forced to depart before Mr Franklin's return, we shall leave a note for him.

Mr Ransom told me about how he met Mr Franklin. I was surprised that, as they have known each other for only a few days, how steadfast in friendship Mr Ransom is.

Mr Franklin is a man of exceptional courage and to whom I, undoubtedly, as with the others, owe my own life.

Read the papers this morning; the incident at Alba Station has become quite a cause célèbre and Mr Ransom hailed as a hero.

My second piece was received well, and although relegated to page three in the Olympian Herald, has provoked an illustration.

Mr Ransom features, though looking more like a wild-eyed American frontiersman than a gentleman farmer, the illustration does lend itself to heroic interpretation.

The High Sheriff's unequivocal dismissal of any suggestion of charges laid against Mr Ransom and Mr Franklin lightened the mood considerably.

I have come to be quite intrigued by the automaton, Karl. I have met several automatons encoded for various tasks, however I have not met one as sophisticated in thought or so forthright in reason. Although he, and I cannot help but think of "him" as a person, is most obviously a programmed machine his fine disposition is evident and in far excess of simple coding. He has expressed numerous emotions, including deep regret for injuring and killing those who attacked us. This led us all on to a somewhat interesting discussion on the morality of killing to defend one's self beyond the simple legal rights and wrongs. Mr Ransom tells me that his father was a virtuoso amateur, as far as automaton encoding was concerned, and he intended to make Karl more of a companion than a servant. Evidently Mr Ransom senior argued that automaton encoding was fine for the battlefield and the servant automaton, but far too linear for truly independent thought and learning. What he believed necessary was some way of encoding a "currere" that was not linear, but eclectic and allowed for experiential learning and reflection. Much in a similar way a human mind learns.

I wonder if there is an opportunity of an in-depth article on those ideas. Mr Ransom assures me that he has retained all his father's journals and records.

Mr Ransom agrees it would make a fine epitaph and would bring his father posthumously some of the appreciation he merited.

Mr Bravett called on Mr Ransom this afternoon. Warrants have been issued for the apprehension of Everheart, Docket and others (I made a list) ostensibly on charges of corruption.

Though nothing has shed light on the question of D Maurier's complicity in the whole matter.

Those apprehended seemed to be in the pay of a second or third party, something Bravett assured us is the customary comportment in the underworld.

Mr Bravett informed Mr Ransom that the man with the monocular apparatus attached to his face, (the one who murdered the two police officers), is still at large.

He has been identified as a certain Uri Knapp, "a notorious hoodlum implicated in a series of slayings and assassinations across the face of the planet." (Direct Quote)

Bravett believes "Knapp" is the alias of one; John Lloyd. Who, under that name, was also the paymaster of the whole enterprise.

I wonder how such information had become accessible in such a short interval. All Mr Bravett will say was "sources had come forward." (Direct Quote)

I am left speculating whether Knapp's movements were already being observed by the authorities. But if so, why did they not intervene earlier?

Bravett assures us that if Knapp can be connected directly to D Maurier than the whole wretched business will unravel. A likeness of Knapp has been drawn up from official records and our description, and is being circulated throughout the city. He has given me a copy for my follow-up article. It is not a face easily overlooked.

For our own safety, several armed plain-clothed police officers will be stationed in and around the hotel and will provide escort until we leave the city.

Mr Ransom ascertained from me my intentions after he leaves for Tharsis. I explained that my intent was to stay here in Alba and submit a further follow-up piece.

Once I receive word Everheart, Docket and the others in the provincial council of Tremorfa, have been arrested I will return there to report the story.

Mr Ransom suggested that I might like to accompany him and Mr Franklin to the home of his father-in-law, the esteemed Professor James Athanasius Flammarion, in Tharsis.

Mr Ransom promises the Professor and his daughter, Mr Ransom's wife, will be delighted to meet me.

Mr Ransom says it was Prof. Flammarion who engaged Mr Bravett and used his influence to get Mr Ransom an audience with Mr Bogdanov, the High Sheriff. Mr Ransom tells me, the Prof, shares our common loathing of D Maurier.

Such a man would, I feel, indeed be worth my while making the acquaintance of. So I have accepted Mr Ransom's invitation.

I wonder what the good Professor and Mrs Ransom will make of the rag-tag bundle Mr Ransom will be dragging in with him.

Mr Ransom then asked me to excuse him as he wanted to spend some time drawing. I asked him why he, being somewhat of an accomplished line artist, spent so much time drawing an ugly little dog in outlandish costumes? He told me that after his daughter's dog, Mr Pug, was abducted he had made up a tale of the wild adventures the little dog was having, to placate her. And, while he was away from home, he would send Tabitha stories and drawings to illustrate the adventures of Mr Pug, now Captain Pug, Sky Pirate, no less.

Sometimes he would also send letters purporting to be from the Pug, himself expounding on his escapades. However, Mr Ransom admitted his stories owed no small part to the tales of derring-do he had so loved as a child himself.

Most of the rest of the afternoon was spent writing my follow up article for the Herald.

Mr Franklin returned just before dinner.

I must say I was greatly relieved to see him. Beyond his careful reserve and kind manner, I must remark that Mr Franklin has a certain air of stoical vitality about him.

Mr Franklin was heartened that Mr Ransom had remained here awaiting his return, though he chided him for such recklessness.

Over dinner, Mr Ransom apprised him of the news Mr Bravett had brought this afternoon.

Mr Franklin would not divulge much detail of his exploits to us other than to say he had been wandering the city and found several places he thought he remembered or at least that appeared familiar.

Ransom was delighted for him, but Mr Franklin seemed troubled and often worked hard to change the topic.

I enquired if he was yet ready to allow me to interview him and he demurred politely but firmly.

Journal of Adam Franklin.

Karl had us up and mustered for our journey at the crack of dawn. It was a shock for me as I had had the first night's sleep in memory unplagued by nightmares and visions. I found myself woolly-headed and it took at least three strong cups of tea and a hearty breakfast before my senses cleared.

We were escorted safely back to the railplane terminus at Alba Station by several burly police officers. I do not know if I felt more a criminal than a dignitary being at the centre of so much attention. Although Edwin and Charity were anxious, the whole thing went off without incident, save some spontaneous applause from a couple of lady commuters who apparently recognised Edwin from pictures in the papers.

Aboard the railplane itself, an elderly gentleman passenger approached us and asked to shake our hands as he congratulated us on our bravery in standing up to "those damned foreign Anarchists." He was about to share with us his insights based on his own extensive military exploits when we were thankfully spared the ordeal by the Clippy insisting he returned to his own compartment. She clipped our tickets, smiled sweetly, wished us a safe and "uneventful" journey and closed our compartment door.

At that Charity burst into a fit of giggles and all three of us collapsed in riotous laughter. Karl sat patiently through our outbreak of hysterics until we had regained our composure before asking what it was we found so comical. We were hard-pressed to explain our outburst other than in terms of the sheer preposterous irony of it all.

The railplane journey was thankfully uneventful, although pleasant enough. The British Colonial Administration built the suspended railway to link Alba and Tharsis when attempts to build a ground-based railway failed time and time again, due to the dust and the harsh unconquered topography.

Edwin enthusiastically informed us the in-cylinder compression engines driving the huge propellers were an extrapolation on an earlier Otto Pyréolophore internal combustion engine design. He was delighted to impart that the engines were powered by biologically produced liquid fuel from dandelions.

Flying due south-west the railplane's monorail track took us over the remarkable landscape of the plain between Alba and the lake of Ulysses, and on towards the three huge volcanos that stand like vast sentinels against the south eastern skyline. It is all so familiar to me and yet also so strange to see as if with new eyes.

To our right, just beyond the horizon, stands the mighty walls of mount Olympus, its vast upthrusted escarpments of red rock shielding the calderas behind. A volcano the size of France so huge it has its own unique weather patterns. Not long after mankind had arrived here Earthmelding had turned those calderas into the vast lakes to feed fresh water to the thirsty agricultural settlements and towns of the plain below. The land over which the towering pylons marched is now a tame patchwork of lush colours; the greens of orchards, vineyards and woodlands, the golds of cereal crops, the reds of native plants, and the swathes of the intense yellow of sunflowers, rapeseed and Edwin's beloved dandelions.

The plain is dissected by vast ancient canals with their lush banks of forest and near jungle, some so long and so wide that, Edwin claims, they are visible from Earth. They reflect the cerulean sky like mirrored ribbons stretching out across the planet. We passed over one of the mighty paddle steamers as it powered its way through the glassy smooth water of the Canali Phlegethon. People waved excitedly up at us from its decks. The steamer blasted its whistle in acknowledgement of our passing and the railplane answered in kind, to the enormous delight of the passengers on both vessels.

Something in the back of my mind suddenly became uneasy with being on the railplane, it was an elusive feeling that presaged an old memory. I had travelled this journey before. Probably in the days of fighting the fathers of those people on the paddle steamer I had raised a hand in acknowledgement to. In actual fact, probably the fathers of almost all of these people, on the ship and the railplane. Maybe I should have gone and reminisced with the old codger who had tried to accost us with his war stories and traded a few of my own.

By early afternoon we passed over the northern edge of the great lake of Ulysses Fossae, and there before us stretching out to the feet of Mount Parvonis and Mount Ascaraeus sprawled the vast city of Tharsis. She had worn many names in her short history; New Jerusalem, New London, Parvonis City, Tharsis Parvonis, but even before my time they had dropped the "Parvonis" and she had become simply Tharsis, synonymous with the city and the state.

Memories filtered back of the last time I came here; a time when the flag of the Union flew over the city and the writ of the British Empire ruled. Today it was an independent republic and, reading between the lines of Beresford's book, Hell-bent on conquests of its own.

The capital city was a stark revelation after the majestic natural grandeur of our journey. In less than a hundred years, Tharsis has grown from a shanty town around an aethervolt landing site to a city to rival any on Earth. At its edges, great houses nestle in lush green gardens set in genteel, almost bucolic, splendour. Beyond that suburbanisation has created a vast ring of homes and businesses, a locus for the aspiring middle classes, intelligentsia and the patrician "Red Bookers." Beyond that the true city stood; where the endless crowded tenements of the indentured working class shelter in the fetid shadows of the vast factories they service. And at the city's heart, veiled in a permanent haze of heat and fumes, there stand the towering citadels of industrialisation, their stacks billowing greasy black smoke into the cold blue sky. These colossal manufactories and workshops had rendered down and refashioned the raw bones of Mars into the tools of its own conquest.

So this was what had been touted as the "Gateway to Eden." Hundreds of thousands of poor, desperate working class families came here on the back of vague promises of building a better life. Gratefully, they gave up the drudge of their hopeless destitution in favour of a dream of a "New Jerusalem." Only to sell their lives to travel millions of miles across space to find the self-same misery under a different sky. Sold on that red penny and little more than indentured slaves, they either fell victim to ochlesis, worked themselves into early graves or died in the incessant wars that have plagued our time on this bloody red rock.

Cheerily Edwin began to point out locations to Charity; the Cathedral of St. George that was converted from a vast Aresian temple, the fortifications of the Old Imperial Casern, the parks, the Grand Freedom Hospital and the spires of the university buildings.

Below us, the thoroughfares thronged with people and every possible type of conveyance imaginable. Above the city the sky is full of flying contraptions; aerostats, balloons, ornithopters and aerial steamers, all vying for space in an insane mid-air ballet. Above all the chaos floated the railplane terminal itself, built upon a huge chunk of gravity-defying rock, it hangs motionless like a tethered balloon over the city. I had forgotten how amazing the sight of it was and sat for a moment simply gazing at it. Here there is a change of motion as the monorail becomes steel hawsers, the propellers fall still, and we are no longer moving under our own propulsion but drawn in like some huge cable car.

Being a Sunday afternoon, the public places below us were teaming with people playing cricket, riding horses or punting on the narrow canals, all without the merest hint of wonder at it all. Few, if any, even looked up as we flew over their heads and onwards towards the terminus.

Charity Bryant-Drake.
Notes to self. 29/9/26
This morning's journey was encouraging.

Mr Ransom was recognised by passers-by in the railplane terminal at Alba and applauded. They recognised him from the illustrations published with my article.

He was also accosted on the railplane by passengers wishing to congratulate him and Mr Franklin for standing up to those "damned foreign anarchists."

This morning the events of the incident at Alba Station had been succeeded on the front pages of the broadsheets by some astonishing lithographs of the maiden voyage of the new aerostat Dreadnaught, the Daedalus, and speculation as to when war with the Thylians may break out again.

However, inside they were full of my article and those illustrations republished in the two other major dailies and with a great deal of editorial speculations.

Some of the other rags left me a little peeved, to say the least, as they had cribbed my story, but did not acknowledge it with even a by-line. I am really irked by that. I will talk to my editor about it.

I hope all this nationalistic furore will encourage readers to equate the events of Friday with anarchists and D Maurier with those "enemy foreigners." Most of the papers are full of bellicose anti-Thylian and anti-Zephorite editorials, along with a great deal of jingoistic sabre-rattling.

Evidently, there has been an incident in the Forests of the Gorgonum Chaos, with various groups of so-called "settlers" fighting over water rights, which seems to have led to the intervention of Thylian and Zephorite mercenaries. The leaders of the Sirenum alliance of Free Settlers, have petitioned our Government to "defend their rights." It is just a repeat of Arabia Ponds; another war by proxy.

Hopefully, in this current political climate, it will bring severe discomfort to that evil little toad and force those around him to rethink their associations.

These days in Tharsis "anarchist" is synonymous with words like; spy, counter-revolutionary and traitor. With the mood of the people so hostile, things are enormously perilous for anyone even suspected as an enemy of the state.

Our journey was peaceful.

Mr Ransom was entertaining and imparted frequent detailed observations about the railplane and features of the landscape.

Mr Franklin was an amiable travelling companion as well until we passed a steamer ship on one of the canals, after which he became withdrawn and took to reading the papers and writing in his journal.

I have not been to Tharsis city since I was a small girl and flying into Tharsis from Alba presents a view of the city that is breathtaking; the city is a vast metropolis, like those I have read about on Earth. It is ten times the size of Alba. In my estimation.

Mr Ransom pointed out the most interesting places as we flew over them. I thought it all equally wondrous until I saw the railplane terminal itself, which leaves one dumb struck with amazement. I remember reading something about it at school and have seen an illustration or two, but nothing can prepare a mind for the sight of it. It is of little question why the people of Tharsis are so proud of their achievement. It looks to all intents-and-purposes like an upside-down mountain, a vast, truncated iceberg, hanging a thousand feet above the city. The top of the rock is, in its self, the size of a small town and that is exactly what it supports. A small town has been constructed upon its flattened surface to service the railplane and AirTrain terminuses and the various landing strips, hangars and runways. All simply hanging there in the sky by some ingenious magic.

I asked Mr Ransom did he know how it was possible. He explained it is thought to be a piece of a third moon that once orbited Mars, Phrike. It had either crashed or was knocked down by a comet, and shattered into millions of pieces. All of which seem to be made of a gravitationally opposed mineral called phrikite, a kind of "anti-magnetic." This piece originally floated over the Acidalia Planitia, but the British had it hauled all the way here to provide a platform for the city's air defences. Mr Ransom says he read that some of the Aresian citadels, even cities, were built on these fractures of moon rock. Ransom explained, we, Earthmen that is, had learnt from the Aresians how to amalgamate the mineral with copper and use it to plate airship hulls, so with the stimulation of a mild electrical field, we can raise such heavy loads on reasonably small blimps, or the balloon envelopes would have to be enormous. In fact, without phrikite, most of our aircraft would hardly get off the ground. But the source is, of course, limited, however luckily they can now produce an artificial material called Cavorite, which has similar properties though it is not quite as effective. Mr Ransom regaled us with a story of his meeting the inventor of Cavorite, an eccentric physicist named Professor Cavor, when he was at university. He went on to explain the physics of it all in great detail. I must admit to having missed much of what he said as I was more interested in just gazing at the rock. It was originally named for the Empress Victoria but since U.D.I now is renamed the "Pegasus Rock." With the sky around the rock so full of ornithopters and other flying machines of all sorts, one could easily picture them as those mythical winged beasts circling their lair.

The railplane drew to a stop between the huge masts and gantries and we took the elevating room down from the platform to the terminus proper. It is the strangest of sensations to stand on what appears to be the firmest of terra firma but is, in fact, floating a quarter of a mile above a city. Mr Ransom was still keen to educate us all in the nuances of the engineering of the elevating room and the method that would take us down to the Central Train Station below. I was about to voice my amazement at the solidity of the platform when suddenly the whole rock – and my stomach - shifted in the face of a heavy gust of wind. Mr Ransom supported me and assured us all was well, but I was more concerned about the height we were to descend and the strength of the winds to pay much attention. Although, as soon as we were on the clacking cable train chugging its way down to the city, I wished I had listened to him. I would have demanded a stiff G and T before ever boarding such an infernal contraption. None of the style and comfort of the railplane itself, but an antiquated old rust bucket. This particular conveyance was a "singular marvel of civil engineering" according to Mr Ransom, as it pre-dates the railplane by two decades, but I found nothing "civil" about it. I can only describe it as a shabby upside down steam engine slung at 45 degrees beneath a huge and alarmingly rusted cable. The intentional design of which seemed to be to inflict as much discomfort and alarm upon its already anxious passengers as possible. That, coupled with being subjected to the engine's smoke and fumes to the point of almost asphyxiation, made the whole journey unpleasant, to say the least. Until, of course, the winds cleared the smoke and we were treated to the view. At which the journey immediately went from merely unpleasant to terrifying.

I do not believe I am a woman of frail disposition, and I believe I have never suffered from acrophobia in my life, but I found myself hanging on to Mr Franklin's arm in a most unseemly manner and unable to let go. Thankfully, Mr

Franklin was in much better humour and most understanding about my predicament.

The cable train deposited us on the platform opposite the main entrance of the Central Train Station. I have never in my life been so relieved to step on the true earth. For a moment we found ourselves alone on the platform and, I for one had a sudden spell of déjà vu. To our relief Carstairs, Mr Ransom's father-in-law's driver, hailed us and, accompanied by two hefty looking young men, Carstairs' sons, whisked us away to awaiting vehicles in short order.

We rode in some comfort in the Emancipation steam carriage while the Carstairs boys and our rather limited luggage followed on a Whitechapel. Ever alert Karl chose to ride shotgun on the Whitechapel although city ordinances do not allow for him to carry a firearm openly in public, even though now he is licenced.

The journey through the city was almost as impressive as flying over it. Mr Ransom fell back into his repertoire of pointing out landmarks and places of interest. Mr Franklin seemed more interested now we were on the ground and engaged us both in speculative conversation regarding the anti-Thylian sabre rattling reported in the press. Mr Franklin was interested in the new dreadnaught, the Daedalus, and the proposition of more ships like her to come. I pondered if he was interested in re-enlisting if there was another war, a man of his obvious talents, experience and abilities would, with a little financial backing, find no problem obtaining a commission. Mr Franklin cavilled at the suggestion insisting he was far too old and not of the right temperament for any military service.

I enquired of Mr Ransom if he knew what his father-in-law's position on this issue was? Mr Ransom said his father-in-law was born into a famous Wilburite family and has often argued forcibly and publicly against violence in all its forms.

Mr Ransom ventured if the Professor was not so well-regarded and indispensable to the Government his forthright views may have gotten him into serious difficulties. Mr Franklin said being a conscientious objector and living here on a planet named after the God of War is a strange and difficult contradiction. Mr Ransom seemed to stop himself on the very edge of a pithy response, instead, he just smiled decorously and redirected the conversation.

I am looking forward to meeting Professor Flammarion.

The Diary of Eleanor Athaliah Ransom (Mrs).
29th September 26
My heart is fit to burst with such gladness! Edwin came home today! I can hardly contain my joy!

We have all been awaiting his return with such anticipation all day. Even Papa was anxious to get Edwin home and safely in the bosom of his family. He arrived just before tea, not at all ruffled by his journey or his perilous exploits since he left here only a few days ago. I have always loved his imperturbable composure and gentle manner.

Oh, it is so good to have him home! The children were so thrilled that I and Nanny could barely contain them. We were all so delighted that I fear our euphoric reception made us look quite foolish to Mr Franklin and Miss Bryant-Drake. But no matter! We almost danced for joy!

Papa dispensed with all formalities and we rushed Edwin and our new friends to the parlour to take tea. I have no idea how she does these things, but Mrs Carstairs had laid on a veritable feast of sandwiches, cakes and scones, more than enough to sate the most voracious traveller's appetite. They were all so parched from their journey that the samovar ran dry three times! As Edwin has led me to expect, Mr Franklin is a tall and impressive man whose striking countenance and reserved manner is belied by his courteousness and ready, self-effacing, humour. I must say, to my deepest chagrin, I did momentarily pause in perturbation when first laying eyes upon his ravaged features. Though, thankfully, to their credit, the children did not show any such trepidation in their greeting of him or take any measure in their conduct towards him. In fact, Tabby seems to have taken a ready liking to him and even going so far as to boldly question him about his scars. Mr Franklin was gracious in his reply, even allowing Tabby to touch his face. Edwin was also accurate as to the nature of his eyes, I have seldom ever seen a man with such compassionate and soulful eyes. Nanny remarked to me that before his accident, Mr Franklin must have been a very handsome and striking gentleman.

Miss Bryant-Drake is a robust young woman with a fair, open and friendly face topped with a shock of auburn hair scooped up into an untidy chignon at the nape of her neck. Her demeanour is charming, but a little awkward and her masculine attire; oilskin duster coat, long laced boots and leather riding breeches, does little to flatter her femininity. She is intelligent, quick-witted with a delightful, although off centre, smile and sparkling green eyes. (Which she seldom takes off of Mr Franklin for more than a few moments.) In conversation, she is quite articulate, forthright and clearly spoken.

After tea, Papa took Edwin, Mr Franklin and Miss Bryant-Drake out onto the veranda to take some late afternoon air while I helped Mrs Carstairs clear the table and Nanny settled the children.

Nanny had almost got them settled back in the nursery when Karl arrived and they were equally clamorous to greet him. He had delayed to make certain there were no undesirables following from the city. Strangely, I was almost overcome at the sight of him standing in the vestibule. It is such a relief of having him back here with us, the children were almost as delighted to see him as they were their father, and clung to him as if he were a favourite, but long lost, uncle.

I feel as though I have been living on the edge of a knife since this turn of events began and now in that moment, I knew we were safe again.

Edwin thanked Papa for his advice and assistance and for the introduction to Mr Bravett and Mr Bogdanov. He feels that without Papa's intervention the situation in Alba would have become far too tangled and precarious. I was horrified to hear him admit he honestly feared he would either end up dead or in prison!

Papa was most truly impressed by Edwin's bravery and the courageousness of Mr Franklin. Miss Bryant-Drake inquired if Papa had ever encountered that man Du Maurier? Papa assured us he had not, though he has, of course, heard of him, Even before last Tuesday evening when he accosted me at the Phileas Society's reception. He has a reputation as an unpleasant, almost rapacious entrepreneur with low morals and little conscience. There is not a club or society of repute in Tharsis that would allow him membership. The Phileas Society alone has blackballed him twice and, last year, the Tharsis Guild of Exploration and Trade refused to even accept his application, submitted for the fifth time. As Papa says; "What passes for commercial enterprise in Zephier will not be tolerated in Tharsis. We may be a new nation, but we are a civilised nation, not one of ne'er-do-wells, popinjays and petty despots."

Mrs Carstairs saw to the visitor's comfort. She has put them in rooms in the west wing away from the hustle and bustle and the noise from the nursery. I picked a few more fetching pieces of attire for Miss Bryant-Drake out of Lenora's old closet. She was delighted to divest herself of her "road clobber" as she delightfully called it. We had a little more difficulty with finding some clean clothes which would fit Mr Franklin but Mrs Carstairs is a marvel.

Thankfully now the house is settled, Edwin and I can spend some time together.

It was wonderful to spend time with Edwin alone this afternoon while everyone retired before dinner. We sat, held hands and talked for hours. My husband is such a man as I dared to believe him to be, still the gentle and compassionate man he has always been with us, but dauntless in the face of adversity. I would never have wished this misfortune upon my dear Edwin, but I am proud of how he has conducted himself. Although, with his customary reserve, he has attempted to play down his bravery at Alba Station. I have carefully read a dozen times what the witnesses said and how he saved that little child's life. Edwin though is full of remorse for killing one of the assailants, and I fear it almost moved him to tears to talk about it. He blames his own obstinacy for causing all this mayhem and anguish. I told him a dozen times; I could not be prouder of him.

We were dressing for dinner when an unexpected carriage arrived in the driveway. Our unforeseen visitant was no less than Lady Niketa. Lady N had been a great friend of Mama's and still descends upon us on a whim, though thankfully less frequently than she used to. She is a wonderful, gregarious and amusing woman, who, within moments of her arrival, had succeeded in creating utter chaos. The children, upon hearing her calling for them, were up and out of their rooms with poor Nanny in pursuit. Carstairs, Dan and Aegy, were engaged in trying to capture and contain Lady Niketa's ever-growing pack of little dogs and the whole house was aroused. Only Papa was conspicuous by his absence.

What with all the day's excitement, their father's return, Lady Niketa showering them with small favours and the fun of chasing seven small yapping dogs around the house, it took all my and Nanny's energy to marshal the children back to bed.

By the time I returned Lady Niketa was holding court in Mama's Orangery with Edwin dancing attendance upon her. Refusing to go unnoticed she had sent Mrs Carstairs to "fetch" Papa from his "dingy den" as she called it. I arrived as she was holding forth about her late Buntie and how he had so loved this house and still does.

She then turned to what I mistook for the reason for her visit. I cannot say she asked Edwin about the events of the last few days, but as is her usual want she simply held forth her unsolicited observations and opinions. One of the few things she and Papa emphatically agree upon is their disparaging attitude towards Edwin's desire to pursue his father's vision. Attitudes which I fear that, through my bemoaning my sequestration and my melancholia, I have only helped entrench. This, muddled up with chatter about Buntie's messages to her from beyond "the veil," led on to what was little more than a polemic on what an evil monster Du Maurier is and how Edwin should have never been so foolish as to have returned to Tremorfa in the first place. All this was very much her normal chatter until the subject turned to Mr Franklin and Edwin formally introduced them.

I have known Lady Niketa for most of my life, but I have never seen her lost for words or react so peculiarly. Mr Franklin greeted her courteously but when she held out her hand, which he took with his left, she went as pale of any of the apparitions she so often talks of. For a moment I thought she was having an apoplexy! Edwin rushed to give her a glass of water, but she regained herself quickly, dismissing it all to the fluster of the journey and the warmth of the orangery.

Edwin went on to introduce Miss Bryant-Drake and we all exchanged pleasantries until Mrs Carstairs announced dinner was served.

I have never had a dinner like it. Papa arrived as we had almost finished the consommé and we were about to move on to a few of Mrs Carstairs' tasty kickshaws. Lady Niketa chided Papa for being so tardy as to be late for his own dinner party, but to my surprise, Papa took the chastisement in good humour. I tried to broach the news of Papa's impending explorative expedition, but he did not wish to talk about it over the dinner table. He can sometimes be so perfunctory in his manner he might appear almost indecorous to those who do not understand his disposition. At the conclusion of the meal, Papa announced that he had specially invited Lady Niketa this evening. I was surprised as he had not confided in me or Mrs Carstairs as to such plans.

Papa declared his reason for inviting Lady Niketa was his wish for her to hold one of her spiritual readings for us. I and Edwin could only stare at each other in complete disbelief. To use Nanny's colourful expression when I confided in her later; we were flabbergasted.

Miss Bryant-Drake was excited, but Mr Franklin's discomfort was obvious by the change in his demeanour. Papa had always disparaged Mamma's interest in Spiritualism and often, in private, made quite acerbic comments about Lady Niketa's practices. "Flummery and table rapping nonsense," was one of his favourite dismissive remarks, and her offer of holding a sitting here not long after Mamma's death almost ended their acquaintance completely.

Still somewhat astounded, drinks in hand, we all traipsed across to the smoking room where Carstairs had set out Papa's antique card table, upon which have been played so many games of cribbage and whist in the past. Now covered with a black drape and set about with six high back chairs gathered from around the house, the familiar old table suddenly took on an almost ominous presence. Papa requested all to sit.

Of course, I have attended dozens of such séances and spiritual sittings as an escort to Momma, and this, though unusual for being in our own home, was initially much the same. With much the same nervous humour as always accompanies these proceedings, we made ourselves comfortable around the small table and, under Lady Niketa's direction, held hands. I had Edwin on one side of me and Papa on the other.

Lady Niketa started with her usual theatrical preamble regarding spirits of the "Other World," her various Spirit Guides and what was to expect and what not to do. All of which Miss Bryant-Drake seemed to find quite amusing. Carstairs and Mrs Carstairs lit the candle on the table and dimmed the gas lights, we squeezed each other's hands for assurance, and Lady Niketa began.

At first, all was much as I would have expected; Lady Niketa's questions as to whether any spirits were present with us were answered by a few indeterminate raps and knocks. She introduced us to the spirits and introduced her Spirit Guide; Whitehawk, a Red Indian Chieftain to us. It is always amusing to hear this deep American accent issuing from Lady Niketa's mouth, though he seems a pleasant fellow and greeted us all warmly and respectfully. It was only when Whitehawk asked what the supplicants quested for, that events took a wholly unanticipated turn. Not that all of this was not already much unexpected.

As Papa cleared his throat to speak, I found myself unable to breathe as I truly feared he might ask a question of Mamma's spirit – but he did not. Instead, he inquired, "I want to speak with the spirit of an Aresian, a First Martian if they have such spirits. I wish to ask a question of him."

There was an audible gasp in the room and we all looked from Papa to Whitehawk. Lady Niketa's expression, illuminated now only by the single guttering flame of the candle, did not change, she did not move, only the voice of Whitehawk answered. His reply was that to seek the Martian spirits was to journey into another realm, one he could not go and one no man should try to.

Though Whitehawk's tone was chilling, Papa was not dissuaded, he replied forcefully, "I am Dr James Flammarion and I wish to speak to the spirits of any true Martian. I call upon you to speak to me." I must admit I almost panicked as I felt Papa might be doing this to publicly mock or ridicule poor Lady

Niketa, I tried to slip my hand from his to break the circle but I just did not have the strength.

Suddenly everyone felt the temperature in the room plummet. The fire in the hearth banked as if stifled by ashes, and we all squirmed uneasily in our seats. Miss Bryant-Drake no longer seemed to find it amusing. I found myself staring into the eyes of Mr Franklin, whose intense glare with furrowed brow was set upon Lady Niketa.

The voice that came out of Lady Niketa now was indescribably strange. A guttural voice both contemptuous and menacing in its tone. It spoke words, but none I could possibly guess at the meaning of, and in no language I could identify. Papa suddenly commanded it to stop in a manner I have not heard since I was a small child. The voice fell silent. Papa asked, "Who are you? What is your name?" But all it would say was it was cold. Papa pushed on and it confirmed it was indeed what we knew of as an Aresian, or First Martian as Papa refers to them, but some of the things it said were incomprehensible to us due to its strange accent. Papa asked it if knew of others, others that were still alive? It only replied; "Many, many, many…." Papa asked if it knew of others alive on Mars. And it laughed. I have never heard such unnerving sniggering and it said; "They await you, old man. Beyond the Hourglass Sea, beyond the Ice. They know you are coming." It, and I can only think of it as an 'it' laughed again and said, "If you do not die trying to get there."

Papa was undaunted but by that time we had heard enough. I asked Mrs Carstairs to raise the lights and as she did, I blew out the candle. That seemed to bring Lady Niketa out of her trance. For a moment, she looked utterly discombobulated, but then she smiled and asked for a gin and tonic. We were all just beginning to relax and discuss the proceedings when suddenly Lady Niketa stood up rigidly and pointed at Mr Franklin. "Him, bring him," the alien voice demanded. "The dead man. He knows the way."

Suddenly she swooned so completely it was lucky Papa was close enough to catch her before she hurt herself.

Mr Franklin looked utterly thunderstruck, his face pallid with the shock of it. I requested Carstairs to escort him through to the drawing room and get him a brandy. I hurried Edwin and Miss Bryant-Drake after them, while I and Mrs Carstairs revivified Lady Niketa with a few waved napkins, smelling salts and a large glass of G and T.

It was only then I realised Papa had left us. I assumed he had gone with Edwin and Mr Franklin but when Lady Niketa had regained herself enough for us to join them in the drawing room Papa was not there. I mounted a search for him only to discover him back in his study scribbling in his journal in a most frenetic manner. When I interrupted him to enquire if he was well he looked at me almost alarmed. For a moment I was sure he did not know who I was. Once he had broken out of his confusion, he said to me, "Nelly dearest," Papa seldom ever calls me Nelly. "I was right! It seems utterly illogical to me, but Lady Niketa could never have known those words! That language! Oh, have I been such a dolt?" I have never seen him so agitated. He rushed around the desk to me and grasped my hands, his eyes searching my face. "They are still here on Mars and Hélène Ramié was right; they can communicate with us. Through our minds!"

I said I thought the Aresian that came through was a spirit of a dead person. Lady Niketa says they are voices of the dearly departed.

"Not so!" Said Papa elatedly, "Nelly my dear, not so! In my quest I have made a long study of their languages, I admit I am still no true expert, but I know enough and... oh and Nelly, here is the rub... when he first came through he said; '!Deráthvérshnu na a y'owu oul-askadaikae'a! Æ gærru pour þáin y'owu gor þou y'owa þos y'ousa. Foolish men and your foolish machines. The sword above your heads is ours, not yours!' It is a clear inference to the Sword of Damocles! The sword over our heads! That means he must know what is happening now, in the last few days, here in Tharsis! It was no spirit, unless they read the Tharsis daily newspapers in their particular corner of Elysium!"

It is so long since I have seen his eyes sparkle with such delight I found myself caught up in his euphoria as he hurried me back to the drawing room. Clasping Lady Niketa's hands, he thanked her profusely for her efforts to the point of embarrassment (which is by far some way for Lady Niketa) before he turned to us all.

He then recounted his evidence for of the Aresians remaining on Mars, the purchase of the aerostat, The Seren Bore, and laid out his plans for an expedition to contact them. He was certain now they still dwell here on Mars and the one that Lady Niketa channelled was no denizen of the netherworld but a living breathing First Martian. One of those that can exercise some form of Mentalistic transference to communicate across vast expanses.

Lady Niketa was flabbergasted, but after another fortifying draught, she conceded that it was the queerest of channellings, unlike anything she had ever experienced before. When Mr Franklin enquired in what way it was different? Lady Niketa could only say the alien spirit was extraordinarily compelling, so much so she felt for a moment that she might lose control of her own physical body and be driven out into some strange limbo. Suddenly she fell quiet and in an almost mawkish manner, truly abnormal for one of her vigorous personality, explained there had been a dreadful sense of evil about it as if the spirit was cruelly mocking us all.

Papa asserted he did not believe it was a spirit at all and someone powerful enough to control another's mind from such a great distance would no doubt leave their receptor feeling shaken and powerless. As for evil, he said, "Evil, after all, is only a matter of perspective. An act that may seem utterly evil to a hen is but a matter of breakfast to a man."

Lady Niketa agreed, but I do not feel that consoled her in the slightest. She was still so traumatised by her ordeal so I excused us both from the conversation and took her back to the Orangery. Where she could enjoy the comfort and the ministrations of her dogs, while I organised a room for her to stay overnight.

By the time I had her and her companions settled and returned to the drawing room, Papa had already enlisted Mr Franklin, Miss Bryant-Drake and, to my great frustration, Edwin, into his expedition, and they were all happily discussing the adventure ahead.

It is now almost midnight and they are still down there even now. This is not what I imagined for the night of Edwin's return to us.

Journal of Adam Franklin.

On the journey from the railplane terminal to his father-in-law's home, Edwin appeared to become pensive and nervous. I asked him if he was anxious about our meeting his family, and I offered to take lodging in the city if he felt there would be any imposition.

He dismissed my concerns, but confided in us that his relationship with Professor Flammarion has not always been on the very best of terms. The Professor adores his daughters, especially Eleanor (Nelly), and, though he has always supported their choices, he has often made it abundantly clear he did not approve of Edwin's decision to return to Tremorfa after his father's death. The Professor felt Edwin should have stayed with his family in Tharsis and concentrated in forwarding his careers and education under the Professor's guidance. After the incident of the intruder and the dognapping, Professor Flammarion insisted Nelly and the children return to the family home for their safety. Something I must say I would have concurred with. Evidently, on the occasion of Edwin's last visit, and thankfully whilst Nelly and the children were elsewhere, the Professor and Edwin had a vigorous and somewhat heated exchange of opinions.

We, Miss Bryant-Drake and I, enquired if our presence would create an uncomfortable atmosphere, but Edwin dismissed it again, saying that the Professor is above all a gentleman and, though he may scold a chap in private, he conducts himself with great dignity at all times. I fear it is the private "scolding" Edwin dreads.

We arrived at the home of Edwin's father-in-law in the late afternoon. It is still a substantial striking early British colonial mansion, though wearied by the ravages of time and, from what I have learnt from Edwin, lack of interest on the Professor's behalf. The house was built by Reynard Augustus "The Fox" Flammarion, who I believe was Edwin's wife's grandfather or great-grandfather, and, although the house still sits in substantial grounds, the lands have been nibbled away at by the termites of financial pressures, taxations and running costs to only a fraction of what it once commanded. I felt, upon viewing it, in some ways the effects of the failures in upkeep have softened the general aspect of the house, making it look more welcoming than some we noticed as we passed.

Edwin's wife Eleanor (Nelly) greeted us at the door with their two exuberant children. Mrs Ransom is an attractive woman, fine-boned, tall and lissom, with long dark hair and large green eyes. Though she is accommodating and kindly, she carries herself with the demeanour of a confident woman who has stepped up to the role of mistress of a once great house. The children are beautiful and a perfect mix of both their parents. Little Tabitha (Tabby) though, has striking grey eyes that seem to search deep into your soul. Both children are precocious and highly intelligent. The boy, James, is tall for his age and a little diffident at first, but he is a fine young man. There is a certain intensity about his manner I have seen in Edwin too.

I must say that our greeting stirred something deep inside me. I was honestly touched by their warmth and welcome of us complete strangers into their home. Especially I, with my formidable countenance. Little Tabitha asked to touch the scars on my face and when I stooped low for her to do so she threw her arms around my neck and held on like she was trying to comfort me and whispered, "Thank you for bringing Daddy home."

Professor Flammarion is a bluff, robust man, solidly built with an imposing halo of white hair and a full patriarchal beard. Obviously not one to stand on ceremony, he greeted us in his smoking jacket and slippers, he has a firm handshake, genial deportment and a keen eye.

We were treated to a lavish high tea while Edwin, I and Miss Bryant-Drake were pressed to fill in the details of our misadventures. Professor Flammarion asked some searching questions, but kept his own counsel at least until his daughter and grandchildren were out of earshot.

As we strolled in the gardens to take in the late afternoon air after tea, the Professor spoke candidly. He stated he sincerely regretted what had transpired, but he hoped some good would come of it; Edwin would now see the sense of returning to Tharsis permanently. Tremorfa is – in the Professor's words – 'a damned misbegotten dust bowl' and no place for a young man of Edwin's talents let alone his responsibilities.

Crestfallen Edwin did not argue the toss, and seemingly satisfied he had made his point, the Professor did not labour on the theme. Our conversation was a little stilted after that, but picked up well when Miss Bryant-Drake explained who her stepfather was; Dr Robert Cromie, evidently a famous Xenoanthrobiologist, whom Professor Flammarion knew from his younger undergraduate days. The Professor seemed pleased to hear of his old friend, but shocked at the misfortune that had befallen him since running afoul of Du Maurier.

The Professor was extremely outspoken as to his low opinion of Du Maurier but cited his main concern as being for the Republic itself. In fact, according to the Professor, all the republics have suffered from the rise of such men as Du Maurier and Efram Edgars to name but a few. Inconceivably wealthy, and utterly ruthless. Magnates whose influence and power has quickly grown to transcend political borders, circumvent national laws and flout international agreements. They are drawing more and more power to themselves. They control vast resources, including water and agricultural as well as mining rights, which should never have been allowed to fall into the hands of individual industrialists. The Professor sees such men as the greatest threat to the Republic since the Declaration of Unilateral Independence.

I proposed the question as to whether the rise of such men was not inevitable. Given that, as from what I understand from reading Beresford's book, most of the republics have allowed for a free market economic activity within their borders and signed up to various open trade agreements that facilitate commerce. Those tycoons with an eye to real influence were bound to focus upon control of those resources fundamental to everyone's daily existence; water, food, fuel, mineral resources. If you have control of those across several nations you have more power than any individual government. The Professor agreed, saying such monopolising of commodities into the hands of a few rich barons who, acting beyond borders and laws, answer to no one save themselves, would lead inevitably to a power struggle between them, the national Governments and the people.

The Professor cited what is happening out in Sirenum right now, where he sees the hand of Windlestraw Volpone from Argyre, another such magnate, who has been buying up mineral rights in the area.

Miss Bryant-Drake asked if the Professor truly feared that men like Du Maurier could cause a civil war. The Professor answered he did not envision "civil war" per se, but a coming confrontation between the industrialists and the citizenship over control of our own manifest destiny. His greatest fear being that governments manipulated by powerful self-interests would side with the Du Mauriers of our world against their own citizens. He went on to talk about the revolution in the Americas, the spring of '48 and how the ideals of Mr Locke, Thomas Paine and Mr Marx, had inspired the Red Hand Secessionists to throw off the yoke of colonial rule.

I listened with interest. I never truly questioned the motivations behind the slogans and rhetoric of the Secessionists. I was a soldier, my duty was to serve the Empire and protect her interests, not to argue politics with revolutionaries, but now the "revolutionaries" were driving the steamcoach and it appeared to me that men like Professor Flammarion are fearing the wheels are about to come off.

And what am I? A relic of a lost war? No more relevant than the smashed hulk of the weed-choked Nutcracker lying at the gate in Alba's garrison? If I had to choose a side whose side would I be on? Or has fate already chosen for me? Dark thoughts assailed me.

I asked if the Professor himself had been an active revolutionary. He paused in lighting his pipe, fixed me over his rimless spectacles, with the same striking grey eyes, his granddaughter had inherited, obviously appraising me before committing himself. 'No, Mr Franklin, unfortunately, I have always been more of a frondeur, a man of ideas rather than daring-do, and I am appalled at anything that leads to violence or loss of life. My ancestors are an extraordinarily heady mix of Chartists, intellectual revolutionaries, humanists and Quakers. Eleanor's grandmother was a niece of William Lovett (I have no idea who that was but decided to enquire later) and she was instrumental in ensuring the post-UDI government in Tharsis extended suffrage not only to all working class men, but to all women as well." He puffed repeatedly to get the tobacco to light and then added; "Here, only the woman of Zephyr and Utopia remain unable to vote or take political office. 'Liberté, égalité, fraternité,' Mr Franklin, is meaningless if half the citizenry is disenfranchised. We might as well be like the Athenians, where eighty percent of the city's population did not have a vote, and kept slaves."

I think if anything has truly surprised me about awakening in this new age this did the most. It underscored so clearly that this world these new 'Martians' have made for themselves is fundamentally different from anything I knew. Women freely voting and holding political office? Amazing. That is like something out of the French Revolution (Which I think is what Professor Flammarion quoted from.)

I have noticed women are much freer in thought and more forthright in opinion and action than I knew, but I must have put that down to the 'Spirit of the Frontier' – as they used to say. But this is different, Miss Bryant-Drake is as resilient and indomitable as any young man of her age, exceedingly well educated and pursuing an independent career. Strangely, it does not sit uneasily with me, for I feel I knew many bright, tough and hardy frontier women in my day, some more than a match for any man. Though I am not sure about voting for a woman?

Unfortunately - or fortunately - just as I was about to call the Professor's attention to the abject poverty I had seen in Alba as proof that some had noticeably not benefited in this brave new world, when Eleanor reappeared. She had organised rooms for us, had our meagre luggage stowed, and had sourced and put out clothes for our evening wear. Each room had a water closet of its own with a healthy sized copper bath already steaming in anticipation. I must admit to spending far too much time dozing in the warm bath water before being summoned to dinner.

The wounds and injuries from our escapades and my impromptu examination on the train were all gone, even the graze to the back of my head where Hood had struck me was gone, not healed, simply gone. As if they had never happened. While shaving, I examined my physiognomy again with great care, if they were right and a man's nature could be divined by the features of his face, what a cruel monster must I be? The landscape of horrific welts and scars were not diminished or softened in any way. It is a face that appears for all intents to have been stitched together out of old leather by an enthusiastic but ungifted ball maker's apprentice, no doubt, over a metal skull.

I did my best to make myself presentable however, my moustache is in need of a trim and my hair a good cut. There is nothing 'regulation' about my appearance. The immaculate clothes provided by Mrs Ransom were for what was to be a formal dinner. Outfitted and brushed up, with a little macassar oil to hold my unruly mop, I looked myself in the mirror and thought that at least I now appeared a well-groomed monster. I tightened the beautiful monogrammed silver cufflinks, straightened the white bow tie, adjusted the cummerbund and, feeling for once like a gentleman, headed down to the dinner.

I had stopped for a moment to admire a collection of Aresian religious artefacts displayed in a case on the landing of the great staircase when I noticed Carstairs hurrying to open the front door. As soon as the door opened, in rushed several small yapping dogs and behind them swept in a flamboyant middle-aged woman in an emerald green cape and dress. She shrugged off her cape, deposited it over Carstairs' shoulder, thrust her green riding hat into his hands, and cried an elated greeting to Mrs Ransom who had appeared at the top of the stairs opposite me. *This flamboyant creature I was to learn was the famous seer; Lady Niketa Chaol Ghleann.*

She is one of those people that spreads a kind of jolly pandemonium about them. The children rushed down from their nursery with their pretty young Nanny in pursuit to greet her as she bestowed small gifts upon them. Making themselves and the dogs more excited than ever. The little dogs, about half a dozen of them, were running riot with Carstairs and one of his sons engaged in a futile attempt to round them up. I decided to join the melee only to be confronted by one small, fearless excitedly yapping mutt bounding up the staircase, I swept it up and on reaching the bottom of the stairs deposited it into the arms of James, who was now assisting in the roundup.

With a great deal of fussing, we finally managed to corral Lady Niketa and her pack of dogs in the 'orangery,' an area somewhat likenable to a conservatory but fully integral to the house. Lady Niketa, who obviously knew the place well, recounted various times she had been here with her husband 'Buntie,' visiting the late Mrs Flammarion and helping her tend the specimen plants that filled the room. It took me until then to cotton on to the fact that Buntie was dead and that, claiming some strange Aeaean art or power, she is in almost continual dialogue with him and various other entities. She is indeed what some would call a Spiritualist, though I have known many who would openly call them other things.

It was only when the conversation turned to Edwin's exploits that he formally introduced me to Lady Niketa. Not wishing to be discourteous by proffering a gloved hand I led with my left and she being an apparently 'modern' Tharsian woman reciprocated by holding out her hand in a manner more like that of a gentleman, presenting a firm and assured handshake.

Her reaction though was unexpected; she took an urgent breath, apparently startled, almost a gasp, her eyes met mine and she tottered as if struck. I could only stand there as I too felt a shock pass between us, like a jolt from the St. Elmo's corona that discharges from the pylons and rigging of airships. It froze me to the spot. Fortunately, Miss Bryant-Drake and Edwin were swift enough to catch Lady Niketa before she swooned and they settled her in a chair.

In that instant in between I experienced something astounding; a flash of saintly inspiration, maybe or perhaps simply a thunderbolt of awakening. It is said that a man's life passes before his eyes at the moment of his death, a fantastic parade of events, people and images, like one of those flip books that create moving pictures or some bizarre magic lantern show. But I have already been, in all respects, dead. I have been to the edges of that dark oblivion and until that moment I had been spared the full awareness of that journey, but suddenly, as if a bulkhead plate had fallen clanging from my mind, the memories were there. They did not 'flood back' as people might say, I was just abruptly aware that they were there. More as if I had pulled a dust sheet from an old chair to discover a book or diary I had long forgotten. Part of me wanted to immediately delve into those memories, searching for answers to the questions that plagued my waking thoughts and nightmares, but another part of my mind held firm to caution, apprehension maybe. The memories did not assail me, but their sudden presence was disturbing, menacing even. As if the Sergeant Major had unexpectedly emerged fully formed, in his blood red tunic and black cap, out of some shadowy corner of the room, his face, my face as yet unruined, glaring at me like some phantom for only me to see.

Lady Niketa had regained herself quickly through the ministrations of Edwin and his wife, though her eyes did flicker occasionally to that dark corner from where I mused the Sergeant Major watched. Miss Bryant-Drake obviously noticed my distraction as she did her best to divert Lady Niketa with some creative badinage until we were summoned to the dinner table.

The meal was excellent, though we were forced to begin without our host, Prof. Flammarion. He arrived late and was quite impolite in the way he spoke to his daughter when she tried to encourage him to talk about some plans he had in mind. I felt sorry for both her and Edwin that they are beholden to such a weather-vane of a patriarch. The meal, though delicious, was at times stilted, though Lady Niketa and Miss Bryant-Drake did their level best to keep the conversation flowing.

At the end of the dinner, the Professor suddenly announced that he had arranged for Lady Niketa to conduct a "spiritual reading." Because of the earlier occurrence, I tried to remain distant from the proceedings by making up some excuse, but Miss Bryant-Drake seized my arm and chattering enthusiastically dragged me along.

We decanted to a small drawing room or study where a table had been set up especially for the event. At the Professor's insistence, I relinquished my after dinner drink, I have apparently acquired a taste for what I am assured is good claret, and reluctantly joined the group at the table. We held hands. I feel I may have been expected to remove my glove, but Miss Bryant-Drake took my hand firmly without hesitation. The gas lights were dimmed and the show, for I fear that was what it was, began. Lady Niketa babbled nonsense for a while about 'spirits and entities' of the 'netherworld' beyond the 'veil,' before she suddenly started talking in a music hall cowboy accent claiming to be the spirit of a long dead American Red Indian chieftain. Whose voice reminded me more of a bad impression of Constable Everheart than what I might imagine a savage raised in the wilderness would sound like.

I was beginning to settle into observing this spectacle with some degree of detached complacency when the Professor was invited to ask his question and everything changed. The Professor, in a forthright manner, asked; 'To call forth the spirit of a First Martian, if indeed they have such spirits. I wish to question him.' The atmosphere in the room changed instantaneously.

Lady Niketa, or whatever was talking through her, warned against such 'questing,' but the Professor would have none of it. In an almost commanding tone, he demanded 'to speak to the spirits of any true Martian. I call upon you to speak to me.'

The temperature in the room perceptibly dropped a few degrees, the fire in the hearth and the gas lamps died leaving us illuminated by only the guttering candle. Mrs Ransom squirmed in her seat nervously, Miss Bryant-Drake gasped and Edwin looked horrified.

If I had harboured doubts as to Lady Niketa's abilities, may she forgive me because the moment the thing that spoke through her, uttered its first words I knew she could not be a charlatan or fraud.

The language I recognised straight away. I, the Sergeant Major that is, had heard it many times before. I could not properly understand the words because back in the day few of us bothered to learn, but the language was, as the Professor prefers to call them 'First Martian,' Kitreenoh Aresian. The voice, in its rasping mocking tone, did not even appear to be coming out of Lady Niketa's mouth, but as if from the air above her head. The Professor questioned it further, but most of its answers were a nonsense mixture of Aresian and English in such a heavy accent that we were at a loss to understand any of it. It claimed there were many more Aresians alive and that they 'await' the Professor beyond the Seas of Sand. I fear from the Professor's reaction that he saw it as an invitation, not a clear warning, as the rest of us did.

I was desperately thankful when finally Mrs Ransom called an end to the séance, or whatever it was, and told her housekeeper to light the gas lights. Lady Niketa seemed so utterly drained and befuddled that I went to fetch a drink from the sideboard for her. As I returned, she suddenly stood up, her eyes rolled in her head, and pointed at me saying, 'Bring him, the dead man, he will know the way.' I almost dropped the glass. I recognised the speaker this time. It was Lanulos' sneering voice.

I had almost convinced myself that the events yesterday were just a bout of feverish hallucinations, a dream brought on by a badly digested meal, or some such. Now I fear that even those small straws of sanity had come away in my grasp.

We were ushered to the main drawing room while Mrs Ransom and her housekeeper tended Lady Niketa. Edwin and Miss Bryant-Drake chattered constantly to me, in an attempt to distract my thoughts I think, but I cannot remember a word of it. Memories of Lanulos, not only from yesterday, crowded in on me. I was back on the operating table with him leering over me. His laughing as I crawled across the floor in my first attempt to escape their torments. I was on my second large brandy when Lady Niketa and Mrs Ransom joined us. The Professor though had vanished back into his study.

Mrs Ransom fetched him. I have seldom seen a man so excited by such unfortunate events. He poured himself an exceedingly substantial glass of brandy, quaffed almost half of it in a gulp and set about explaining himself. Something I feel is unfamiliar to his normal conduct.

It appears that the Professor believes that he has evidence that the Aresians never left Mars after the battle of Tyrrhena Mons (Which I read about in Beresford's Book, it happened the year after my aerostat was shot down). He showed us secret reports from the Tharsis Aethervolt Navy of sightings of unknown spacefaring ships entering and leaving the high atmosphere and in deep space. Ships that by the description of their configuration can only be Aresian. I read over some of the depictions written, and sketched, by young officers and they obviously had no idea what they were looking at. But the Professor was right some were most definitely Aresian aethervolt ships. He had a plethora of other sightings and encounters. His theory was that beyond the great plains of red sand there were Aresian cities the Tellurians have never laid eyes upon. Cities where hundreds of thousands, if not millions, of First Martians still live, and one day, if we do not make peace with them, they will return in force and wipe us off the face of this planet.

I asked why they had not already done so. They could have finished the job at Tyrrhena Mons instead they chose to withdraw. Maybe they simply did not wish to engage in warfare anymore. Maybe, like the mediaeval Swiss, they had had their fill of blood and butchery. The Professor agreed and said that he prayed that was the case.

Miss Bryant-Drake suggested that it could be possible that the Aresians had some other reason for withdrawing from Tyrrhena Mons. Could it be to do with the possibility of some other greater menace? She confided that her step-father always claimed that the Aresian civilisation never originated on Mars in the first place, and that they had other settlements, not just in this solar system but 'out there' in outer space. He believed there had once been an Aresian Empire across several star systems. Maybe they had some other threat more pressing. Even the Professor seemed to find that stretched credulity too far.

Edwin enquired as to what the evening's spirit channelling had to do with all this? The Professor explained that he did not believe that that which spoke was the spirit of any dead First Martian, but one very much alive. He apologised to Lady Niketa for his deception, but he does not believe anyone can converse with the dead, but he does believe in, what he called; 'mentalistic transference of thought.' A form of higher sensory communication that can reach over vast distances. He believes that some of the First Martians have that ability. Not just to communicate, but to control minds. Lady Niketa was exceedingly upset at the idea that she had been controlled by an alien, but after a pacifying drink or two she admitted it was a strange 'channelling.' I asked in what way different. She explained that she felt 'taken over' as if she had almost been pushed out of her own body, and there was a dreadful sense of malevolence about that spirit. If indeed it was a spirit. The Professor dismissed her concerns by saying it is only a matter of perspective, and that a person exercising such power would no doubt leave their 'recipient' shaken.

He explained his plan to mount an expedition to search for these lost Aresians. He has purchased an aerostat for the purpose and he claims to have the backing of 'high-ranking members' (He would not say whom) of the Tharsis Government for his endeavour.

The Professor revealed that his expedition departs tomorrow morning at 8 am! And that he would like us, Edwin, Miss Bryant-Drake and myself to accompany him. He has assembled an exemplary team and has an excellent Captain and crew, everything is poised for the off if we wish to join. I believe we were all astonished.

Miss Bryant-Drake accepted the invitation readily on the proviso she would be the expedition's official correspondent. An idea that seemed to delight the Professor. Edwin vacillated, after all he had just got home and he could not see how he would be able to make any worthwhile contribution to the endeavour, but the Professor persuaded him by explaining that he needed a steady right-hand man, a good engineer and someone he could personally rely upon to lead the expedition home if, indeed, something untoward did happen. The Professor also pointed out that they would make no secret that Edwin had embarked upon the expedition, which would put him far from the reach of Du Maurier's persecutions. "If that esurient alliaphage wishes to pursue you out into Mars' frozen wastelands he will certainly find that he and his thugs will have bitten off far more than they can swallow." In that I noticed a certain gleam in the Professor's eye, a 'man of peace' he maybe but I think the Professor would have no qualms in leading Du Maurier's murderous henchmen a merry dance to their doom.

I asked if it was wise leaving Mrs Ransom and the children alone in the house. Edwin too appeared uncomfortable at the thought. The Professor assured us that such eventualities had been thought of, with Karl, Carstairs and his two boys, plus the groundsmen, who will provide additional security by lodging on the premises for the duration, Mrs Ransom and the children could not be safer.

As for me? The Professor said that he had read about me in Edwin's letters to his daughter and in the newspaper reports and that, however 'cloudy' my origins might be, he feels that I am a 'stalwart chap' possessed of the skills he prays that his expedition will never require. I asked why was he inviting me? His answer was; "I have had installed on the aerostat - at great cost - two brand new Cogswaine steam driven rotation guns. Not out of the desire that we should use them, but in the deepest and heartfelt desire that there should never become a point that we should need to. Nonetheless if we need to do so, to protect the ship and our lives, we will. From what I have learnt of you, Mr Franklin, I believe you are a man who understands all too well, such a point of view, and you are the kind of man we could all turn to if such a situation demanded it." To that, he added he was not inviting me but directly offering employment.

My role, he clarified, would be to ensure the physical safety of the members of his expedition team. I was unsure whether to be flattered or appalled at his presumption. Although the thought of paid employment does resonate with my current needs and shepherding a group of would-be explorers and scientists on this wild goose chase can be no more onerous than going to war.

I have accepted his offer, so tomorrow morning I assume the post of the Expedition's Master-at-Arms. My reasons? The evidence that the Professor seeks, should he indeed find it, may also hold the answers I need. I pray this venture, if successful, might provide me with resolutions to the questions that plague my thoughts, more so now than ever before my encounter with Lanulos.

Diary of Aelita Fontenelli (Mrs).
Sunday, September, 29th. MY.26
Dear Diary.

Giovanni has been in one of his moods all day, his 'l'oscurità dell'anima,' as he calls it. After Church, he rudely stalked off without even a by-your-leave to Father Ignacio.

I have tried all I can think of to lighten his disposition, short of outright tomfoolery. By his terse manner and disdain towards myself, I fear the dark melancholia is seated in my determination to accompany him on Professor Flammarion's expedition. Last night over dinner he took great exception to my resolve and became somewhat difficult. I understand his concerns for my physical safety. However, I do wish he would not concern himself with my sensibilities. Bless his heart, but I am no cosseted feeble debutante who has never known somatic adversity, let alone emotional affliction in her life. God has seen to it that I have travelled a path in life that has been singular in its adversity - however, I am no Job - and I believe myself to be all the more resilient for it.

I will attend upon the departure of the Seren Bore tomorrow, and I am resolute that I shall sally forth with it into whatever adventure awaits, with or without my esteemed and greatly adored husband.

Oh Diary, as I have written so often, life here often leaves me envious of the animals in the zoo. They too are caged but at least they are visited and admired for their natural beauty or fierceness. I am sequestered away from prying eyes only to be permitted to venture into the world on singular occasions, then only to be paraded like a prized pet or some novelty.

Oh, dear! That seems so ungrateful when consigned to ink upon a page. My husband is a wonderful man, so emotional, expressive, loving, generous and kind. I have never known anyone with a greater heart. He has been so benevolent to me that I could never repay him should I live a hundred lives. I have a wonderful life, I want for nothing. I have a fabulous home, my pets and interests and even a few personal friends who regularly call upon me but...

Often I feel less like a woman and more as one of those curiosities he keeps in his study to regale visitors with his encyclopedic knowledge of.

And that in truth is why I must go; my husband professes to know more about me than I do (even including matters of my own health). He knows more about my kind, my people, my race and culture than I have ever known. Once we had a visitor from Chryse, a bloated, pompous old coxcomb, who brought with him an American Indian servant, a young valet, his skin as dark and lustrous as rosewood, his hair and eyes as black as coal, but he had been born here on Mars and knew nothing of Earth let alone the prairies and wildernesses of the Americas. One of the guests was even so crass as to make a jest about "redskins" in the presence of both of us. I felt for the young man, even more so, when Giovanni suddenly took an interest in him and began to entertain everybody over dinner with his extensive knowledge of the Americas and its people. Although Giovanni did not mean to harm the valet's feelings I could see the distress in the young man's eyes. I could not help him, but knew all too well his feelings, for almost all that I know about my people, I have learnt either from school, my husband or from the books he has provided for me to learn from.

And yet... there are those recurring dreams.

I dream of my twin brother Gethen, and of my mother and father. Especially of my father, though I hardly had time to know him. In my dreams, Gethen and I are footloose and fancy-free children running through fields of dandelions – why dandelions, I don't know? We laugh and play and Gethen spins me tales and wondrous secrets in a language my waking mind cannot grasp. He so desires me to understand, but it is as if he is imparting a secret he himself does not fully comprehend. Then there is the dream of the White City. A city out in the snowy wastelands, a city made of ice and opaque glass, where I endlessly wander its desolate boulevards and forsaken plazas. Empty but only just, as if I might suddenly turn the next corner and happen upon them all. Sometimes, in my dreams, it is night and I chase glimpses of fleeting spectres through the eerie streets. And I dream of my father; so tall and proud. He too speaks to me in a language I cannot understand and remains just beyond my touch, but the meaning of his words are always clear in my mind. He tells me of his abiding love and gives me advice, guidance I have always followed. These last few nights I have only dreamed of him.

While Giovanni was in his study nurturing his lugubrious disposition, Ursula and I packed the travelling bags. Ursula brought up from the basement the roll top steamer trunk Giovanni takes with him on his expeditions. I knew he kept all sorts of useful things in it and we transferred most of them into my luggage and packed most of my clothes into his trunk instead. If he chooses not to join me in this adventure at least I shall have the proper equipment for the task ahead – assuming that I can fathom the intricacies of some of his apparatuses. It was my intent to leave Giovanni's galvatronic odic pistols in his trunk, but Ursula impressed upon me that I should ensure I have them with me, if only to defend my honour! I assured her that I would be in no such danger being in the company of both Sir John and Professor Flammarion, but she insisted.

Dear Diary. This evening, Giovanni and I had another disagreement. So unseemly in front of the servants. I had to dismiss them in the midst of serving dinner. Giovanni became so demonstrative that I likened his behaviour to a childish tantrum. He did not appreciate the simile.

He strictly forbade me from joining the Professor's expedition and has told me I must stay here in the morning. I reminded him I am the daughter of an Aresian Ambassador, and I see it as my duty to chaperone this expedition. If they are fortunate enough to discover remaining Aresians my presence could be of immeasurable benefit in establishing a cordial dialogue.

Giovanni scoffed and with great incivility reminded me that I was merely a small child when my father died and I have no knowledge of any of the dozen or so known Aresian argots, let alone their customs and the correct conducts. He also pointed out that they may see me as a collaborator or worse still, a marionette in the hands of their enemy. I told him that I would go to them with an open heart and open hands and let the Lord be my guide. He mocked my faith! He told me I am deluded, that I am little more than a pampered massaia, and that I have no idea of what hardships will lay ahead for those foolish enough to partake of the Professor's ludicrous, and undoubtedly fruitless, escapade.

I believe it was then I emptied the tureen of gazpacho soup over his head and retired to my solar. I have instructed Ursula to have a hansom cab arranged for myself tomorrow first thing.

I have also resolved to no longer take Dr Hammond's treatment either. I feel so much better in myself without those ugly little pills.

Extracts from
Beresford's History of the Martian Colonies.
3rd Edition. Milton and Dante.

Chapter 8. The Last Aresian War; Tyrrhena Mons, the Tellurian's Last Stand.

March the 7th, 1874. After thirteen days and over 50 percent casualties, those surviving souls besieged on Tyrrhena Mons were on the verge of collapse. News had reached them by early morning that Jahns and the First Negro Volunteer Brigade, the Blacks, had failed in their third attempt to break out of the Siege of Hellas and were still trapped in Dao Vallis under heavy attack.

The free colonist's air support was now virtually non-existent, as over 80 percent of their air and space-faring craft had been destroyed or put out of action by this point. Munitions and food supplies were almost as exhausted as the defenders themselves. With dysentery and Lange's disease running wild amongst them, the surviving defenders of Tyrrhena Mons were almost at breaking point.

There had been several isolated instances of insubordination and desertion, however, only one truly serious event. On the night of the 12th day of the siege, when elements of the predominately French-speaking Zephyrian Mechanised Legionnaires mutinied, killed five of their own officers and tried to desert their position on the Southern Wall. General Junker von Darmstadt, "The Flying Hessian," personally led a detachment of the Thylian Rocket Troops to secure the position and quash the rebellion. Unfortunately, most of the deserting Zephyrian Legionnaires were killed in the action. By the morning of day 13, discipline had been fully re-established amongst the defenders, but morale was at its lowest ebb.

By midday, rumours had turned to confirmation that a huge force of Aresian aerobarges and sandflyers were moving up from the southeast to reinforce the attacking Aresian land forces. The news was accepted with, as Major A. K. Whedon of the Olympian Highlanders recalled; "cold stoical horror." xii.

There seemed nothing left for the defenders of Tyrrhena Mons to do other than to accept the opportunity to die valiantly while depleting the numbers of Aresians that would live to be thrown against the defenders of Hellas.

Major Whedon, who would later go on to be known as a great literary scholar, in his now famous address to his troops that late afternoon, quoted not the Bard, but the American author Melville; "To the last, I grapple with thee; from hell's heart I stab at thee; for hate's sake I spit my last breath at thee." xiii.

In his memoirs, he remembers giving the orders to his men to "brew up" and to share out the last of their food and ammunition between them. When one of the younger soldiers asked what were they to do once all the ammunition was gone? Major Whedon overheard his Warrant Officer, Sergeant Major Naylor reply, "Then, Laddie, we fix bayonets and charge the buggers." xiv.

March the 8th, 1874. By the dawn of the 14th day of the siege, the anticipated attack had not materialised. At 10.41am scouts of the 1st Free Women's Colonial Militia confirmed that all the Aresian emplacements on the North and West sides of the mountain were completely abandoned.

The Aresians had gone. The attack never came.

Page 621-622

In July 1878 Major A.K. Whedon, writing in a letter to his brother the Honourable J. Hill Whedon, wrote of that morning; "I felt like King Priam, walking through the debris of the Mycenaean's forsaken encampment; my heart full, not of relief and euphoria, but confusion, and heavy with the dread that I should chance upon some great wooden horse." xv.

Page 624

Notes.
xii. . Major A.K. Whedon. Rtd. MY. 15. "Hearts of Iron." Reminisces and Remembrances of the Martian Wars. P. 115
xiii. . Major A.K. Whedon. Rtd. MY. 15. A.K. Whedon quotes Herman Melville's "Moby Dick," 1851. "Hearts of Iron. "Reminisces and Reembraces of the Martian Wars. P. 120.
xiv. Major A.K. Whedon. Rtd. MY. 15. "Hearts of Iron." Reminisces and Reembraces of the Martian Wars. P. 124.

Mathew McCall

xv. Hon. J.H. Whedon. 1878. "Foot Steps of Treachery." The Secession of the Martian Colonies. P. 311.

"... Come, my friends,
'Tis not too late to seek a newer world.
Push off, and sitting well in order smite
the sounding furrows; for my purpose holds
to sail beyond the sunset."

ULYSSES.

ALFRED, LORD TENNYSON.

PART TWO

PROFESSOR FLAMMARION'S EXPEDITION

"Second star to the right, and straight on 'til morning."

PETER PAN

J. M. BARRIE

DAY ONE

THE STAR OF THE MORNING

P.E.S. Seren Bore.   **8.00/30/09/26**
Ship's scrap log (excerpts from) Captain R. K. Llewellyn.

Ship ready for Mister Charles' full inspection by 5 A.M. All in readiness. Nothing more to report.

Staff meeting 5.30A.M.
Chief Engineer's report; all in readiness. Nothing more to report.
Purser's report; all in readiness. Nothing more to report.
Final crew briefing 6 A.M.
All ship's crew on deck for inspection and welcome salute. Ruffles and Boatswain's pipe aboard.
Prof. Flammarion and several members of his party arrived just before 7 A.M. His son-in-law Mr Edwin Ransom, Miss Charity Bryant-Drake and Mr Adam Franklin.
The Professor has informed me that Mr Franklin is to take on the role of Master-at-Arms for the expedition. He will be solely responsible for the safety of expedition members when they are off of the ship. As instructed, I have issued him with a key to the Gunner's arms locker and put him under the direction of Master Gunner Gwenlan when on board as to avoid any duplicating of rolls. The man has the physical bearing of a veteran and has obviously seen combat. We can only hope he is as proficient as he appears.

Miss Bryant-Drake will be working closely with the Professor, I believe she will be chronicling the expedition.

Mr Ransom, I am told, is to be considered by myself as the Professor's proxy in all matters.

The Purser saw to their accommodation on the shelter deck.

Sir John Sydeian boarded at 7.10A.M. Shelter deck.

Colonel Carter Jahns boarded at 7.15A.M. He has brought with him six Negro "escorts." Their luggage seems to consist of military packs and weapons. Mister Charles advised me that they are of the Olympian Highlander Regiment of Foot. I have insisted their rifles be stowed in the Gunner's arms locker.

I have accommodated Colonel Jahns on the shelter deck, but his "escorts" I have had billeted in the orlop away from the main crew and expedition members – especially the ladies.

Dr Octavius Spender and his daughter, Miss Parthena Spender boarded at 7.20A.M. Main deck.

Mrs Fontenelli arrived with her lady's maid (an automaton) at 7.40A.M. I am informed that her husband will not be joining her. Due to these unusual circumstances, I have had her accommodated on the shelter deck between Prof. Flammarion and Mr Franklin's quarters.

The ship received and passed to Prof. Flammarion two telephonograph messages. One from Professor G.P. Serviss, one from Mr Henry Giffard, Esq, and a letter delivered by a messenger from Cav. Giovanni Fontenelli, Dr.

7.55A.M. The Professor postponed departure until further notice. I ordered Signalman Turner to inform the Airdrome Master of postponement.

8.00A.M. The Professor has advised me of a possible change of itinerary. Awaiting further instructions.

8.45A.M. Meeting called by Prof. Flammarion in the wardroom. Myself, Mister Charles and all members of the expedition in attendance.

At the conclusion of the meeting, the Professor instructed me of a change of plan. We are to lay a course for Ransom's Farm, Tremorfa. An estimated three days returning to berth.

9.35A.M. Navigation complete. Course laid. Aerodrome Master informed.

9.45A.M. Departed for Tremorfa in good order.

Diary of Aelita Fontenelli (Mrs).
Sunday, September, 30th. MY.26
Dear Diary.

This has been both one of the worst of days and yet one of the most exciting. Ursula woke me before dawn and I was readying myself to leave when Giovanni appeared at the bottom of the stairs. I fear he had not slept in his room, but had reposed upon the chaise lounge in the drawing room with the intent of catching me before I departed. He looked most dishevelled and was already in the foulest of temperaments. He ordered me to put away this "foolhardiness," as he called it, and return to my room.

When I stood by my resolve, refusing to follow his instructions he became almost incandescent with rage. I have never seen him so angry, but his remonstrations only served to harden my determination. He went so far as to accuse me of being an undeserving and ungrateful wife and to threaten to publicly denounce me as an adventuress of low morality. I thought he would surely raise his hand to me, but he stayed such cacoethes in the sight of the milling staff.

The Good Lord himself knows that my purpose is true and righteous and I entreat him to shine the light of wisdom and compassion into Giovanni's heart. Before we left I again implored him to accompany me, but he flatly refused. He asked me if I had adjudged the reality that if I continue to disobey his commands, then I shall no longer have a husband, let alone a home, to return to. He swore before God that it would be so.

Over the last few days, my thoughts have gained such pellucidity, as if these events were shining a guiding light through the brume that has befuddled my mind for so long. I do so love Giovanni, but I will not be swayed from the resolution I know is right. If indeed he wishes to divorce me for such disobedience, I shall face such chastisement stoically.

In his rage, he even went so far as to command the staff not to assist me to the awaiting hansom cab, but with Ursula's help we loaded my baggage and left to the resounding report of Giovanni slamming the front door. My heart sank as we rode away and a great wave of despair overtook me, I felt I might drown in sorrow. Ursula, bless her, did her best to console me though I wept quietly most of the way to Covingdome Aerofield.

The cabbie sensing my distress was most helpful and dropped us as near to the airship's hangar as he could. I wonder if he would have been so kind if he could have seen the colour of my skin under my heavy veil?

I entered through the great doors and stood for a moment, staring up at the behemoth that hung floating above me, suspended on nothing more than thin air. The airship is truly an enormous thing, it congests the shelter with such a colossal presence that seems to strain at both the capacity of the building and credulity of one's mind.

Several of the men from the ship's crew came down to collect our impedimenta (as Giovanni calls it) and took it up the long wrought iron steps and gantries to the ship. We followed, climbing the latticework treads cautiously. Upon boarding, I was greeted by the Professor and the Captain to the accompaniment of two young crewmen with pipe and drum, and introduced to some of the senior crew members and some of my fellow expedition members. Many of whom I had not met on my last visit; Mr Ransom, who is the Professor's son-in-law, a Miss Drake who is to be the expedition's chronicler.

The Captain was somewhat disquieted by the news that I would be joining the expedition without my husband's presence or approval, but the Professor was most supportive saying that he believed my contribution alone would be invaluable. Captain Llewellyn said he felt that a lady of my standing travelling alone upon such an expedition was most irregular and might lead to "difficulties." He would not elucidate upon his fears. Though he had to concede that his concerns might be a rather outmoded when Miss Drake pointed out her mother and aunts fought for Tharsis in the Air Wing of the First Free Women's Colonial Militia and her mother was decorated for bravery twice. In the light of such womanly valour, what in comparison is my little exploit? I assured him that I am no simpering girl, but a woman who has endured far harsher hardships than we shall face aboard this vessel.

Something I was certainly confident of until I saw the dimensions of the cabin allocated to myself and Ursula. We have larger broom cupboards at home.

The airship is called the "Seren Bore." Captain Llewellyn explained that it means Morning Star, in the language of his "father's."

I have only flown three times and one can hardly compare a short jaunt on the AirTrain or the railplane to such a truly magnificent skyship. Although the cabin is more than a little cramped the general accommodation is comfortably ample. After I changed into something more befitting the circumstances, dispensing with my hat, veil and under bustle, and leaving Ursula to unpack, I went to join the others in the wardroom.

Parthena Spender, looking quite the adventuress in a man's tweed hacking jacket that had obviously seen better days, a daring pair of khaki flared-hip breeches and riding boots, greeted me warmly. Parthena breathlessly explained to me that Mr Ransom and his friend Mr Franklin - a fearsome looking man with a dreadfully scarred face whose cold-eyed scrutiny, I found hard to endure, had possibly discovered an Aresian Royal tomb on Mr Ransom's farmland. When I arrived Dr Spender, with Sir John's support, was arguing forcibly that it must be investigated.

I listened intently to Dr Spender's impassioned argument with mounting disquiet. Suddenly the Professor asked me a question and all eyes turned to me. Taken aback, I apologised and wished him to repeat himself. His question was simple; what were my thoughts?

Aware of the feelings of my fellow expedition members and choosing my words carefully; I explained that I understand that antiquarianism, and the new archaeology, are noble arts and seek to bring us all a greater understanding of the history of our shared pasts. In many ways, I agree with my husband, Giovanni, who believes archaeology, when done properly, is the most analytical and impartial of disciplines, far more truthful than anything found in any history book. But I also fear that done in haste and without good measure, it can appear to be little more than despoliation.

When I had finished I was surprised to find Parthena's hand in mine, she looked at me and gave me an encouraging smile.

Dr Spender's face though was less reassuring, for a moment he looked quite cross and snorted loudly. His shoulders dropped a little and he sighed, "Yes, madam, you are right, unfortunately, some antiquarians have behaved with little regard or empathy for the niceties of the cultures they have investigated."

"And some behave more like tomb robbers," added Parthena pithily.

"Yes, indeed, some do," he added reflectively. "But forgive me, as from what little we know about this find, I truly believe it may indeed be an undiscovered Royal tomb, of your people. If it is so, then it is in great peril, being that it most probably already being sought out by men whose singular aim is to plunder such sites for profit. If we do not get there first and secure the tomb who knows what we may lose to some antiquarian's private collection, and what indescribable damage may be done in the process. Madam Fontenelli, Parthena and I have seen the results of such men's work; utter wanton vandalism for personal gain. That an intact Royal tomb should fall into their hands would be a catastrophe, for us all."

"How can you be sure it is a Royal tomb?" I asked.

Miss Drake interjected; "Mr Ransom's man, Karl, told us that it has a large, hexagonal, pale blue capstone, a type of amazonite. That would indicate that it's an ancient Peerrohs Aresian Royal tomb."

Dr Spender clapped his hands and exclaimed, "Bryant-Drake, of course. I knew your late mother, Rosa. Such a great loss. Your stepfather is old Dobbin Cromie!" He seemed delighted. "How does he fare these days?" Miss Drake said regretfully that her step-father's health was failing him and he had retired all but for a little writing and research on botanical matters. By the way she spoke of him I feel there is a great bond of fondness between them. "Well, he has taught you well. Yes, a type of blue feldspar, it is the traditional colour of Royal capstones of the early dolmen tombs of the Peerrohs."

"Well, that seals it, so to speak," said Sir John. "It cannot, in all good conscience, be ignored. We have to go take a look, at least."

The Professor agreed but still put it to the group to gauge any dissent. No one opposed the proposition that we begin our expedition with a visit to Ransom's Farm to locate the tomb.

We retired to the passenger lounge, for a little late breakfast. I was unsurprised to find that we are to share our post-repast relaxation with the gentlemen as there is no separate Ladies' lounge on the ship. Parthena, like Sir John, drank only a little thick black coffee and excused themselves to smoke those disgusting cheroots on the outer deck. I talked for a while with Miss Drake. She is pleasant, but exceedingly inquisitive. She too wears manly attire, and no corsetry at all, not even a ribbon! When I asked her about it, she said, freeing the body helps free the mind. Though I must admit the idea of such freedom tempts me, and I can see the sensibleness of dispensing with long hems, I cannot imagine going without even my waist clincher.

When I returned to my cabin, Ursula and I examined more closely the few items of Giovanni's expedition attire that had been carried over into my luggage in our haste last night. Anyone, who by chance overheard us, would have thought we had either lost our minds or been imbibing too much port, so ruckus was our amusement. Save for trouserettes for riding I have never worn trousers, let alone my husband's.

When the invitation came to watch our departure from the Captain's bridge I venture forth self-consciously in a pair of Giovanni's breeches and one of his shirts under my sturdiest woollen bolero (I am not brave enough yet to give up my corset.).

The view from the Captain's bridge was astounding. The other set of bay doors had been drawn fully open and one could see across the whole of the airfield; a vast grassed arena circled by a dozen other enormous hangars and populated by ground tethered aerostats and flying machines of all types. From this vantage point, the ground crews and observers looked like tiny marionettes. Far across the field, a crowd waving flags and bunting had gathered around a band of brightly dressed men, from our viewpoint all the size of toy soldiers, who were playing brass music to accompany the launch of a steam-powered dirigible. It reminded me of a great silver cucumber belching black smoke as it rose into the cold morning sky.

Captain Llewellyn gave orders in a calm and effective manner and no sooner had the crew acknowledged him than the Seren Bore obeyed. No oompah band or flag waving to see us off, only the steady tones of the Captain's voice and the rhythmic chugging of the great engines somewhere in the heart of the ship. The Professor, noting the other departure, pointed out that our ship's engines, though much bigger and more powerful do not exhaust such huge clouds of black smoke and steam as they are now, with his modifications, far more proficient. He went on to explain how and why this was but I must concede that though it all sounded wonderfully ingenious it was all far too complex for my mind, uneducated in such matters, to grasp.

We floated forward from the hangar and, with a few shouted orders and a toot of a steam trumpet the Seren Bore began to rapidly rise. I found myself holding on to the edge of the map table for security. As we glided upwards the whole of Tharsis city came into view, and then the mountains beyond. An officer on the deck was counting off feet. "One hundred, one hundred and ten, one hundred and twenty, one hundred and thirty,...."

Parthena took my arm and began pointing out locations we knew; Horsell Park, where, as young ladies, we had both learnt to ride, Maybury Hill, where we could just make out the roof of my summer home, Cobham, where Parthena grew up. St. Mary's Cathedral with its majestic spires, though it has never lost its Aresian pantheon mien. Parthena said it reminds her of pictures of a cathedral on Earth called Hagia Sophia. Mr Ransom joined our conversation, pointing out a few other locations. He seems such a thoroughly pleasant and earnest young man.

I spent quite a lot of the rest of the morning gazing out at the landscape below us. My own home, my world, but I have hardly seen it, and know so little of it.

After luncheon, I took the opportunity of a stroll with Sir John along the Promenade deck. I do enjoy his company so, he is a delight and ever the truest of gentlemen. He was concerned but not surprised that Giovanni had refused to accompany the expedition, and feared that it was very much a reaction to his own presence. Though I tried to assure him that Giovanni would never suggest any impropriety between us, he has never truly forgiven himself for what he still considers was his own failure to safeguard me. We both know how ludicrous that is. It was an unavoidable and unforeseeable situation.

Sir John, though, was outraged at Giovanni's conduct towards me and his refusal to assist me in what I believe is the most important endeavour of my life. He has promised me that, if Giovanni is serious about his threat of divorce, under no circumstances should I fear being left friendless or homeless upon our return from this expedition.

I retired before dinner. Ursula and I spent a little while further examining Giovanni's strange apparatuses and contraptions, most of which we could scarcely make out what application they were for, let alone how to use them. More interesting, if not a little exciting, are his pair of galvatronic odic Pistols, gun belt and holsters. I have never seen him wear this array of weaponry, but he does tell many a vivid tale of audacious daring-do featuring these trusty armaments.

Ursula contends I should gird myself with them at all times, let alone if I should need to leave the ship. Which I find ludicrous as not only are they tremendously heavy and cumbersome, but I have no idea how to fire them. I would present more a danger to myself and my companions than any would-be assailant. After quite a quarrel, I have agreed that we shall both keep one loaded and close to hand in the cabin. Ursula has insisted that, whatever I decide, she will be armed with her little pepper pot when escorting me at any time I should disembark from the Seren Bore. Though she feels the Odics would be far more off-putting to any ruffian or mughunter (a type of pickpocket, she is most concerned about). I relented and agreed I will take one of the Odics in Giovanni's satchel if I feel at all concerned for my safety or need to leave the ship itself, and I have suggested that maybe I should ask Sir John to teach us both how to safely discharge such complicated and fearsome weapons.

Though what would be the purpose, as I could never actually injure or kill another person, it is the gravest and most unforgivable of sins.

Journal of Adam Franklin.

Today I met a Martian.

The Professor had not, in fact no one had, provided me with any form of warning. I stood with my mouth agape like an awestruck fool, hardly able to believe what I was gazing upon.

We had risen early in the morning and breakfasted well. Though Mrs Ransom had not joined us, instead sending apologies for her feeling unwell. Though through Edwin's unusually unforthcoming demeanour it was evident the night had not gone well.

The Professor was imperious this morning, puffing furiously on his pipe like some inpatient steam engine, while loudly hastening everyone along. Edwin hardly got a moment to say goodbye to his children, and Lady Nikita missed our whole departure.

On our journey, Edwin confided to me that his wife and he had had the sharpest of words overnight. It took no great feat of logical deduction to understand why. I asked Edwin whether she had set her face against her father's whole venture or merely his participation.

He laughed mirthlessly and told me that she was a great support to his father-in-law in all things, "It is that she has had such a distressing time worrying about my exploits lately, only for me to hurry off on some other escapade with hardly time to sip a cup of tea." He looked away from me as if his attention had been taken by something we were passing on the journey. "I am no adventurer. I am a simple man, one destined, but for a twist of fate, to be an academic, a conceptual engineer, who gave it all up for the corybantic life of a dandelion farmer, and not particularly exceptional one at that. Now for my troubles, I have been chased out of my home and off my land by murderous thugs. Nelly is right; I am truly not the stuff that adventurers are made of." He took off his spectacles and rubbed at the lenses furiously with his handkerchief. "The Professor does not need me on this venture, it is just to distract me from my own foolhardiness. I should forget all this nonsense and go back to my family."

We sat together in silence for a while as our cab followed the Professor's little caravan of vehicles to the airfield. In due course Edwin added; "I am not a brave man like you."

I assured him I am not a 'brave man.' I told him that I think he has been much more courageous than I. Not just in the last few days, but in everything he has done with his life. I recounted to him the fable of the old warrior and the impoverished farm boy who wanted to run away from the drudge of the family farm to be a hero. The old warrior explains that the real hero is the boy's father who toils at the plough and the hoe to scrape enough from the earth every day to feed his family. Being able to kill people is not heroic, being able to keep them alive, is.

I reminded Edwin that those men who pursued him off his land are still out there, Everheart and the man with the mechanical eye. And what we are doing here, by embarking upon this quest, was not unlike the bird that feigns injury to lead predators away from her nest. It is a terrible truth from which he could take a modicum of comfort, but if this man Du Maurier posed a threat to Mrs Ransom and the children it would have manifested already.

It was then Edwin told me that the man with the prosthesis had been identified as one 'John Lloyd' posing as a Thaumasian called 'Uri Knapp.' I had an icy shock of recognition, a shiver down my spine. I know that name, but why do I know it? Edwin looked concerned and commented, "I say old chap, are you alright? You look as if someone has stepped on your grave."

Indeed, he was right. John Lloyd was the name of the Navigation Officer of the aerostat I was shot down in. The Doctor, Democritus, if that was his name, and if that whole experience was real, said that the co-pilot survived their experiments but went mad. My God! Was that him?

I desperately tried to remember their faces, the man at Alba Station and John Lloyd, the bon vivant balloon jockey, I knew long ago. A rakish profligate who spent most of his energies beyond his service pursuing young women far above his station in life and inflicting the tales of his God-awful romantic misadventures on his fellow junior officers. Could that have been

the same man? If so this was no accidental meeting, in fact, none of this could be accidental. Suddenly I felt like one of the hapless characters in those classic tales we were taught at school; toyed with by capricious Gods. Or the man that Plato wrote of, trapped in a cave mistaking shadows for a reality he could never comprehend
(I have read Plato? When?).
A nauseating sensation of certainty settled upon me. When I attempted to fully realise those two faces in my mind's eye, they were indeed the same man. Under the damage, what had looked like pockmarks were burns, and behind the cruelly bolted on apparatus, was indeed the face of the man I had once known. Older, coarser, with little trace of the humanity or humour I knew, but it was him. Only the pencil thin moustache remained of the vestments of whom he had once been.

Edwin inquired again. What was I to say to him? The man who Du Maurier sent to kill you, the man that went toe to toe with Karl, is little more than a reanimated corpse? And how exactly do I know that?

I begged his pardon and insisted my reaction was simply a wave of mal de mer, caused by nothing more than my overindulgence at breakfast.

Edwin was of sounder mind this morning than I would have credited him, for he produced a few hastily scribbled notes on a fictitious background he had concocted for me. "Something to tell if anyone should ask," was all he would say. I gathered by that he expected someone would. As a distraction we ran over the details a couple of times, with Edwin filling in additional oddments of information, it was a fascinating fabrication worthy of any good novelist.

I feel so guilty that I cannot share with Edwin what I now remember of my true past, but am forced to maintain the pretence of continued obliviousness. How could I tell this young, gentle, idealistic fellow the truth? That I am nothing more than a reanimated monster, formed, in part, from a foot soldier of the most implacable enemy his nation ever faced?   That is one conversation I cannot broach.

Covingdome Airfield is a vast open space west of the city. I remember it as little more than a field of red dirt we used to call the "Pan." It was the assembly area and landing ground for our operations during the wars. There had been almost nothing there back then, hangars and depots were dispersed off-site to restrict their vulnerability to attack, leaving just a few shacks and gantries around the edges of the Pan. Now the huge space was turfed as flat as a cricket pitch and ringed with huge aerostat and aerodyne hangars, gantries, scaffolds and mooring masts. Our little cavalcade of vehicles skirted the landing field to arrive at the side doors of one of the largest hangars, a colossal barnlike structure with a skin of red brick over a skeleton of wrought iron that served as dock and repair yard for the aerostats and dirigibles.

Inside frantic preparations were ongoing to ready the airship for our departure.

The Professor gathered us together and proudly presented the Seren Bore, pointing out features of the aerostat with the aid of a long-stemmed Tyrolian pipe he seems to have adopted for the purpose. The Seren Bore is almost 200 feet from stem to stern with five decks and twenty-five crew, plus another dozen taken on for the expedition. The balloon itself is over 300 feet long and contains two and a half million square feet of aeaea gas, which, with the electrificated copper phrikite plating on the hull, gives the whole airship enough potential lift to raise almost twice her unballasted tonnage. With the Professor's own modifications to the engines, their power output has been doubled. In test flights, he claims she has reached over seventy knots and can run constantly at 40 knots for as long as fuel reserves last. The modified engines not only generate the magnetic field to charge the phrikite plating, but also generate a strong enough power to provide electric current to run the ship's independent Oersted electromagnetic bi-rotating external aerial manoeuvring rotors and other electromagnetically powered motors, allowing the engines to conserve their power for the twin main propulsions. As normal, pyrolytic gas from the two-stage fuel combustion process is used to provide night-time and below deck lighting, but with the addition of a Davy de la Rue electrically powered radiance system modified by the Professor. Charity was astounded by the thought of electrically produced illumination on board an airship!

The Professor seemed delighted at Charity's enthusiasm and expounded upon the point by explaining that his design for the electrical accumulators and storage apparatus were based upon the St. Elmo energy harvesting array that illegal gatherers used to harness lightning. When Charity asked if the Seren Bore could gather lightning, the Professor only smiled and said that such a thing was far too dangerous, although wasting all that free energy was such a pity.

As the crew attended to the various bags and luggage, we followed the Professor up the wrought iron steps. He continued his narration by pointing out that the ship was well provided for in the 'extremely unlikely event' of hostilities. I enquired as to what type of 'hostilities' he was referring? His answer was vague, though he cited the dangers posed by some of the denizens of the wilder reaches of the seas of sand.

Charity enquired about the menace posed by airborne buccaneers?

The Professor chuckled, but avoided the question with the deftness of a man who has spent far too much time around politicians. He explained that the Seren Bore, as a Free Merchant Trader, had already boasted a substantial defensive armoury, even before he had brought her and upgraded her. I have experienced far too much insincere obfuscating by officers to not be able to perceive that there was more than a scrap of real concern behind the Professor's bluster. Not wishing to be alarmist, I suggested that the Master Gunner should apprise me further when he familiarises me with the armoury and security on board. The Professor agreed and added that a colloquium, presented by Sir John Sydeian, on flora and fauna we might view on our journey is scheduled for tomorrow. Sir John, apparently a noted hunter and adventurer, would be expressly focusing on anything that might pose a danger in any way to expedition or crew members.

We were piped aboard with great ceremony and greeted by the Captain and senior crewmen. The Professor, with a flair for the dramatic, announced his appointment of myself to the post of Master-at-Arms, his appointment of Edwin as his assistant Expedition Leader, and Charity's appointment as the expedition's Diarist and official Correspondent. After salutations and handshaking, we were shown to our rather cramped accommodation. The berths are well-appointed and the bunk beds on the small side but comfortable. Luckily I have little to stow and Edwin travels light.

Charity has taken the berth next to us which I feel provides her with a modicum of assurance.

While others arrived, I took the opportunity to talk to the Master Gunner, Gwenlan. He showed me the well provisioned arms locker and provided me with a key, also to the gun cabinet in the wardroom, nothing more in that than a few good shotguns and a couple of elephant guns for shooting the wildlife. I do not require such familiarisation with the battery, but requested that he generally familiarise me with the ships defences and drills.

Although drills will have to wait until we are underway, he was delighted to show me the two Cogswaine's. 'Fulcrum mounted steam driven water cooled rotation guns,' no less. One on the fore and one on the aft deck. Gwenlan is most proud of them and keeps saying "State o' the art, they ar'." Which they are indeed. He claims they can fire a thousand rounds of good old .303 in a single minute over a range of 800 yards or more. A truly devastating weapon.

Of the old fittings there remains the two amidships mounted 3lb'er Picaro pneumatic repeating cannons, deck-mounted and rather old now, almost antiques, but damn reliable. I was impressed with their maintenance. They have an eight-round magazine and a range of six thousand yards or more. The ship also boasts three Puckler's, hopper fed rotary rifles. Best anti-boarding guns in use when I was.... alive.

I remarked to Gwenlan that maybe the Professor was expecting some serious dangers on the journey. He volunteered that there had been a lot of 'talk' lately about trouble in the Neath area. What troubles? I asked. *"Privateers and such like,"* he said, *"Also I 'eard that in tha papers only ah couple o' days ago ah merchantman out of Aeria wos attacked and wrecked by a Pirate Nautilus, not a single survivor."* He shook his head dolefully.

I did not ask how it was known what attacked the said merchant ship if there were indeed no survivors as he attested.

The Martian Phrikite Nautilus (not Pirate) is, as far as I am aware, a solitary hunter, preferring to ambush prey from its lair within dense clouds and thunderheads far out over the Red Seas. No doubt a decent sized one could take down a small dirigible, but bringing down even a medium sized merchant ship sounded preposterous. A point I would take up later with Sir John Sydeian.

Our conversation was interrupted when a rating arrived to escort me to the 'wardroom,' for an official introduction. With a small but adequate library, good chairs, a magnificent table, chandelier and automaton attendant, it was a room more befitting a gentleman's club than an airship. The Professor had gathered all members of the expedition together for the introductions and a briefing.

The Professor introduced me to Dr Octavius Spender, a tall man with a shaggy moustache, in his sixties who I can only describe as weather-beaten, in appearance and apparel. One of those men that somehow always looks dusty. An archaeologist attached to the university, once a bit of a gallivant from what I have learnt, though he fancies himself more the brave adventurer type. His daughter, Parthena, who can only be in her early twenties, affects a similar weathered appearance, wearing mainly practical male clothing with her hair cut unfashionably short. Though her forthright demeanour appears deliberately masculine, she is indeed an exceptionally striking and highly educated young woman. Charity seems most taken with her.

Sir John Sydeian cuts a slim but wide shouldered silhouette, keen-eyed and clean shaven. Bedecked in hunting tweeds, long boots and casual open collar. His manner seems a little affected, and I feel that it is a shallow act. The Professor introduced him as a famous adventurer and big game hunter, and Sir John raised to the part.

Colonel Carter Jahns, I knew the name immediately from Beresford's book, is an imposing elderly gentleman with a characteristic military bearing. He too had come dressed as if for game hunting, his whiskers heavily waxed and his unusually long iron-grey hair tied back in a ponytail. He observed me intensely, if not distrustfully, from beneath wildly bushy eyebrows and was curt, if not almost impolite, to Sir John. I have since learnt that though he insists he is 'retired' he has brought with him six Negro men from his old regiment. Members of the Blacks Brigade, no doubt. Ostensibly they are to provide additional manpower and protection for the expedition, but even the Professor seems a little apprehensive about the idea of the Colonel having his own private army on board.

The Professor explained his proposal to postpone the original aim of this expedition for a few days while we returned to Tremorfa to investigate the 'tomb,' or whatever it is, Karl has told us is out on the edges of Edwin's property.

Dr Spender, his daughter and Sir John were most insistent that the tomb should be investigated as it may well be an untouched example of an ancient Peerrohs Aresian Royal tomb. Edwin was especially excited and Charity, who had led us to this conclusion, emphasised that (without naming names) grave robbers working for collectors and dealers were already operating in the area.

Colonel Jahns was unable to see the importance of the whole thing and exasperatedly declared it an "inconsequential digression" as there could be nothing in a dusty old tomb that would have any bearing on this expedition's purpose.

It was at that point the wardroom door opened and a rating ushered in two ladies.

I did not immediately realise the first was an automaton, not unlike Karl, but deliberately smaller and more feminine in construction, more 'androidic.' Dressed as it was, inappropriate attire, it would be easily passed on the street for a refined young woman, although its alabaster countenance would raise misgivings. Nothing as sophisticated as this, nor Karl for that matter, existed in my day. Automatons were often little more than clanking steam boilers with clockwork legs and arms, or scaled down versions of the Nutcrackers. Nothing like these, nothing like me.

I was musing on that fact when the Professor intruded upon my reverie to introduce me to the last member of the expedition.

Suddenly I was face to face with a Martian. A red skinned, Peerrohs Aresian. For a moment I could not comprehend what I was seeing.

She was as tall as I, elegant and graceful in movement. Her skin, without blemish or imperfection, is red, a carmine red. Her eyes sparkle like pieces of polished fire opal set in stark contrast against the pure white of the sclera. Her hair is as black and glistening as wet coal. She smiled and spoke a few words to me in greeting. Snow white teeth against the lighter red of her lips. I heard not a thing she said, for I could only wordlessly gawk at her like some country yokel at a fairground. She offered her ungloved hand, I took it, held it for a moment, noticing how white the nails are against the fingers, how delicate her hand was against my black leather gauntlet. She withdrew in perfect motion, moving on to her next introduction. I felt like I had been struck with something. She is profoundly beautiful.

Charity nudged me in the ribs with her elbow and beamed up at me. "Why Mr Franklin." She whispered conspiratorially, "Tut-tut! She is a married woman after all."

Obviously, my shock had been so apparent that Edwin joined us and, in a hushed voice, explained. She is Madam Fontenelli, the wife of the famous explorer and cartographer Giovanni Fontenelli. By some terrible, tragic circumstances, she was orphaned as a small child and brought up in a convent school on

Mount Olympus. But I have been told again and again that all the Aresians have withdrawn, gone from all contact.

Charity put it into a context that my confused mind could grasp, "She is no more an Aresian than I am an Earthling. She was brought up from a small child as one of us. Inside, no doubt she is as human as you or I. She once said she cannot even remember her own family let alone her language or culture."

I queried how she could be so sure? Charity explained that she did a biographical piece on Fontenelli when he was about to be awarded some gong or whatever. "He's not much of an explorer really, just a dreary old map maker. But Aelita Fontenelli, his seldom-seen wife, now there was a story." Charity sighed, "Pity I never got to publish it." We both asked why? "Fontenelli is an enormously private man and he has powerful friends. And to protect the last Aresian in Tharsis... well, they felt it might be in bad taste."

Without our awareness, the conversation had returned to the subject of investigating the tomb. Dr Spender, apparently still smarting at the Colonel's casual dismissal, was talking passionately about the need to save all Aresian sites from the hands of looters. The Professor suddenly held up his hand to halt the archaeologist's invective and turn to put a question to Madam Fontenelli. What were her thoughts on the matter?

Obviously surprised she appeared to flounder briefly before giving as concise an answer as anyone could have asked for. She spoke with great avidity of her reverence for archaeology as a 'noble art' and the need for an understanding of "our shared pasts." I noticed Dr Spender's hackles rose noticeably when she decried some archaeologists as little more than tomb robbers.

I also found it interesting to watch Parthena as she slid her hand into Madam Fontenelli's to reassure her. There is a certain abundance of compassion in her manner, regardless of her unusual dress style and boyish haircut. Her father ploughed on with his insistence that the expedition should investigate the grave as he agrees with Charity that it may well be an undisturbed Royal sepulchre.

It was hard to read Madam Fontenelli's expression, but the fear that an ancient Royal tomb of her own people might be under threat from looters seemed to gain her acquiescence to act.

I find myself entranced by Madam Fontenelli; the flawless line of her profile, the elegance of her neck, the graceful economy of her every movement, the intensity of her regard. This exquisite creature, whose presence captivates me so, is the child of my sworn enemy. I had waged war on her kind, without pity or remorse.

Though, in truth, I seldom saw the Peerrohs themselves on the battlefield as anything other than officers or leaders. Leaving the front line fighting to the Yellows and Greens Spookers. Nonetheless, I can remember witnessing the aftermath of the handiwork of the Peerrohs' elite warriors, the Hómoioi. After the battle of Lasswitz Ridge, we were set the task of discovering the reason for the failure of our diversionary attack when we came upon a scene of utter carnage in the eastern gulch. Half a regiment of Cimmerian Grenadiers, sent to flank the Yellow's defences, had been cornered and slaughtered like pigs in a pen. A lone surviving Cimmerian deliberately left as a witness, told of unstoppable towering red devils, in armour and cloaks, eschewing firearms for falchions and axes. A bloody, bloody business, indeed.

Oh, how I had hated back then. In war, it is easy to hate, but now? As I looked upon her? Where is my hatred? My wrathful friend? I felt no such empathy when I shot Lanulos or the Doctor. Just cold rage, but now? I know that if she came to me as if in a dream and asked me to follow her to the very Mountains of the Moon, I would do so. Without hesitation, without thought.

Charity, assuming my distant reverie was due to boredom, formally introduced me to Sir John. Polite small talk is not my forte and so, armed with foreknowledge that he was to give a symposium on the dangers posed by some of Mars' more outlandish denizens, I enquired if he thought a Phrikite Nautilus could possibly grow big enough, let alone bold enough, to take down a fairly large merchant ship, as reported in the papers? He agreed that on personal experience they certainly grow huge but he had never known one to be so bold, nonetheless out there in some of the remoter areas, it was the only one of two apex predators and like many such creatures, its full adult size may be solely dependent upon the abundance of food and resources. But they are rare creatures and getting rarer – in fact, so rare as to be considered extinct in some regions.

He laughed at my thoughtful expression as assured me there were enough horrors out there to justify my salary.

For elevenses, I took some coffee and tiffin with Edwin, Dr Spender, Sir John and the Professor. Colonel Jahns did not join us preferring to return to his cabin for a nap. While the ladies diverted themselves with discussing suitable attire for the expedition, the Professor and Dr Spender began to deliberate on exactly what "investigating the tomb" would entail. I have scant knowledge about the complexities of archaeology and excused myself from the table. I spent some more time acquainting myself with the layout of the ship.

During my meanderings, I made a deliberate effort to discover where Colonel Jahns' men had been billeted. I discovered them roughing it in the orlop, amidst the cables, taking turns to smoke their pipes out of a single porthole. Though the insignias were gone from their kit they were defiantly Olympian Highlanders by their accents and their kit. I had previously acquired some cigarettes on my travels (from the hotel) and, after sharing them out, passed a few minutes trying to make small-talk with the men (easier for me than with Sir John and the others). Decent enough fellows of good humour and, though cautious about their words, it was obvious enough to tell that they were experienced soldiers and probably still in service.

I got their names;

Freddy "Red" Rawlings, Albert Kline, Rex Gordon, Harry Capon and Smith and Weinbaum (did not get their first names). By their ages, facial hair and barring I would say they are all at least the rank of sergeant. According to Beresford the last surviving members of the First Negro Volunteer Brigade were amalgamated into the Highlanders after the last Aresian conflict. Though these men were not old enough to have been with Jahns at Hellas.

So Colonel Jahns has not brought his own private army with him, these men are regulars, veterans no doubt, and very much still part of the Tharsis army, I would wager.

I left them with a pledge that I would see to it their quarters were made more comfortable and I might accept their invitation for a game of cards in the evening.

We were all invited to the bridge to watch our departure, but I made my excuses after only a short while. Madam Fontenelli was there with Sir John very much in attendance. I found it uncomfortable being in their presence and took a few turns around the shelter and promenade decks to clear my head.

I have not felt so bewildered since the incident on Clerval Street, is someone playing with my mind? My emotions seem no longer to be manageable by coherent thought. I cannot look upon the woman without the strangest obsessional contemplations coupled with insane flights of fancy. I have resolved to maintain my equanimity, let alone my sanity, to distance myself from her and, as much as one can on a ship, avoid being in her presence.

Until dinner, I occupied myself by reading. The wardroom has a small, but heterogeneous, library and several good wing-backed chairs. I entertained myself perusing selections from a historical gazetteer, "The Gazeta de la Novità," which seemed to be little more than a tri-annual collection of scandal and rumour mongering columns from several broadsheets and a strangely prophetic novel by Mrs Shelley, "The Last Man." The automaton steward, Jakes, is most attentive and informative. Before fully settling to my reading I asked him how long he had served on the Seren Bore, he informed me he had been with the ship only seven months. Before that he was a valet to an elderly statesman, though originally he served on one of the biggest paddle steamers to ply the great canals, the Old Glory, a gambling ship until it was gutted to the waterline by fire. He proudly showed me the patternation on his bronze skin from the fire damage.

After a couple of hours, Edwin rousted me from my reading to join him, Charity and Miss Spender, in viewing the sunset from the fantail. We stood, sipping tea from mugs, wrapped up in our dusters and overcoats.

The plateau below us is an impressive sight, more as now as it is mostly cultivated. Decades of farming have tamed the wild terrain and settled the red dust. Up here the air is fresh, cold and above all clean enough for us to risk dispensing with filters and masks altogether.

Standing there watching the sky and the passing panoramic, in congenial company, I felt, for the first time, truly relaxed. We spent some while debating which of the Canali, with its glassy water and wide belts of vegetation, we were following, was it the Phlegethon or the Nilus? We laughingly reached the deduction that the sum of our joint geographical awareness was somewhat lacking.

Edwin was most excited as he had spent the afternoon familiarising himself with the Professor's plans and making arrangements and contingencies for the investigation of the tomb. He chatted incessantly about the particularities of who would be doing what, and who was in charge of what. I must admit I gave the whole thing only scant attention, as what more than myself and a couple of armed crew members would be required to provide safety for the excavations.

Dinner in the beautiful wood panelled saloon was awkward, though initially, I considered myself lucky, seated at the far end of the table away from Madam Fontenelli and Sir John who appeared to be engrossed in each other's company, I soon regretted it. I was placed with Dr Spender, his daughter, Charity and Colonel Jahns. Although I did my best to engage in the customary small talk my attention, like a loadstone to iron, kept being drawn away to Madam Fontenelli. Each time I had to make the effort to wrench my eyes from her.

As ill 'luck' would have it Colonel Jahns arrived late resplendent in his mess uniform, with all his medals on parade, and deposited himself almost opposite me. He hardly waited for the first course to begin before launching into his interrogation of me. He rightly assumed that by my comportment and, of course, my ruined physiognomy that I too had some military background. Luckily, through my reading of Beresford and Edwin's careful tutorage, my claim to have been a member of the Free Companies injured at Arabia Ponds fighting Thylian land grabbers and illegal prospectors was enough to mollify him. Though obviously, by his manner, it did not completely convince the old warhorse.

As Edwin and I had thought, Jahns, being much the traditional soldier under that flamboyant hair and bluff manner disdained the role of mercenaries and guerrillas. He dismissed the battle of Arabia Ponds as a settler's skirmish and moved on to how I, what he assumed as a lowly mercenary, knew Professor Flammarion?

I explained that I only met the Professor yesterday, but I have been working for Edwin for some time and we had grown to be friends, and so when the attacks happened I stood by my friend as any decent man would. Jahns, at least, approved of that.

Then the conversation turned to the events of the last few days. Miss Spender and her father were fascinated by the specifics. Though I was somewhat surprised at how detailed the Colonel's awareness of the reported events are.

Dr Spender knows of Du Maurier only by reputation, both as a collector and 'benefactor.' He made an odd gesture with his fingers when he said the word. In neither role does he consider the man's repute being anything above that of an ill-mannered cheap autocrat, only one step up from a common criminal.

Dr Spender also knows Charity's step-father, Dr Robert 'Dobbin' Cromie, as he had studied with Charity's late mother. He knows of the harm Du Maurier has done to Cromie's reputation simply because the man had refused his advances. Charity, seated beside the Colonel, illuminated the conversation with some details on the ruthless underhand machinations Du Maurier used to try to bring down her step-father's career— mostly spreading salacious rumours and outright bribery but ending in several incidents of clear-cut intimidation. All this merely for refusing to work for him, this Du Maurier is truly a man who does not like not getting his way.

The Colonel voiced a similar opinion to Professor Flammarion on the threat posed to the integrity of the state, whichever state, that is, by overly mighty industrialists like Du Maurier. I construed from his comments that there was more to his assertion than a simple personal opinion. I asked the Colonel why the Government has not acted to curtail the activities of such men.

The Colonel just glared at me for a moment before answering, "That would be unconstitutional, Mr Franklin. And thus we could never do such a thing. After all, we are not the Thylians, this is a democracy, not a stratocracy."

"Not for long," I countered, "It would seem, if nothing is done to stop it, you are looking at a plutarchy." I was amused to see that word received with raised eyebrows.

Dr Spender, citing historical precedent from the Ancient Athenians, asked if it was not the role of the military to protect a democracy against such an incipient plutarchy. Especially if those emergent tyrants and their families are using malfeasant means to obtain political influence and wealth?

"Ah, there, as you are fully aware, Mister Franklin, these emergent moguls are cunning, they work through clandestine influence, blackmail and corruption, and they act only through third and fourth parties. Never directly, never openly. They are

truly blameless men, careful never to commit criminal actions in any location where they may become exposed." Jahns sipped his wine, his eyes never leaving mine. "We all know that Du Maurier is behind everything that has happened to Edwin but the proof is scant, and certainly too meagre to satisfy any Court of Law."

I pretended to consider his remark for a moment before replying, "Then maybe it is time, as the good Dr Spender here said, that the Government used the military to deal with the problem; if you cannot seize the men themselves then neutralise their intermediaries and seize their assets?"

"Unfortunately, or more rightly; fortunately, that is not legal in our country Mister Franklin."

Jahns smugness was beginning to get under my skin. "Then, Colonel Jahns, you are going to have to watch as exactly what the Professor and Dr Spender fear is going to happen happens before your eyes. These 'moguls,' as you call them, will grow ever more powerful until your Government answers to them, not to its people. Then where will your 'free Mars,' your revolution be? Sold to the highest bidder or, in this case, stolen by the most cunning thieves? And on your watch too."

Jahns flushed under his collar.

Miss Spender was a little more forthright calling Du Maurier "an ugly, deranged little gong-farmer," with a Napoleon fixation. Which reduced our end of the table to guffaws of laughter. Even the Colonel raised his glass to that one.

After the meal, I tried to excuse myself, partly as I had another engagement and partly to avoid being anywhere near Madam Fontenelli, but the Professor buttonholed me. Firstly, to ask if I had been given the tour by the Master Gunner? I dutifully affirmed the fact and presented the set of keys I had been furnished with. Although it would now have to wait until the morning for drill practice. Secondly, he wanted to know if in the morning I would give the once over to the plans for the excavation, security wise, that is. I really had not troubled myself much about it. I had assumed that I and a couple of armed crew members would be enough, but the Professor's caution made me reconsider. The Professor told me I could deploy the Colonel's men if I wished. I promised to give it some careful thought, but wondered if the Colonel would be in complete agreement with his men taking orders from me.

Finally, in a conspiratorially low tone, the Professor asked my opinion of my fellow expedition members? He accepted a succession of non-committal observations until I got to Sir John.

"Don't you think he's being a little too attentive to Madam Fontenelli?" The Professor nodded slightly in their direction, "I mean; he practically fawns over her. Extremely unseemly."

I concurred, but deliberately understated, "They do appear to be friendly. I believe they have known each other for some time before today."

"He's a good chap, you know, but he has gained himself a bit of a reputation as a libertine. Much through fault of his own, I must add. Would you keep an eye on them for me? I cannot afford for Sir John to get Madam Fontenelli into any more discord with her husband than she already is."

My heart, or whatever contraption is in my chest, sank.

"And will you watch over Madam Fontenelli, I cannot emphasise how important she is to the success of this expedition."

My heart sank a little more, but it was what I was being paid for. I promised I would watch them both carefully.

I was finally able to take my leave to retire for the night, and almost out the saloon door, when the Colonel, re-entering from a stroll on the deck, seized my elbow and leant in close to me.

His breath was heavy with claret and cigar smoke, but under those profuse brows, his eyes were piercing. "Ah, there, understand me well, sir; I do not know who you are or what your game is but I do not like you nor believe a word of your story."

For a moment the Sergeant Major was back again, I bit back his blinding fury and vicious tongue. How dare this jumped up Red Hander, this stinking drunken traitor to Queen and Empire, touch me. The Sergeant Major's voice echoed in my head demanding I put this half ratted toss-pot on his arse and tell him exactly what I thought of turncoats and traditors like him. My God, he dared to still wear the medals awarded to him by the British Empire alongside those of his traitorous revolutionary masters.

The Colonel must have seen something in my eyes as he released my arm and pulled away slightly. "If you were at Arabia Ponds," he hissed. "Who was your commanding officer?" He looked pleased that he had fallen upon something with which he could catch me out on, or maybe even verify.

I fought to keep my expression passive. "Theophilus Ransom, Captain Ransom, Mr Ransom's uncle. Tharsis Albannach Volunteer Irregulars. He was killed by the same homemade mortar round that got me and seven other lads." Jahns' expression was a mix of frustration and rage. I continued, "Hit our punt amidships as we were launching a knock-up on one of the Sourdough's barge forts. Swanwick Pond, complete fucking balls-up. If you don't mind my language. Sir."

The Colonel humphed, thrust his cigar back into his mouth, and pushed past me.

On my way through the ship, I snaffled a couple of bottles of claret, meant, I suspect, for the Colonel himself, and headed down into the bowels of the aerostat.

I had spoken to the Purser, Mr Grant, earlier and requested that some home comforts be afforded the Colonel's men in the orlop. The chaps welcomed me heartily. The Purser had been quite generous and their ad-hoc billet looked a great deal more comfortable and supplied.

We sat on casks and old boxes, cracked the claret, smoked, and played a few hands of poker for pennies. I joined in with the idle banter and chit-chat until they were all relaxed in my presence, and the claret had done its work, I turned the conversation to Colonel Jahns.

It is now way past the witching hour and I must admit that the effects of today's bonhomie are finally beginning to take a hold, so I will keep this short;

It is as I suspected, Jahns' 'semi-retirement' is only in name, in truth, he is still a senior member of Tharsis' Military Intelligence, the, so-called, Republican Defence League. Mostly he is viewed as a pompous old claret soaked buffoon who rests upon his renown, but his men know under that he is still a sly old fox. Why he has brought them on this expedition they have not been instructed but, as serving soldiers, they are under his direct command. So far they have received no orders and are bored stiff stuck down there bulling boots and cleaning kit.

They have learnt through shipboard gossip that the expedition is going off into the "nether regions" looking for leftover "Spookers." They have heard there is indeed a "Spooker" on board but thought the crew members were pulling their leg.

I confirmed there is indeed an Aresian lady on board and that I had been charged with her welfare, so they better behave courteously around her. They joshed me a little, in the usual soldier's indelicate manner, but took my cautioning in good humour. I like them (all but Weinbaum, who is a cold-eyed truculent cove with an offensively good ability at cards) but I fear that there might be a point where their Colonel and I might not see eye to eye and these chaps and I might have to come to blows.

Strange, I have another twenty-seven years on them, but still I am apparently younger than all of them. For the first time what I am, the machine inside, gives me the assurance of indomitability. I hope it is not a false sense of confidence.

I did not push my queries any further and, once the claret was done for, I took my remaining few pennies and bid them a peaceful night.

I returned to our cabin to find Edwin had fallen asleep sitting at the fold-down desk, writing and illustrating stories for his children again. I packed away his journal and drawings and put him to bed. Checked the Lancenett pistol I have selected from the weapons locker and placed it under my pillow, the slide is tucked under the mattress at the end of the bed. Now it is time for me to turn in as well.

An unpleasant night. Bad dreams. Madam Fontenelli figured in them, a lot. So did Lanulos. I can still see his evil grinning face. They were dancing at a ball full of dead people. Also something about tombs and being buried alive. Disturbed Edwin by shouting in my sleep.

By Courier
Mrs Eleanor A. Ransom.
Locksley Hall.
Machen,
Tharsis.
September 30th. M.Y. 26
Dear Nelly.

I am so deeply regretful of our bitter words last night and our cold parting this morning. I apologise with all my heart for the disappointment my decision has brought you and the children.

I will miss you terribly and count off the minutes until I return home again to your loving arms, but this thing I do, I am resolved to do.

Almost immediately upon embarking on the journey to Covingdome, my resolution deserted me, but it was Adam that erased the ambiguity from my mind. I do not wish to alarm you further, but until this whole Du Maurier situation is cleared up, I am, as you have so often said, in certain mortal danger. And that danger brings with it peril to all those within my purlieu.

Du Maurier's agents are set upon the chase like hounds, and so long as I am running I carry their interest and in that draw them away from our little fox home.

It was Adam that spoke the unthinkable this morning; that if Du Maurier meant you harm, he would have made threats or taken action long ago. I know it is hard for you to understand, but I sincerely believe that you and the children are by far safer without me there. You have Karl, Carstairs, Dan and Aegy, and Minnie, Joshua and the others will be with you in a day or two.

We are going back to the farm firstly to investigate the tomb Karl spoke of. Your father has convinced everyone (except your friend the Colonel) that it is of utmost importance. I am really rather excited about the whole thing. To think, a Royal burial chamber! On our land! I must have ridden past it a thousand times without the slightest inkling. I must though, wonder why my father never mentioned it. I never took him to be a superstitious man.

Once we have secured it, we will return to Tharsis to refuel so I hope that I can see you all very soon.

All my love,
Your devoted husband
Edwin.

The Flammarion Expedition Journal of L. Edwin Ransom.

Dear reader,

I am writing this journal as a personal record of the following events. I would request if this journal, and other papers accompanying it, have come into your hands by any other route than through the effects of my family, that you would please do me the great service as to make sure it returns unto the hands of my wife and children, or whosoever remains of my descendants. So that they may glean what solace they may from the knowledge that I tried my very best. And did not perish in vain.

Day One. 30th 9th. 26.

We, myself, Adam Franklin, Miss Bryant-Drake and Professor Flammarion, arrived at the aerostat at ten-to-seven this morning. It is an impressive airship, quite beyond anything I had expected.

We were piped aboard with great ceremony and introduced to the Captain, the First Mate Mr Charles, and the Chief Engineer Mr Beer, a cheery fellow who insists upon being called "Gregory," and the Purser, Mr Grant.

Captain Llewellyn is quite a redoubtable fellow, the very model of what one would expect an aerostat Captain to be; a bear of a man, with a closely cropped beard and thick hair that forms a white mane around his ruddy complexion. He is jovial and has a ready wit in small talk, but can use his deep, sonorous voice to great effect on the bridge. He still retains a strong accent, Welsh I believe, and has a habit of calling any below his status "boyo" and using other oddly endearing idioms. He runs a tight, well-ordered ship and I can see why the Professor has put his faith in him.

I am to be the Professor's Deputy in all matters and have spent most of the day in the Professor's company familiarising myself with the course plans and itinerary for the expedition.

I did manage to dash off a missive to Nelly and the children before we departed. I feel so awful about leaving them so swiftly after my arrival. I have promised myself that once this adventure is over, and when Du Maurier is in prison, I shall sell the farm, as a going concern of course, and return to Tharsis. My days of dandelion farming are all but over.

The Professor called the expedition members together for introductions and to discuss his decision to defer our embarking upon the mission so as we may be able to scrutinise the tomb that Karl says is on my land. Miss Bryant-Drake, Dr Spender, his daughter and Sir John are most insistent that we should. I fittingly kept my own counsel, as the Professor had requested me to.

The resolution was made, swayed as it was by the intercession of Madam Fontenelli, whose mere presence was enough to hold the room spellbound. She has certainly had quite an effect upon Sir John and seemingly the opposite on Adam.

Adam seems terribly fraught in her presence. I do not think it is because of her race, as she seems a most pleasant young lady, and he has not expressed anything but an appreciation of her clarity of judgement. Still, I fear her presence has stirred some deep disquiet in him.

Before changing for dinner, I badgered Adam into joining myself, Miss Bryant-Drake and Miss Spender on the fantail deck to watch the sunset. The Purser issued us with a few immensikoffs to wrap ourselves in against the cold and several mugs of tea. The Captain will not allow good china on the decks.

From up so high, it afforded us the most astounding view of the heavenly extravaganza and the breathtaking landscape below. I so love this land, this world, though I have known no other I cannot for the life of me imagine what it would have been like to have been born on that far twinkling celestial body, Earth.

Miss Bryant-Drake and Miss Spender were sparkling company and I think the event raised even Adam's spirits, let alone mine.

Dinner was surprisingly delicious and went down very well. When I could attract his attention away from Madam Fontenelli, I had occasion to talk to Sir John about his adventures and what he knows of the areas we will be travelling into. He turned to me earnestly to warn me about the "Dread Winds of Tremorfa" and that it was a ghastly enclave where no man of good character should venture! The sparkle in Sir John's eyes gave away his true intent; a humorous reference to a notorious penny dreadful novella penned several years ago by Thomas Hailey that had everyone in the region up in arms. I took the joshing in good part, agreeing that the wind in Tremorfa is indeed considered lazy, as rather than be troubled to go around one it simply blows straight through. Though, on the whole, the region was far less remarkable than Hailey had made it out to be. Though Sir John observed that from my own accounts, it was no less dangerous.

I steered the conversation to the real point, Dioscuria, the frozen deserts and the ice cap beyond Elysium. Sir John's knowledge of the weather patterns was most insightful. He has spent quite some time in Elysium and knows the surrounding geography exceptionally well. Colonel Jahns' only reflexion, though famously associated with the campaigns against the Utopians in that region, was that it was "damned bloody cold, truly bone-achingly cold," and that he was too busy trying not to get his "head blown orf!" to have taken much notice of the meteorological conditions.

After dinner, I joined Sir John, Madam Fontenelli along with Miss Bryant-Drake and Miss Spender for an impromptu firearms lesson off the top deck. Madam Fontenelli and her automaton maid, Ursula, wished to be taught how to use a pair of galvatronic odic pistols they had brought with them. The other young ladies initially came for the spectacle, but soon dashed off to retrieve their own side arms. The Purser furnished us with some fluorescent dyed clay balls the crew use for such target shooting. I fear that I allowed myself to be burdened with the duty of launching the balls off into the darkness. Thankfully, my days on the University's cricket team put me in good stead, I still have a good roundarm.

The odic pistol is a frightening looking thing that is made even more alarming as it lets out a terrifying mechanical scream as it charges loudly to reload, the report on it is a deafening metallic crunch. Madam Fontenelli did not hit anything but, by God, she would scare even the most hardened sky pirates out of his breeches with that thing. More alarming though, was the lethal accuracy that Ursula, the maid, showed with the gun's twin.

On impact with its target it does not shatter or explode it, nor pierce it cleanly like a Lancenett, but completely evaporate it. Leaving only a burning trail of luminous dust.

Once the supply of clay balls had been exhausted and the cold had become unbearable, we adjourned to the wardroom for tea or something warmer.

There we were entertained by a selection of Sir John's whimsical tales of adventure, or more rightly, misadventure. He is an excellent raconteur and remarkably self-deprecating, placing himself in the midst of his narratives, but, I feel, amplifying his pratfalls for comedic value to underplay the glamour of his notable achievements. The ladies, especially Madam Fontenelli, were enthralled by him.

He has lived a wildly exciting life of adventure, while such as I have spent theirs with our noses in dusty books or pressed into the soil. He is personable if not dashing, humorous, valiant and charismatic, all facets that I find my personality lacks. Is this how mortal men felt standing beside great Achilles or in the shadow of Alexander?

The Professor, who was already sharing a bottle of port with Colonel Jahns and Dr Spender, listened for a while, before excusing himself for bed. The Colonel soon followed and I took that as my cue to bid everyone a good night and retire to my cabin.

No sign of Adam. I would so have wished to speak to him before sleeping.

I checked the time on the Frodsham half-hunter my children chose for my birthday. Twenty past twelve. The great surprise they were so excited about, as if I need to tell you, is the intricate lithograph of them that has been engraved into the inside of the back plate of the pocket watch. Done with such exquisite skill that it almost seems like a bas-relief. I sat for a while in the quiet of the cabin and I shall do a little more work upon Tabitha's "Adventures of Captain Pug," before I finally turn in. At least I can imagine what being a hero is like.

The Diary of Dr James Athanasius Flammarion.

30th Sept. 26th.

And so we are off. At last! I could not be more expectatious. Everything is prepared.

Captain Llewellyn, being a fellow of considered deed, has welcomed the short journey out to Tremorfa as what he terms a "shakedown" for the ship and her crew before we embark upon our true mission.

Edwin is proving to be much greater assistance than I expected. And he agrees that having him here with me on this quest is far safer for him and for our family. I am intrigued also by his companion, Mr Franklin, who is an impressive man with a military bearing and impeccable manners even when goaded by the Colonel. He is not at all as I imagined from what Eleanor read out to me from Edwin's letters. I have tasked him with the protection of the expedition members when off the ship. I feel he will be more than up to the task. I am also awfully interested to have a look at that hand of his, Edwin mentioned in an earlier letter that it is mechanical and of great artifice, but I shall leave that until we have all grown to know each other better.

I am only disappointed that Serviss did not join us this morning, but it would appear from the letter I received before departure that he is indeed intending on joining us. We may have to mollycoddle the old fool, but his knowledge and insight will be useful.

The letter from Henry has though been most welcome news. The Government has indeed sanctioned my endeavour and I may consider myself as an official representative of the Republic of Tharsis in this matter. I have given this news to only Jahns and Captain Llewellyn so far. They, the Government that is, have also agreed to provide assistance and some financial remuneration for my expenses on our return. I do not think that this offer covers our little shakedown voyage, but I will be pleased to hoist the banderol of the Republic on our official departure.

I also received a vile communiqué from Giovanni Fontenelli. That man is a brute. Though if his fears are amplified by the presence of Sir John on board I can understand his suspicions. Although alien, she is a very pulchritudinous young woman and has led an exceedingly sheltered life and Sir John, for all his famed audacious intrepidity, is a profligate and a womaniser. I have asked Mr Franklin to keep an eye on them, as I would not wish our return to be tarnished by an unseemly scandal.

Dr Spender and I have laid careful plans for his investigation of the supposed tomb. Edwin has been most useful in this. We will circumnavigate the area, avoiding, as best as may, attracting attention, and approach the location from the North East. It might put another half a day upon our journey, but it should forestall any problems. I doubt if Bogdanov has had those warrants served yet, and, even if so, I should think the situation within Tremorfa Township is fraught with dangers.

Llewellyn has informed me of his intention to have Mr Charles and the Gunnery Master run some crew drills in the morning as we should be out over open terrain. A number of the expedition seem to be enjoying an exceptionally late night tonight and a 3lb Picaro cannon will make as good a wake-up call as any window tapper.

For myself, I am both excited and trepidatious. I have been pawing over my notes and records and I am utterly certain they are still out there. They have to be, but the nagging doubt is whether I am looking for them in the right place and if so will they meet with us.

This quandary reminds me of a quote from Henry IV;
" I can call the spirits from the vasty deep."
"Aye, so can any man; but will they come when you do call them?"

Indeed, will they come when we call upon them?

(Identifying information redacted)

Date; Sunday, September, 30th. MY.26

Transcript of a discussion witnessed and recorded by Agents ▌▌▌█████████ ███████ ██████

Location; First Class Passenger's Private Chartered Waiting Room 101, Alba Central Train Station.

Time; 8.03AM   (Subject 1 arrival)   9.00 AM   (Subject 2 arrivals)

Individual subjects identified as

(Subject 1) Eleuthère Du Maurier, Industrialist, Zephyrian National

(Subject 2) Lucius A. Everheart, prospective Constable of Tremorfa, Tharsis, Naturalised Eridanian National.

Two other unidentified individuals presently believed to be subject's automaton bodyguards.

Subject spoke throughout in Zephyrian French. *Translation*

Subject 1. You read the papers this morning?

Subject 2. I did.

Subject 1. This whole thing is getting out of hand. I want the putride (?degenerate?) dandelion farmer dead, and Flammarion.

Subject 2. I rented (?hired?) a boat and crew, as you suggest. But it will be expensive.

Subject 1. Tell the Captain, I will reward him...

Subject 2. Her.

Subject 1. ... her? Oh. Then I will reward handsomely for his (?her?) trouble.

Subject 2. I have arranged a reserve, full payment, if necessary, by both parties and they can (?pick over?) choose (?) the bare bones.

Subject 1. This woman Captain can (? I?) trust?

Subject 2. Whenever one of them can, a little more than most. I know her well.

Subject 1. And as for Mr Knapp?

Subject 2. It is already on its (? his?) way to rendezvous with the ship.

Subject 1. Alone?

Subject 2. No.

Subject 1. You know what to do if I (? he?) fail me again.

Subject 2. It was not my idea to hire (? him?). I got it all by hand, but you insisted.

Subject 1. (*Indecipherable words*) I sent a team to the site.

Subject 2. The farm? Is it not a waste of time? You have more pressing concerns (?than your?) gem collection, Eleuthère.

Subject 1. (silence) (*indecipherable words*) (?It?) is important. Just make sure there are not loosen ends.

Subject 2. No loose ends. This will cost.

Subject 1. Flammarion has friends in high places, dangerously high places, and it blends (?) in my business. You must do this to stop. Whatever cost. Ransom, (?the?) journalist and Flammarion. No witnesses.

Subject 2. There will be a lot of blood spilt before you can bury it, Eleuthère. The death of a poor farmer in the dirt boondocks would not raise an eyebrow in Tharsis. The death of an academic, inventor and foreground (?). A man close to the most powerful men in Tharsis, will upset a cart-load of horse shit. And then there is the daughter of Cromie, the journalist. The journalist who has publicly blamed you. Consider, Eleuthère, do you have enough money to bury all this?

Subject 1. Do (? not?) treat me like you are my equal. You are not. Just do what I'm doing (?) you do. Or I'll find someone who will.

Subject 2. As (? like?) Knapp?

Subject 1. (*shouted indecipherable words*) Do what I (?pay?) you to do!

Subject 2. Left at 9.06AM.

Interview statement taken from Prisoner 452, Henry Avery, aka "Long Harry." On the 43rd, October. 29. Tharsis Panopticon.

Convicted crew member, "rigger," of the aerostat The Wyndeyer.

We were moored in Princess Alvilda's couloir, a defile we used to use as a hithe, about a half mile and a half out of Cowbridge Station on the 30th September, 26.

Captain Dullahan (1) she had like a meeting arranged with this fella. So we had to keep our heads down for a day or so's. Then this flyer turns up with this bloke in it. Right one he was. A bizarre little ginger cove in a huge fur coat with a huge filter helmet on his head (2). The Captain, she was like all really puffed up, full of swagger. Made him wait for half an hour before she deigned to see him. So he comes on board totting this big old portmanteau. She hurried him into her cabin and locks the doors. But a few of us know where you go to have a look-see. Anyways. She and the Quartermaster, Old Roger (3), are in there, when out of the case the toff pulls several bundles of notes. Tharsian Pounds notes, big fresh looking white tenners. Enough lucre to buy the whole damn ship, crew and all. Can't says what they talked about as she had that music box thing playing loudly to cover their words. But they was really haggling over something.

Deal was done in a few minutes. Off he went.

No, I never heard that name mentioned. Then, that is.

Captain called us all together for a chin wag. That's when she told us what we'd been hired to do.

She told us we had been offered a hiring, but not by whom, to take down some old masher's exploration ship. An easy mark as she reckoned it. We'd all receive twice our share and a bonus on completion. We'd even get our usual share of what prize, we take from the ship as normal, which would be full of clever tat. To sweeten the deal further she had some lucre to spread around. We all ayed for it.

No, she didn't give much detail. It don't usually work that way. And with the paper in me pocket I didn't give much of a thought to it anyways.

Yes, it was unusual business. But Dullahan had contracted us out before. There was good money in it.

We left the couloir about noon headed for the Valley. Captain told us we were picking up some "specialist," on route. He was the patron's factor, so we weren't to bother him.

No, the crew didn't much like the idea, but we'd taken on plenty of pilgrims, as we called them, in our time. A lot of privateers will take paying steerage, especially if the pickings have been sparse and the pilgrims is willing to pay well.

Anyways, he didn't turn out to be no pilgrim. Well, lest not what we'd expected.

(1) Identified as Colleen Ann Dullahan.
(2) Identified as Edward Roger Seegar.
(3) Identified as Eubulus Phattitude Docket.

Discovered amidst my grandfather's expedition papers. Torn in four pieces and in its original envelope.

James Ransom

Professor J. Flammarion.
By Hand.
Dear Sir,
I insist that under no comdiziton that you allow my wife Aelita to accompany in any way upon your expedition.
It is a husband's duty to protect and guide his wife in all things. And I forbid her to attend your ridiculous excursion.
She is little more than a wilful child and of a delicato fragile nature. As though she may feel she knows her own mind she is given to wild flights of fantasia.
She is not the intelletto to comprendere what dangers she is in doing such a foolish thing. Also, by her innocent comportamento, she may cause dangerous confusione and upset amongst the gentlemen upon your ship.
I will expect you to compel her and her automa, which too is my property, to return home immediately.

Yours faithfully,
Cav. Giovanni E. Fontenelli. Dr

Ps. She is not of vigorouso health and I fear she has left without her medicine.

Fontenelli.

The Diary of Eleanor Athaliah Ransom (Mrs).
Sunday 30th September.
Oh, how heavy my heart is this morning. Edwin insisted that he must join Papa on his expedition and we argued furiously into the early hours of this morning. It is not my position to tell my husband what he may or may not do. I have supported him in his every endeavour, though these times apart have caused great anguish, not just for we two, but to the children as well. Nevertheless, this is almost too much to tolerate.

I regret terribly my harsh words of last night, but how could I stand by and say nothing? Yet it did not stop Edwin from leaving with Papa this morning.

I could not attend upon their departure, for if I had, there would have, without a doubt, been an inexcusable breakdown of dignity on my part, which would have been both unseemly and discourteous to the others. So I hid in my room, feigning illness, only to watch the two most important men in my life leave on an escapade I cannot truly be sure either may ever return to me from.

My resolve deserted me at the last moment and I rushed down to the front hall in nothing more than my nightdress and Edwin's dressing gown, but I was too late to even wave them farewell. If it had not been for the presence of the children and staff I fear I would have collapsed sobbing on the threshold like some overly demonstrative Gothic heroine.

Why are men so pig-headed? So easily set upon a course of action and yet so damnably unable to change such courses? Can they not see even what is in front of their very noses? Such prideful absurdity!

So I am now deserted again. Bereft of both of them. To hold the fort. For how long, I have no idea.

I took a late breakfast with Lady Niketa. She is such a darling and she has agreed to stay with us for at least a few more days. I am so grateful to have someone to talk to. She has a level head and more experience than I could gather in several lifetimes.

Although she did not approve of Edwin leaving so abruptly, nevertheless her counsel is wise and understanding.

Strangely the chaos she and her pack of maddeningly excitable little dogs have had a great effect on distracting the children, if not the whole household, from Edwin's and Papa's absence.

It was also good to have Karl here, his calm presence is reassuring, though, after breakfast, he did little to settle my fears as he insisted that we discuss what precautions should be taken to secure the house and grounds. Carstairs told me that Papa had given him express orders to take whatever such provisions he considered necessary. In that, he had issued Papa's shotguns to Dan and Aegy, and to three of the younger groundsmen and had organised regular patrols of the gardens. The gates are to be locked and manned until further notice. Karl also insisted that we must forgo all but the most unavoidable excursions into the city.

It was difficult to agree to such things. Not only would it alarm the children, but it, I can imagine, will rapidly begin to feel as if we are living under siege.

Karl promised that as soon as Minnie and the others arrive he will be able to make better arrangements.

Just before noon, a courier arrived with a letter from Edwin. I was so relieved to receive his words, but they were no less unsettling. He truly believes that his presence here would draw the unwanted attention of Du Maurier's men to the house and that his inclusion on Papa's expedition will serve to lure them away from us. I feel so confused, I understand wholeheartedly what he is doing and why, but I want him to be here with us.

I showed the letter to Lady Niketa who she said she believes that Edwin was doing the only thing he can do in the circumstances. Though she believes it is also the safest thing he could do for himself as she doubts that Du Maurier has the resources or inclination to pursue the expedition out into the wilderness. She offered to do a reading of her crystal for me this evening. I am unsure as I do not wish to think what I will do if it foretells anything untoward.

Edwin wrote that he believes the expedition ship will return to Tharsis in only a few days to refuel and re-equip, and I shall see him and we shall make our peace.

So we spent the rest of the day securing the house. At least an hour and a half was wasted in trying to locate and account for the keys for all the door locks on the ground floor and outbuildings and the stable. Some of which I have never known to be ever locked. Oh, what a lackadaisical life we lead here! Even after the abduction of Mr Pug, how have we grown so complacent?

I have given strict instructions that no weapons shall be carried openly in the house, by anyone other than Karl, and none shall be left unattended where the children may have access to them. James is fascinated with Papa's collection, but I do not want him touching them. Children and guns are a dangerous brew.

I had the children and Nanny take dinner with myself and Lady Niketa this evening, a rare treat that I can only indulge them in when Papa's not here, but their excitement livened the meal and lifted all our spirits. Lady Niketa remarked how James grows more and more like his father in comportment and appearance every day. It has been difficult for him to grow up without his father's presence, but he does have such a similar forbearance in his manner.

Once the children were in bed and the house locked up for the night I decided I would take up Lady Niketa's offer of a reading. We adjourned to Papa's smoking room where the card table, from last night was still in place. Mrs Carstairs pulled the drapes and lit the candle before leaving us.

Of course, I have had a few readings done before, but tonight seemed so full of portent that I felt like one of the tiny moths drawn to the candle flame (or, in our case, tiny fruit flies that escape from Mama's orangery).

Lady N's crystal ball was already on the table, covered with a black satin cloth.

"I know your heart is full of doubt, my dear," she said to me. "Let us see what the crystal can help us see." She pulled away the cloth and drew close to the ball. I could see little save her reflection and that of the candle, but she gazed intently into the depths of the sphere.

Papa would say that if one stares too long into anything one will see one's own imaginings within it. Like patterns on the curtains or clouds in a sky, but I am sure as I can be that after a short while flickering images, like those of a zoetrope, did appear within the heart of the crystal. I swear that for a fleeting moment I saw Edwin's face.

Lady N began to move her hands over the surface of the ball and talk in hushed tones. "All is well. The journey goes well. Edwin is safe. I can see him. They are all well. I can see no threat in their immediate future."

I was so relieved to hear that news. When suddenly the darkened room became profoundly darker, not as if the candle dimmed, but as if some blackness had pervaded the room. I did not feel the change in temperature, but suddenly I could see our exhaled breath in the air. In my alarm, I went to speak, but Lady Niketa quickly took my hand and squeezed it firmly, a finger pressed to her lips.

We sat there for what seemed an age as something moved about the room

I cannot truly explain it. There was a presence in the darkness, huge and pervading, yet subtle and insubstantial. As if we had come under some keen awareness. The sense of being more than watched; studied. As one could imagine being closed in the darkness with a bear, one you could feel but not touch, sense but not see. I thought I caught a glimpse of whatever the presence was at the edge of my vision. A distortion, like one of those amusing mirrors one sees at a sideshow or fair, but it moved. I am sure, I heard it move, I felt the air disturbed about me, but as my eyes focused to searched the gloom, even into the inky black recesses, I could see nothing, only shadows in the darkness.

Lady N, squeezed my hand again to gain my attention and began to speak softly, intoning what sounded like a prayer. I could tell by the way she looked into my eyes, she needed me to join in, and so together, in the darkness we sat, continually repeating words that I had no idea in what language let alone what they meant, until the sensation of the manifestation left us.

"It is gone now," she said softly.

I had to ask what it was. Was it that thing that came through last night? Lady N, was reticent at first to talk, so I had to implore her to tell me. Firstly though she insisted we return to the warmth and comfort of the sitting room and take something fortifying before she would continue.

"My dear child, it is so very difficult to explain these things to the uninitiated and I can only tell you some of what I know. I am a member of the Voynich Society, we were formed several decades ago by the leading mediums, philosophers and mystics on Mars, and those that reached Mars with their minds, like Hélène Ramié, a long time before Stranger, or any Earthman, set foot upon this soil. We have taken upon ourselves the sacred duty to explore what we call the Novagnosis, the Sophia Mustikós, of the Universe. We work for the enlightenment of all mankind. We believe that through our understanding of the Novagnosis, the new knowledge, we can play an important part in guiding the future, therefore we are privy to many secret and hidden things that must stay so until the time is right for them to be shared with all mankind. To share incomplete knowledge of the Amen, the Hidden Universe, is, by far, more dangerous than to share none.

Consequently what I tell you, you must not repeat. It is not for the idle gossip of the servants or chattering ladies at tea."

I was a little taken aback that she would suspect such a thing from me, but I needed to know more and so I promised, with great solemnity, not to discuss it with any other, not even Edwin. After I had made my declaration I sat quietly spellbound as she unfolded the most extraordinary story to me. I know I agreed not share it, but I have had to write it down as the whole thing seems so incredible in its scope that it is the only way I can truly grasp what she told me.

"This may be too difficult for you to understand, but we of the Society believe that Yâho, One True God, the Pangenitor, withdrew from the Earth after he had created it, to move on to create other worlds and other heavens. Unfortunately, without His presence, other entities took control of man's destiny. You know them as the God's of the old religions, but they were all false God's. Some may call them fallen angels and devils and that sort, the creatures that inhabit the edges of Avitchi, the darkness. They crept into the material world and gained power over men's minds. On Earth, it was mankind's darkest hour.

"But cometh the age of awakening, the Golden Dawn of Mankind; mighty men of power, enlightened rulers and great thinkers, philosopher kings, who had transcended the mortal realm, arose to rid mankind of the yoke of superstition and destroy those false Gods. Their minds are now so expanded through oneness with the Universal that even though their bodies have long since fallen away, their consciousness remains. As it was on Earth it was here on Mars.

You see we in the Voynich Society understand all the worlds of men that are now free of the old God's rule were led there by The Enlightened or Great Old Ones. It is they who helped mankind cast off the old Gods, and it is they who still guide the fate of mankind."

"Are they like Angels? I asked.

"They cannot be thought of in such simple Christian values. They are neither good nor evil. They seldom interfere with mankind. Mostly they bring peace, knowledge and order, but sometimes, because they understand the future and the past far more than we can ever comprehend, their actions may seem strange and aloof, harsh even. Here on Mars are the strangest, and most powerful. Alien minds, several thousands of aeons cold."

I sat for a while, sipping my tea and trying to digest her tale. When I was ready to hear more I asked if it was one of these "Enlightened Ones" that came through at last night's séance.

"Oh, no," she answered softly. "That was something dreadfully different. My dear girl, as I said, there are many other strange beings that inhabit the Amen, most are completely indifferent to our existence. Some you may call good and some you could call evil, though such human moral designations are meaningless to them. As you might call a man who murders another man 'evil,' but what of the gardener who pours boiling water into an ant's nest and kills tens of thousands in one act? You would never think him a murderer, would you? Unless, of course, you were an ant. To some entities out there in the Virl, we are less than ants. That pneuma that came through last night was truly powerful, I have seldom encountered such malevolent intent."

So what was that thing in the room this evening? I had to know.

"That entity is what we call an Egorg Egregoroi, a Watcher. To you, I can only describe it as an elemental spirit. It was sent by a Magician, someone potent enough to bind and control it. I have encountered them before, but never one so brazen. They are usually little more substantial than the shadow cast by smoke."

My credulity was beginning to stretch too far, but I wanted her to go on, I asked how she knew it was controlled by a Magician?

"It bore a mark, a seal, of the one that sent it."

I begged to know whom?

"I believe it to have been the Zephyrian Thaumaturge, Jeteur de Sort, he calls himself Le Grand Bête. A man who sells his 'powers' to the highest bidder."

I begged her pardon, but even to me, this all sounded more like some fantastical tale Scheherazade concocted to keep her head. Such stories I would read to the children; with its djinns and magicians and all.

Lady Niketa was not at the least irritated. She sat calmly and took my hand. "Even though your mother had such interests and you have seen what you have seen, it is good, healthy even, that you find such revelations understandably difficult to accept at face value."

I had to admit that these events had indeed been extraordinarily real to me, so had those Momma had taken me along to as a child, but if consulted over breakfast the next day Papa would always be able to conceive some perfectly rational explanation. I can particularly remember the time when the celebrated society spiritualist Freddy Voleckman and his wife were exposed as frauds in the Tharsis Herald, Papa had a lot to say about that.

We talked on far too late into the night, and after such an emotionally taxing day, I was absolutely overcome by enervation. I had just made my bid to take my leave of Lady Niketa and retire, when she took my hand and pressed upon me a tiny pistol that she carries in her purse, She made me promise to keep it with me at all times.

As I have a mounting abhorrence of firearms I tried to refuse as graciously as possible, but she would hear none of it. With the most earnest of expressions, she explained that, though she prayed ardently I should never come to the point of needing it, these are truly dangerous events unfolding about us, and even I should be prepared to gird one's loins and, if necessary, to defend myself and my family.

Her intensity disquieted me so much so that I had to ask if her fears were based upon something she had witnessed in her crystal? She promised me that was not the case, though her expression belied her declarations, but she would not say any more.

So, with my mind, even more, disquieted, I came to bed.

I doubt if I shall sleep. My mind is a milkmaid's churn full of worries, and my eyes are ever drawn to the little, pearl handled, double-barrelled, pistol lying amidst the brushes and perfume bottles on my dressing table.

I dislike guns, especially those created for one purpose only, and I find it difficult even to look at, let alone touch it.

"Answer me, you who believe that animals are only machines. Has nature arranged for this animal to have all the machinery of feelings only in order for it not to have any at all?"

VOLTAIRE

DAY TWO

<u>THE STORM</u>

The Flammarion Expedition
Official Journal
31st Sept 26

Making good time. Crowded air traffic.

6.20 AM. Headwinds causing slight buffeting.

The ship's crew completed numerous drills throughout the morning. Including firing of main armaments, anti-boarding actions, fire drills and emergency descent.

We landed at 11 AM and all disembarked for ten minutes or while the crew finished their emergency landing and evacuation drills.

At breakfast this morning, Professor Flammarion advised the expedition members that the expedition now has official approval from the Government of the Republic of Tharsis. This was greeted with applause and congratulations.

The general mood of the expedition members and the crew is good.

5 PM. Sir Sydeian gave a demonstration of his single manned propulsion apparatus on the Weather Deck.

7 PM. Passed due south of Alba city to avoid congestion.

The Captain estimates arrival at Ransom's Farm, Tremorfa for approximately 6 AM given good winds.

The weather ahead good. Though rain clouds to the South East may gain on us before we reach Tremorfa.

C.L. Bryant-Drake

The Flammarion Expedition Journal of L. Edwin Ransom.

Day two. 31st. 9th. 26.

I was awoken by the crew firing off a volley from the ship's guns. Blank rounds I am assured, but every bit as alarming as the real thing. For a few seconds I must admit to having been totally discombobulated by my environs and, in my alarm, struck my head upon the frame and almost fell out of my little cot. As my wits returned I was left with the confusion as to how I had ended up in the bed in the first place. Adam's cot was as immaculately made as it had been last night. I wondered if he had returned at all or whether he had slept in it and straightened it this morning without disturbing me.

I dressed and carried out my ablutions (as best as one can do in such cramped conditions upon a moving vessel) and went in search of both a toilet and breakfast, preferably in that order. I had to queue in the little corridor outside the closet designated for the gentlemen. I passed the time in small talk with Sir John, who was in a wry sense of humour, but appeared a little worse for wear from last night's shenanigans.

Breakfast had been laid out in the saloon. All in all, I had had a good night's sleep and ate heartily in the company of Dr Spender and his daughter. They insist on informality and I am to refer to them as Octavius and Patty, I had likewise reciprocated as I do feel it is more suitable for such time as we have to spend together. Miss Bryant-Drake arrived complaining that one of the "heavy guns" is situated directly above her cabin and when it went off she was not only shocked awake, but so panicked by the noise she almost fled out onto the deck in her nightwear!

The other's filtered in over the following half hour. All except Adam. Intrigued and a little concerned, I asked the automaton steward if Mr Franklin had been down to breakfast. He informed me that Mr Franklin had taken a light repast earlier with the morning watch and was now engaged with the various drills being carried out by the crew members.

It has now been officially decided amongst the members of the expedition to refer to each other by their Christian names, all except, of course, the Colonel and the Professor. Miss Spender and Miss Bryant-Drake say they find all this formality stuffy and overbearing, and I am inclined to agree, but my upbringing will not allow me to refer to the illustrious Dr Spender by his given name.

The Professor, Colonel Jahns and the Captain joined us to announce that our expedition has been given the approval of the Government of the Republic, and we are now to consider our original purpose as official. The expedition's members and the crew were delighted and we all toasted the success of our endeavour with a glass of champagne, provided from the Captains own reserve.

I joined the Professor in his cabin and spent the morning reviewing the material that he has accumulated regarding the possible Aresian encounters over the last twenty-five years. He desired me to aid him to reanalyse the evidence with fresh eyes. Was he making an erroneous assumption or overlooking something? He insisted that I be as sceptical as possible and challenge his every deduction and assertion. Dr Spender joined us and together we played our part with the zeal of the Spanish Inquisition.

Nevertheless, the Professor is right, the evidence stands firmly upon its own foundations. His interpretation is purely logical and his conclusions are sound. If ever I doubted his assertions I do not now. The weight of the evidence is overwhelming; Aresian aethervolt ships are being regularly encountered by our aerostat and aethervolt craft. The witnesses are most often of the highest quality, Navy Captains and Commanders, in one case a Rear Admiral, and these are often not singular events. By luncheon, we had agreed that we believed, upon the evidence as is, that there must be some active base or populated settlement of notable size within the search area the Professor has identified. The Dr and I wondered that if the Government knew of the substantial weight of this evidence, why had this information never been acted upon before?

The Professor admitted he was at a loss to answer that question. Up to only a few days ago his assertions and deduction had been all but dismissed by those in authority. Sometimes with an attitude of barely concealed ridicule. He cited a letter he received last year from the office of the First Admiral, which was most caustic in its tone. It categorically rebuffed the reports by his own officers, some of high rank and standing, as unreliable and possibly delusional.

Dr Spender ventured that possibly it was a simple matter of belief; men like the First Admiral and even the President himself simply refused to believe that such a thing could be. That all we have achieved in the last twenty-five years has been on the edge of a knife blade.

At that the Professor repeated to us what the voice had said at the séance; "Foolish men and your foolish machines. The sword above your heads is ours, not yours." Although the Professor feels this is an allusion to the new aerostat, Damocles, the Dr felt it was probably more a thinly veiled threat.

Dr Spender recited the tale of the war aerobarges he had witnessed at the battle of Tyrrhena Mons massing for the final assault. They were like none he had seen before. Great biremes, triremes and quadriremes, some bigger than any he had ever seen before and in huge numbers, possibly thousands. All were flying war banners he did not recognise, and as a junior officer of the Intelligence Corps, it was his job to know every sigil and nobori of every city and every alliance. Beneath them, the red dunes were swarming with sandflyers, war machines and regiments of mounted troops. It was not a strike force as it has often been portrayed as, but an armada. He had no idea why they did not attack, or where they went, but they, to our knowledge, were never engaged, never fought, let alone defeated.

With a heartfelt earnestness, I have seldom encountered, Dr Spender assured us both that such a fleet could have swept all resistance before it. When he learnt they had not fallen upon Tyrrhena Mons he spent a dozen sleepless nights awaiting the dreadful news that they had struck elsewhere. In the decades since, he admitted, that he would have even doubted his own memories of that day if he had not kept his handwritten notes for his original report and sketches. He fetched them from his cabin to show us. Hurriedly scribbled annotations in his personal field journal weaved their way through equally rushed pencil and watercolour representations of the innominate war banners.

The Professor and Dr Spender explained to me that they use the term nobori for them, a Japanese word, for they have a similar composition, a long rectangular flag attached to its upright and supported by a top bar at 90°. Each is a mixture of geometric symbols and text, much like Ottoman war gonfalons of the Middle Ages. The complex use of colour and lettering being often as important as the text. I got a little lost in Dr Spender's use of obscure heraldic terminology, but found myself compelled to ask the most obvious of all questions; could he interpret these "nobori"?

"I have tried," he said. "But their meanings are often of high ritual significance. Something they kept traditionally secret. Even the written words are in some form of cryptography, possibly akin to medieval magical texts like 'Liber Razielis Archangeli.' I took the foundation of my research from the banners we knew that belonged to kingdoms and states we were familiar with and started from there. Bloomfield's Compendium of Aresian Heraldry, a slim but useful volume that we were all issued by the War Office, was invaluable. But in the end, it is just a compilation for identification, not translation.

"From what I managed to record," he pointed at a collection of five sketches. "These are the nobori of Royal houses, and this...," With a flourish, he flipped over the page to reveal another sketch. An intricate and detailed red banner, "That is something else. This one was displayed prominently upon a quadrireme, one of the largest four decked warbarges and upon several others. I think it might have been the nobori of an over-king."

The Professor and I both spoke the same words simultaneously; "An Imperial banner?"

"Yes. I can make the argument clearer if you wish me to fetch my copy of Bloomfield's and my other notes, but in my opinion, that is the only Imperial war banner ever recorded. The nearest to it, I could discover, now resides in the Aeolis Central Museum of Arts and Sciences; a ceremonial Imperial nobori from the Tiziraou Dynasty. It is over two thousand years old. A dynasty that, as our scholars were always led to believe, died out a millennium ago at the hands of the quasi-Empire of the Malacandrians."

"It could not be a Malacandrian banner?" I asked.

"No, most certainly not, my boy."

We simply stood and looked at each other in amazement. The Professor, who had been assiduously packing his Tyrolian struck a match and puffed it into life. "So, by what you are saying Octavius, the Aresians could have been under a Greater Imperial rule the whole time, right back to the first Earth settlers, without us ever knowing. And that Empire could be well over two thousand years old?"

"Yes. Exactly. Or, possibly, Imperial rule had been restored under a new dynasty."

We ended our postulations while we joined the others for luncheon. I was pleased to see that Adam joined us for the buffet. He was exceedingly cheery as he had been keeping busy with the crew, assisting in their drills and familiarising himself with "every nook and cranny" of the ship. After we had finished the meal Adam requested to know whom amongst our team members had military practice or felt capable with a firearm.

I admitted I hate the things but, as everyone is aware, I have had cause to become far more familiar with them than I would have wished in the last few days. Charity and Parthena both had demonstrated last night that they were dab-hands.

Aelita though questioned why we should all need such things? Her observation was that if this mission was one of peace, then why do we need so many armaments?

The Professor deferred to Captain Llewellyn, "With all due respect, Madam. I would not wish to alarm anyone of you, but, and here's the thing; you have to understand that beyond the pale of these bright cities, the laws of civilisation do not reach. Even some of the places we may have to call at are more riotous and more perilous than the most dangerous districts of Alba. Frontier communities full of desperate people and some exceptionally bad men. Out there, in the wildernesses itself, there are bandits and pirates aplenty. It is my responsibility to make certain of your safety upon my ship. To which she is armed accordingly.

"It is Mr Franklin's responsibility to make sure of your safety whenever you should have reason to leave the protection of my ship. In that even you, Madam Fontenelli, have to accept it is your duty to assist in maintaining your own personal safety."

"Poppycock!" Colonel Jahns interjected loudly. "I have six good men, well-trained veterans who served under my command and they will provide more than adequate protection for all." He pointedly gesticulated towards Adam with the vertex of a half-eaten cucumber sandwich. "This man is naught but an undisciplined guerrilla. Not fit to be trusted, let alone with the responsibilities of protecting the ladies."

Captain Llewellyn raised a hand as if in benediction to silence the Colonel's tirade. "Professor Flammarion has placed those fellows under my authority and I have placed them at Mr Franklin's disposal." The Professor nodded his agreement but the Colonel blustered and refused to countenance it. At that, Captain Llewellyn put down his tea and stood up. "Sir, those men are upon my ship. By law, as Captain of this vessel, they are thus under my ultimate authority whatever. They shall either serve as I see fit or I shall have them in irons until I can remove them from the ship. I will not have your private army running amok on my ship! Do you understand?"

The Colonel looked apoplectic with rage. His neck, from his collar to under his mutton chops, flushed angrily. I would suppose a man like Jahns has been seldom spoken to in such a way, but I had to admire him for having the good sense to keep his own counsel.

At that, Adam spoke up. "Captain, I am here only to ensure the safety of the expedition members. As the Colonel has rebuked me for, I am indeed a guerrilla fighter by experience, not a regular soldier, but I, with the support of your crew members, am more than equal to the task. I have no need for the Colonel's men above that of the role of bodyguards, which perhaps would be a waste of their undoubted skills. Maybe they would be better remaining under his command and your authority."

The Captain and Colonel Jahns remained glowering at each other. "May I suggest that their expertise would best suit a Marine role under the Colonel, who, of course, is far more experienced in such actions?" Continued Adam. "In case we do indeed encounter hostiles." Whether it was the reasonableness of his tone or the logical practicality of his suggestion, but it seemed to go some way to defusing the antagonism within the room. All eyes turned to the Captain then the Professor, who seemed bemused by it all, and then back to the Colonel.

Finally, Jahns huffed once more and said, "They are not my 'private army' Captain. They are reservists of the Olympian Highlanders, veterans, on active service under my orders." People began debating that point amongst themselves immediately but Jahns ignored them and ploughed on. "The War Office believed that official approval from the Office of Foreign Affairs of this expedition's aims was only a formality, and so, under my recommendation, they provided a military escort."

Charity asked directly; "Then Colonel Jahns, you are saying that you are still on active service?"

Jahns turned to her, "Ah, there, yes indeed, madam, I am semi-retired from official duties, but I am still attached to the Military Intelligence, the Republican Defence League."

The Professor finally stood up. "Thank you, gentlemen. I believe that I owe a debt of gratitude to Colonel Jahns. Of the few military men with access to the ear of the

President, he has been almost the only one that has taken up my cause. I must admit I was alarmed when you arrived with your men in tow, but I will ask you to forgive the Captain and me in our little deception. Nevertheless we needed to establish for what purpose you brought those chaps on to my expedition."

"What did you fear, James? That I was here to stop you?"

The Professor nodded. "Yes, Carter. That indeed was what I feared."

Jahns laughed boisterously. "Ah, there, damn it, James! How long have we known each other?"

"Longer than I would care to admit."

Jahns laughed again, and this time I was relieved that his guffaws broke the atmosphere of the room, and everyone relaxed. When the chortles had finally died down the Colonel addressed the room. "Ah, there. It is true, I am a fellow of little forbearance and even lesser imagination, a practical, if not prosaic, man. Not given to flights of fancy or wild speculations. But, I must say that I, and several of my colleagues in the League, were persuaded of the validity of James' deductions from the first time he mooted them. Since then I have personally uncovered enough evidence to convince myself that not only is he correct in his assumptions, but that there must be an imperative to our action." He now had all our attention. "We in the League and some concurrent minds in the War Office, believe that 'something' is afoot. I am not at liberty to elucidate further, but there has been an expediential growth in the sightings of what the gnomes at the War Office refer to as Anomalous Airborne Entities,

AAE's, in the area between the Cydonian Plane and Laplace Land over the last twelve months."

"Neath!" said Sir John. "It is slap bang in the middle of that area."

"Indeed," said the Colonel.

Extracts from
Beresford's History of the Martian Colonies.
3rd Edition. Milton and Dante.

Chapter 3. A New Eden; the Flora and Fauna of Mars.

Few would have expected the diversity of wildlife that existed on Mars. Most having close parallels to terrestrial life forms; birdlike creatures, various mammals, fish and insects that are analogous, or even almost identical, to creatures on Earth. All of which suggested that either some form of cross-fertilisation (v) of both planets had occurred or indeed the hand that created the green Earth created red Mars. (vi)

This was initially a happy discovery for the early explorers and pioneers. Most of the Martian flora and fauna were no more dangerous than anything encountered in their home countryside, let alone the jungles and remote territories of Earth. And most of the inhabitable lands appear to have been cleared of truly dangerous creatures by the Aresians themselves.

It was only as Tellurians moved out into the more remote areas that they encountered some of the unique and exceedingly hostile creatures that inhabited those harsh deserts, the abandoned canals and the skies above. Sholes of the deadly Maiden's Tresses, the Aresian Man-o'-War, the incredible Phrikite Nautilus, the voracious Plains Strider, the horrifying Red Sand Worms, the Sand Krakens and the Canal Sharks. Though all superficially resembling earthbound lifeforms they have no true terrestrial parallels.

For example, the Phrikite Nautilus, the Aresian Man-o'-War, the Great Parasol and Maiden's Tresses resemble sea creatures of Earth, as indicated by the names given to them by early explorers, but on Mars, they swim, not the oceans but the skies and are of vast size. Pioneers often encountered these wondrous creatures to their detriment.

As colonists finally began to expand from their established footholds on Mars into the hinterland, creating satellite communities and settlements and opening up the wilderness to wider human occupation, there was a growing need to protect their infrastructure and populations from such marauding monstrosities.

The Colonial Governments placed bounties upon the "big five" as they became known, but this brought about little effect as only the most intrepid or foolish would dare hunt such creatures. In May MY 2 during the first Biannual Intergovernmental Summit, ostensibly to settle remaining border disputes, an Extermination Directive was issued jointly by all the represented Governments. The Directive tasked all military personnel to destroy these creatures on sight unless it interfered with their specific missions. By the end of MY 4 over seven hundred Phrikite Nautiluses were recorded as destroyed, two thousand Man-o'-War, five thousand Planes Striders and three hundred and eighty Sand Krakens, most often by military firepower. Warships often actively sought out these creatures for target practice.

The Extermination Directive was rescinded by most nations by MY 8 after the Melas Canyon Incident, and other scandals, where the directive had been deliberately misinterpreted to facilitate the destruction of a large number of other indigenous life forms, including the extermination of tens thousands of aboriginal Anemoi. (iiv)
Page 192.

Notes

v. C. Derwin. 1884 The Origins of Martian Species.
vi. Bishop J. Uri Knapp. 1885 God's Almighty Hand. Meditations on the Divine Creation.
iiv. The Anemoi. Volans Lacerta Simiae.
A race of reptilianoid, hirsute and winged humanoids indigenous to Mars and Selene. Although intelligent, having, apparently, rudimentary language skills, elementary tool-making abilities and living in semi-organised extended communities, eyries, they have never been considered anything more than a lower order of sentient life. Naturally restless and, favouring cliff faces, living in some of the most inaccessible parts of the world they have never come into direct competition with human settlers over resources or access to territory. Some sub-groups were hunted to near extinction for trophies and because of unsubstantiated claims of livestock stealing. The now extirpated colonies on Selene have been attributed to deliberate conveyance by Aresians for some purpose, as yet, undetermined, though many theories abound.

The Flammarion Expedition Journal of L. Edwin Ransom.

Day two. 31st. 9th. 26.

Cont.

Sir John's seminar on the dangerous and exotic creatures of the wildernesses and Red Seas was a much appreciated diversion. His manner was not at all didactic, more like that of a raconteur or entertainer. His narration was accompanied by a hand cranked magic lantern moving picture show, a plethora of illustrations and some astounding trophies. I must say that a few of his tales often verged upon the risqué, even improper, but were simultaneously ghastly and hilarious.

His trophies included; the three foot long metallic lanceolate baculum of an immature Plains Strider that he occasions to use as a walking stick, and the crested head of an Anemoi, a type of flying lizard monkey creature that still infests the more remote gorges and canyons.

He began in earnest with the terrifying Plains Strider, a monster that glides on a cloud of ionised gas it creates beneath itself. It was one of these very horrors that my brother, Philip, died fighting when it attacked the iron miners at Mount Erebus. Not wanting to sour the tone of Sir John's presentation I decided to say nothing.

For such a huge creature, Sir John assures us, the Strider moves extraordinarily fast indeed. In fact, it is able to outrun a horse over short distances. It glides through the air by rippling flaps along its sides and attacks using a pair of fearsome mouthparts that look like legs with which it rends and tears its unfortunate prey apart. However, its real mouth is a massive disk-shaped apparatus ringed with teeth, used to crush ore and hard-bodied prey. Although really a carnivore, it often digs out and ingests large amounts of iron ore, which it metabolises into its armoured shell, otherwise the carapace would remain no harder than hippopotamus hide.

I must admit I was both fascinated and horrified by the slabs of two-inch thick armour from the carapace of one of the creatures that Sir John handed around. There were also pictures of Sir John with two or three he had downed himself. Charity asked with what could you kill such a behemoth, if it is covered with iron plate? Sir John chortled and said a few solid 3lb'ers are needed to crack the carapace, it is incredibly hard but brittle. The creature lacks much of an internal skeletal structure, so a couple of explosive rounds often finish the job.

Then, like a mischievous stage magician, with great flourish, Sir John presented us with a monstrous preserved 'head.' I believe it the most ugsome thing I have ever seen! A vile trophy twice the size of a flattened rugby ball and arrayed with teeth, pincers and antenna. This was a !D'ol, – we had great amusement pronouncing that – Sir John compounded our disgust by assuring us it was only a youngster of no more than three or four years.

The !D'ol, or Giant Aresian Red Worms, are huge, aggressive creatures found in the Northern Red Sea deserts. Some are gigantic reaching up a hundred feet long. They prefer to ambush their prey at night by burying themselves in soft, deep sand where they wait patiently for something unfortunate to happen by. It strikes with its extendable spike-tipped labium which is chock-full of razor-sharp teeth. The biggest are known to attack with such incredible speed they can cut a horse, or man, instantly in half. They are highly cunning, if not intelligent, but seemingly rely for hunting upon vibrations or disturbances in their immediate environment. To maximise their chances of success when faced with a larger or numerous prey, they can spray streams of quick hardening engleimous rheum in a wide arc, up to twice their body length, hoping to catch anything, or anyone, who happens to be in range. Some, a cave dwelling variety, have been known to use the viscous slime to form web-like structures to illaqueate the unsuspecting.

We inspected the vermillion carapaced head in the glass box with a mixture of mounting horror and disgust, as Sir John, with obvious relish, told us of his various encounters with these monsters. Including this particular one that took up residence in the latrine pit of a railway workers camp. He spared us the worst of the details, but the creature accounted for several men caught unawares, literally with their trousers down, before Sir John was called to dispatch it.

Another set of slides introduced the Aresian Sand Urchin. Even stranger still, it is another truly unique creature, with no ostensible eyes and a hidden mouth, it gives the impression of being little more than a huge, armour plated pin cushion; about five feet high with an array of three-foot spikes protruding from it. They can be recklessly aggressive and their spikes have often caused festering injuries. These things mainly graze upon the peerrohs viriditas, the red zizany, but where they are, a Plains Strider is often not far behind. Sir John told us how the miners and hunters would harpoon these creatures from aerostats, drag them out into the wastelands and use them as bait for Striders, adult Red Worms and Sand Kraken.

Then Sir John read us a piece from his latest biography;

"A Man Alone. Escapades and adventures in Amazonis."

"We were travelling across the Medusa Trough on a cool afternoon in May, the cinnabar dust was rolling across the plains to the north, and I could swear that in the distance I saw a disturbance in the clouds. At the beginning, I doubted the evidence of my own eyes, until I turned to my guide who was nearby, his hands trembling as he took down his telescope.

He swayed his head and whispered, "Air Kraken. Sir."

(We all gasped.)

"I emitted a short guffaw at the words, but was cut short as the dust cloud parted and I saw a creature more of mythology than reality. Yet very much live and before my very eyes, drifting through the air, a colossus of awesome proportions..."

He stopped cranking through a few images and then, from under a cloth on a side table he revealed what he explained to be the glossy black rhinotheca of a beak, almost fifteen inches wide and two feet long! We sat awestruck as Sir John continued on; "Ladies and gentlemen, may I introduce one of the most impressive and minacious denizens of the Martian skies; the Aresian Phrikite Nautilus." He hoisted the beak. "This monster was a good two hundred and fifty foot from the tips of its extended front tentacles to the back of its shell."

"You killed it?" asked Aelita incredulously.

"No my dear lady, we never got near enough to that one to try to take her down, and she was a big one, bigger than this, biggest I have ever seen. This, though, is from one I found in the desert several years ago, it had been downed by some truly heavy ordinance. Probably military as they had not gone after it for trophies."

"Maybe they were too damaged themselves," suggested Adam.

Sir John paused. "Yes, possibly."

"They attack airships?" Parthena asked as she examined the rhinotheca.

I caught an odd look pass between Adam and Sir John before he answered, "Possibly yes, there have been some unsubstantiated claims that truly big ones have attacked smaller aerostats and dirigibles."

From one of his many boxes and cases, Sir John produced several small flat pieces of what looked like fantastically coloured precious stone. He handed them to the ladies first who cooed over their beauty. He revealed that these were shards of the shell of the fallen nautilus.

"They are such wondrous creatures, they superficially resemble the nautilus of the oceans on Earth, and no doubt, somewhere along the line they are somehow related, but nothing their size, let alone their ability to fly, ever existed on Earth." He explained that the creature metabolises phrikite like the Strider does iron ore, although no one is sure exactly how they up take the mineral. It produces a gaseous vapour within itself and uses it to fill the chambers of its shell creating buoyancy like a dirigible. The creature itself superficially resembles a cross between the terrestrial squid and the nautilus from which it takes its common name. The creature can, as some squid back on Earth, change, even pulsate, colour across its body and even the shell, giving it a chameleon-like ability to hide in plain sight. Though their favourite lair is within thunderclouds. The hood and shell can not only change colour at will, but is almost entirely made up of metabolised phrikite which is stimulated by the lightning in the thunderclouds. Sir John explained that these monsters can fly both forward and backwards and attack either using their tentacles or by ramming their prey. They have other nasty tricks such as creating a cloud of thick black vapour around themselves and are able to discharge powerful blasts of atmospheric electricity.

He introduced us to what he quite rightly believes to be the most dangerous monstrosity of them all; the Aresian Sand Kraken. Another colossal ambush predator, akin to the octopus of Earth's seas. It is said these creatures can be hundreds of feet long and 'swim' through the deep sand

and dust of the Red Seas like their Telluric cousins swim through water. Though they are probably no closer relative to the octopus than the Phrikite Nautilus is to the nautilus of Earth's oceans.

We digressed a little into a debate on the subject of the approximations of such names. Though numerous Martian creatures and plants resemble, sometimes closely, those of Earth, mostly – we were assured by the Professor – they bare no provable connexion. "The fauna and flora of Mars are unique to the Martian environment and none of these creatures actually have any connection with creatures found on Earth." He said authoritatively. "Explorers and adventurers, upon encountering these exciting new creatures, and not being in any way experts in such things, simply labelled them in a perfunctory manner based upon cursory and often superficial semblances. Much like the Prattan which took some time to shake off the label of 'Martian Sabre-Toothed Tiger.' Being it is not even a feline, though, particularly cat-like, the ferocious creature is, in fact, a kind of marsupial, more like, but certainly not akin to, the thylacine of the Australian continent."

Sir John moved on with images of the Sand Kraken. Though the images only showed us parts, mainly huge limbs, and anatomical illustrations from books. One photographical image showed a dismembered tentacle, impossibly long and as thick as the height of the men standing beside it. That particular leviathan evidently had been dynamited out of its lair, the ruins of its body parts scattered about a huge crater. In another picture, a crowd of navvies and well-dressed officials were gathered around a huge eye, the size of a pouffe, as one old man in a top hat poked at it with the point of an umbrella.

After a short break for refreshments and to take some air, Sir John introduced us to the Aresian Man-o'-War and the other high altitude "jellybirds" as he calls them. The Man-o'-War and its kin are so similar to their namesakes found in Earth's oceans that in some respects they are identical, suggesting strongly a common origin, in his opinion. The major differences being, of course, these creatures, when they grow to enormous sizes, no longer inhabit the seas and canals of Mars but the skies. Much like their Earth counterparts, they are not aggressive, but are highly dangerous, especially the Aresian Man-o'-War, because of their lethal discharges.

He went on to discuss various other less impressive, but equally dangerous creatures and plants that we might see or encounter on the expedition, but as he was closing Adam asked the most pertinent of questions; "What, Sir John, is the true chance of us encountering any one of these animals? Truly, without actively hunting them or seeking them out, what are the odds?"

Sir John appeared to muse upon the question for a moment before answering, "Quite remote really. Of these creatures I mentioned, I would say that the jellybirds are the creatures we are most likely to actually see, but Llewellyn is an exceedingly experienced and knowledgeable Captain and will easily avoid encountering their shoals. Of the others, well, most were already rarely encountered before the first Tellurian settlements were established here on Mars, and, as a threat, are now, thankfully, virtually extinct."

The news was greeted with some great relief by all.

After a light tea and taking some air, I took the time to talk with Adam. It was good to have the chance to spend some time in his company, his demeanour has somewhat changed over the last couple of days; he gives the impression of being by far more relaxed. He put it down to having some responsibility, a purpose in life. We nattered like two old ladies in a Corner House about last night's dinner and his exchanges with the Colonel, a man he dislikes strongly. He told me that he has used the fictitious background that I suggested to good effect. Strangely I was rather pleased. Though, in truth, I must reflect upon the fact that if a man like Adam had been with my uncle then he might just still be alive to this day. We also discussed the question of the Professor's request for Adam to watch over Sir John and Aelita Fontenelli. Although their behaviour has been in no way unacceptable, Adam told me he finds being close to Aelita unsettling. I presumed to understand, suggesting that the presence of an Aresian might be too much for him to tolerate being he is still unaware of who he really is, let alone the events that brought him to such a low ebb. He waved me silent and clarified the point he was trying to make; he has felt a great attraction to Mrs Fontenelli, almost uncontrollably so. His disdain and aloofness towards her is nothing but an act, a method of creating a distance between them from the fear of making an utter fool of himself.

Smitten! I might have laughed if he had not been so desperately earnest. I promised I would talk to the Professor and take him off such duties, of course, without mentioning his predicament.

We returned to the wardroom for Dr Spender's briefing regarding the proposed investigation of the Aresian tomb on my land.

I must say I am extraordinarily excited by the prospect, not least about seeing my own home from the air. The Captain has agreed he will allow me to collect a few things from the house while Dr Spender, Parthena, Sir John and the Professor investigate the tomb itself. The Dr has brought along a picturegraph apparatus, a Maddox camera, that he has asked Charity to record the event with. She is most eager to try it out.

As the Seren Bore will be nearby, the Colonel's men will look after the team members and crew until Adam and I return.

What I thought would be a simple procedure looks to be anything but. Dr Spender will enlist several crewmen in excavating the site to establish if it is a tomb and if it is indeed undisturbed.

If it is undisturbed the Dr must, by law, secure the site and alert the Tharsis Bureau of Antiquarians. He expects that, as protocol dictates, he will be appointed Director in charge of any official excavation. If it is indeed a tomb, but has been disturbed, then we are free to investigate more thoroughly.

Whatever the decision, there will be a great deal of measuring, drawing and recording to be done. Aelita has volunteered her artistic skills, she evidently is no mean watercolourist and sketch artist.

As for myself, I am torn between earnestly hoping it is a unique and unsullied discovery of great importance and wishing, like an eager child at Christmas, to open it up and discover what magical things lay within. I have secured a promise from the Dr that if it definitely is to be opened, he will await my return from the house.

After Dr Spender's briefing, those interested were invited up onto the Weather Deck to see a demonstration by Sir John of his single manned propulsion apparatus. He says he has adapted it from a German built, Benz and Cie, rocket pack used by the Thylian Rocket Troopers. Over thirty years old now, and extensively modified by Sir John himself, he extolled the virtues of the apparatus's durability and reliability over more modern imitations.

The Colonel, who had come along, as he said, "Out of interest," argued that the Royce Skyrocket was by far a superior machine. Sir John agreed that the Royce was indeed lighter and more manoeuvrable but was really designed for Marines dropped from aerostats directly into the fray. than for long range or high altitude use.

In truth, though, as he had to concede, there is little of the original apparatus left, as Sir John has comprehensively redesigned the machine to his own specifications. His adaptations are mainly to facilitate his hunting and explorative exploits. He then treated us to a demonstration of its capabilities and his own skills in flight.

He took off, carried out some breathtaking balletic manoeuvres, circumnavigated the entire aerostat and landed with pinpoint accuracy before us.

He claims that with his modifications he is able to fly up to 6000 feet and 50 miles without refuelling, an operating range of 25 miles at a maximum speed of 60 miles an hour. I found myself so in awe that I had to question him thoroughly over dinner later. It would seem he relies upon a blend of super-refined Tarax with additions hydroxide of phrikite and a couple of "other ingredients" that he promised, with a knowing wink, to tell me of in private. The power centre is an Aresian Radium Coalescing Interaction device he salvaged from "somewhere." Another wink.

The ladies were delighted and Parthena pleaded to be allowed to have a go. Though apparatus without thrust is quite a substantial weight she shouldered it manfully – womanfully, I should say – and with little instruction from Sir John, she rose several feet and kept up with the Seren Bore's momentum. We all applauded delightedly.

Parthena made Sir John promise to teach her to use it properly and, in good spirit, he did. Though, of course, contingent upon her father's agreement.

Sir John showed us the various other pieces that make up his flying kit, his armoured panoply of leather and metal and a truly fearsome helm into which an airflow is pumped, that allows him to push the boundaries of both speed and altitude. He then introduced us to his beloved 'Betsy,' the gun he had built from his own designs. A hefty brute of a thing, powered from this flight apparatus. It launches over a mile, up to 24 superheated iron jacketed rounds, each with a core of mercury or molten lead. With his usual ebullient yet wry humour, he told the graphic tale of blasting his way out of a Reaver's ambush in the Myrmidon's with 'ol' Betsy,' and the damage she wrought upon all that got in his way.

The Colonel seemed extremely interested in 'Betsy,' and later queried whether Sir John would ever wish to discuss the gun's design and capabilities further? I noticed a gleam of something cunning in the Colonel's eye.

At the Captain's invitation, we partook of some light refreshments on the fantail to watch the sun set over the stunning landscape and the far lights of Alba city's suburbia that sprawls out of the caldera of the extinct volcano to our North. Behind us, to the South East, there is a colossal onrushing storm front pursuing us off the Northern Plateau. The Captain advised us that the storm will either peter out or overtake us, probably as we arrive at our destination tomorrow.

We remained to watch in awe as the sky fully darkened and the storm on the horizon displayed its ferocity in light and sound.

I suspect it, as so many such wet storms do, swept up from the Bulge, the Southern Plateau, over the mountains and Tharsis itself, and now would, as the Captain so rightly predicted, either die out on the plateau or be channelled between Olympus' towering walls, and cooling waters of the Alba's canals and fossae, to follow us through to Tremorfa Province.

If it does, it might cause us numerous inconveniences for our plans tomorrow, and I dread what damage its winds may wreak on my plantation. Still, I could only stand transfixed by the sonorous clamour of the boiling thunderheads and the menace of the lightning prowling the horizon.

I hope Nelly and the children did not get too frightened by the storm's passing and it does not leave too much damage in its wake. Though a wet storm is always less egregious out here than the dry storms that blow in from the West or far North.

Dinner was pleasant and, as I mentioned, I had time to talk to Sir John about his flying apparatus and the modifications he has made, his attention though, was drawn to more flirtatious dialogue with the ladies, Aelita and Parthena, than with my dry engineering inquiries. Though he did offer to show me how to fly the contraption. I declined respectfully, as my natural acrophobia is let alone challenged enough by being aboard this ship.

During our after dinner drink and cigars in the wardroom, Adam broached the subject of the safety of expedition members again. This time should there be any of a number of emergencies. He ran through them; an emergency abandoning the ship, preparing for a forced crash landing, a fire on board, and even, God forbid, an attack upon the ship. Much of his advice to the expedition members was simply to do exactly as either common sense or crew members instruct them to do. He belaboured the point that at the site tomorrow, though Dr Spender was in charge of the archaeological investigations, expedition members must not meander or go off alone for any reason, and, should anything untoward transpire; must do precisely as the Colonel's men instruct them. Which, in most probability, will be to return to the ship post-haste.

Afterwards, I was invited to join the Captain, the Colonel and Dr Spender in a few hands of whist. The others engaging in conversation, reading or excusing themselves for early rest.

We were about to begin our second rubber when suddenly the Captain put down his cards and asked to be excused. "It would appear that that storm has caught up with us earlier than I expected." He then hurried off.

I must say for myself that I had not noticed any indication of such, but, of course, the Captain has far better senses for such things than someone like myself.

The Colonel huffed at the departure of his partner. "I think I'll turn in then. Before it gets too choppy to sleep."

At that, we all bid each other a good and sound night's sleep before heading off to our respective cabins.

I must say that the strength of the wind and rain on the deck was surprising. As I had been so oblivious to it only minutes before.

I made it back to the cabin, a little damper and more windblown than expected but ready for my rest.

The storm is now growing in intensity and buffeting the ship quite noticeably. I shall endeavour to get some sleep now as to slumber through the worst of it, hopefully. At least it will have exhausted itself by morning.

The electrificated lighting system has been turned off, no doubt due to the dangers of attracting the lightning, though I do prefer to write by oil lamp, and so I shall leave the lamp lit for Adam, as he has still not yet appear

Edwin Ransom.

Journal of Adam Franklin.

Strange day.

Up at Five AM. I left Edwin still snoring in his cot. Quick breakfast of tea and biscuits with the crew and spent until midday running drills. The Captain and Mr Charles train these men well.

We landed the ship for ten minutes to run an evacuation drill. Crew excellent, but organising the expedition members is like herding confused geese. Dr Spender being the worse. The Professor also saw no reason to partake until Mr Charles personally ordered him off the ship.

Evidently our expedition to find the Professor's lost Aresians now has official approval from the Tharsis Government. Whether that means anything or not is yet to be seen.

Before luncheon, the Professor summoned me to his cabin. He and Captain Llewellyn wanted me to know that they had shared misgivings regarding the personal armed retinue the Colonel had brought aboard with him. They believed them to possibly be mercenaries. Both agree the Colonel is a good fellow, but why would an officer "retired" from the service require an armed escort? The Professor feels that allowing them to stay upon the ship is to place the determination of any outcome into the Colonel's hands.

They asked me for my thoughts. I told them that I believe the Colonel is in no manner "retired from service" and that the men are not mercenaries, but most probably regular army, highly experienced veterans, but still in service.

The Professor was no more relieved at that news, but could understand it now in light of the communiqué received this morning.

They enlisted me in a deception to be played upon the Colonel, more to see which way he jumps. At luncheon, the issues would be brought up and the Captain would challenge Colonel Jahns directly over the question of authority. If our suspicions were right Jahns should come clean and at least go some way to admitting the truth. If not, I was to have twelve crewmen and the

Master Gunner armed and ready to arrest Jahns' men immediately.

As it was, luncheon went well, and though Colonel Jahns became rather irascent when challenged by Captain Llewellyn. He did admit to the truth, as I expected him to; he and his men are here to ensure that the Government's interests are met. He knew from his contact in the various ministries that the Professor's expedition would get the blessings of those on high, especially once it was underway, at his own cost. Thus he and his men, were here to "protect" the expedition.

I found it enlightening that once the Colonel has fessed up they were all so ready to happily accept the presence of the soldiers on board. These Tharsians have an apparent trust in authority that I find perplexing. After such a bitter struggle for freedom against the colonial powers and a violent revolution, they were still inherently, well, British about it all.

Jahns does not like me at all. He sees me as some sort of irregular. And he seems to despise me for it. I must admit I find it amusing, as it is the part I am playing, but for him, a traditor to the Crown and the Empire, to feel so haughty to look down on someone he believes to be a partisan. I never betrayed my oath.

Somewhere in the back of my mind the Sergeant Major constantly questions whom it is that I now serve? I do not know. My employer? My friend? Myself? Do a dead man's loyalties really matter? Do they not go to the grave with him? I certainly do not serve Tharsis, a Government made up of men like that damn traditor Jahns.

In the afternoon, as a diversion, I attended Sir John Sydeian's much-vaunted seminar on the more fearsome wildlife of the Red Seas. I listened courteously, though often resisting an amused chortle. He was an engaging speaker and, though most of it was entertaining nonsense, his self-aggrandizing was tempered by humour and a sardonic wit.

It was also my first opportunity to watch closely the interactions of Sir John and Aelita Fontenelli. This afternoon, and this morning during the disembarkation exercise, they seem to be a great deal more reserved towards each other. Madam Fontenelli's behaviour is almost withdrawn, although she did enliven during the seminar itself.

Afterwards, I took the opportunity to share some of my misgivings with Edwin, especially my difficulties with the task of observing Aelita Fontenelli and Sir John.

(The Purser, Mr Grant, advised me that Sir John did not sleep in his cabin last night.)

Dr Spender explained what his aims were in investigating the tomb, if we indeed find it. I, on the Professor's orders, will be escorting Edwin back to his home to collect some personal belongings, and leaving the guarding of the Archaeologists to the Colonel's men.

It would seem that if it is an intact tomb, then we will get no chance to investigate it, so we are left hoping that it is not intact, but that will probably mean it has been thoroughly looted and of little interest. Edwin admitted to me just before dinner that Dr Spender's news was disappointing.

Sir John has brought with him a single manned rocket propulsion device that he says he has used often in his escapades into the wilderness. It is a Thylian Rocket Trooper's apparatus, probably 35 years old or more, which he has tinkered extensively. For all his bravado he is a man of an inestimable nerve, to be flying about in that thing is tantamount to playing Russian roulette with a reservoir of fuel strapped to your backside. I was immensely engaged to see Miss Spender insist her way into having a go. She even flew a few feet.

The young women of this age are beguiling, independently spirited and forthright. If there is any one single thing that makes me glad that I have "returned" to see these days it is that, it is a pleasure to see. They remind me of the women of the frontiers, especially the settlers' wives, who were a match for any of their men.

Dinner was interesting. I spent most of it avoiding the Colonel's watchful glare while trying not to appear to be observing Sir John's flirtatious behaviour with Madam Fontenelli and Parthena Spender. I am beginning to question the validity of whether he is indeed the rapacious libertine, he presents as, or if it is all some kind of act. Interestingly, of the two, I presume eligible, young women aboard, Charity and Parthena, Sir John shows no interest at all in engaging Charity in any way. Though Charity and Parthena Spender do seem to be drawn to each other's company. I am managing to control my own enthralment with Mrs Fontenelli, as, when in her company, I am forced to play a disdainful role.

After dinner, I had a chance to talk with the whole expedition team regarding what to do in the case that something problematic happens tomorrow. As I have been tasked to escort Edwin back to his home tomorrow I will not be readily available to supervise. I calculatingly ran through some of the possible incidences that could possibly occur while I was away. My real motive, however, was to emphasise to them all, that in the event of an incident, all expedition members were to remain calm, follow their common sense and do exactly what the Colonel's men instruct them to do. (I tried to be as diplomatic as possible, but had to point out that Du Maurier was probably far from finished with Edwin, and his men were still at large.) I also reiterated that they must not wander away from the site or the ship at any time, and if for some reason they are separated from the others, they must do everything possible to return to the safety of the ship immediately. For once the Colonel made approving comments in supporting my advice.

The storm we noticed earlier has now caught up with us and, though our ship is still making good headway, we are being battered about a bit by some enormously strong winds. Due to the threat of lightning strike, the electrificated lighting system has been switched off. I have been furnished with a hurricane lamp to write by.

Miss Andromache Spender.
180 Merchant Street.
Ilgenfritz.
Syria.
Ophyr Province.
Tharsis.

Dear Andi,

I hope this finds you well, beloved sister. What adventures we have embarked upon! I have such delightful news.

Father is well and you are always in our prayers. He assures me that he is taking his medicines regularly. They seem most efficacious, more so than the previous prescription. Although he is exceedingly enthusiastic about the possibility of finding an intact tomb, I am managing to keep him from becoming too agitated.

The other team members of our coterie are extremely interesting. As I wrote about Professor Flammarion, that old windbag Colonel Jahns and the beautiful Madam Fontenelli before, so, of them, I shall not bore you further.

I have now met Elinor Ransom's husband, Edwin. A pleasant, but quietly spoken, studious gentleman, apt to stumble over his words when he gets too enthusiastic. Not at all what I expected. I am surprised that he has survived the reported attempts on his life. Well books and covers, as Mr Tulliver said.

Edwin has brought along his friend, Mr Franklin. Mr Franklin has had some terrible injury to his face, which renders his visage somewhat less than divine, but his demeanour is more virtuous. I have never encountered a military man with such excellent etiquette. Though I took him to be taciturn upon our first meeting, he is erudite and courteous in his statements. He has taken on the duty of seeing to our safety when we are not on the ship and I have total faith in his abilities. My new friend believes he is the most courageous man she has ever known.

Sir John Sydeian is a revelation! Not at all as I would have expected. He is fascinating, dauntless and entertaining, often to the point of audacious. He gave us a seminar on the more horrid denizens of the wilderness (Though I must admit some of his assertions were flamboyantly embellished) which was exceptionally good fun.

Do you remember our encounter with the red worm in the Altoura ruins, Lybia? I doubt either of us has ever run so fast in our lives!

Sir John though, has raised a few eyebrows due to the lavish attentions he is showering upon Aelita Fontenelli. If I did not know she was married (Though I shall, in circumspect, not affix "happily,") I would suspect Sir John of setting his cap firmly in her direction. Oh, what delicious manoeuvring! As I have told you, her husband is a bumptious Latin bore, much older than herself, who, indeed, as rumour has always suggested, keeps her under lock and key as if she were a curio in his cabinet. She has shown such spirit joining our adventure, apparently against her husband's most fervent wishes.

Sir John also gave a demonstration of his flying apparatus. Yes, of course, I had to have a go at it myself. It took some imploring, but he did relent and allow me to fly just a little. It was so exhilarating that I almost forgot to breathe! For a moment I imagined I tasted what it would be like to be a bird in the air. It was an utterly magnificent sensation. I have secured a promise from him that he will teach me to fly the machine properly. What fun that will be.

I have one other piece of news. Something wonderful. I have met someone special, aboard the ship. Her name is Charity Larissa Bryant-Drake, she is twenty-two years of age, a journalist from the city of Alba. We have become firm friends in such a short time. We share many of the same interests and persuasions. She even rides a monowheel! She has the loveliest auburn tresses and the brightest viridescent eyes that sparkle with mischievous humour in any light. She tells me that her parents were of Irish extraction which is where she obtains her colouring, her wry wit, as well as her abiding sense of justice. Her stepfather is Dr Robert

Cromie, the Xeno-anthropologist, who you will no doubt have read about.

Charity has such a courageous indomitable spirit, she makes me feel like a giddy child in her presence and she is also so kind. She is a journalist and occasional private investigation agent, which is absolutely exciting stuff. We have already spent many hours together talking, it is so good to finally find someone with whom I can be completely honest. As she is with me.

I feel these days upon this expedition may be the happiest in such a long time.

Give my love to Philip, tell him not to worry, we are in extremely safe hands.

I so wish you had been well enough to accompany us. There is already so much I would have wished for you to have seen. Father brought the Maddox with him and Charity has offered to help record pictures of all our exploits, so we shall have lots to show you and Philip upon our return.

All my love, your adoring sister,

Patty.

Journal of Adam Franklin.

The storm has overtaken us. It is now midnight and the winds and rain are buffeting us remorselessly. I have no idea how the Captain can hope to make headway in this, let alone stay on course. I could feel us climbing earlier but, in the last few minutes, I can feel we are losing altitude.

Half past Midnight.

The Purser, Mr Grant, informed those of us still in the wardroom that the Captain has decided that it is too dangerous to try to ride out the storm. Due to the enormity of the weather front, the ship has been unsuccessful in attaining enough altitude to rise above it, even if we started to dump ballast we are too burdened. Therefore he has made the decision to ground her. By that, he means to find as sheltered a location as possible, drop the ground anchors and wait out the storm.

The Professor and the Captain have made the decision not to arouse the other expedition members as it is probably best they remain calm and in their cabins.

Ten to One. A.M.

On the bridge the discipline was exemplary, but the air was thick with palpable anxiety. Nervous faces glanced up from the instruments, their eyes watching for the merest signal from their Captain. Up there, with the great panoramic viewing windows, the tempest was truly awesome to behold.

The storm is growing so fierce that it is difficult to find a good location to drop anchor. The pyrolytic gas-powered search beams were not strong enough to penetrate the rain and the inky darkness. A consultation in hushed voices in the corner of the bridge established there were only two alternatives, if we were to land; flying blind this low to the ground in hopes of an opportune moment presenting itself, before disaster strikes, or reinitiating the Davy de la Rue system in a thunderstorm and risk attracting a direct lightning strike that could knock us out of the air altogether. The Professor was no daedalist and could make no clear decision. The Captain shook his head in frustration. "Damned if we do, damned if we don't."

I offered my penny-worth. A thought that came to me earlier when they had ordered the Davy-Rue shut down; when we came aboard the Professor stated that the electrical accumulators and storage apparatus the ship uses for powering the copper-phrikite plating is based upon the St. Elmo energy harvesting array that the old lightning gatherers used.

"That's the problem, Mr Franklin; we do not need extra electronic power. Our batteries are full." Llewellyn growled back at me. "We need a way of earthing the ship, and we have no earthing cables long enough. To go lower would not be to court disaster, but to invite it."

"And a direct lightning strike could blow the entire electrical system or blow the plating right off the hull."

I let us all take a breath before I explained my idea. "Turn on everything, every light, not just the external Tasker lights. Every electrificated apparatus on board. Put as much drain on the batteries as possible."

"We would attract the lightning like a copper rod!" Blustered the Professor.

"But are we not exactly that already, with all that copper plating below us?" I explained. "Tether your earthing cables to the accumulator system and the Faraday net. If, as you fear, we draw a direct lightning strike there should be enough resistance in the system to stop overloading, replenish the batteries, and disperse the rest over the Faraday net."

"There are reasons why what you are suggesting is illegal, Mr Franklin." Llewelyn glared at me.

"Yes, Captain there is. But we are not doing it to harvest energy. We are doing it simply so we can get a look at the ground."

We were shouting now, not in anger, but over the roar of the storm.

"It is still putting everyone's lives in danger, Sir."

"They already are, Captain, and once you turn on those electromagnetic manoeuvring rotors for landing you might as well turn everything else on anyway."

"He is right," said the Professor.

"I know," agreed the Captain with a sigh. "Have you done this before, Sir?"

"Yes, Captain."

"Did it work?"

I replied honestly, "I think so."

He shouted orders across the deck that were greeted with "aye, ayes" from the crew and relayed down speaking tubes to the engineers in the bowels of the ship.

One o'clock A.M.

I kitted myself out in a crew member's foulies, I purloined a second set and awoke Edwin. How he could sleep through this I had no idea. A clear conscience, no doubt, but I knew he would not wish to miss such excitement.

I raised him and set him to officiate over the task of rigging the earthing cables to the batteries and Faraday net. After my explanation he looked at me with bleary-eyed disbelief, and mumbled something about the fact I was every bit as insane as he had always suspected, He chuckled, slapped my shoulder, dressed and set off to find the Chief Engineer.

Fifteen minutes past One A.M.

I had joined the hands on the exposed decks. The Master Gunner had set me the task of spotter for the forward harpoon grapple. The shout went up and the Davy-Rue system came on, the ship lit up like one of those paper lanterns, and I found myself hanging over the rail resembling some demented whaler searching for prey. I suddenly realised how "alive" I felt. A ridiculous statement, I appreciate, nonetheless out there, in the teeth of the howling wind and driving rain, I felt wonderfully invigorated. Since the incident at Clerval Street, I have slept well, hardly troubled by nightmares, though Aelita Fontenelli seems to haunt the corridors of my dreamlands. I cannot remember feeling so hale and hearty.

The lightning wasted no time in finding us. We were struck high on the balloon itself, but thankfully it was weak. A second strike lit up the night around us, but missed the stern by what seemed only feet.

It was in that fraction of a second that I, and the grapple crew, saw the other ship.

She had no navigation lights and was running dark, less than five hundred yards to our starboard and a good hundred feet above us. An aerostat almost as big as the Seren Bore, but sleeker, more contained. The grapple crew swore oaths of disbelief that anyone should be so foolish to fly so close in this weather, and without lights? As I saw realisation dawn on their faces, I pulled the young Tasker light operator off his station and told him to inform the Captain, and only the Captain.

Within a few minutes Grant, the Purser, was by my side shouting in my ear; "Most of the crew on the starboard had spotted her. Not to panic, it's probably just another ship blown off course." I emphasised the lack of lights, not even running lights. He nodded, "Could indeed be privateers, but they will not try anything in this weather." He finished speaking, gave me a cheery grin and stepped away into the path of an incoming shell that tore his entire right shoulder off. I watched the shock of realisation cross his face as he tried to say one last thing to me before he fell dead.

I shouted to the crew to man their posts as I ran for the Picaro. The gun crew were already struggling to get the pallings off it when I got there. I wasted no time. I ripped the covers off, loaded the magazine as fast as I could and prayed for the next blaze of electricity to light up the sky. I did not have to wait long. We took a direct hit from the lightning, the water around us effervesced and steamed, the system held, and I eyed our pursuer clearly once more.

I have no idea whether their shot that killed the Purser was by more luck than judgement in these conditions but I had no such *concerns. I felt the strange invigoration of the Sergeant Major's fury resurfacing in me. I levelled the Picaro, balancing her for our yaw and wind resistance. The Sergeant Major knows these guns well; they kick to the right and up, the explosive's shells I had loaded her with tend to deviate left and down by around 2° more than standard over a hundred yards. Always squeeze the trigger in a fluid motion, hold then release. Everything seemed to slow into a dream like state. I pulled the trigger rapidly and sent eight 3ld explosives hurtling towards the other ship's superstructure, my aim was guided by where the Sergeant Major's voice told me their bridge would be.*

I could no longer see their ship, but I could see the impacts. I felt the cold pleasure that I had made their taking Mr Grant's life cost them dearly.

The Gunnery Master had drilled the crew well, they had the gun loaded again quickly enough for me to fire off another eight standards in quick succession, this time aiming for the centre of the blurry silhouette still imprinted on my vision. A stab in the darkest of dark, I knew, but worth it even if only a couple of shells found their mark.

We waited nervously, dreading and praying for the lightning to return. Suddenly it did, three bolts in rapid succession, stalked out across the sodden night shrouded landscape, but there was no black silhouette of the Reavers' ship to be seen.

Quarter to Two A.M.
The crew fired off their harpoon grapples and dropped the land anchors. With extraordinary exactitude, the manoeuvring rotors took us down to what must be only twenty feet above the ground. Here we are in the lee of a heavily wooded elevation that provides us with some small shelter from the prevailing winds and driving rain.

I stayed at the gun until the Master Gunner ordered me to stand down. I went to find the Captain and the Professor. I found them on the bridge, along with Edwin.

We talked about what had happened in the night. Edwin was sure the pirates were hunting us, probably in the pay of Du Maurier. The Professor was not so convinced; Du Maurier is ruthless, yes, but to go as far as to let loose such hounds upon us? To the Professor it seemed an unlikely venture. Pirates like that are not free to hire out like chimney sweeps or washerwomen. The Captain felt that it was just as likely that we simply surprised a ship up to something nefarious by suddenly lighting up like that, and that they thought we were stalking them. Though what any privateer is doing within this proximity to Alba is questionable.

I listened carefully. It was true that we may have surprised them as much as they surprised us, and that is maybe why they loosed off a few pot-shots at us and fled. Nonetheless they had hardly changed heading when I had my chance to take my crack at them. As for hiring out like some country beaters, yes, I believe some do indeed sell their services as mercenaries. So I had to agree with Edwin, there is good cause to assume that this may indeed be the work of Du Maurier.

We stood in silence for a while, sipping tea and lost in our own thoughts. When the Professor finally spoke it was much as I expected; "Captain, I want you to tell the crew not to speak of this incident to the expedition members or in their presence. I do not want them alarmed, especially the ladies. Should they ask then tell them Mr Grant was tragically killed by accident during the storm, a harpoon charge missed fired or some such. I believe that any damage can be patched up and attributed to the storm. I shall talk to the Colonel and apprise him of the true situation. Mr Franklin, Edwin, I am going to trust in your discretion in this matter. The crew will remain on highest of alerts in case the blighters should return for whatever reason motivates them. I believe, Mr Franklin, from what I hear, whatever their motive for attacking us, that you may have given them cause for reconsideration should they think of confronting us again."

"The gunfire?" I asked.

"Firing off flares and the harpoons," replied the Captain. "Hopefully they will not have heard much over the thunder and

anyway, if they did sleep through that storm, I doubt if a few cannon shots would have disturbed them!" We all nodded solemnly. Captain Llewellyn pointed out that the Seren Bore was hit two other times, luckily suffering nothing major, but a full inspection and repairs may hold us here for at least a day. We grounded just after dawn.

Interview statement taken from Prisoner 452, Henry Avery, aka "Long Harry" on the 43rd, October. 29. Tharsis Panopticon.

Convicted crew member, "rigger," of the aerostat The Wyndeyer.
Cont.

Night of the 31st? No. Wasn't us.

We was nowhere near them by then. Captain Dullahan hated flying in storms, even when there was urgency about it. So's we grounded the Wyndeyer.

The Shenandoah.

No, a Free Trader. Didn't have the guts for much other.

Running contraband out to Cebrenia. Charlie "Sea Sick" Frankston was the Captain back then, scared of his own shadow but he was a storm chaser.

Afeart of getting caught so would fly nights and ground up during daylight if he could. She was a good ship, fast for a hand bomber, but they blow more smoke than a buffer in the head.

You find plenty of holes to hide in on a regular route. He preferred flying in bad weather.

Thought the Seren Bore was a Preventer an' started firing out of panic.

Got more than he bargained for though. Got raked up pretty bad.

Think he lost four or five crew. In his panic, he dived and clubhauled the ship to get out of range.

Ripped a kedge right out the starboard and almost wrecked her. Splinters flying through the wheelhouse took the old wandrought's eye out.

Couldn't help them much though. No time and our "Passenger" was having none of it either.

Anyways, best for them. They were ducked and them being only runners. The Shenandoah didn't carry much other than a couple of ancient old Armstrong's.

Dullahan, was a merciless bitch, if we'd been free to, she'd have snuffed old Sea Sick's candle and had the crop in a trice.

No. As I said; we didn't layover. Just long enough for our sawbones to hav' a look at their Captain and the other wounded in trade for information.

Well, he wos alive when we moved on. Probably died of his wounds or his own crew 'ad him. No honour amidst thieves or smugglers, know wot I mean?

The Diary of Eleanor Athaliah Ransom (Mrs).
Monday 31st September.

Though tired from last night, as my sleep was disturbed by unpleasant dreams, this morning began well. Karl brought me breakfast in my room and apprised me that all was fine in the household and the grounds, the night had passed off without incident.

The children, Lady Niketa, Nanny and Lady N's pack of little rascals, were gaily enjoying a spot of morning sunshine on the lawn by the time I reached the morning room.

All in all, it was a pleasant day. The forecast in the newspapers was for a storm coming in from Syria, but the day was so sunny and calm that it was easy to believe that the forecasters had got it wrong again, which was a grave mistake. Taking advantage of agreeable weather we opened the house up fully to help get some fresh air into the rooms.

I busied myself with organising housework, and in the mid-afternoon, I even joined in beating rugs on the line, something that I always find seems to have quite a therapeutic effect upon one's spirits.

For entertainment, Mrs Carstairs dressed young Michael up in the rather moth-eaten prattan skin rug from Papa's study, and he, the children and the little dogs, with Nanny in close pursuit, had great fun hunting each other around the gardens.

I adore Papa, but, I almost dare not think this, the household is far more relaxing when he is away, and the children are so much more ebullient. I know Papa says I am over-indulgent, but it is hard for the children that they must have to spend their young days either cooped-up in the day nursery, or tippy-toeing around the house to avoid disturbing their Grandpapa at his work. He has become such a curmudgeon since Mama died.

Because it was such a lovely afternoon I suggested to Mrs Carstairs that she should allow the rest of the staff to take their tea with us on the lawn in an impromptu picnic, something I loved when Mama used to allow it. It always made me feel that we were more of an extended family than simply a household.

I did not attend to a stitch of real work, other than picking flowers for the dining room and entrance hall, until, in the late afternoon, when we were abruptly driven back indoors by the first few heavy droplets of rain.

It was not until then I realised how the time had marched on. I had been at least expecting word from Minnie today, if not her arrival. But there was no news or sign, which was a little disconcerting.

While I attended to the household accounts and the children returned to their studies, Lady Niketa amused herself in the music room. She is quite an accomplished pianist, far better than I, even after the years of interminable lessons. She left the doors open and the melody, accompanied by the sound of the rain, spilt out. I did not know the piece, a piano concerto by a young Icarian composer, Jëpha Õyena, Lady Niketa informed me later, but it was such a wonderful composition. The sound touched me deeply, evoking memories of long summer afternoons when Mamma used to play for us, and the house was filled with music and laughter.

I decided to take dinner early enough for the children to join Lady Niketa and I again. I find it oddly comforting, and James is so grown up in his ways, it is almost like having Edwin here. And Lady N delights in the children.

I spent the rest of the evening working on my tapestry and talking with Lady N. We talked about the news in the papers this morning; the sister ship of the Daedalus, the Talos, had been unveiled and named. It was evidently a new kind of aerostat, an Ironclad, and bigger even than the Daedalus. Illustrations showed the mighty leviathan, bristling with guns, as it raised from its moorings, above cheering, flag-waving crowds. I wondered, almost pensively, what hand had Papa in the creation of this great warship.

President Bradbury's address to the crowds was full of praise for the military, sloganisms and thinly disguised threats to other nations. Lady N feels that it is plainly the rhetoric of aggression rather than defence. I wondered if Papa had known that the second ship of the Damocles Project would be described, rather chillingly, by our leader as "the iron hammer to deliver the fatal blow into the heart of our enemies."

Lady N brought to my attention to a tiny footnote column, buried amidst the advertisements for chocolate Oxfords, stockings and Electric Manipulator machines for curing diseases at home (Lord knows what 'diseases,' they meant). It talked of the Aethervolt Navy being placed on high alert in readiness for some unmentioned reason. One ominous line talked about the development of some new weapon that could be used from the outer edge of the atmosphere.

Lady N scoffed at the ideas, her late second (or third?) husband, the much vaunted Colonel Brewster 'Buntie' Blithe-McFadden, was evidently quite high in the War Office Procurement Department. (I only met him twice and he appeared as just a rather jovial, though immensely portly man, with a large rosacean nose, along with a penchant for too much port and a tendency to fall asleep at the drop of a hat. I remember he would doze off with his remarkably little chubby hands curled up under his beard, like some enormous, but amusing, dormouse.) Evidently, Buntie had told Lady N several times that Tharsis' 'Aethervolt Navy' barely existed beyond the wistful thinking of those fellows over in the Air Navy. What there was, consisted of eight ships at best, and most of those could hardly make it off the ground, let alone into the void itself. None of the others are First Rate ships. When I asked why things had gotten to such a bad state of affairs, Lady N explained that Tharsis, as much as any of the other nations, no longer has the expertise or resources to maintain the engines. The technology is simply dying out. There has only ever been a handful of engineers, men of genius, much like my father, that can truly even understand the technology we adapted from the Aresians, and they too are a dying breed. Consequently when an Aethervolt Displacement Drive breaks down there are precious few knowledgeable enough to repair them, and those that can, have often to resort to cannibalising one engine to maintain another. Buntie told Lady N that no new aethervolt ship had been built in the last twenty years. Not a single one on the whole of Mars.

As if to make things worse, there was also much talk in the papers about a military 'encounter' between Tharsian Expeditionary Forces and 'unknown forces', possibly Thylians, near the city of Sirenum. Lady Niketa fears that the word 'encounter' is simply a substitute for saying that some poor woman's husband or son will not be coming home again. The columnists claim that all contact with Sirenum has been lost, and they fear it has been occupied by these 'unknown forces.' Lady Niketa, though she questions greatly the validity of some of the wilder claims, seems to believe it is the first steps on a road to yet another war.

Rather than be impolite by disagreeing with Lady N, as I do not think our President is doing anything more than sabre rattling to caution the Thylians and their friends the Zephyrians and Utopians, against such voices amongst them that would either see our nation weak or that would advocate anything impetuous, I agreed with her abhorrence of the waste and suffering of war.

I had just steered the conversation away from such fears and on to a happier topic when there came an urgent pounding upon the front door. It awoke the whole household, including Lady N's pack of dogs we had kennelled in the orangery. Carstairs and his eldest, Dan, reached the door first. I, from the upper landing, cautioned circumspection. They waited until Aegy arrived to arm them with Papa's shotguns.

The pounding became urgent, voices called through the door. This time Carstairs called back. I did not hear what the reply was but swiftly Carstairs threw back the bolts on the door and flung it open.

I was a little taken aback as, accompanied by a huge gust of wind and driving rain, several hunched figures staggered in. Bundled up in heavy coats and hats and sodden through. For a moment I did not recognise them, until one discarded her ushanka and cried out my name. It was Minnie! At last!

I ran down the stairs to greet them. I threw my arms around her in total abandon and she clasped on to me as if we had not seen each other for a lifetime. I could not have been happier to have seen my sister Lenora arrive. Minnie has always been as close to me as an elder sister, closer I fear than my own sister Sarah, and the very best of friends. My composure gave way completely as I threw my arms about each one of them as they shed their drenched coats and capes. Joshua, as rough and down to earth as ever, chuckled warmly, David and Eli stood transfixed like a cat suddenly beset by an overexcited puppy, Out of relief bordering upon euphoria, I hugged them all, even young Bowen. And then there was Neriah, cautiously waiting with her baby in her arms.

She is little more than a child herself. How can one truly judge harshly the rash actions of young love, as if we too were not all once young and foolish and in love? And, as Edwin said, after all, as she is Minnie's niece, and with no one else to turn to, she is part of our family and so, as Edwin said, mimicking his father's gravelly rumble, "T'is Ransom's business, and we Ransoms will always look after our own."

Though the Lord Himself alone knows what my Papa will say when he sees her, as there will be no avoiding presenting the situation to him anymore.

The baby is beautiful, a little girl, named Minerva after her aunt. Little Minnie! I embraced them both and cuddled little Minnie, a sweet smiling child, no worse for her rough journey in such atrocious conditions.

By now the whole house was up, even the children, and it took quite an effort to get everyone settled again. All Joshua and his sons wanted to do was see Michael and get some sleep. Mrs Carstairs took Bowen, who was shivering and sniffling like a half-drowned rat, to show her where she could find something hot to eat and to make her up a bed by the scullery hearth. Lady Niketa saw the children back to bed while Nanny took Neriah and little Minnie off to the old nursery, where there was a cot and dry clothes for the baby.

Minnie and I found our way down to the main kitchen. Minnie made tea while I raided the cupboards and larder to find her something for everyone to eat. Within moments Mrs Carstairs appeared and set about driving us out of her kitchen, but Minnie would have none of it. So together we made tea, and a few sandwiches, for all those awake and desperate for something warming.

Once all those that required it had been fortified with tea and settled, Minnie and I finally had a chance to talk.

It had been an awful journey for them all. Edwin's message did not arrive until Thursday afternoon, thus there had been no possible way that she could get everything organised to leave until Friday morning. It was a terribly tense night from which neither she, nor anyone else, managed to gain much in the way of sleep. On Friday morning she sent for Neriah and the baby, paid off the day workers and told the others to take the time off. She was so worried because of having to pay out almost everything in the cash box, even some of her own savings, and still she could only cover a couple of weeks wages. There had not even had enough to pay Joshua or Bowen.

Minnie also feared for the house, and so decided to take as much of the family's personal belongings as possible, just in case. That, she could not manage to get onto the train, is now stored in Mrs Phillipott's barn. Along with Edwin's beloved Trago, who had found his way back to the guest house a few days before.

On Friday afternoon, as they were packing the waggons and preparing to leave for Tremorfa, three men came to the house. Their leader was wearing a badge and proclaimed himself Deputy to the new Constable, and he wanted to know where they were going. He was an obnoxious character who became quite aggressive when Minnie refused to tell him anything. Only being disarmed and ordered to leave the farm at gunpoint by Joshua finally persuaded them to go.

Understanding the danger they were in, Minnie said they rode as fast as was humanly possible, what with the baby and all, to Mrs Phillipott's. Which was so hard on the poor drays that she was surprised they survived the journey. She was also quite sure the supposed Deputy and his men trailed them all the way.

Edwin's telephonograph had reached Mrs Phillipott and she was readily prepared for their arrival, including going to the trouble of enlisting her brother's sons to aid in securing the guest house. Minnie was quite taken aback to discover Mrs Phillipott was actually the eldest daughter of the late Mordecai Uwharrie, the progenitor of the Uwharrie clan. Minnie admitted at first she could only see them as a dreadfully outlandish group of yahoos, almost more frightening than the Constable's thugs, but actually, though a little unruly and rough in their comportments, she found them to be very respectful in a childish manner.

Before they left Mrs Phillipott's, Oldman Hezekiah Uwharrie himself came to visit Minnie and impressed upon her if the Ransoms ever needed his help then they need only send a message via Mrs Phillipott and he would come. Though he is in aspect every bit the grizzled hirsute Goliath of rumour, Minnie was surprised by what a courteous old gentleman Oldman Hezekiah really is. His demeanour utterly belied his formidable reputation, and she found him actually quite charming, though deadly earnest in his declaration, to which he had, even gone so far as to write a personal note to Edwin;

Tremorfa Township 29th September 0026

Mr Ransom

Sire,

My family and I keep our business rightly to ourselves and donte mess in no businesses of townsfolk or you farmsteder folk. It is not our ways. Our types of people just donte rightly get along. But by reading the newspapers as I do I was already rightly aware of your situation. I two have heard of Mr Demauirae but I have not had interaction with him as his concerns and ours ainte crossed ways before. Least before your stay at my sisters Gest House for Gentlepersons. It is not for common knowledge but Delilah Jane Phillipott is my sister. Though Pappy did not approve of her marrage I hold to no such concerns and we were long ago reconciled after Pappy's death. God Rest His Soul in Heaven.

I was mightily angered when I heard of the attack upon my sisters Gest House. Putting as it did her life in jepody and that of little Abigail Rose. Be sure I do not hold you to blame as Delilah has insisted you were most brave in defending the house and protecting her and her ~~dowtger~~ daughter.'

We exchanged incredulous glances over the edge of the paper as she read it aloud to me. What Edwin will make of this I have no idea.

'I am a man of slow temper an as I said afore my family donte wish to get involed in townsfolk business but I am rightly vexed by what occurred. Now I knows that this Mr Demauisae has no rightful business with me or mine nor has He or his hirerlings crossed my path and woe betide him if he did but I will not be at rest until I have repaid the insult and distress that he caused my sister.

I admire any man who stands up for his family and his rights no matter what He be or where He comes from. Two many peoples round here ainte got no backbone lest any real fight in them. If you happen to have any more of such predicaments then you may call upon my assistance at anytime. You may easily get a message to me through Delilah Jane and I will come to your aid directly.

I am indebted to you. Sire.

As the Good Lord says. The enemy of my enemy is my friend.

Yours sincerarly

Hezekiah Uwharrie'

Minnie remarked wryly to me she could not remember that part being in any Bible she had read, but at the time she was in no position to argue scripture with the head of the Uwharrie clan.

By Saturday morning rumours abroad in Tremorfa had reached Minnie's ears. Several of the High Sheriff's agents had arrived in town and had immediately started serving warrants and arresting people, including three Aldermen and the Deputy Mayor. In the afternoon Joshua learnt that another Alderman had committed suicide and his son had been killed trying to escape arrest. Alarmingly though there was no trace of Everheart or Docket.

Minnie explained that Tremorfa was eerily quiet, and the train station platforms deserted, when Oldman Uwharrie's men saw her and the others to catch the train on Sunday morning. She felt that there was an air of nervous expectation as if the whole town were holding its breath awaiting something terrible to happen. But nothing did. Whether the threat had subsided, or it was the presence of a dozen armed miners and hewers from the Uwharrie clan, but all went off well enough.

Minnie felt she should have been safe on the great overlander but fear had settled so deeply into the pit of her stomach and she could not rid herself of it. Before the conductor could show them to their allotted carriage, Minnie, as always as bold as brass, palmed him a considerable gratuity and requested he relocated them to another compartment on the upper deck or another section of the train. Once done, she made sure he understood that the consideration was also to ensure his silence upon the matter. As it transpired her fears were not unfounded.

Joshua had warned her that if there was to be trouble then it might come if the train stops at Alba Kirk or when they arrived at Alba Central Station. So it was with huge relief that, though the signal had been raised at Alba Kirk there was no one readying to either board or alight, consequently, though the huge steam engine slowed, it did not stop.

Ensconced in their alternative carriage Minnie and the others were oblivious to other events until the conductor came to inform her later that two men, of a disreputable nature, from Third Class, had been seized by porters trying to get into the First Class compartment of Carriage 42. The original carriage Minnie was allotted. Upon searching the ruffians it was discovered they were armed with knives and guns. The Chief Conductor had them held in the baggage compartment until they reached Alba and then had them handed over to the Police, on suspicion of attempting to rob First Class passengers.

Upon reaching Alba Central Station Minnie discovered that, for some reason that no one in authority was willing to explain, the railplane was not running to Tharsis, so Minnie had been forced to use the last of her savings and some of Joshua's to hire rooms for them all at a local Guest House.

On Monday morning they presented themselves at Alba Central only to discover that the Railplane was still not operating. No proper explanation was forthcoming, but rumour had it that some of the pylons outside the city had been discovered to have been deliberately damaged by what were possibly explosives.

I was shocked to hear her solution, but Minnie, ever the practical one, understanding that this could leave them trapped in Alba for several days at least, sent Joshua into the city to sell some of her jewellery - as she says desperate times lead to desperate measures. Joshua luckily, upon the recommendation of the Guest House owner's wife, found a reputable jeweller who gave her a reasonably fair price for the items.

I was devastated by such news and promised her I would have Carstairs dispatch a telephonograph to the jeweller first thing in the morning to buy those precious things back at whatever cost. I will not have Minnie impoverishing herself because of our misadventures.

With the money, she paid for passage on an airship, the Albatross. Though it was little more than an old rust bucket given over to more of a tramp steamer than a passenger ship, the accommodation was Bohemian, to say the least, it was at least the only ship that was still leaving regardless of the weather forecasts.

They had had quite an adventure already, but nothing had prepared Minnie for the passage on the Albatross. The airship found itself heading into the storm front. Unable to gain enough altitude to rise above the storm, and buffeted ferociously, the airship was driven off course several times. Neriah and Bowen were indisposed with mal de mer, and the baby fretted endlessly. Finally, they were forced to ground and wait out the worst of it, but the moorings broke and the Albatross was only saved by dragging her anchors until it fastened on to something.

Once the Captain had regained the ship he decided, mostly out of foul-mouthed rage at the storm, to plough on to Tharsis regardless of the headwinds and driving rain. The airship took a terrible battering, and so did its crew and passengers.

Their arrival at Covingdome airfield was even more traumatic than their journey. For want of the technical terms, which neither of us can guess at, she explained that as the airship was descending to land one of the upright propeller blades broke off and ripped a hole through the balloon's envelope. Luckily they were only a few feet from the ground otherwise, all on board would have been killed, as it was, the entire ship crashed to the ground. Minnie and the others had to be rescued by the ground crew.

By this point in her story, she was hysterical with incredulity. I laughed too at the insanity of it, though, thanking God, that no one was hurt.

"I was left there, standing in the middle of the chaos of the shattered passenger lounge, the roof now completely gone, exposing us all to the full force of the wind and rain, with a screaming baby under one arm, and two hysterical girls hanging around my hips like some caricature of the Raft of the Medusa." She became dramatically serious, "It was then I decided..."

Decided what? I asked.

"I decided that no matter what happens, I shall murder that man De Maurier myself if I should ever chance upon him! If I have but a shoe to hand, I shall do for him on sight!"

It was a joy to laugh, even at such misfortune.

Once safely rescued they were whisked into an awaiting steam carriage provided by the Aerodrome's Controller and brought here forthwith. As far as Minnie knew their luggage, all but for a few items they arrived with, is still inside the wreckage of the Albatross on Covingdome Field.

"So here I am, to present myself to you, dearest Nelly, like some shipwrecked waif; Sodden, penniless, tired almost beyond endurance, somewhat windblown and bereft of anything other than the remains of my ragtag household, a bag full of Edwin's ledgers and the clothes I am standing in." Her sardonic humour bravely masked the tremor in her voice and the quiver of her chin.

I hugged her closely, "But you got here! And now you are safe."

We sat holding on to each other for what seemed an age, neither of us willing to let go.

Now the house is quiet and everyone is abed. And maybe I can sleep a little sounder tonight.

Though it is a relief to have Minnie and Joshua safely here, at last, I miss Edwin and Papa so. They are chiefly in my prayers.

*"Filled with dreams I begin to wander
through this maze of alien wonders
into glades with ponds of starlight
ethereal beauty beyond human might."*

WORLD OF BLACK AND SILVER

CRYSTAL EYES

DAY THREE

<u>AMANTHOR</u>

The Flammarion Expedition
Official Journal
32nd Sept 26

5.30 AM. We have grounded about half a mile from the ruins of the Aresian city of Ananthor.

In the night we were overcome by a terrible tempest and the Captain has required us to stop to establish if any major damage has been done to the ship.

The Captain has announced that the checks and repairs will mean a lay day.

Intention to cast off before dark. 7.30 P.M.

The crew and Expedition members were terribly distressed to learn that during the attempts to find a suitable location to ground the Seren Bore, an accident occurred; a charge for the ground anchor exploded prematurely and killed the Purser, Mr

Grant. His family will be notified as soon as we return to Tharsis.

Mr Grant's remains have been stored in an annex to the cold storeroom.

C.L. Bryant-Drake.

Charity Bryant-Drake.
Notes to self. 32/9/26

I find myself forced to write balderdash! We have been told by Captain Llewellyn that Grant, the Purser, was killed in some kind of accident last night during the storm. Utter claptrap! I heard the gunfire, and those were not flares they were firing.

When we landed, I took Patty and, in the guise of taking the air, had a long look at the ship from the ground. There is a hole, as big as a man's two fists, in the right side of the front (I will have to check the correct terminology) part of the ship. Patty thinks there is also one high on the balloon's skin itself. But my eyesight is not as good as hers. I had left my spectacles in my room.

Unquestionably, someone took shots at us last night in the storm with some sort of cannon, witnessing the size of that hole, and we fired back.

I am utterly convinced Mr Grant was killed in the attack.

The crew are all pretty tight mouthed and I doubt I will get a great deal of information out of Adam, but I shall beard Edwin as soon as I can get him alone and find out the truth.

Has that draffsack Du Maurier sent pirates after us? Nothing like the craft that pursued me to Alba Kirk would be able to even get airborne in such weather. It would have taken a fairly large ship, and one fitted with heavy ordnance, only pirates and reavers have ships that are capable of that.

A horrid thought assails me; there is actually another kind of ship that would carry such weapons. An Air Navy ship, but that's too awful to contemplate.

Damn men! Why do they insist upon such secrecy in everything?

Patty and I cornered Edwin this afternoon after we returned from our constitutional. We caught him as he was coming out of the gentlemen's conveniences on the weather deck. Nothing easier to manipulate than an embarrassed gentleman in a compromising situation. Patty bodily manhandled Edwin back into the washroom, (she is surprisingly forceful when she wants to be, quite the Amazonian) and we questioned him thoroughly.

Eventually, he admitted that we had actually been fired upon by another ship during the storm and that we, well rather Mr Franklin, had fired back. Enough to drive them off. The Purser had been slain by a shell fired from the other ship, it almost tore the poor man in two!

We could have all been killed in our beds if it was not for the bravery of Mr Franklin.

Accordingly the Captain and the Professor decided to make up the accident story to avoid alarming us! The ladies!

As if we were nothing more than timorous debutantes!

I became so irritated I was about to storm the bridge and have it out with Llewellyn and the Professor there and then.

Patty stopped me. It was true that we were not as easily frightened as they expected, nevertheless, she feels we must think of her father and, of course, Aelita.

Patty fears that her father will only fret all the more about the whole expedition and, as his heart condition is far more advanced than one would suspect, such anxiety would be no good for him.

As for Aelita, Patty is right, she is travelling alone, and with relative strangers, on what is possibly her first ever journey without her husband. Although he may indeed be an overbearing old flapdoodle, he has shielded her and been her protector for two decades.

If it is not necessary to alarm her, well both of them, maybe we should allow them the comfort afforded by such innocent obliviousness.

Patty has invited me to accompany her and her father to view the ruins of the Aresian city of Ananthor which lies near here. I jumped at the chance. I have passed it on the train but never had the chance to actually visit it.

It will be wonderful to spend some time adventuring with Patty and her father.

The Flammarion Expedition Journal of L. Edwin Ransom.

Day three. 32nd. 9th. 26.

An exciting night! Though tinged with tragedy. I must admit that I allowed myself to get lost in the mayhem and exhilaration of it all.

Adam aroused me from my slumbers. The storm had overtaken us and the Captain needed the Davy-Rue electrification system so he could use the electrificated Tasker lights to have any chance at seeing the ground in this wretched weather, but was worried it would attract a lightning strike. And so they wanted me to help Mr Beer, the Chief Engineer and his men, jury-rig, the main batteries to the Faraday net! I told him he was insane but he just laughed and told me that if it was an insane idea then I was exactly the right chap for the job!

So, resplendent in heavy oilskins over my pyjamas and dressing gown, I sallied forth. It was a ludicrously dangerous idea, something lightning catchers used to use before the practice was banned decades ago, but Mr Beer seemed to be up for it.

So only a few moments hence, regardless of my childish acrophobia, I found myself hanging from the rigging by my fingertips hundreds of feet above the ground in a raging tempest. Trying to affix extra earthing cables to the Faraday net that protects the balloon envelope itself from lightning strikes. My hat went, I had to dispense with my spectacles or lose them to the storm, I was sodden, freezing cold and battered, but oh how alive! Maybe I have stumbled upon some method of dissipating one's fears and phobias through the auspices of confrontation! I am sure that I shall never again be overcome by nervous timidity merely surmounting a library ladder.

Once we had jury-rigged the cables I rushed back down to help Mr Beer's men anchor the other earthing line, which they had extended as far as they could by cobbling five lengths together.

All the time I was loudly praying that there would not be a strike before we had made all the connections or we could all be killed instantly. I do not know how, probably by the Grace of the Almighty, but we did it!

Mr Beer informed the Captain as I loudly beseeched God and threw the switch. The Davy-Rue came on, in fact, everything bar the manoeuvring rotors came on. The whole ship lit up like a beacon.

Moments later we took a hit, everything fizzled, crackled and sizzled, but the batteries did not explode, the resistors held, inductors and capacitors survived.

Like a mad man whooping with joy, I ran up onto the deck, but instead of joining me in my delight the crew were busy going about their appointed tasks. And so I made my way to the bridge, in time to pass the Purser on his way out.

The Captain and the Professor thanked me for my endeavour and I was in the process of excitedly explaining how I and the engineering crew had managed such a feat when chaos broke out.

Someone bawled the news that Mr Grant the Purser had been killed! I stood, mouth agape, unable to grasp what had just been declared. The man had only just passed me in the hall, "How?"

The Professor seized my arm and pulled me back towards the rear of the bridge, "Edwin, there's another ship out there," he leant close to my ear. "We are under attack."

I had hardly any time to comprehend his words when the lightning struck us again and our starboard gun opened fire. I had a fleeting glimpse of a long dark shark-like shape a good ways off and higher than us, black against the illuminated thunderheads. I remember thinking at that moment, why did it not have any running lights? Of course, I understood why; it was a sky pirate ship.

"My God, sir! To attack us in this? Who in God's name....?" The question died in my mouth.

The starboard gun rattled off again.

"Indeed, Edwin." The Professor's expression was grimmer than I have ever seen it. He chomped upon his pipe and growled. "Let them try us. Come any closer and they will find out what those Cogswaine's can do. We will blast them out of the sky." There was a steely anger about him that I hardly recognised. This was the father of my wife, the grandfather of my children, my mentor and teacher, the man who I have so often listened to argue passionately against warfare, in fact, against all forms of violence, even the horrors of capital punishment. Suddenly he wore a forbidding mantle more given to an old warrior, like Colonel Jahns, than the kindly Professor I have always known.

Together we peered out through the rain-lashed starboard windows and waited. The whole bridge appeared to hold its breath in silence with us. Suddenly the lightning came again, this time it did not strike us, lighting up the sky in several quick bursts, but no sign of our adversary.

I wondered if we had shot it down. Captain Llewellyn thought it unlikely our gunner had even hit it, let alone done any real damage. Probably it had been just enough to scare them off.

The ship's crew then set about locating a safe place to land the ship. I, in the meantime, and the Professor went in search of something to calm our nerves.

We were joined by the Colonel in the saloon, still dressed in his nightwear, dressing gown and cap, the gunfire had awoken him. The Professor explained what had occurred. The Colonel listened carefully and offered his advice. For all his usual blustering pomposity I must admit I found his presence and calm practicality assuring. He advised that we should not alarm all the expedition members with tales of pirates, unless, of course, they return tonight, but downplay the entire event, to an accident or some such. The crew can be put on the most alert of footings without unduly unnerving the others.

It was while Jakes, the automaton Steward, was pouring the tea that he informed us that it was Mr Franklin who had had the presence of mind to return the pirate's cannon fire.

"He is quite a man, your 'friend' Franklin." Observed the Colonel pointedly.

"Why Carter, that was almost admiring. I thought you did not even like the man," replied the Professor.

"James, dear chap, I do not. But he certainly seems to be the kind of man you would want around when you are in a fix."

I, far too tired to verbally spar with the Colonel, chose to hold my own counsel and, I fear, promptly fell asleep in the armchair. When I awoke Jakes told me it was almost dawn and the ship had just finally landed, or 'grounded' in the vernacular of the air ways. I apologised for my unseemly behaviour but Jakes informed me it was on the Professor's express commands that I was left to sleep.

I joined the Captain and the Professor on the bridge not long before Adam arrived. I stated that I believe this was the act of pirates in the pay of Du Maurier. While the Captain and the Professor seemed more willing to consider other alternatives. Though I cannot see any real logic in their musings. At least Adam, knowing how far Du Maurier will go in his ruthlessness, supported my view.

I found myself agreeing though with the decision to tell the others as little as possible to avoid unnecessarily distressing them. Mr Grant died in a terrible tragic accident and that will be all that is to be said.

Adam went off to aid the crew in tethering the ship down.

I returned here to the cabin and I intend to try to get a few hours' proper sleep at least!

The Field Journal of Octavius Spender, Dr
32nd of Sept 0026
Ananthor.

As serendipity would have it, due to unforeseen circumstances, we have been forced to land close to the ruins of the Aresian city of Ananthor.

I have not been here since I finished my studies. Though tinged with a little sadness at the loss of a crew member, I was thrilled that the opportunity to visit the ruined city had presented itself.

After breakfast Parthena, her new friend Miss Bryant-Drake and I, prepared ourselves to set off on the half-mile journey to the northern edge of the city. The Captain provided us with a steam carriage, a strange old clunker with its own universal railway track instead of wheels, hoisted down from the ship's internal bay. The driver had it fired up and ready for the off in only five minutes. The Captain also insisted we were to be escorted by four of the Colonel's men, who were to ride ahead in a similar but smaller contrivance.

These are truly remarkable conveyances, these machines. I have ridden, of course, in a number of steam carriages, (I even owned one once before it became too expensive to maintain on an academic's stipend) but never ones that can so easily and speedily traverse the rough ground made boggy in some parts by last night's storm. Although they are quite some bone shakers. The young crewman driver informed me that the Professor himself designed them specifically for this expedition, basing them upon an old tarax oil driven Hornsby (whatever that is) extending the body and adding these amazing self-laying track thingamabobs that he had taken from a design by Messrs Edgeworth and Wroński. This one, he claimed could reach almost thirty miles in an hour over the roughest of ground! Though I fear no bone would go unbruised.

We were packed up with a picnic and all and about to be on our way when Sir John and Madam Fontenelli requested to join us.

I was delighted to have their company, though, as we approached the outer limits of the city, I began to have reservations about the propriety of taking Mrs Fontenelli into such a place.

Though she did not seem to be anything other than as fascinated as the others. I myself felt apprehensive, after all, Ananthor holds a singular place in the history of the early conflicts between the Aresians and Tellurian settlers.

Ananthor had once been the home to more than twenty thousand Kitreenoh Aresians. Living as they did in their strange pristine houses made of a natural exudate, or mucilage, amalgamated with rock deposits to form resilient honeycombed structures of ineffable beauty. Not the brutality of the rough brick and stone structures of us Tellurians, but pale translucent shards of crystal-like material, that seem to have more been grown than built.

Here there was nothing as obtuse as gas light or fireplaces, the fabric of the edifice itself absorbs the sun's radiance and stores it within the matrix of its structure in the form of light and heat. Every night each uniquely formed building would have been aglow with an inner light, the defused shadows of the occupants playing out their humble lives upon the virtually transpicuous backdrop of their walls. Only one of so many wondrous technologies that the Aresians never deigned to share with us, their Tellurian obtruders.

Without inhabitants, the very buildings seemed to have died. Although the sun still shines, the buildings themselves barely illuminate the gloom of the night, seen often by travellers passing by on the railroad as nothing but a ghostly luminosity in a darkened landscape. It is as if there were once some relationship between occupants and structure, some form of biological mutuality, a dependent co-existence.

No Tellurians have successfully inhabited such places, as the technology, if it be technology, of that mutuality is beyond our kind.

Here at Ananthor two utterly different societies had encountered each other, on the edge of a frontier far from the restraints of their respective supremacies. As Earth's own history taught us, it is at the frontiers of cultures, far beyond the pale of their social elites, where extraordinary things happen.

At Ananthor, so history tells us, Aresians and Tellurians interacted with open cooperation. Reciprocity and freedom to barter, led to a free trade not just in material goods but ideas and culture. Eventually, Tellurians were even allowed to inhabit parts of the city and build their own dwellings nearby. Ananthor became a centre for commerce. As more and more settlers flooded westward from Alba's growing conurbation and British political control, Tellurians settled these areas and came to rely upon Ananthor for succour.

The ruler of Ananthor was the Suzerain of Amhoria who grew wealthy upon the city's trade, regulating it as and how he saw fit. The British Colonial Government at Tharsis though was concerned for many reasons, not least for the fact that this major trading centre on their borders was not providing a tax revenue. Ananthor's protection was guaranteed by treaty but the avaricious eyes of Imperialism soon turned towards the city.

For a short "golden moment" Ananthor was a beacon of hope for another way, another future. A future where

Earthmen and Martians could live together, even side by side, in peace.

Nevertheless, though the gutter press and penny broadsheets of Tharsis continuously circulated preposterous stories of "unnatural goings on" in Ananthor, portraying the place akin to a post-Biblical Martian Gomorrah, in an ill-conceived attempt to stir up public odium against the city, nothing happened. The Colonial Government was too enmeshed in other conflicts to spare the resources to effect yet another annexation and the ensuing protracted warfare it would bring.

As our clunking vehicles entered the deserted city, I could imagine how this beautiful place once was, and its proud people, Earthmen and Martian, yet to be laid low by the coming of the phthisis pandemic.

What the Colonial Administration could not, or would not, do by force, the malaise did equally and as ruthlessly. Helped on its deadly progression by the Colonial Government's denial of medical supplies or Doctors to go to the inhabitant's aid. Some records, of those few that were kept, let alone survived the revolution, speak of twenty or thirty percent of Tellurians, and sixty or seventy percent of the Martians, within the city succumbing to the disease. The Tellurian population that could escape fled for their lives. Only to find themselves refused entry into Alba and Tharsis and thus be forced to suffer in the wilderness. Then, or so the tales go, the Suzerain of Amhoria ordered that their people remain in self-enforced quarantine. A city in isolation, its people left to die on mass.

Ananthor, a once beautiful city of shimmering crystal, that had been for a fleeting moment a ray of hope for us all, was finally extinguished by the Colonial

British forces in 1876. A railway was to be built from Alba running south of Ananthor, out towards the newly proclaimed Tremorfa province and beyond.

To make it safe for "civilised travellers," settlers and prospectors, the Imperial Administration ordered that Ananthor, "that plague-ridden cesspit," "that den of thieves," should be "cleared."

That winter when the soldiers deployed they found a place of ravaged poor, where a few thousand destitute Martians and several hundred failed Tellurian settlers had been cast off by misfortune to scratch out a living in the ruins of their once magical city. Poor they were, ravaged and desperate, but still proud, and still living in peace with each other. Still endeavouring to rebuild their city. But the Suzerain of Amhoria was long past and there was now nothing to protect the inhabitants from the guns and artillery of the British. Those Tellurians and Martians alike who escaped, what I can only call an act of horrific brutality, were driven out at bayonet point to die in the frozen dust.

I remember, to my eternal chagrin, that as a nascent young man, my chest full of bravado and my head ringing with jingoisms, raising to a toast over the broadsheet's headlines screaming the news of the clearing of Ananthor. What did we know or care for such alien vermin and Human detritus? I, like so many of my cohorts, was born here, on Mars, in Tharsis, yet I saw myself as no colonial child, but British and proud of it. We were brought up with visions of our own glorious destiny manifesting before us, unlike the Americas we had no "Western frontier," we had a whole world to conquer and civilise in the name of the British Empire and mankind.

We rode in silent awe, through streets of shattered buildings. Years of military service taught me that intelligence has no defence against cunning, and that beauty, innocence and truth, are the first casualties of any war.

I tried to shake off my torpor and began to point out some of the most interesting of the ravaged buildings that remain. Sir John was engaging, and obviously noting my struggle to dislodge my reverie, began to ask questions, intelligent questions. Trying to avoid the history of the city's demise I endeavoured to explain some of what little we know of the city's infrastructure. I kept it to an anthropological and archaeological perspective by focusing on construction techniques, the layout of the city, municipal services, buildings of significance both secular and religious, and the various indicators of technologies and the nuances of Aresian culture now lost to us. All very fascinating, I am sure, but of little real interest to my companions.

After a short time, we reached one of the piazzas, an open square, hexagon rather, that used to serve as a public meeting area, market, and recreational space for this quarter of the city. It was once just a simple open area seamlessly floored with the same material the homes and buildings around it were constructed of. But now vegetation grew in the cracks and the red dust had claimed a large swathe of it. But still, the "square" was impressive. At the ladies' behest, we stopped the carriages and got out to stretch our legs.

Glad to be able to climb down off the bone shaker I too took the opportunity to walk around a little. I was explaining to Miss Bryant-Drake what little we, as archaeologists, know of the complex structure of Aresian societies, when Madam Fontenelli approached me and asked me the most dumbfounding question.

She fixed me with those intense peculiarly coloured eyes of hers and asked, in all solemnity; "Is this place haunted, Doctor?"

I stood speechless. There had been much talk on board the ship of séances and other ludicrous goings-on, and in some social circles, I understand they are de rigueur these days. I, though, have no interest or time for entertaining such twaddle. Normally, as a gentleman, in such a situation, one would have felt compelled to have said something purely to have humoured her, but faced with Madam Fontenelli's earnest enquiry, all I could muster was to answer, "My dear Lady, if any place on Mars deserves to be haunted, Ananthor would be it."

She gave a winsome, yet nonetheless sad, smile and almost whispered. "I do believe it is."

In that instant, I was struck by how beautiful she is and how magnetic her disposition. Regardless of the hue of her skin, if I were not such an old man, then, husband or not, I would set my sights upon her. No wonder Sydeian fawns over her like an obsequious lapdog.

(How odd? I have never even looked at another woman, let alone felt any such stirring of emotions, in the ten years since I lost Damaris. And suddenly now? Here, with this alien woman?)

I found myself watching her closely. Here in this place where she so obviously belonged. Something about her presence transformed the feel of the place, as if the atmosphere itself had altered. As an archaeologist, I have tried to cultivate the childlike skills of imagination to envision the past in one's mind's eye. No mean feat for any hoary old academic like myself (and one so many of my fellow scientists fail miserably at) but suddenly here, in her presence I could so easily imagine the city whole and vibrant, so clearly it had almost a hallucinatory quality.

For a moment I felt as if I were conveyed into the past, into the piazza on some market day, vividly overflowing with the noise and hubbub of life. I stood, as if I were some ghostly spectre, amidst Ananthor. Not this dead husk of a city, but Ananthor alive!

Lost in my enchanted daydream I saw wondrous things I could have never have thought to imagine; a city bustling with Aresians and Tellurians of all colours and shades, creatures of burden I have never heard even talk of, conveyances the like of which I have never known. And others; other aliens, strange and awesome, walking casually amongst the trader's stalls and weaving their way amidst the crowds.

I was both delighted and awe-inspired, but it was only a vision. At least that is what I believed even though the longer it lasted the more tangible it seemed. As that thought crept into my mind I noticed that the people no longer walked by me unnoticing of my presence. Heads began to turn, quizzical expressions appeared upon faces, an Aresian child pointed.

Abruptly an irrational panic leapt into my chest like I was some discovered felon or heretic. I turned to flee from the anticipated hue and cry only to suddenly see her; Aelita Fontenelli.

Dressed not in the travelling clothes of today, but in the sumptuous flowing zaffre robes of the highest born of her people, and about her a glorious radiance hung like some Renaissance artist's halo. A small crowd was gathered around her, each reaching out to touch her, not with rough grasping hands but with genteel reverence. As I turned so did she and our eyes met. And suddenly it was as if I understood, everything.

I awoke here in my cabin to Parthena's gentle ministrations. Hushing my excited babbling, she explained that I had passed out in the piazza and struck my head badly. They had had to rush me back here. Mr Holley, the ship's Medician, gave me a good going over and ascribed it to over-exertion, lack of sleep and my lackadaisical approach to taking my medication.

Once regaining my senses properly I, like any good patient faced with a stern and unimpressed nurse, took my scolding like a man and kept my thoughts to myself until I could write down this report of my singular experiences.

Upon reflection of completing the above, I am frustrated by the knowledge that in the hallucination, for, regrettably, I must assume that is what it was, I had that sensation of revelation, almost omnipotence. As if a drape had risen and now it had fallen again as emphatically as any theatre fire curtain. My rational mind understands that it was not real, just one of those strange sensations people experience in a delirious dream state. No truer than the content of the bizarre vision itself, nevertheless it has left a peculiar yearning in me. I feel as if the delusion were trying to convey some deeper message.

Or maybe a warning, as the anxiety that overcame me in the hallucination still resides in my chest.

Diary of Aelita Fontenelli (Mrs).
Tuesday, September, 32nd. MY.26

Dear Diary,

I am utterly discomposed. Truly I am enjoying this undertaking amid such exciting company though I have found myself torn between my heart and my loyalties. I fear I shall be constantly treated like a porcelain doll if I continue to behave like one. And so, after the events of yesterday, I resolved to take a firmer hand in all matters that concern me. However, as soon as I endeavoured to take such control more and more bewildering are the events that overtake me.

I found it difficult to sleep last night, what with the storm and all the other commotions, and when I finally did, I found myself beleaguered by strange dreams. I was prowling the abandoned streets of the White City again, chasing fleeting shadows, but not with childish curiosity but with a heavily burdened heart, desperate to find comfort in some company. I felt like a lost child anxiously searching for the parent whose hand had slipped from hers in a crowd.

Ursula was beside my bed when I awoke as I had been calling my father's name out loud. Ursula was so concerned she suggested I might consider taking one of Dr Hammond's tablets to soothe my nerves, but I will not be frightened by the workings of my own unconscious mind.

I feel that was why, when Sir John suggested that, due to the airship having to stop over for repairs, we could accompany Dr Spender and the others to see the remains of the city of Ananthor, I readily agreed.

I have heard the place often mentioned in conversation but know really little about it. After all, it was, I believe, the nearest surviving major Aresian city to Tharsis. There is nothing left of the Aresian city of Carthoris, the wondrous capital of Malacand, that was once where Tharsis now sprawls, apart from the walls of the Old Citadel and Great Temple that now is absorbed within the fabric of St. Mary's Cathedral. A place I used to spend as much time as I could as a child. Of course, only when the Nuns would allow.

Sir John made the necessary arrangements. Dr Spender had opted to use a vehicle provided by the Captain. Unfortunately, we took the last two seats, therefore Ursula could not accompany me. She was very concerned and demonstrated her displeasure by bestowing upon me yet another sermon regarding Sir John's "ungentlemanly" attentions.

Though, I must add that we did have quite a disagreement, I am all too aware of the truth in what she is cautioning, I'm afraid I have to admit that for all her protestations, and the veiled "counsel" from the other passengers, Sir John's "attentions" are not at all ungentlemanly, and not, for that matter, unpleasant. And, if I am to free myself of the shackles of convention, I must learn to do as I wish, not as, so-called, polite society dictates. Although there is nothing truly "polite" about the morning room gossiping and malicious innuendos society uses to coerce women into obeying their mores.

The company was pleasant, of course, but I must say that I find the curious glances of the soldiers somewhat irksome. Though they are courteous enough and respectful in my presence, I should be used to such reactions by now. The crew members of the Seren Bore are much better, though Ursula puts that down to good instruction. I cannot help but find such things disquieting. I am not an aberration or some sideshow exhibit and I grow tired of being stared at as though I were.

Dr Spender appeared a little distracted throughout the entire journey into Ananthor and we relied mostly upon Parthena and Sir John to edificate us as to what we were actually observing. And what wonders they were.

Much like the city in my dream the entire city appears to be grown out of crystal. Parthena tried to explain how but, even in this abysmal state of ruin, I was lost in the romantic beauty of it all. Sir John said that this was a city of the Kitreenoh, but still my people. Though I know little or nothing of them, only what I have seen in paintings and old daguerreotypes, and read of in tales and stories. I have never seen them with my own eyes. Well, at least I do not remember ever seeing them.

Dr Spender had our vehicles stop when we reached a large open precinct. The others were all so wrapped in conversation as they perused of the marvels about them, that they did not pay me any attention. Which, not for the first time in my life, I was grateful for, but as I stepped down from the steam carriage my attention was taken by a lone child standing only a few yards away. I thought his presence rather odd as the Doctor had informed us that the city was completely deserted and had been so for some considerable time.

My instinct was to immediately turn to remark upon the child to the others but something about him caused me to hesitate. Though it was indeed a child, and clearly visible to my eyes, there was a translucency about him, like an image held up to the light. I glanced around but it was obvious that none of the others had noticed the boy, and so, gathering my wits as best as I could, I followed Giovanni's advice (that I have so oft heard repeated) that when faced with something curious or unexpected one should focus upon what one is observing with great assiduousness. As I watched the boy seemed to coalesce, no longer a diaphanous waif, but a solid child, as real as the stones of the plaza and the broken buildings around us. A tall child of no more than twelve years of age, dressed in a simple, pale blue, smock and leather sandals. A blond boy with fair skin, I thought, but the skin was not "fair" but luteolous, a striking amber, and his hair was the palest gold. As I stared at him he smiled, as if acknowledging my scrutiny, a charming, welcoming smile that reached up to his strange bright yellow eyes.

Abruptly I realised I must be looking at a ghost! I cast a glance around but none of my companions seemed to be able to see him, not even Sir John who was now standing only inches from my elbow. As I realised this, the child slowly raised a finger to his lips in an exaggerated hush, as if he knew I was about to call attention to his manifestation, and then he promptly faded from my sight.

I became aware that Sir John was enquiring after my well-being. I reassured him that I was perfectly well, just a little giddy from the motion of the vehicle.

As soon as I could, I made my way over to where Dr Spender was elucidating on some particular aspect to Charity and asked him whether he thought the city was haunted? He considered the question for a moment and agreed that if any place deserved to be haunted then this place did.

I would have asked more of him but I was becoming aware that there were more of the apparitions appearing out of the edges of my vision. All around me translucent figures glided silently.

Feeling no alarm or apprehension I turned away from the Doctor and tried to focus my mind on what I was witnessing.

At that moment it all became absolutely clear.

I was still standing in the same plaza, but it was as if I were transported to another time. Around me the city was alive, the buildings whole, the square chockfull with market stalls of some marvellous bazaar and teeming with buyers, sellers and gawkers. There were people of all kinds, and the more I concentrated the more came into focus. Everywhere there were Kitreenoh Aresians and other races I could not even guess at; some tall reptilian creatures, with too many arms, though exceptionally proud looking, others more like hulking apes and cat-faced men. Through a gap between stalls I spied a man-like creature with the head much like that of a praying mantis as it passed by engaged in animated conversation with another. The entire plaza was frenetic with comings and goings. There were creatures of types I can only explain in terms of vague likenesses to those I have read of, or viewed in the Tharsis zoological garden; several were elephant-sized shaggy beasts of burden, trunkless but with great reptilian heads and six legs! There were many humans here too, going about their business, indifferent to the exotic people they rubbed shoulders with.

Wonderful conveyances, machines and contraptions of transportation abounded.

My attention though was drawn unto searching out my own kind. If the Kitreenoh and the little green Prahsino, were here, where were my people?

For all the wondrous creatures that inhabited this delusion, I could not understand why I could not see my own kind.

Suddenly the Kitreenoh boy was there again, this time much closer to me, with his kind smile and profoundly empathetic eyes, with their strange lozenge shaped pupils. As he tentatively reached out towards me I realised there were others, Tellurians and Aresians, gathered around me all reaching for me, their faces full of curious wonder. Without the merest ounce of apprehension in my heart, I too reached out to them.

For a moment, probably only a second, I could feel their warm fingers, their gentle touch against the skin of my hands, arms and face. A strange sense of compassion and longing swept over me and I felt myself almost becoming lost, as if swept off my feet by some extraordinary euphoria, much akin, I imagine, to the rapture at the End of Days that Father Lacunza wrote of.

There was a sudden shout of panic and the spell was instantly broken. Poor Dr Spender had suffered some fugue, no doubt brought upon by our exertions, and had fallen and struck his head on the footplate of the vehicle.

We were now lost in the frantic chaos of rescuing Dr Spender. The soldiers bundled him into their steam carriage and set off at a breakneck speed back to the airship. We, our hearts full of concern, quickly followed on.

I could do little to help but hold Parthena's hand while Charity and Sir John spoke reassuring words to her, and I feel it was my helplessness that led me to gaze longingly at the ruins of the city around me as we sped along.

It was the most strangest of sensations, even stranger than the visions in the square, for I could both clearly see the devastated ruins around me and, as if in my mind's eye but imposed upon the real; the city in its grandeur. Thoroughfares thronged with ghostly apparitions, shattered structures were also whole, broken edifices were at the same time again magnificent. I can only describe it as if I were looking at two images through a stereoscope, one before the calamity that had befallen Ananthor and one after, but this was no static sepia image seen through a viewer, this was as tangible as reality; moving, vibrant and alive. These apparitions were unlike any ghosts I have ever read of or heard tell of, no white-sheeted phantoms or wailing dead. These people were alive, going about their daily routines, as oblivious to our passing as my companions were to their existence.

Dr Spender was rushed to his cabin where the ship's Doctor attended upon him. The news is good and we have been informed that he is conscious and none too worse for his ordeal.

I, on the other hand, find myself perplexed, even mystified. Unfortunately, at this point I have no one I feel I can speak of about my experiences in Ananthor save Ursula, and she was as pragmatic as ever. Of course, to her, the concepts of "ghosts" or enduring souls is beyond understanding, but her questions, as usual, were thought-provoking.

In some way, I know I must have been seeing ghosts, or at least shades of the long lost past. That I can understand, if indeed, I can accept such things are even possible. It is tempting to think in terms of Heaven and Hell. After all, few Aresians accepted Salvation through conversion, preferring to remain paganus. Maybe it is that their souls, being neither evil nor at peace with God, are trapped in Limbo, (Giovanni would be incandescent at such talk!) but I can hardly believe market days occur in Gehenna.

And the boy seemed to know I was there and they touched me, I felt their warm hands against my skin. Not even the shades of the Odyssey are warm to the touch.

If not ghosts then what? Some form of waking dream? But it was most definitely not that White City in the snow, whose forsaken streets I often meander in my slumber, although it bore a close resemblance. Maybe simply a hallucination conjured up from my "childish" (as Giovanni often dismissively alludes to them) imaginings and desires? But Giovanni also chides me for having little or no truly creative imagination, and certainly not one fertile enough to envisage such things as I witnessed.

I am left with the deeply held conviction that not only what I saw WAS real, but, (and I have no idea how this could possibly be) what I saw IS real. Another kind of "real." Another existence, possibly? I feel like the little girl in Mr Carol's wonderful story, suddenly privy to another reality existing the other side of the mirror. It seems almost too preposterous to contemplate such things, but my skin still tingles from where their warm fingertips caressed my face.

I think... I am certain that the Professor is right; my people did not leave this world. They are still here, but in some way that is beyond our simple understanding.

I have decided to approach the matter with Sir John this evening after dinner. He is a dear friend and has had many curious experiences during his adventures, some more than equal in high strangeness to mine. I shall value his judgement and trust upon his discretion.

I visited Dr Spender before dinner, he was asleep but Parthena (Patty, as she insists) says he is resting well. She fears the true cause behind his syncopia is his laxitude towards his medication. Something upon which she intends to take a much firmer line with him on. I sat with her for a while at his bedside and we had a most pleasant tête-à-tête, the first time we have really had a chance to talk in private. She is a most remarkably engaging and perceptive young woman, and unlike any other I have ever known.

*The Flammarion Expedition
Official Journal*
32nd Sept 26
Cont.;

11.23A.M. Watch reported a plume of smoke on the North Eastern horizon. Estimated over 5 miles away. The Captain and the Professor decided not to investigate.

12.30 P.M. Dr Spender, Miss Spender and myself (Charity Bryant-Drake), accompanied by Madam Fontenelli and Sir John Sydeian, set out to explore the nearby ruins of the Aresian city of Ananthor, with an armed escort of four of Colonel Jahns' men.

1.45 P.M. Group had to return to the Seren Bore because Dr Spender collapsed due to lassitude.

2.30 P.M. Mr Holley, Medical Officer, has informed the Captain that Dr Spender is well and recuperating. The incident has been attributed to Dr Spender not maintaining his proper medication regime and not getting enough sleep last night.

3 P.M. Because of the pleasantly mild weather, and good air conditions, the Captain allowed afternoon tea to be served picnic style near our landing site. The gentlemen of the expedition organised an impromptu light-hearted game of cricket between themselves and members of the crew. Colonel Jahns' men, of course, played for the expedition team. The expedition members, notably Mr Franklin and Sir Sydeian, won by a lot of runs. Mr Ransom has an excellent bowling arm and scored numerous goal – or whatever they are called - successes. The experience was awfully enjoyable for all of us and raised all spirits considerably.

4.30 P.M. A large grazing herd of Martian Giant Tardigrades was sighted by the crew members when collecting fresh water. Sir Sydeian and the soldiers went out and bagged a brace for the stores. Not pleasant looking creatures but delicious, or so I am informed. Sir Sydeian commends that one should always taste native Martian game before one sees it in the wild. They also brought back several braces of wild waterfowl.

8 P.M. Before dinner, the Captain gave a short eulogy in memory of the Purser, Mr Horatio Cedric Grant, and prayers were said. Mr Grant's body will remain with us until we return to Tharsis and he can be returned to his family. The Captain also announced that all repairs and checks had been completed and that the ship would be continuing on her voyage after dinner.

9.35 P.M. We resumed our journey. Calm weather and clear skies.

C.L. Bryant-Drake

The Diary of Dr James Athanasius Flammarion.
32nd Sept. 26th.

It is difficult to endure the responsibility of the death of an employee. Last night, in the grip of a tremendous storm, we were attacked by another ship, and the Purser, Mr Grant, an affable chap, was killed, in an act of unmitigated murder.

I have always been a man of peace. A rational man who believes in the inviolability of human life, but if I had been on the deck last night I would have seized the Picaro and, without mercy, fired upon that ship myself. As it was, as every shot was fired, I ardently wished it to find its mark, God forgive me. So indignant and so angry was I.

I personally interviewed Grant for the position. I have even met his wife. And now she is widowed and their children without a father. I shall endeavour to assure their needs are supported for as long as it needs be.

Nonetheless, this is a sacrifice we must all be willing to pay in this quest for knowledge and peace. I can see it as no less than the quest for mankind's salvation, even if only for those here on Mars.

We fool ourselves. Even our calendar maintains the lie. It has been almost fifty Earth years since Unilateral Independence. Our societies have grown but for little other purpose than to serve the needs and constant demands of internecine warfare. Our technologies are archaic, even backsliding, our culture stagnant, and our future bleak. We have been abandoned and probably forgotten by our Earthbound progenitors. Birth rates across Tharsis and her allies are dropping rapidly. Atmospheric conditions are worsening. There were more days of unbreathable air conditions in Tharsis as a whole last year than ever recorded before. The red dust and our own industrial pollution will, in only a few more generations, make this planet's air unbreathable. Across Mars, over the last five years, there has been a .9% overall loss of arable land back to the sands and the red weeds; farm and plantation lands are dying. Even the forested margins of the canals, created by the Aresians themselves, are retracting. Forestation and planting initiatives, part of the overall Earthmelding programmes so vital to our continued existence, are being skimped on to spare resources for military expenditure. In our cities; poverty, social unrest and lawlessness abounds.

In addition, (what no one dare talk about openly, let alone publish in the newspapers) there is the grave news that the peoples of Noachis Territory have, after three consecutive failures of their crops, abandoned their rural communities and migrated to Hellas and Argyre. That is those that were allowed to, large numbers may have been forced to flee elsewhere. Noachis Territory now exists in little more than a name on the map, and one sprawling shanty town, Noah. More disquieting still is the word that all contact has been lost with the city of Sirenum. Rumour, at higher levels, has it that the city was savaged by the maddening disease St. Anthony's fire, or something far worse. I was privy to one report that claimed that Sirenum was seen to be in flames.

As I write this I fear that, unbeknownst to ourselves, we may, even now, be at war. Our enemy may already be upon us.

How can we fare against Mars, the God of War, himself? Historically speaking we have been on this planet such a short time but at what cost? Since we arrived here there cannot be a handful of square feet that has not been soaked in the blood of Earthmen and Martians. We have fertilised the red sands with our blood, our sweat and an ocean of tears. The children of Earth have known not a moment's peace since they first stepped onto Mars' red sands.

As Friar Godfried wrote; "This is not a world to be called home, it is but the bloody altar of an ancient War God, upon which we are sacrificed."

I truly feel that this expedition is not only tasked with re-establishing contact with the Aresians, but with the heavy burden of saving mankind. If we remain isolated we, as a species on this bloody red rock, are surely doomed.

As for our attackers of last night; I do not believe in happenstance nor coincidence, and although Captain Llewellyn has put forth the possibility that the incident was simply some chance encounter with smugglers or some such, I am inclined towards much the similar conclusion as Edwin's.

THE DANDELION FARMER

Edwin fervently believes that the ship that attacked us was under the direction of Eleuthère Du Maurier. The man is a true cacodemon with seemingly inexhaustible financial resources and a veritable army of homicidal brutes at his beck and call. Nonetheless, I am not wholly convinced that I can see his hand in it. I know there are many other forces, even more ruthless and resourceful than Du Maurier, ranged against us; I fear that even elements within our own Governmental structure would enthusiastically, if not actively, see us fail. People who have staked their reputations, if not their careers and fortunes, on me being little more than a raving lunatic.

To cap it all Octavius collapsed today on a field trip to Ananthor. I fear he is far iller than he has divulged even to his daughter, possibly too ill to even complete this expedition. Which is truly unfortunate as I believe his experiences during the last Aresian War, along with his academic and archaeological knowledge may be crucial to our venture.

Llewellyn has informed me that his men have effected the repairs necessary and we shall be ready for departure after dinner.

I would dearly like to abandon this diversion, no matter how important Octavius suspects it is, and strike out North but the mood of the expedition members seems to have set. Edwin particularly is determined to return home, even if only for a truly flying visit.

Llewellyn informed me that the apparent closeness of the friendship between Miss Bryant-Drake and Miss Spender has led to rumour mongering below decks. I have requested that he deals with such impropriety sternly and he has set Mr Charles upon the task. He, in turn, has bidden me remind the young ladies that they are aboard a vessel crewed primarily by men. Good, hardworking, men but drawn from a lower social order, and thus less liberal-minded, than the ladies may have normally associated with. And that open displays of sisterly affection, and such night-time meanderings, might be misconstrued.

I will speak to both of them as soon as the opportunity presents itself but the growing closeness of Sir John and Madam Fontenelli is of far greater concern to me than two high-spirited and unbetrothed young women playing nug-a-nug in the privacy of their own cabins. I fear that upon our return any scandal involving Sir John and Madam Fontenelli could be used to eclipse and discredit any achievements we accomplish.

Mr Franklin has kept me apprised as to their comportment and all seems to have been, so far, quite respectable. Though I shall have to insist that Madam Fontenelli's automaton maid chaperones her at all times.

I hear that Madam Fontenelli has also been the subject of deck hand's speculation, mostly admiring in their coarse colloquial ways, but warnings from Mr Charles regarding loose mouths resulting in loss of pay have meant that it has been kept to a minimum.

I have authorised Mr Charles to heavily garner the pay of any crew member found to or believed to, be making lascivious remarks or spreading gossip. Persistence will result in summary dismissal from the crew.

Captain Llewellyn informed me of an Air Naval tradition, going back to the days of the Empire, it is called "dropping off," and means just that; a barbaric practice where the unfortunate dismissed crew member is abandoned with only their personal possessions and three day's supply of food and water at the first convenient landing site. Regardless of its proximity to civilisation. Tantamount, I fear, to a death sentence, and something I could not be party to.

Before dinner, I spoke to the assembled expedition members (Octavius took his meal in his room). I said a few utterances in the form of a eulogy for Mr Grant, though we are still maintaining that he died as result of an accident. Miss Bryant-Drake suggested a collection be made towards funeral expenses and to help support the man's family. I assuaged their concerns and assured them that Grant's wife and children will be looked after.

After dinner, I took a spot of lunting on the weather deck ostensibly for my constitutional, whereupon, by chance, I had the opportunity to speak to Miss Bryant-Drake and Miss Spender in private. It was a tricky subject to tackle, being the true problem is other's presumptions, but the ladies seemed to be understanding of the situation and took it in good part. Although I did do my best to impress upon them that sapphism presents no personal dilemma to me in any way.

I bearded Sir John in the forward stairwell and invited him to join me in my cabin for a cigar and glass of port. I had noticed that Madam Fontenelli was extremely reserved at the dinner table and did not join the others in the wardroom afterwards. This was my "in" so to speak; I enquired if she was unwell or if there was some problem that I might be of some aid in solving? Sir John assured me she was perfectly well, however, perhaps, still a little shaken from witnessing Dr Spender's collapse.

While on the subject I took pains to clarify to him my concerns regarding his friendship with Madam Fontenelli. He listened carefully without interruption, something I did not expect from him. When I had explained myself to the best of my abilities, without, I hope, offending him, I invited him to speak.

He replaced the port decanter on my desk and sighed loudly.

Sir John first encountered Madam Fontenelli when he was travelling on the Grand Equatorial Express, the day the Utopian Anarchists blew up the railplane from Lybia to Tharsis. In the ensuing chaos at Altoura Station, Madam Fontenelli and her attendant automaton became separated from her husband's entourage and missed the departure. Isolated, her anxious attempts to disguise herself and thus go unnoticed in fact resulted in making her behaviour all the more suspicious to the confused, hysterical and angry crowds of trapped passengers madding about the station platforms.

Luckily Sir John, himself travelling back from a hunting expedition in the Hesperian wilderness, with all his kit, several bearers, loader, dogs and attendants, noticed the ladies desperately trying to secrete themselves away from prying eyes. Sir John put it down to the "predator's eye," that one slowly gains over the years of hunting.

Concerned that several undesirable members of the crowd were already taking an unwarranted interest in the ladies, Sir John decided to act. Hence trailing bearers, dogs, trophies, attendants and all, he descended upon the ladies and hurriedly swept them along with him.

He had an entire carriage booked on the next train and a salon room had been made available from which to await its arrival. Madam Fontenelli, although concerned about disclosing her identity to a stranger, was desperately grateful for his timely intervention. When finally she gave her husband's name, Sir John knew enough, through reputation, to recognise who she was. He grasped her need to remain concealed from the gaze of the masses.

Consequently he admits that he half rescued, half shanghaied, Madam Fontenelli against her determined resistance. She ardently believed her husband would return immediately to find her. Nevertheless, as Sir John knew, that would take at least a whole day for Mr Fontenelli to return, there was nothing for it; he sent word ahead to the various terminals on the way and as politely as possible hustled Madam Fontenelli and her maid on to his train carriage as soon as it arrived.

Just in time as it turned out. As the newspaper sellers started shouting the headlines that conflict had broken out along the border of Utopia and Amenthes, alarm spread through the already frustrated crowd. Upon the arrival of the Express, a tremendous kafuffle broke out as the jostling lower class passengers turned pugnacious in their desperation to board the train. At Madam Fontenelli's insistence, Sir John and his men plucked a number of distressed women and children to safety from the pandemonium.

And so, what was to have been a relaxing post hunt journey back to Tharsis in the comfort of his private carriage, in the company of his attendants and servants, turned out to be a chaotic rescue more akin to the retreat from Kabul.

I must say Sir John talks about it all in quite amused terms, but it was obvious, from what he implied, that the whole situation at the station got quite hairy and the couple of days' journey in a train carriage packed with distraught women, squabbling, hungry children, hunting hounds, his own retinue and Madam Fontenelli and her automaton, was actually far from a jolly adventure. Or even some illicit romantic interlude as it would seem Giovanni Fontenelli suspects.

Finally, Sir John addressed the crux of my concerns; No, he and Madam Fontenelli were not conducting any form of an affair. They are simply the very best of friends. Yes, she is an extremely beautiful and captivating woman, but, though she has disobeyed him in this instance, she is still exceedingly devoted to her husband. A man of whom Sir John holds in nothing but abject contempt.

I expressed my relief at Sir John's assurances. He smiled wryly and said that it was not for want of trying on his behalf, but she is a Roman Catholic lady of the highest moral exactitudes. Though, if her husband does, as he so cruelly threatened, disown her upon her return to Tharsis, Sir John assured me he will redouble those efforts. "A man like me, in this stage of life, needs a wife. And what a couple we would make!"

He is quite a contradiction, both libertine and hero, and, though I despair at his apparent moral ambiguity, I must admire his resilience. Though I reminded him that while a member of my expedition she is under my guardianship and shall be accorded the utmost deference.

Charity Bryant-Drake.
Notes to self. 32/9/26
(Cont.)

I am so furious I feel I could explode! I have never been so brazenly insulted in my life.

Professor Flammarion approached Patty and I this evening after dinner. I had finished my duties and we were amusing ourselves with watching the stars and trying to spot Earth, from the weather deck.

We greeted him and passed pleasantries for a while. Then he said he had a rather delicate matter to discuss with us. I must admit that I immediately stiffened at his tone. And Patty feared it was to do with her father, but it was nothing so expected.

It would seem that our friendship, Patty and I's, has in some way offended certain "members of the crew"! He asked that we abstain from such "overt displays of affection" that might be "misconstrued," by the men of the lower decks.

I was so confounded that I lost the ability to speak. If it were not for Patty's firm grip on my hand, I think I may have slapped him in the face right there and then.

Patty handled his "request" courteously and with a sense of humour and dignity, I could never have managed. I have not had anything like the "proper lady's" upbringing she has had.

After he had left us, no doubt to badger someone else, Patty tried to calm me, but I was far too angry to be reasoned with.

How dare they? How dare they judge us! **WE have OFFENDED them**?! Well, they, with their stupid, narrow-minded, bigotry offend me!

I wanted to go to Flammarion's cabin and demand he tell me who it was that had made such comments, and I would have their guts for garters, I swear. Patty would not allow it. She is far more tolerant of these things than I. I do not know how she bears it, but she says that after so long a while, such things are water off a duck's back to her.

She told me of the mistreatment she has suffered, even at the hands of the academics and colleagues her father works so closely with. If I ever believed we lived in a more enlightened age, then any such misconceptions were quashed tonight. Women of Mars have achieved so much in sense of status and respect, even political franchise in the more enlightened nations, but still, even here in Tharsis, we are not thought of as truly equal. Women and girls like us are treated with disgust.

Desist ladies for you may frighten the ship's cat! Or turn the cabin boy's head!

In the name of a loving God! What utter stupidity!

I will **NOT** be dictated on how to comport myself with someone I care for by some ignorant lackey from the lower decks. Patty and I are happy together, it is the first time I have been truly happy in this way, for years. In fact, ever since leaving boarding school.

Sitting here now, I wonder if Flammarion was lying, whether "crew members" was just a cypher for that pompous old blowhard, Jahns.

I vow to myself, and to Patty, that I will find out.

We may be far, far away from the old Empires and have fought a bitter war of emancipation for our freedoms, fought for by both men and women, but it is evident that those Empires have left their indelible smear upon our culture.

Damn them! My mother fought for this nation. She flew Le Bris Sparrow Hawks both against the Empires and against the Aresians. She was commended as the best daedalist of any flying machine in the 1st Free Women's Colonial Militia and braver than any man, but still some people – some men - still cleave to those ridiculous old pre-revolutionary attitudes.

Patty, still clowning about in an attempt to raise my spirits, joked that she shall go down in the morning in an open-necked crewman's blouse, displaying her tattooed décolletage and bosom rings! That should outrage the old puffins enough to put them off their breakfast. She proceeded to play act Colonel Jahns choking on his bloater and falling off his seat in shock, spluttering "Ah, there!" endlessly. She is so wildly funny. I suggested we slip an eccoprotic into the porridge in the morning as it may help to unconstipate the old fools.

Patty proposed that if we have outraged some nameless, spineless crew members, we should get blind drunk and act as mischievous as possible to vex them even more. She has just gone off to fetch the bottle of Mons Parvonis Dry Gin and some of her father's Winslow's Efficacious Tonic she has secreted in her cabin and we intend to drink the lot and misbehave terribly!

Huzzah!

Interview statement taken from Prisoner 101, William Coppinger, aka "Butler, Bill" on the 45th, October. 31. Tharsis Panopticon.

Convicted crew member, "Loadmaster," of dirigible The Shenandoah.

We had to ground her where we could.

Not much choice when we'd been all shot up like that in the middle of a storm. Half the bridge like was ripped open and we were on fire. It was a bloody miracle that we didn't crash the old scow.

Sea Sick (1) had dropped the starboard kedge an' almost wrecked us, an' got half the wheel straight through his cheek for his troubles. The bos'n was dying and four others were dead, including the most bona pilot we had.

By morning the bos'n had croaked too. We had wounded all over the ship and we were left waiting for the Preventer to come finish us off, grounded that we were, like.

Comes morning and I almost dropped my load when this other ship appears, like. It was the Wyndy (2).

We couldn't have fought them off, no more than we'd could a Preventer. An' we all knew the Wyndy by repute, like. So we struck the flag and bellied up, like.

But she (3) weren't bothered about what we were running. Just what had happened to us, like. They even had their crow (4) patch up Sea Sick an' a few of the others.

Then they were on their way, like.

Yes, a huge bastard in a big coat with a cape. Wore a billycock and had some sort of contrivance in his face. Like an eye-scopic thingy. Sort of bolted on, like. Never spoke to us, just stayed back puckering to the Mistress and eyeing us up. (5).

About noon, I was helping Snotty John and Sawney jury rig something to steer the old scow with, like, when the watch calls out that there was something approaching.

We were all on a razor's edge, expecting trouble. So we grabbed our irons and went to take a look-see, like.

Turns out it was this aeronaut. Flying a rocket pack right at us. He comes in hard and fast and we're still standing there like lemons waiting for the squeeze, like.

He landed right there in the open loading bay doors, like, an' just starts shooting up everything.

I swear, I myself got a good shot at him, like, most of us did, but it had no effect. He just kept coming. Nothing stopped him, like. So those of us that had any sense, ran.

Tall. All armoured up with a big nasty looking helmet, like them Orientals used to wear. Seen some things in my time, like, but it was the querist get up I've ever seen. And he had this gun, huge gun, like some sort of Maxim, or something like, but he swung it around like a Martini.

I jumped the ship and hid in the scrub and didn't go back until I saw him drop some flares and then fly off. Like some big angry bug.

The front of the gondola was alright, but I needed to get me kit and see if anyone was alive in there, like.

He'd killed everybody, like. Even the cabin boy. Even Sea Sick's bloody cat. Who troubles to kill a bloody ship's cat, for God sake?

It was carnage, like. Absolute bloody carnage. Only me and two of the others were left alive, like, and they was pretty banged up too. Jimmy the Stoker (6) and Birdlime Harry (7).

No. We didn't use your real names, in fact, you mostly use monikers, like. That way you keep your anonymousness, like.

Jimmy and Birdlime helped me manage to get the fire under control, like. At least as long as it took us to get some supplies out of there.

Loaded everything we could on a bl'oat (8), like, and got out of there as soon as we could.

I know nothing about that, like. We only took the one bl'oat. Maybe not all the other crew were goners after all. We didn't do no 'exhaustive search' nor nothing like it. Like.

1. 'Captain' Charles Jonas Frankston.
2. The Wyndeyer. A privateer.
3. Taken to indicate 'Captain' Colleen Ann Dullahan.
4. The ship's Doctor.
5. Identified as John Lloyd, under the alias of Uri Knapp.
6. As yet unidentified.
7. Identified as Harold Fowler.
8. Colloquial contraction of Balloon Life Boat.

The Diary of Eleanor Athaliah Ransom (Mrs).
Tuesday 32nd

After the excitement of last night's arrivals, today has been spent organising the chaos. After such a late night, I was up at an ungodly hour this morning and I was barely able to keep my eyes open this evening. I have retired early and I think that this entry shall have to be brief.

Everyone is settled now, Joshua and his sons are to aid Carstairs and the grounds staff in looking after the house and keeping us safe.

Mrs Carstairs kept Bowen busy all day with a hundred little tasks that she has been meaning to get around to. Bowen is not a particularly bright girl but she is industrious, hardworking and cheerful. This is the first time she has been to the house and she is so excited by it all.

Little Minnie is settled in the nursery, and Neriah has been helping Nanny with the children. I understand she may feel embarrassed by her situation, so I have not made any demands upon her and allowed her to spend the day with Nanny and the children. Though I will have to insist that she, as a member of the family, at least joins us for meals tomorrow. I cannot have her skulking around in the shadows, afraid to be seen or spoken to, like some ghost of a shameful secret.

It is wonderful to have Minnie in the house. It has been a fine day today. The air was particularly sweet and clear, and we all decided to take Lady N's pack of little mutts for a long walk around the grounds in the afternoon. Karl and Mr Lutchins, our gardener, escorted us.

The rest of today was taken up with household business, though I did have the opportunity, before dinner, to go over Edwin's ledgers and have a conversation with Minnie regarding the farm. Though with a heavy heart, she agrees with me that, this current unfortunate situation aside, the enterprise as a whole is barely clearing a profit of a few shillings. With the projected costs of repairs and maintenance that has been put off for so long now, let alone the losses incurred by the suspension of all production and the failure to bring in this year's second harvest, the farm, as a business, is unsalvageable.

Minnie, bless her heart, also confirmed to me that she has been using her own resources, including her inheritance and meagre compensation for Philip's death, to support the household, in fact, to put food on the table. I know, even though Edwin does not know I know, that he too has used up almost every penny his father left him.

I did not worry Minnie with my thoughts, but I believe that complete failure is no more than three or four months away.

When Edwin returns, as I pray passionately he will do so soon, we shall have to have an extremely difficult discussion.

Oh, how trifling these thoughts of money are against the real dangers Edwin and Papa face, but they distract me from my greater fears.

So to bed.

"In this world, which is so plainly the antechamber of another, there are no happy men.
The true division of humanity is between those who live in light and those who live in darkness.
Our aim must be to diminish the number of the latter and increase the number of the former.
That is why we demand education and knowledge."

VICTOR HUGO

DAY FOUR

THE ATHENAEUM OF HARENDRIMAR TAI

P.E.S. Seren Bore.   **8.00/33/09/26**
Ship's scrap log (excerpts from) Captain R. K. Llewellyn.

Ship ready for First Mate Mister Charles' inspection by 7 A.M. All well.

Staff meeting 7.30 A.M.

Chief Engineer's report; Repairs holding well. All routine maintenance, signed off 7.43 A.M.

Purser's report (Given by Mr Harkett, acting Purser); Supplies holding well. 8.00 A.M.

Master Gunner's report; Watch continues to be double manned.

Ship's Medical Officer's report; Dr Spender is somewhat recovered from his collapse and insisting on being up and about.

Miss Bryant-Drake was not able to attend breakfast due to a touch of mal-de-mer.

One crew member reporting sick at First Watch; James Birkett, Able Airman. Breathing difficulties (Sand Lung).

New course entered in Navigator's Log.

Estimated arrival at destination 3 P.M.

Making good time. Weather ahead fine.

Mister Charles has entered the names of three members of the crew in the Reprimand Record for spreading scuttlebutt regarding members of the Expedition Team. These appear to be the ringleaders of the malcontents.

Name.	Position.	Punishment.
Cooper. Shane.	*Stoker.*	*First warning.*
Fined; 10s.		
Fairlie. Mara.	*Engineer (oiler), 2nd Class.*	*First warning.*
Fined; 10s.		
Howe. Darragh.	~~*Rigger, 1st Class.*~~	*Second warning*
Fined; 10s.		
Insubordination; 20s		
Reduced to Rigger, 2ndClass.		
As of this date.		

Mister Charles delivered a strict warning to all crew that such scandal-mongering and malicious talk will not be tolerated.

Mister Charles has voiced further concerns about Mr Howe's deportment.

Chief Engineer Beer informed me that Howe is a vagarious man of ill temper who has voiced an extreme enmity towards Madam Fontenelli because of her Aresian origins, and toward Sir John Sydeian, due to his closeness with Madam Fontenelli.

If his behaviour does not improve beforehand, I am minded, upon recommendations, to drop him off near Tremorfa Township. Whatsoever, I will have him paid off at Tharsis upon our return. We can ill afford a rabble-rouser amidst the crew.

I will advise the Professor of my decision.

Journal of Adam Franklin.

Editor's Note; 3 pages have been roughly torn from the journal and have never been accounted for. As the removed pages comprised the first part of the entry included below, we feel that by the weight of evidence it is probable that it was the entry for the previous day.

James Ransom.

...... involving Charity and Parthena getting very inebriated and practicing a dance called the "polka," in the main corridor late last night. Parthena arrived at breakfast as I left. She was more reserved than usual and appeared to have had little sleep.

I checked my arrangements with Edwin. He still insisted upon returning to his homestead to retrieve some personal objects and books. I cannot say I do not understand his impetus, but fear that it is one that others might well anticipate. Du Maurier has shown a flair for patience and forward planning previously.

Before luncheon, the expedition members gathered in the wardroom to discuss final preparations for the landing and tomb investigation. Colonel Jahns will personally supervise security. Mr Charles will roster several crew members to aid with any clearing and heavy work.

The Captain would provide Edwin and myself with one of the tracked Hornsby's, a driver and one of Jahns' men as an extra pair of hands.

I had a bad feeling about this whole excursion. I suggested to Edwin that he furnishes me with a list and that I go alone with the driver but he will not hear of it. I thought to appeal to the Professor but feared that might leave Edwin feeling as if I were treating him like a rebellious child.

We returned to our cabin to change into more appropriate apparel for our afternoon goings-on, but, instead, ended up having a fairly heated discussion. I told him that if I were Du Maurier I would have men crawling all over the farm, let alone those searching for the tomb, and ready to pounce should he return. I also reminded him that, as far as we were all aware, Everheart and Lloyd are still at large. Du Maurier seems to have a veritable army of such hoodlums willing to do his bidding. That, added to the fact that we have no idea where the airship that attacked us went, made his idea of returning to the house tantamount to courting disaster.

Edwin would not be swayed. He is an especially decent and honourable chap, but possibly one of the most singularly bull-brained men I have ever met. His counter suggestion was that he should go alone, (wearing a different coat and hat as a cunning disguise!) so as not to endanger me or any crew members. Utter bloody-minded stubbornness.

I insisted, that if he could not be dissuaded, he would have to follow my instructions and, for once in his life, do as he was told. Finally, after some further badgering, he agreed.

The ship was making good time and so I spent the remaining couple of hours making sure that all the others knew what to do should there be any alarm or threat. I must admit I was in no small part annoyed at being called away to escort Edwin when I should be overseeing the safety of the whole expedition. I had to rather forcibly insist to the Professor and the Captain that no expedition, nor crew member leaves the ship unarmed, including Dr Spender and the Professor himself.

The Professor made light of it, saying that in an emergency he would be more of a threat to himself than any assailant, but Edwin reminded him that he was indeed a fine shot with a shotgun. Then again, the Professor countered, that was shooting ducks or pheasants for the table, not shooting men.

The Captain expressed the opinion that we should alert the team, those that did not know already, as to the truth of how Mr Grant's death came about so that they will appreciate the real dangers. The Professor, Edwin and I agreed (though I believed that only Madam Fontenelli, the young ladies and Dr Spender were the only ones not to have been officially told beforehand).

We gathered for an early tea and the Professor calmly explained to everyone what really happened the other night, and why they must be cautious. All took the news rather stoically and agreed that our precautions were only reasonable in the circumstances.

To remain unnoticed by the locals, or any undesirables, we circumnavigated Tremorfa Province's border, below the horizon. In fact dropping low enough to brush the treetops and headed out towards Edwin's farm.

Through careful planning, we entered Edwin's lands from the North following the irrigation canals across to the place Karl had described. We lost only a few minutes as Edwin struggled to gain his bearings, but at almost 3 P.M. exactly we arrived at the location.

Thus far so good. We had done our best to reconnoitre the location as we arrived, but, for safety's sake, Sir John strapped his flying apparatus on and took a "look-see," as he called it. The man's antics border on the insane, but he wants for no ounce of courage or adventurous spirit. Within a few minutes, he was back to report he had noticed nothing unusual or worrying in the area.

With that confirmation, the Captain ordered the grounding of the ship.

By 3.30 the Hornsby was almost ready for Edwin and I to depart. I was double-checking the equipment with Sergeant

Rawlings, who had been sent along with us by the Professor, when Sir John approached me and made a suggestion. It was a fair one and on my agreement, he pressed a Very pistol into my hand.

We set off in the Hornsby at a surprising speed. The young driver informed us these machines were another brainchild of the Professor. The man is quite the genius and, I have to admit, in mass production they would make excellent military vehicles. If you could equip a cavalry division with these you would have an incredibly effective strike force. If, of course, you could get the horse-jockeys out of their saddles. The machine was one hell of a spine-rattler, but the driver's estimate of thirty miles an hour over even rough ground was no exaggeration. We held on with grim determination as the Hornsby acquainted us with every knoll, dip, rut and furrow on our journey.

Following Edwin's directions, we reached sight of the house in less than an hour. As Edwin said there was a field of sunflowers that backs up to within almost a few yards of the rear of one of the barns west of the house. Though battered by the storm, most of the sunflowers were still standing at over 10 feet high and afforded excellent cover through which to approach the homestead. Leaving the driver with the Hornsby, the three of us picked our way through the rows of towering plant stems carefully, as not to announce our presence by creating too much disturbance.

We had gone well armed, I had insisted, though Edwin was still certain that no one would bother to watch the house for so long on such a faint chance of his return.

Almost at the edge of the plantation, we stopped and surveyed the area between the storage barn and the house itself. It was clearly a potential killing ground. Edwin's father had, most probably unbeknownst to himself, built an all too easily defensible home.

Jahns' man, Freddy Rawlings, had brought a good set of binoculars and we did our best to scour the area for any signs of a trap. Nothing. No life signs. No fresh footprints in the soil, no suspicious movements in the curtains, no smell of recently extinguished tobacco. Not a thing. So we waited.

Soldiers and hunters are trained to wait. They are taught to be patient, calm, quiet. There is a lot of waiting to be done in both warfare and the hunt. You learn to be aware of your smallest movement, the sound of your own breathing, the scent of your own body, the tiniest noise you make. You learn to control everything, you create silence around you. Patience is as valuable a skill in battle as being able to fire a gun.

The kind of men that become hired brutes for people like Du Maurier not only lack that skill, they have never been taught it. They have never sat quietly for long periods awaiting their prey, whether animal or human. They have never shared their space with an unsuspecting enemy.

So it was only a matter of time.

A stifled sneeze followed by a muffled curse hissed through clenched teeth.

There were at least two watchers along the edge of the field to the south of us. A position from which they could observe the western gable end and the front of the house. I would expect there to be a similar pairing to the northeast. Four men, not skilled, to watch the outside. Economical but effective.

I left the discombobulated Edwin in the safe hands of Rawlings and moved down to where I could come upon the sentries from behind.

They were hefty fellows, more brawn than muscle, though, shabbily dressed, but well-armed, too well armed for mere henchmen. I came at them from the verdure. Always take the biggest one down first. It demoralises their lesser brethren.

A big man, maybe over six feet seven, big bearded and barrel-chested. I felled him with a kick to the inside back of his knee and clean punch to the back of the head. As he went down I took his rifle from him and slammed it into the face of his surprised friend.

I dragged them a few yards back into the rows of sunflowers and took a better look at the two of them. The big one was covered in tattoos, and I was surprised to find him wearing a rusted old vest of chain mail under his heavy grimy overcoat. His rifle was some eight barrelled thing, like an old-fashioned boarding gun, that looked as if it had been cobbled together by an enthusiastic, but not experienced, blacksmith. He also carried another two pistols and several blades, including what looked like a falchion. The Sargent Major's voice hissed from somewhere at the back of my mind; this man did not care for his weapons, and a man who does not care for his weapons is a fool, often a dead fool. The other was a smaller, stouter man, dirty, with a dark scabrous beard, lank hair and, under the blood, he had the deep sun tanned outline of a breather mask permanently marked on his face. He stank of alcohol and stale sweat. He too carried a ridiculous number of weapons, two pistols, almost antiques, four blades and a battered Martini-Henry with some odd viewing contraption built onto it.

I needed to question them, but the smaller one was dead, I had driven his vomer a good three inches into his face with the rifle butt. The big one was still breathing but he had a fist-sized dent in the back of his skull that was seeping gore and thick blood into the soil. I was sure he could not live much longer. They were not going to tell me anything without the aid of Lady Niketa. Human bodies were obviously much more fragile than whatever the machine that those monsters Democritus and Lanulos had built inside of me.

I decided that there was only one thing for it. Assuming they existed, I would have to take down the other guards on the northeast side. I shouldered the boarding gun along with my own rifle and ran, as stealthily as I could, back along the inside edge of the rows of towering plants. I did not return to Edwin but went on further to where the plantation ended. There was a gap, some kind of track for farm vehicles, between the sunflowers and another huge field of mature dandelions.

I do not know how fast I can run, but my speed at yesterday's cricket match had been a surprise to everyone including myself. I sprinted across the trail and dived into the cover of the huge dandelions. Though obviously plumped up by the rain they stood between two and three feet high, I remember my shock at first seeing them, what must be only a few days ago, but alas, they were still too short to provide cover, even for a crouching man, so I threw myself into a tiger crawl. It was filthy, mucky going, but exhilarating. I felt like a prattan on the hunt.

My quarry were exactly where I expected them to be. Under the cover of a small stand of fruit trees on the far north eastern edge of the dandelion field. Two rogues of equal stature, but otherwise much like their brethren. One wore a metal breastplate, under an old duster overcoat, and bowler hat, the other; a shabby, moth chewed, immensikoff and an old Royal Regiment of Artillery issue full faced gunner's helmet. Tough looking, but grubby men, armed to the teeth with an array of guns and edged weapons. The one in the immensikoff was boredly slashing at the dandelion heads with a cavalry sabre, while the other was watching the approaches to the house through an old spyglass.

I got as close as I could do unobserved, and launched into them. I did not rate the boarding gun as much of a firearm, but its immense weight and crude brass-bound stock made for a splendid club. All those years of bayonet and butt training came into good use. I took the sabre wielder down first, with a hard blow to his upper back and a sharp clout on the side of the helmet. His head must have rung like a bell in that thing. I drove the brass-bound stock as hard as possible in the centre of the other one's breastplate, right over the solar plexus, and gently tapped him on the top of his bowler as he went down.

I must have underestimated the one in the big coat because he recovered quickly enough to take a good swing at my back with the sabre. If it had not been so blunt it would have sliced through my overcoat right down to the skin and what was below that. Instead, it felt more like being whacked with a blunt iron bar. I swung around and in a fit of annoyance rammed the boarding gun's stock as hard as I could into his faceplate. This time he would not be getting up and if he was still alive, he would not have much of a face to talk through.

The other however was gasping for air and very much still alive. I quickly divested him of his eclectic collection of weaponry and slapped his senses back into him. Once I had his attention, aided by the closest possible look at the gaping barrel mouths of the boarding gun, I enquired if there were others. He nodded in affirmation. Where?
"In..in..in the h... house."
How many?
"Th..three."
It was then I noticed the earring; a lump of silver, the size of a cobnut. Of, course, the other two had had them too. I warned him

truthfully, *"Do not lie to me, I would as willingly kill you as let you live. What ship do you hail from?"*

He did not pause, *"The Wyndeyer."* There was a certain expectation of recognition in his tone, a touch of pride perhaps.

The name meant nothing to me. *"All of you?"*

He nodded nervously.

"Where is she grounded?"

"About five miles that way." He nodded westward. The Sergeant Major's voice started cursing loudly in my head. *"How many of you?"*

"Four dozen of us in all."

I did not expect much of an answer to my next question, but it was worthwhile trying as he would never be so honest again, real fear can loosen the tightest mouth. *"Who sent you? Who hired you?"*

He looked utterly panic-stricken at the question. I thrust the barrels closer to his face and let the Sergeant Major speak to him. I saw his eyes widen in horror.

"I do... do, don't know... I don't... know... there's this Passenger... he's paying the piper. I don't know his name."

"Describe him. What does he look like?"

"B... big... like you... scarred up too... got a thing built into his phys..."

Lloyd. *"Where is he?"*

"In the house."

I cannot honestly remember if I left the man alive or dead. The Sergeant Major was so furious, his anger was almost blocking out any reasoned thought. It was hard enough simply concentrating on getting back to warn Edwin and Rawlings.

When the red mist of the Sergeant Major's rage abated, I found myself not back with my cohorts, but standing at the foot of the steps up to Edwin's house. It took me a few moments to gather my wits. There was no time for planning, no time for subtleties, I was there now and they, whoever "they" were, would know it.

Better this way though, no one else to worry about, just them and me.

I pulled the Very gun from my belt and fired it into the air and tossed it aside, swung the lever-action rifle off my shoulder, levered a round into the chamber and started up the steps to the front door. It felt like an age since I had first walked up these steps, though it had only been but a few days. These farmstead buildings were all much of a muchness, rammed earth constructions, plastered to resemble old Earth red brick, and built in a style that echoed the elite homes of a civilisation several million miles away across space. Each an encapsulated testament to the power of British colonialism. Much like me, I suppose.

The door was ajar. An inviting trap. Would they know I had taken down their brethren? If not, they would think their trap was still well set. I did not want to disappoint them. I pushed the door open with the muzzle of the rifle and stepped inside.

Enough light spilt in from the front door and the coloured glass around it to illuminate the cluttered interior. The once spacious hallway was filled with a chaotic jumble of a couple of life time's worth of accumulated paraphernalia; long cased clocks, pictures, trophies and numerous anomalous objects brought into the house for some purpose that never made it beyond their first resting place. The staircase ahead of me, with its thread worn carpet and similar accretion of objects, choking its treads, led to the upper hallway and bedrooms. No fancy balcony, just a simple landing that split off in three directions.

On the ground level, six doors, none of them fully closed, led off the entrance hallway, two to each side and two that flanked the staircase. From my left; the morning room, the dining room, the door to the kitchen and servant's quarters, I had no idea where the door on the other side of the stairs led to, but the next one was the drawing room that led through to Edwin's study and finally to my right; the dayroom. All seemed quiet. I stepped through the front doorway.

"Do come in, old bean."

The door to the day room swung open and there stood the man from the train station. Without the Inverness to hide his frame I could see how skeletal he was under his blazer. His face was like rotting old parchment pasted over a skull, the ridiculous moustache was mangy and looked as if he had pencilled the bald areas in with mascara. His left eye was gone, replaced by some makeshift ocular contrivance of lenses and brass that was crudely bolted into his flesh and from which a corposant glow emitted. But for all of that, he was still instantly recognisable.

"Lloyd." I levelled the rifle at him.

"Sergeant Major Franklin." He reciprocated by levelling the Lancenett in his hand at me. "So good to see a familiar face." He smiled, or grimaced, it was hard to tell, but as his thin, cracked lips pulled back over metal teeth he made a noise like a clogged drain. "And you look so well, indeed."

"More than I can say for you, Lloyd."

He made the noise again in a vague approximation of laughter. "True. It did not go as well for me, dear boy. All got rather ballsed up, I'm afraid." He tried to chuckle again. "Still better than being dead."

"Is it?" I asked incredulously.

There was a flash of something in his remaining eye. Lloyd had always been a ne'er-do-well, a would-be libertine if he had had better breeding and a higher rank. A droll chap with an amusing line in self-deprecating patter, mostly regarding his failed pursuits of eligible and ineligible women of a higher class. Nevertheless there had always been those cold, glassy black eyes of his. "Fish eyes," some of the men had called him behind his back. Dead eyes, but sometimes when the chiding got too near to the bone, something would flash deep in those cold eyes and people knew to back off. Gossip had it, and the barrack rooms were always full of gossip, when he was not spending all his pay chasing fine ladies, he liked to knock about with the girls of the street, the ones in the city not around the Citadel, and he liked to hurt them. Hurt them a lot. Animals too. There had been a lot of disquieting rumours about him, all unsubstantiated and unproven, of course. As they say, though, there is no smoke without fire.

I fought the compulsion to shoot him right there and then, but the old interest flared and I wanted to know more.

"What is it you want, Lloyd? Why are you doing this?"

"Oh, my dear chap, don't you know?" He feigned surprise in the most mocking tone. "Haven't you worked it all out yet? Well, I am shocked."

I gritted my teeth and tried to block out the raging voice in my head, screaming for me to kill the murderous bastard.

He continued in the same mocking tone, "Oh, Adam. May I call you 'Adam'? After all, we have known each other for such a long, long time and been through so much together. Even shared a grave and our resurrection. I feel we are almost brothers. You and me."

There was a delicate looking long cased grandmother clock standing between the day room and the drawing room door frames. The area around its face was mirrored, and in the silvered reflection, I could easily see the hand of someone inching the door behind me open. On the edge of my vision, I could see another thug had appeared at the top of the staircase, trying to hide his presence behind the cover of the wall.

"We are not relatives, Lloyd. The only thing we have in common is we have been turned into monsters by the same maniacs. Oh, but you already were, weren't you?"

Lloyd's smile dropped. "Now, Adam, don't be churlish. We have both killed our fair share of innocents. I have just watched you murder four men in cold blood. One of which you tortured to death. Monsters? We were both monsters a long time before they dug us up out of the ice."

There was a question I wanted to ask, and that moment seemed the perfect opportunity. "I am a soldier. I took the Empress Queen's shilling a long time ago and if I have to kill, whether, with a gun or bayonet, I look my enemies in the eye. What were you? Nothing more than a balloon jockey? You dropped a few bombs with the bravery born of being beyond the range of the enemy's guns, and the peace of mind of never seeing the faces of those you killed or maimed. Grandiose talk, Lloyd, but you flatter yourself, you were never much of a soldier and not much of a man either." I knew he would not be able to resist answering that.

His cadaverous features, contorted with resentment. "Oh, dear chap, you really know nothing about me. I've killed, oh so many; whores, doxies and rollers, chavos, urchins and assorted street scum by the dozen. Even one of those little Nipponese Nuns, for the fun of it. And that's not the half of it, old bean. All fair game to me. You had no idea. They had no idea. That's why their indoctrinating didn't work on me," He tapped his temple, "You see, they couldn't make into a soulless killing machine, because I've always been one. Just... like... you."

That was when I decided I was going to kill him, and this time I would make sure there would not be enough left for them to resurrect.

The one behind me had now opened the door sufficiently to step through and begin to slowly level her shotgun at the back of my head. "Why are you here, Lloyd? It is no coincidence. What have you to do with all this? With Edwin? Du Maurier?"

"Us, dear chap. Us. You and me. All this is but chaff in the wind, merely smoke and mirrors, they sent me to kill you." In that instant, I saw an involuntary flicker of his eye to the Lancenett.

So I shot him. High on the right of his chest, sending him staggering back as the blast from his pistol went flashing into the wall. In a single movement, I dropped, pirouetted, levered another round into the chamber and shot the woman who had come out of the morning room in the face. The big shotgun went off simultaneously, over my head, in the direction of Lloyd. Without hesitating, I threw myself into the cover of the staircase, my back against the kitchen door, as a hail of bullets from above tore through the hallway.

The problem with hurdy-gurdy guns like the Bira is that you have to be immensely strong to aim it and crank it at the same time, or it just sprays bullets wildly, and they take an age to reload. Good for keeping your enemy's head down, but when you have run out of ammunition you better have a backup plan. I suspected he would not.

As the last report sounded, I vaulted up and over the handrail and bounded up the stairs. As the gunman stood there struggling to unstrap himself from the Bira's harness, I put two shots into his chest, but then, as he collapsed, his overcoat parted, and I noticed he had a piece of boilerplate strapped to his chest, like some improvised cuirass. Crude but effective. He threw his hands up to ward me off and cried out, but there was no time for mercy. I am, as Lloyd so rightly pointed out, a monster.

Lloyd? Where was Lloyd? I turned just in time to see him stagger into the hall. His already skull like visage had been shredded into a bloody pulp, the contraption on his face, shattered, and the metal beneath his flesh exposed for all the world to see. He must have caught the full force of the shotgun blast from his own henchwoman.

He came out screaming like a wounded animal and firing the Lancenett wildly at me. All sense told me to dive for cover, but the Sergeant Major's voice in my head held me motionless. I just stood there, with the blaster's beams flashing about me until the screeching totenkopf reached the bottom of the stairs. I took careful aim and emptied my last rounds into his grisly physiognomy. He went down with the sound of an airship crashing.

All abruptly fell into silence.

I inhabited the sudden stillness, letting it flow into me. I watched the gun smoke flowing in the air and the tiny motes glittering in the daylight through the stained glass of the window panes above the front door. Lloyd lay there like a broken mannequin and I stood surrounded by death. Again.

After what could have been an age, the big grandfather clock between the day room and dining room doorways struck the hour, followed closely by its companion grandmother across the hall. Other clocks elsewhere in the house joined the chiming cacophony. As I stood there, transfixed by the sound, Lloyd began to move.

His body jittered as if galvanised back into life. After a few seconds, he let out a sound, an ugly mournful noise, and slowly sat up. Not as a man, or even an automaton, would do, but more like one of those clockwork tin toys do. I watched in sickened fascination as, in jerky mechanical motions, he slowly clambered to his feet.

It was only as he began to step towards the stairs that I dropped my rifle, pulled the pistol I had been issued with and emptied round after round into him. Each shot blowing away a little more of the vestiges of his once human husk, staggering him but not impeding his progress. At the bottom of the staircase, he stopped and slowly bent over to retrieve the Lancenett.

As he straightened back up, I discarded my pistol and took up the boarding gun. Though obviously as dangerous to its user as to their target, the gun unexpectedly felt hearteningly potent in my hands. Lloyd, or what was left of Lloyd, seemed oblivious to me, lost in his own slow spasmodic world.

I stepped down to meet him and rammed the brass-bound butt of the boarding gun into his face. And again and again. I have no idea how many times I struck him, but eventually, he crashed back down again.

This time though I had no time for morbid fascination, I slammed my boot on his chest, pushed the barrels of the boarding gun into the remains of his smashed eyepiece, cocked the hammer and pulled the trigger. In my fury, I did not even envisage for a moment that the humongous weapon might not fire, or worse; explode.

The gun roared and bucked violently, blasting a huge hole through Lloyd's head, Edwin's hall carpet and floorboards beneath.

As the smoke cleared part of me, though sickened, was yet still somehow relieved, to see blood, bone and brain matter dripping from inside the metal encased carapace of Lloyd's skull.

We are not automatons, we are not machines. Inside his shell, within a shell, he was still a human being. I stood as if mesmerised. I am still Adam Franklin, I am still alive.

Suddenly the front door flung open, I whirled to meet the challenge levelling the empty gun, but it was merely Edwin and Rawlings coming to my aid.

I gave Edwin the briefest of explanation of events. Though both he and Rawlings were almost too fascinated by the half-man, half-automaton that lay dead in his hallway, to take in much of what I told them. Rawlings though, used a word I have never heard before, "Golem." A machine man, not simply with augmentations for damaged arms or legs, but a true hybrid; half-man half-automaton. He had heard of such things, but he thought it was just fiction.

Edwin was horrified. "In God's good name! Anyone could be one of these things. Even one of us. How would we ever know?"

I laughed at the absurdity of it all. "No doubt it would be indeed exceedingly difficult to tell."

Edwin started to witter on about giving these men a good Christian burial, so much so that I had to be extremely forthright with him. We had no time for social niceties. The men with Lloyd were from an airship, the Wyndeyer, probably the same pirate ship that shot at us the other night. No doubt they would be here soon, especially if they had seen the signal flare I had fired off to warn the Seren Bore. Nonetheless to assuage Edwin's concerns I offered to take the corpses out to the edge of the field and cover them with something so at least they would not stink out the house, while he and Rawlings collected whatever it was that he required. Edwin unenthusiastically agreed.

Without a great deal of ceremony, I dumped Lloyd and his two henchmen at the corner of the sunflower field, with the first two I had dealt with. As I promised Edwin, (after, of course, relieving the big one of the rest of his ammunition for the boarding gun) I laid them in the furrow and covered the bodies with a few fallen sunflower stems. I returned to the bodies of the other two sentries and dragged them further into the dandelion field and covered them with foliage too. There was something apt about that, I thought.

As I stood over them, covered as it were in their shroud of dandelions, it occurred to me I had slain seven men, brutal hardened myrmidons no doubt, without receiving a scratch. Even Lloyd had been no match for me. Am I the machine-man that Lanulos and the Doctor were trying to perfect? Am I their monster, their golem?

By the time I returned to the house Edwin and Rawlings were loaded up with various books and suitcases. Evidently, Minnie, Edwin's sister-in-law, had taken most of the important personal things with her when she left. I made a mental note to kiss the woman when I saw her again.

I hurried them out of the house and back towards the waiting Hornsby. With all Edwin's luggage, we could not make it back through the stands of sunflowers so we had to use the track between the fields. We had made but a few hundred yards when from the southwest, low over the fields came a small fast moving dirigible. Edwin and I recognised its configuration immediately as the one that had pursued Charity to Alba Kirk. It had a disagreeable insectoid look about it, with those peculiar lightning swathed toroidal electrificated engines thrust out each side of the gondola.

Aware it was looking for us, and knowing how heavily armed it was, we dived into the cover of the sunflowers. We eyed it keenly as it circled the house a couple of times. Only two crew; a gunner and a daedalist. The gunner was acting as spotter, almost hanging out of the machine's cockpit, to get a better look and, because of the roar of the engines, communicating with hand signals to the pilot. We suspected they were awaiting a sign from the house, but none would be forthcoming. Eventually, they would understand that none was going to come, then they would either begin searching for us or take off back to warn their cohorts.

I could not allow that. All the time we had been watching the machine I had also been reloading the boarding gun. The dirigible was fast and manoeuvrable but its altitude was low and, if I could get it in range, a volley of eight 16-gauge solid lead shots would do a lot of damage to one of those engines, if I could not hit the pilot with my rifle. I was preparing myself when suddenly the dirigible spun on its axis, and with a blast of black smoke and breathtaking speed, it shot a good 30 feet further up in the air.

Edwin exclaimed in alarm and dived further into the verdant cover of the sunflowers. I roughly propelled Sergeant Rawlings after Edwin, but myself, I stayed where I could observe the dirigible and its crew through the binoculars. The gunner was frantically trying to operate some mechanism, probably to bring the Gatling guns to bear, but whatever it was it was not responding. Something was causing them great alarm and I was sure it was not because of us. I took the chance to cast a glance around the horizon – as much as I could without betraying my presence to them.

There, in the distance, I saw it. A quick glance through the glasses confirmed my intuition; like a big black bug on the horizon was Sir John in his flying apparatus. As good as his word.

I turned my attention back to the dirigible crew in time to see the pilot reach forward to slap the gunner across the back of his head and, once he had the other's attention, signal something. A simple but urgent gesture of drawing his thumb quickly across his throat. The gunner nodded in compliance. The little dirigible whirled about and, in another blast of oily black smoke, took off over the roof of the house and out of my line of sight.

I stepped out and waved vigorously to attract Sir John's attention. He landed only yards from me in a great cloud of dust, dirt and fumes, pulled off his helmet and mask, and greeted me with; "Wot oh, old chap! Dreadfully sorry for my tardiness. Looks like the blighters have cleared off then. Would you like me to give chase?"

There was no doubt he was up for it, but I demurred explaining that we had more pressing business. My principal concern now was to get Edwin and his 'few items' back to the safety of the Seren Bore. What I required of the intrepid aeronaut was that he return immediately and alert both the Captain and the Professor, that the pirate ship that fired upon us is around here somewhere.

Sir John looked horrified. "Damn it! The chaps had just actually entered the sepulchre when I left. They'll be dreadfully disappointed."

Extracts from
The Death of Malacand.
The History of the Human Conquest of Mars.
R.M. Scott.

In 1852 Capt. Edmond Rudnick Hamilton was an adventurer and a member of the doomed von Lasswitz expedition, the Prussian Government backed expedition to discover a route through to the White Sea from the River Kemijoki in the Gulf of Bothnia.

It was a lunatic escapade premised upon little more than the wistful, if not, mystical thinking of Kurt Von Lasswitz himself and encouraged by the desperation of the Prussian Government over its failure to defeat Denmark in 1851 and thus ensure its access to the North Sea.

Lasswitz was a self-styled visionary, natural philosopher, amateur scientist, inventor and would be adventurer who, though he had powerful friends in the Prussian Court, some exceedingly close to the King himself, had no experience of exploration and no other support for his scheme than a purportedly ancient Viking map that he had obtained in Stockholm – under questionable circumstances – and a series of dreamlike "visitations." Due to escalating costs and unforeseen problems, the expedition failed to set off until late September 1852.

Hamilton joined the team in August. He had tenuous family connections to Lasswitz and used that, along with his experience as an airship Captain to obtain a place upon the expedition when the first appointed Captain met an untimely demise. In his autobiographical exposition Hamilton suggests that agents of the British Government not only had a hand in the various setbacks that plagued the Lasswitz Expedition's preparations, but that Hamilton himself, who had served in the Royal Naval Aerostat Service in India, was encouraged to offer his services to Lasswitz under the direction of the British War Office.

The 20 man steam-powered airship, the Herkus Monte, designed by Jules H J Giffard, set sail on the 1st of September 1852.

According to Hamilton's autobiography; plagued by continuing technical problems and exasperated by Lasswitz inept and indecisive leadership, the Herkus Monte had reached 60 miles North East of Tervola by late October. Flying into – not unexpected - atrocious weather conditions.

In the grip of a sudden and violent hail storm, there was a fire on board, believed to have been caused by an unsecured oil lamp. The blaze precipitated a series of unfortunate events that led to the airship becoming virtually rudderless in the storm. The crew valiantly fought the inferno while Hamilton and the flight crew struggled to regain control of the ship. Unfortunately, the fire breached the hydrogen envelope and the resulting explosion tore the airship's balloon apart.

According to Hamilton, Lasswitz himself and twelve other members of the crew were killed in the explosion and subsequent crash. Of the remaining seven, three were too badly injured to survive more than a few hours.

After burying the dead and salvaging what little supplies could be found, Hamilton and the four other survivors struck out in a South Westerly direction in hopes of finding their way back to civilisation. They were not successful.

Within five days, two of the others were dead from a mixture of exhaustion, starvation and exposure, while a third had simply wandered off in to a blizzard in the grip of some Fata Morgana type delusion. Hamilton and the other survivor pushed on for another day or two before they too were overcome.

Hamilton wrote that he remembered sitting down in the snow beside the already dead body of his shipmate and just hoping that sleep, hastened by exhaustion, would overtake him before death's icy grip stilled his heart.

Hamilton wrote that he became aware of an enveloping light and warmth and that he fought to open his eyes, expecting to see angels or some other fetch sent to retrieve his immortal soul.

Instead, he was surrounded by figures in what he first mistook for silver armour, with roundish helms upon their heads. To his befuddled mind, they looked as if they had stepped from the pages of some Arthurian romance, medieval knights in shining armour. Save their helmets were glass and their fair faces strangely set?

Hamilton claims that he "passed out," and thus was unable to explain his transferral from the frozen wastes to a comfortable bed upon, what he first thought upon awakening, was an airship.

Hamilton soon discovered that this was no ordinary airship nor were his rescuers ordinary men. They were, in fact, alien interlopers and he was now aboard their ship heading back to their homeworld.

Their leader, one called Verilhon, took great pains to explain the situation to Hamilton over the course of their journey. These were no normal men, their skin was as yellow as dandelion heads, their hair as blond as straw, with amber coloured caprine eyes. They were lithe and handsome and kindly.

They claimed they were explorers from another world that had been visiting Earth since the beginning of time. They assured him they meant no harm. They came as observers and occasionally as missionaries of a sort when they felt Earthmen needed gentle guidance. Verilhon showed Hamilton their astounding ship, not an airship but a spaceship, a colossal avian machine that flew with effortless grace upon gossamer wings through the endless night between the planets.

Hamilton asked why they had saved him and not the others of his crew. Verilhon said that regretfully they were not infallible Angels, only fallible men much like himself. They had simply come upon him and his dead companion by accident. Rather than leave him there to die they decided, as an act of mercy, to save him if they could.

Verilhon showed Hamilton the Earth and the Moon from space, he showed him the planets, more than any Earthbound astronomer had ever surmised, and beyond it; the vast Heavens themselves. Hamilton was astonished.

Verilhon invited him to accompany them to their homeworld, Uarius. Hamilton, admittedly unthinkingly and recklessly, readily agreed. After several days the ship arrived at a point just beyond the Moon where Verilhon explained there was a lacuna, like a rabbit hole in the aether that the Uarians use to travel the far distances across the void to their own homeworld.

Hamilton wrote that being on the deck of the Uarian spaceship as it entered the lacuna was the most magical and spectacular experience of his life. He likened it to crossing the Bifröst, the mythological burning rainbow bridge, which reaches between the realms of mankind and that of the Norse Gods.

In what to him felt like nothing more than a few moments the ship was hurled through the vast enormity of space, far across the solar system to another world.

It was only as the great burning red sphere appeared in the heavens before him that Hamilton realised the world that Verilhon called Uarius, the home of these extraordinary spacefarers, was, in fact, the planet we know as Mars.

Hamilton stayed several months as an honoured guest of Verilhon, who in fact was a great noble amongst his people. Hamilton lived within Verilhon's compound in the city of Carthoris, the capital of a nation known as Malacand, ostensibly the greatest nation on Uarius. For they too had nations and different peoples like Earth. He lived alongside its yellow-skinned inhabitants and learnt much of their ways.

He also had the freedom to travel and explore, visiting other cities, sailing the great canals, hunting in the red forests, even taking a yellow-skinned Malacandrian woman as a lover. He learnt of and met many different races; including the Red and Green Uarians, emissaries of other nations, and other exotic peoples and creatures. He was welcomed and feted over at the tables of many powerful politicians, nobles and even royalty. He learnt that Uarius was a truly peaceful world. Life could be hard, especially for the farmers and those that mined the raw materials, but all knew their place within harmonious societies and the strife of war was unheard of.

A few months into his stay Hamilton began to feel the wistful nostalgia of homesickness. For all its astounding beauty, for all its enchantments and for all its wonders, this was not his home. After a long journey of exploration, Hamilton returned to Verilhon and broached the subject of his return journey to Earth.

Verilhon said that he regretted it deeply, but there could be no return to Earth for Hamilton. For returning would expose too much of their world to the people of Earth, and the Great Council of Elders would never agree to it. Also, he reminded Hamilton, they came upon him only moments from death. This was not only a new world for him, but a chance for a new life. Verilhon would provide him with a home, servants, all his needs would be met. He was free to come and go as he wished, but he would never return to Earth.

"I felt as like Gershom; a stranger in the strangest of lands. I was a prisoner in a prison without walls, a hostage beyond any hope of ransom, but held by the tenderest of captors." (1)

Hamilton wrote that his initial heartbreak began to subside as this new life began to settle upon him. He was a luminary, a celebrity, and was regularly petitioned and invited into the spheres of the most powerful, even of other nations, who in turn saw to it he wanted for nothing.

It was during one of these sojourns, a prattan hunting expedition in the company of the Suzerain of Tyrr, Hamilton first encountered Joseph Stranger, another Earthman guest of the Malacandrians. Unlike Hamilton, Stranger claimed to have found his own way to Mars in a spaceship he built himself, but that on arrival, he had crashed and almost died. Thankfully, he was rescued from his burning wreck by a Green Malacandrian farmer who nursed him back to health.

Being the only other Earthman the other had seen, and both British to boot, they became firm friends. As they compared notes on their adventures, it soon became clear to Hamilton that maybe things were not all that they were presented as on Mars. Hamilton's suspicions were aroused.

Stranger told him that during his time with the Green farmer and his family he learnt much of the realities of their life. The Green Malacandrians were not the jovial rubes that the other races portray them as, far from it, they were, in fact, serfs, little more than slaves. Their lives are harsh and their treatment often brutal. Hamilton was reluctant to accept such things as his friend Verilhon had been so kind and open with him, and their society was so peaceful. Surely Stranger was wrong, possibly his saviour was just a disgruntled individual. Stranger discounted Hamilton's notions as naïve, adding that this was no peaceful world. This 'peaceful world' was in fact riven with constant internecine warfare. Nation fought nation, race against race, ideology against ideology, often with a level of utter ferocity seldom seen on Earth.

Hamilton protested, pointing out that he had travelled freely and spoken to so many and never seen or heard of such horrors. Not even a hint.

Upon their parting, Stranger warned Hamilton that he must open his eyes and see what was about him. He was being duped. Yes, the Malacandrians were kindly hosts, but they were liars and illusionists, and Stranger feared to contemplate what else they were lying about.

Although he does not state so in his autobiographical memoir, it is clear that Hamilton and Stranger did not part from that first meeting on good terms.

Upon returning to Carthoris, Hamilton was plagued by curious dreams, though he does not go into the detail of them in his writing, he does clearly indicate that something had changed in how he now viewed his erstwhile rescuers.

A single incident a few weeks later, led to a further revision and deepening of his disquiet. Possibly motivated by concerns brought on by unsettling dreams, Hamilton began to observe carefully the comings and goings of his host's household and especially those of his host, Verilhon, and his own Malacandrian lover, Lorquas. One morning Hamilton followed Lorquas through the maze of buildings, winding paths and secret spaces that formed the compound into Verilhon's inner sanctum whereupon he eavesdropped as she relayed in careful detail all his activities, his every movement, and every word he had uttered for days.

Shocked and with a heightened sense of paranoia, Hamilton began to re-examine his entire understanding of Malacand. Hamilton wrote that he felt as if he were a child that had managed to take a look behind the curtains of some all-encompassing theatrical pantomime, or a magician's sideshow, only to discover that it was all nothing more than a cynical deception of smoke and mirrors. A veil of tissue shrouding an edifice of lies.

Within days he had resolved that he must try to flee Malacand, in fact, to escape Uarius and return to Earth. He fled Carthoris and made his way to Tyrr, in hope of finding Stranger and hatching a scheme to escape their captivity.

Hamilton found Stranger living an ascetic lifestyle on the edge of Tyrr. In Stranger's own words;

"As if no longer of interest to my imprisoners I was discarded to a point almost beyond the pale, and left to my own devices, only to be occasionally summoned and trotted out like a once prize palfrey, now grown too long in the tooth." (2)

Stranger was also ill, he had contracted the disease we now know as Dust Lung, and his general health was failing. The Malacandrian physicians did not seem to be able to treat the illness as it was utterly unknown in the native populations.

Hamilton heard much from Stranger that contradicted almost all of what he had come to believe about the Malacandrians. To illustrate his claims Stranger took Hamilton to show him the graves of two previous Earthmen who had been brought to Mars by the Malacandrians, both had died of the illness he now endured. One of them was a French man called Maurice Marcel-Ray, abducted in 1793, whom Stranger claimed he had spoken to before he died. Joseph Stranger also detailed the bloody wars the

Uarians wage against each other, the brutal slave labour basis of their societies, and the true reasons behind their expeditions to Earth. The Malacandrian interlopers were scouting and spying on Earth in preparation for what Stranger had no doubt would one day be a future war of conquest.

Stranger feared that when the Malacandrians finally unite Uarius under one strong ruler, their technology with its flying barges, floating cities, death ray weapons and aethervolt spaceships would crush any army on Earth.

Hamilton wrote that he was so horrified he could hardly believe what Stranger was telling him, but he knew that whatever the ultimate truth was; he had to escape.

Stranger warned Hamilton that he must not even think of escape. When Hamilton asked why, instead of answering the question; Stranger posed another of his own, "What language do the Malacandrians speak Capt. Hamilton?"

I immediately replied, "Well, English of course...." but it was then it dawned upon me. Every Malacandrian I had spoken to, whether Yellow, Green or Red, even those of other nations, spoke English as well as I did.

Stranger pounced upon my realisation. "I have even spoken Scots Gaelic to them, the language my grandmother taught me, and they replied in that tongue."

"That is impossible," I exclaimed.

"They do not speak English, Captain. They do not speak Gaelic either, in fact, they do not speak our languages at all; they read our thoughts." (3)

So as not to stimulate suspicions Hamilton returned to Carthoris for a few days, ostensibly to inform his host that he would be spending some more time travelling with his new friend. As Hamilton wrote; Verilhon seemed unconcerned and even provided Hamilton with a small aerobarge for his own use. Though he did suggest that Lorquas accompany him as she grew more and more morose each time he was away. Hamilton, freely admitted in his memoirs that he was in love with Lorquas but he had resigned himself to abandoning her along with his comfortable imprisonment. Verilhon's insistence made that impossible.

Hamilton, with Lorquas in tow, returned to Stranger and the two men hatched their plan of escape. Leaving Lorquas at Stranger's remote home the two friends travelled into the desert of the Hourglass Sea, where their privacy was assured.

It was only once they were far away from anyone that Stranger revealed his plan. Unbeknownst to his captors, Stranger had been constructing a means of escape. Hamilton wrote that his heart almost somersaulted in his breast when he saw what Stranger had laboured so long and hard over.

Several months before their meeting Stranger had discovered the abandoned hulk of a Malacandrian aethervolt ship in a couloir in the desert hills. Being a gifted engineer and utilising the wreckage of his own vessel, and much he had scavenged, Stranger had succeeded in almost rebuilding the ship, aptly naming it The Chimera.

Stranger explained to Hamilton that most Uarians shared a taboo against disturbing the dead, so when in battle a warrior, a fighting machine, even a ship, fell they were often left where they lay. Especially out in the deserts. To the Uarians, especially the Malacandrians, salvaging such things was considered desecration.

To Hamilton and Stranger, it was a godsend. They spent at least another month together under the most primitive of conditions refitting the aethervolt with parts from the various crash sites, and battlefields, that Stranger had scouted out over his years of exploration.

Although Stranger was initially against it, Hamilton insisted that they take Lorquas back to Earth with them. Partly because he was in love with her, but partly because she was living proof of the tale they would have to tell. It would be so much easier to make the people back home believe what they had to tell them if they had proof to show them. The beautiful, golden and utterly alien, Lorquas would be their living testimony.

On the pretext of showing her something wondrous they had discovered they lured Lorquas out into the desert and bundled her onto The Chimera.

Hamilton wrote that their escape in that hodgepodge of a craft was the most frightening and the most exhilarating thing he had ever done.

Within a week they crashed their spaceship on a common near Worplesdon Hill in Surrey, England. They surrendered themselves to a passing Police Constable and an amateur astronomer and part-time correspondent for the local newspaper, who lived nearby.

Due to his untimely death, in a fly fishing accident less than a year later, Hamilton never wrote about his experiences post his return home, but the events are well documented.

Alarmed by Hamilton and Stranger's news, and goaded into action by the evidence of the spacefaring ship and Madam Lorquas, the British Government, fearing that a Uarian armada of conquest might arrive at any minute, at once set about building a fleet of their own aethervolt ships with the express aim of "bringing the battle to the enemy," as the First Lord of the Admiralty, Viscount Halifax, put it. (4)

In great secrecy, the industrial might and resources of the Empire were quickly brought to bear and the first British Imperial Aethervolt Dreadnaught, H.M.S.S. Icarus, designed by Mr Brunel with the assistance of Mr Stranger, was launched on Christmas Day 1854. The Malacandrian base on the dark side of the Moon was stormed by British Colonial forces on New Year's Day 1855 and the conquest of Mars was soon on the agenda.

Joseph Stranger received a Knighthood for his services to the Empire and his contribution in facilitating the British scientists and engineers deciphering of the Uarian's technology. The newly created British Imperial Aethervolt Fleet within six months of the taking of the moon base consisted of eight First Rate ships of the Line and several dozen other warships.

Spurred on by rumours that the French had discovered the remains of a crashed Uarian spacecraft in the Alps, the British

Government resolved not to be beaten to the punch and initiated the first military expedition to Mars.

The race to conquer Mars had begun.

Introduction. Pages 1 – 5.
"A Hostage to Uarius." Capt. Edmond Rudnick Hamilton, 1854. P.101. (1)
"A Hostage to Uarius." Capt. Edmond Rudnick Hamilton, 1854. P.285. (2)
"A Hostage to Uarius." Capt. Edmond Rudnick Hamilton, 1854. P.335. (3)
"The Eve of Conquest. The Speeches that Doomed Mars." 1867, P.885 (4)

The Field Journal of Octavius Spender, Dr
33rd of Sept 0026

What an utterly unexpected day, the events of which have left me both shocked and euphoric!

Even if one is most fortunate, such an event can come but once in a lifetime!

With the Professor's support and the willing aid of all those involved, including, in no small part, my daughter, we easily located the site that we sought. Mr Ransom's automaton had been quite accurate in the details and directions he had noted for us.

We had located the tomb and had begun scrapping back the mound of soil and weeds before elevenses was served. Unlike similar tombs on Earth, this was not a true tumulus as such, for the Aresians of the period did not bury their tombs deliberately, this was simply the accretions of several millennia. I could not contain myself and had to carry on, trowel in one hand and delicious scone in the other, like a lunatic!

By the time the men were back from their respite I had touched the silky smooth surface of the azure amazonite capstone. The men returned to work with renewed vigour. I was correct in my initial estimation of the size of the hexagonal table at about 70 square feet, which makes it amongst the largest of this type of tomb yet discovered.

As we cleared it back, I was thrilled to notice that the 3-foot thick quoit was undamaged, there was not even the smallest stress crack. As I expected, in line with other such sepulchres from the earlier periods, the tomb reveals as a featureless hexagonal box. Fashioned with such intense perfection, it belies any doubt as to the true extent of Aresian technological achievement.

We took a break for tea and considered what must be done next.

I cannot record the following events in my report or my official journal, but as I was explaining to Professor Flammarion, the Captain and the Colonel, that as there were no signs of damage to the tomb, I cannot do any more than secure it and report it. Our discussion was becoming quite heated due, in no small part to my own frustration, and therefore I was unaware of what was happening until the gunshot.

Sir John had borrowed Madam Fontenelli's odic pistol, walked past our gathering and fired at the tomb. As we all rushed over, he calmly smiled and said, "I say, Doctor, there is definitely some damage, old boy. I think you must have missed it." A piece about the size of a rugby ball had been blown off the south eastern corner joint of the supporting menhirs.

I stood in open-mouthed disbelief at the audacity of the man.

"Definitely looks to me like some scoundrels have tried to break into it. What do you think, Doctor? Professor?"

I was still so dumbfounded by Sir John's actions I could barely form thoughts yet alone words. The Colonel patted me on the shoulder and consoled me, "There, there, old chap, don't fret so. Even the best of us occasionally miss something obvious. Now, as you were saying, only if the tomb is damaged in some way, thus indicating previous disturbance, would you be allowed to investigate further." He patted me once again harder. "Well, looks to me as if there is quite definite evidence that someone, at some time, has tried to blast their way in."

Sir John added, "Quite so! Who knows what damage the buggers might have done? I think, old boy, it's your duty to investigate further. Don't you?"

I was about to stridently declare how I could not countenance such deliberate despoliation when

Parthena took my hand and whispered closely. "They are right, Poppa. As the Professor was saying; we have no way of protecting the tomb until the proper authorities can organise an excavation, and who knows how long that will take. Now we have discovered the tomb is damaged, we, you, must investigate further."

There was another loud bang. I spun around to see Sir John thrusting that odic behind his back like a naughty child caught in mid-act. "I say, it looks like the damage was worse than we thought, old man."

Blinded with rage, I flung myself at him, only to be restrained by the Colonel's men, and I shouted at him to stop it immediately and to get away from my site. Luckily, a few moments later, he seemed to have discovered some "urgency" and promptly left.

I shall be forced to have to record, in my official journal, that I discovered the damage while examining the tomb. I am proud to say I have never falsified a report in my entire career, but at least I can say, in truth, I never actually witnessed anyone damaging the tomb before my work began. Nonetheless, for all of the Professor's homily about it "being for the best," cutting such corners - no pundigrion intended - the whole thing still does not sit squarely with me now.

Parthena requested Charity to take a picturegraph of the tomb in the state in which we "discovered" it, as evidence of the pre-existing damage. While I organised the preparations for lifting the capstone.

The Professor had amassed quite a variety of lifting and moving contraptions, mostly of his own design, and brought them along. Some of them had already been unloaded by the crew and it took no time at all to have one of the heftiest steam-powered apparatus deployed in moving the capstone.

Within no time we had managed to lift the southern side of the quoit a good 4 feet. After properly securing it with props, of course, we all rushed to the ledge with lanterns and a couple of the Professor's amazing clockwork hand-lamps he had furnished us with.

We gazed into the cold, dusty gloom like expectant children, their noses pressed against the Christmas decked window panes of a toy shop, and with an equal level of anticipation.

I expected to behold the lavish burial of some unknown ancient Aresian noble or King, lying in great ceremonial state within the cist. Though my experience over these years has taught me I should never "expect" anything, I was indeed shocked to discover nothing more than a dusty platform leading to a staircase descending into inky darkness.

I was still absorbing my bewilderment when Parthena sprang over the edge of the menhirs onto the platform and thrust her hand-lamp forward revealing that the staircase descended far beyond the reach of the beam.

We were all so excited that there was almost a scramble to climb over the ledge to join her. Together we crowded on the landing peering breathlessly into the murkiness.

"Well?" The Colonel asked pointedly. "I would hazard a guess by your reaction Dr Spender; this was not what you were expecting?"

The Professor interjected before I had a chance to answer. "Ranolph, despite your efforts to doze through Octavius' briefing the other day, you know full well this is not what anyone expected."

Charity insisted that before we ventured any further she must take a picturegraph of the four of us gathered at the top of the steps, posed gazing into the void. It was then I noticed that Madam Fontenelli was still sitting beneath the comfortable shade of the parasol of her easel, observing the goings on over the edge of her sketchbook. I immediately requested her to join us, for if any of us should be here it was she. At first, she was reticent but the gentle imploring of Parthena and Charity soon changed her mind.

Excerpt from;

Diary of Aelita Fontenelli (Mrs).
Wednesday, September, 33rd. MY.26

I had been restless all morning. In all these years of Giovanni's imposed seclusion, I have seldom felt so trapped.

Although he too seemed distracted, Sir John was kind enough to agree to accompany me to watch the digging.

So as to do our part we assisted by taking down refreshments for the workers. While Ursula carried down my paint box and easel.

It was a surprisingly warm, bright day and I felt the opportunity it presented for me to paint might calm my disposition.

By the time we arrived the crew members had cleared most of the top of the tomb to expose a pale blue hexagon of some size about which Dr Spender was most excited.

He is such a pleasant man and so enthusiastic. It was delightful to see him so animated, especially after his bad turn yesterday. I can see why Patty is so fond of him.

Patty explained to Sir John and I that, though it was wonderful, if not incredible, to have found a tomb apparently undisturbed and undamaged, this meant that Dr Spender was not allowed to do anything more than record it and report it to the authorities. Who would, in their good time, organise an investigation themselves. At first, I thought this sounded a reasonable requirement, but Patty pointed out that with unscrupulous men already in search of the tomb, the Professor would either have to leave several people to guard the site or it was almost certain that by the time the authorities should get around to initiating their own excavation, the tomb will be robbed and everything within it lost to archaeology and science.

There was quite a debate going on over luncheon as the Professor, though obviously understanding of the situation, was trying desperately to explain to Dr Spender that the expedition, let alone the ship, could not spare several men to guard the tomb for what could be an indefinite period. The cost alone would be substantial, and he, the Professor, was trying to explain that he simply could not afford to finance it. He too is such a dear man and I could see it made him uncomfortable not only to talk about such private things, but to deny his friend in such a moment of triumph.

I was pondering what possible resolution they could reach, apart from reburying it and praying to Almighty God that it would not be discovered before the authorities could act, when Sir John took me gently by the elbow and led me a few feet away. He asked me a question I had never fully considered before; how did I feel about opening the tomb?

I admitted I had never truly considered my 'feelings' on the matter. I know from what I have read and learnt that my father's people had several taboos about 'disturbing,' as some might see it, the dead. And I, brought up as a Catholic, truly believe that one day, upon the heavenly clarion call, all souls, no matter who or where they lie, will rise to be judged. Though my feelings are that; opening any place of rest is wrong, if it were simply to avoid the inevitable, it would be best done to prevent wanton desecration by thieves. The Commandment is; "Thou shalt not steal," and to leave this grave unprotected would, in my opinion, be little less than aiding grave robbers.

Sir John listened patiently to my meanderings with a kind smile on his face. When I finished, or rather simply ran out of words, he squeezed my hand and assured me that I was indeed making perfect sense. He asked me for my galvanic pistol, without hesitation, or real thought as to why, I took it out of my painting satchel and handed it to him. He gave me an impish smile and advised me to stay where I was. He then walked past where the Professor and the others stood and over to the tomb and, to my astonishment, fired at it!

Dr Spender was enraged, but Sir John explained that obviously now that the tomb was indeed damaged it was perfectly acceptable to investigate further!

I know it was inappropriate, so I had to hide myself behind Ursula's shoulder to stifle the onset of giggling that burst out of me. And then, as I had just about regained control of my mirth, Sir John, with a wink and all the mannerisms of a mischievous child in a nursery, did it again! Dr Spender was furious and started shouting at him. I, though had to step away, feigning a coughing fit to hide my laughter.

By the time I had recovered my composure Patty and Colonel Jahns had calmed Dr Spender enough for him to understand that Sir John's actions had decided the issue. Although Dr Spender is a highly principled man, the tomb was now undeniably damaged and consequently further investigation could be justified.

Sir John returned my pistol to me with great flourish and a remark about Alexander and the Gordian knot. I replied that at least he had not had to use a sword or we would have been here all day watching him diligently chipping away at the stonework.

We were giggling and whispering like a pair of conspiratorial children in a nursery until Ursula interrupted to point out a falling light in the sky. Sir John said that was his signal to 'fly' and raced off back to the airship to get his aeronautical apparatus. Leaving Ursula and I to watch the crew members as they erected some exceedingly complicated looking steam-powered lifting equipment and set about raising the lid of the tomb.

They hoisted the lid up a few feet and rushed to view the interior. Which I was to learn was not as the Doctor had expected for it had revealed a simple landing and set of steps, rather than the fabulous burial he, no doubt, had expected. Patty, intrepid as always, was first in, gracefully leaping over the wall, followed by the ungainly struggle of the elderly men.

Charity, who had been recording the whole event with a Maddox camera, called them all to attention for a picturegraph of the great Archaeologist and his chums at the doorstep of their discovery, all looking awfully pleased with themselves.

After the picture had been taken Dr Spender called myself and Ursula over and asked if I wished to accompany him. He could not vouch for the lack of danger, but he said that he felt that I, as the only representative of my people, had more right to be beside him than anyone else.

I was flattered by this proposal, but I felt uneasy, especially after yesterday's experiences. I believe the dead are but sleeping souls awaiting their summons to rise and account for themselves before God. It is not for me to disturb them in their rest, but the others argued forcefully, especially Patty and Charity.

Patty finally took me aside and spoke to me in hushed whispers. She reminded me of the conversation we had yesterday as we sat beside her father's bed, and the hopes I had shared with her. She told me that this was why I was here, this was my journey, my adventure, and I must not fail it or myself. If I was to ever truly leave my world of shuttered drawing rooms and walled gardens, my 'gilded cage' as she called it. She believes I must do this. I must cast off the mentality of the heavy veils and the closed carriages and be courageous and venturesome and I must be at the forefront of this undertaking.

She, of course, was right, but as soon as I acquiesced in the smallest portion she marched me back to the airship to change into something more rational for the exertions. I could do nothing else but follow her.

The Field Journal of Octavius Spender, Dr
33rd of Sept 0026.
Continued;

After Madam Fontenelli had changed into something more "appropriately adventurous," we gathered again for another picture, the five of us and the automaton.

After Charity had taken the image, I was about to ask Parthena to extinguish her cigarillo, when she pointed above me to the underside of the quoit. I was astonished to realise that above me the entire stone was carved in bas-relief pictograms. I have never seen anything like it; a complex profusion of stylised images and cryptographs. At first sight, it bore no relation to any Aresian language I have seen before, not even in the Great Temple in Tharsis.

The Colonel reminded us, we had a task in hand and limited time available. He was right, of course. So I requested Charity to make some images of the pictograms while we prepared to negotiate the narrow steps down into the undercroft.

Ever the most fearless of my children, Parthena insisted on going first. Madam Fontenelli and I followed with the Professor and one of the Colonel's chaps following. Jahns had decided to stay above and would escort Charity down when she finished her photographications.

We descended into darkness. Our lanterns and hand-lamps fought valiantly to pierce the pervading black, with limited success, forcing us into feeling our way trepidatiously downward. The smallest sounds echoed strangely and our voices, forced into whispers, were distorted by the smooth walls and the parabola of the arched ceiling above our heads.

Down we went with Parthena ahead counting and narrating every step. She counted off fifty before she reached the bottom. Here the walls were flat, but no longer smooth, rough with tool marks and imperfections. Ice cold to the touch. Our breath steamed in the cold air creating strange shadow patterns in the beams of our lamps. After a dozen yards down the sloping corridor, we came upon another staircase. This one plunging even steeper into the black.

I must say that at no point did any of my companions suggest turning back. Parthena counted off another fifty steps before we reached the bottom. The corridor we stepped into widened out to what I estimated was fifteen feet, and at least double that in height. At first, we took the roughness of these walls to be no more than the tool marks of corridor above, but here the entirety of the walls and the ceiling were carved in the same shallow bas-relief style as the capstone. The illumination of our lamps and lanterns was far too paltry against the oppressive darkness to allow us to grasp the scope of the illumination.

The corridor led on another hundred yards or so before we reached an obviously sealed portal. I tapped upon it with the handle of my trowel and we all listened with bated breath for the cavernous echo, but none came, just a dull solid thud.

I informed the others that meant one of several things. Either the wall was extremely thick, the area beyond the seal had been backfilled or, as was most likely, in a hypogeum tomb like this, that it was a ruse, a misdirection to confuse would-be tomb robbers.

The Professor speculated if it was a decoy the actual tomb could be anywhere, behind any wall, in fact, there must be a possibility that there was no tomb at all.

I was explaining that it was most unlikely that there was no sepulchre within the complex when Madam Fontenelli unexpectedly grasped my hand and, in that instance, my whole understanding of reality was changed forever.

Whether it was a dreamlike state or a mirage, it was obviously one we both shared.

Suddenly she and I were no longer standing in the gallery of the tomb, but as if in space itself. About us, the heavens glittered with a million bright stars. I know little about astronomy, but enough to know this was no nightscape seen from Mars. Around me, I could still see the faint flickering edges of the carved reliefs and as I watched they came alive. Like some strange magic lantern moving picture show.

The hieroglyphic script flowed like telegraph tape in the wind, images of extraordinary spacecraft took flight into the void, fabulous cities and planets came into sight and faded. Unknown champions grappled with each other in life and death struggles. Towering war machines strode over devastated alien landscapes and vast armies of bizarre beings marched against each other. And there, in the darkness above the chaos, presided a monstrous evil, a cephalopodic demigod that writhed ecstatically in the throes of their euphoric carnality.

All in the utter silence of the stars.

I found Madam Fontenelli clinging to my arm and I could do nothing more than hold on to her. Around us, an indescribable universe continued to unfold its story in strange two- dimensional moving images. Vile Cecaelia like beings reached out across space and time, and in their umbra spread the madness of an endless war.

Then, in the confusion of images, I recognised the elegant construction of some of the ships; the Aresians. Battles in the deep void were played out before me; a vast war between numerous alien races, a mortal struggle against an ancient enemy. My heart began to pound elatedly as the Aresian ships fell upon wave after wave of invaders pitilessly destroying all in their path.

Nevertheless, slowly the myrmidons of the horrific Cecaelia turned the tide against them. A war erupted across the cosmos, empires fell, planets burned and stars were extinguished. The insanity raged on until the peace of absolute exhaustion fell upon the universe. The images showed me endless destruction; the burning ruins of a thousand mighty civilisations. Starving children of strange races scavenged for scraps in the ruins of once magical cities, people burnt their history books for warmth. Cultures spurned their reason and their Gods, slaughtered their leaders, and made rulers of fools. Death became a God to be worshipped.

Then, in one desperate last act, the Aresians and their allies arose one final time. Throwing down the ancient Gods of the Cecaelia and driving them back beyond the darkest holes in space.

The images faded, the walls around me coalesced. I was back in the real world, well as 'real' as I can know it to be.

My mind was left racing as fast as my pulse. Was it another hallucination? A vision? It was like no other experience I have ever had, not even in the square at Ananthor. How long have I, as man and boy, wished I could just peep behind the veil of time and see the past for what it really was? It is probably the most heartfelt desire of every historian, antiquarian and archaeologist that has ever lived or ever will, and now, by some means unfathomable to me, I have been witness to a history I could have never, even in my wildest imaginings, have envisioned.

Part of my mind rebelled against the nightmare phantasmagoria and the terrifying knowledge, it brought with it, but I knew the actuality of it with absolute certainty. The images had shown me the truth, a truth so utterly terrifying that it felt I had been pushed to the absolute edge of the precipice of insanity. I felt urgently compelled to impart the knowledge as warnings to my companions, I looked about me, but the others were oblivious to my revelation.

My companions were still engaged in good-humoured, but facetious, speculative conversation. I quickly realised that what had felt like an age to me could have only been a matter of moments, nothing more than a few heartbeats, and that I must regain myself before I can truly understand what I have experienced.

I looked at Madam Fontenelli, she was still clinging to my arm, her eyes as wide as saucers. Though my attention had been totally lost in the narrative throughout, I could at all time feel her steadfast grip on my arm. I enquired if she needed to rest. She looked back at me as if confused, then whispered; "Did you see it too?"

Excerpt from;
Memoirs of Aelita, Lady Sydeian.
The Athenaeum of Harendrimar Tai.

It was then that the truth of the gallery revealed itself to Dr Spender and myself.

This was no tomb, but a repository of information, a wondrous archive of knowledge. I know the Doctor did not see what I saw, but I believe you gain only the knowledge you seek from such places. For those who can interrelate with it, it provides answers to specific questions rather than overburden them with the sum total of the knowledge it has. To do so would undoubtedly reduce a mind, even one as great as Dr Spender's, to that of a simpleton.

Since that day many have inquired of me; as to what did I see? Was my experience as that described by the late Doctor in his works on the subject?

As I have attested to before, my recollection of the events in the Athenaeum differs from Dr Spender's account only on the content of our personal experience of the gallery's narrative. I cannot, and will not, speak to the validity or veracity of the Doctor's personal vision. It is left only for me to say that I knew him to be the most honourable and trustworthy of men and one neither given to flights of fancy or childish over exaggeration. Nothing before, or after his untimely death, has challenged my confidence in him.

I can only explain what was revealed to me: most of which only makes sense to me in the light of the years since the events.

For me it was a personal revelation; it showed me who I am. Or, more rightly, who I could have been, were it not for the events of my past. It revealed to me things I did not even know about myself. The most overwhelming being that we, the Peerrohs, are not as Tellurians, born either side of a physical gender divide, but that we are all born female and remain so until the onset of what I can only describe as puberty, which occurs much later in our kind than in Tellurians. At that point, our gender is chosen. The Athenaeum showed me the choices to be made, rituals observed and ceremonies completed. I saw my father and mother make their pairing and their choices, becoming not who they were but what they would be, and those, the epicenes, who elected not to choose.

The greatest shock to me was the sudden realisation that I never had a brother. Gethen was not my twin, he was the other side of me. He was the 'me' I may have chosen to become if I had understood the choice was mine to make, but the determination had been made for me long ago by the Nuns in the orphanage. The name, the clothes, the upbringing. They had solidified around me as I had settled into the Tellurians world, as a young woman, unknowing of my own true nature. But until the rites were observed to bring my body into balance I could not be wholly one or the other, simply a sterile epicene masquerading as a young woman. By the age I was when I joined the Expedition my consignment had been long overdue, and, although full of potential, I knew little or nothing of truly being a woman. While, inside me, the humours surged like a thunderhead raging in a teacup.

Since that day in the Athenaeum, I have learnt much, especially apropos to the danger such things brought to my physical and emotional health and those around me. On the Seren Bore I had somehow been aware, but naïvely oblivious, to the impact of my presence upon some Tellurian men, especially Sir John and other members of the Expedition.

Before I fled the confines of Giovanni Fontenelli's lavish oubliette, that I had once called a home, to join Professor Flammarion's adventure, my interactions, as an adult, with the world beyond had, apart from once, been always carefully structured, even stage managed. Fontenelli had not only kept me from fulfilling my true nature, he had hidden the very knowledge of it from me. I had not been his 'wife' but, as I had always feared, an anaesthetized specimen. A captive creature to be studied. His hand never reached for me for any other reason than to chastise me or stroke me as one would do with a favoured lap dog.

Now the Athenaeum had laid it all bare for me to know, but my childish mind, so long closeted from life, hardly grasped the meaning of what unfolded before my eyes.

I saw my father. I heard his voice. Not with my ears, but as one does in a dream. He told me of this world before the Tellurians came. He showed me the Malacandrian Empire. The Empire of the Kitreenoh Aresians, firstly vibrant and vigorous but slowly decaying into depravity. Their merciless rule had broken the natural order of things, an affront to the intricate rubrics and conventions so ingrained into all Aresian cultures. Few outside of the Empire's direct control, even amongst the non-Malacandrian Kitreenohs, would easily consent to be ruled by these despotic overlords. Continual warfare sapped their strength, cruelty and oppression sowed the seeds of rebellion, greed and lust for power bred intrigue as powerful families bribed and murdered their way to the steps of a powerless Empress's throne.

I saw their aethervolt craft travelling to Earth, Venus and Jupiter, even beyond to the stars themselves. Desperately searching for something to prop up their dying Empire. Their technology failing them, their power waning, and so, out of fear, they became more and more despotic.

The figure that appeared as my father raised a hand and there above his palm spun Earth. Giovanni had a globe of Earth in his study, but this was no painted papier-mâché sphere, but a real planet that shone brilliantly with pulsating life.

Here there was a secret, hidden deep within, the one the Malacandrians had lost. A strange and terrible secret, aeons old.

Their missions failed.

And then, as if the terrible judgement of Almighty God was against them, came the Tellurians, like the plagues upon Egypt. In what in reality could have been only moments, I feel like I was witness to it all. The fall of Malacand, the destruction of the other great Aresian nations, the endless, pointless conflicts, the greed of the Tellurian Empires and the bloody avariciousness of the settlers. Savage, brutal wars in which no one and nothing was spared. Not even my own mother and father.

The last image it showed me was of two small, terrified children, huddled on the cold flagstone floor of the orphanage dormitory, clinging to each other so tightly it would seem to the observer they were almost part of each other.

They were. They, were me.

The Flammarion Expedition Journal of L. Edwin Ransom.

This day has been one of unimaginable horrors. And a day that, no matter how deeply I wish to, I will never forget. Several times today I feared we might not live to see the end of it.

The day did not begin well. After breakfast, Adam and I had words over my insistence on returning home to collect the rest of my belongings. I felt that because he was so obviously a soldier in his former profession, that he has little sentimental attachment to what to him must seem simple objects. I tried to explain that, though I pray that Minnie has removed most of the most valuable and obviously sentimental items, I have to check, and I know that there will be items, especially amongst my books, she would have overlooked.

I could not believe that Du Maurier would go to the ridiculous trouble of posting and maintaining guard on my home simply on the off-chance I might return. How wrong I was.

Before luncheon, the Professor held a meeting in the wardroom to make the final arrangements for the day. I would help pinpoint the location that Karl had given us so that Dr Spender and Parthena could narrow their search as much as possible. Once we were grounded, Adam and I would scoot off to the house in one of the Professor's tracked steam carriages as fast as we could.

Unfortunately, while Adam and I were getting changed into more suitable attire for our labours the subject of my determination arose again and we had an extremely serious difference of opinion, including some very strong words. Also, I reasoned, that the locating of my personal items would be far speedier for me, than any number of well-intentioned others. If there were indeed sentries set to watch the house would it not be better for me to slip into the house unnoticed and gather the things I require. Adam insisted that I draw up an inventory of items and that he would go, list in hand, to collect them like some porter or footman. I understood his concerns, but I would not be frightened off by a group of louts from returning to my own family home or treated like a child for that matter.

It was decided by the Captain and the Professor that before we, the Expedition members as a whole, arrive at the "site" (as Dr Spender calls it), we should make a clean breast of the events of dangers that we may face.

I must say that the ladies took it in the most robust manner. Charity admonished us all, saying that, though she appreciated the reasons for our lack of candour, if the women of this team were to be allowed to make a worthwhile contribution to this endeavour we must not treat them, herself and the other ladies, as if they were some flighty little stable-minded girls who might go off in a muzzy-headed swoon at the mere mention of danger. Her heated tone left us all in no doubt of their shared annoyance.

The Colonel, reddened in the face, attempted to remonstrate, but was pulled up sharply by Parthena whose language can be unusually colourful for one of her breeding and status. Though, luckily she delivers it with enough charm and good humour to disarm even an old warrior like the Colonel

Though it was a difficult discussion afterwards, everyone agreed that it was only sensible for us all, even Aelita's maid, to go armed today. The Professor himself claimed that with a gun he would be more of a potential threat to those around him than any possible reprobates. I reminded him that he was one of the finest game shots I have ever seen.

We finalised our preparations, and I assisted the Navigation Officer in circumnavigating Tremorfa and locating the spot Karl had marked on the map we had drawn up.

Sir John took to the air in his flying apparatus and reconnoitred the area while the crew grounded us. We were down and ready for the off on the dot of 3.30pm.

I do remember noticing that the storm had moved a lot of dust dunes close to the edge of the plantation, although the lynchets and hedges appeared to have held back the worst of the sand. In more normal times I would have scheduled the area for clearing before the sand breached the barriers and clogs the irrigation ditches, which, of course, would have meant that I would have paid it much closer attention, but all I could do was shake my head in despondency.

I never thought to give it a second glance, or remark upon it, and that was an unforgivable blunder that I must take full responsibility for.

I was further distracted by how good it was to be home on my own soil again! I found myself torn between desperately wanting to join in the search for the tomb and the desire to get my most personal belongings from the house. I promised Dr Spender that I would be there and back as soon as physically possible.

The Captain loaned us the use of one of the Hornsby's along with a driver and the Colonel sent along one of his chaps, Mr Rawlings, an imposing and redoubtable black fellow with a keen eye and a droll wit.

Adam maintained that we must go overland rather than use normal paths and tracks and so off we set at somewhat an unnerving pace. I had been warned by Dr Spender about what a bone shaker these things were but one has to experience them for oneself. I swear that if I had not been securely strapped in I would have been thrown clear out of the vehicle several times. Adam and Sergeant Rawlings seemed almost at ease in comparison to my discomfort.

I made a mental note that there was no possible way I could convey anything fragile in this.

I guided us across to the eastern sunflower field that backs onto the house. And so as to not be noticed if there was indeed sentries, we disembarked and trudged the last half mile on foot through the sunflower stands. It hurt my heart so to see them untended, a goodly portion felled by the storm winds. I would not be back in time to supervise their harvest, nor even that of the dandelions. Half a year's crop wasted, and at my expense. If I were a man of ill humour I would have vowed revenge upon Du Maurier for that alone. Such a loss would impoverish most independent farmers, thankfully my family's fortunes are not dependent solely on such vagaries. We marched on through the stands at a pace set by Adam.

In my mind, I had tried to compile a list of the possessions I needed to save, if that was the word, from what had been my home. It was difficult. How can a man reduce his entire home, a lifetime's belongings, to the contents of a trunk or two? Hopefully, Minnie would have had the good sense to take as many of our most treasured things as possible with her.

So it was a strange fusion of eagerness, sadness and anxiety which came over me as I saw the house begin to loom above the flower heads.

I directed us to the rear of the main storehouse. There we stayed. Adam handed me the binoculars and asked me to give the house a look over to see if anything was out of the ordinary. I must admit, I did not notice anything unusual, the house looked somewhat deserted to me, but Adam and Mr Rawlings were insistent that we make absolutely sure. And so we waited.

I was just about to protest that we were obviously wasting time when someone sneezed and a rough voice growled an obscenity in reply.

Adam's scarred face wrinkled into the most unpleasant sanctimonious grin as he hushed me once more, I did not know whether to be chastened or infuriated.

Adam and Mr Rawlings proceeded to talk in some kind of rudimentary sign language before he beckoned me closer and whispered, "Stay here, with Rawlings, there's a good fellow and keep your head down. If I am not back in under twenty minutes get yourselves out of here, sharpish." With that, he scampered off into the foliage.

Mr Rawlings and I dutifully obeyed Adam's commands, but strained at every sinew to listen out for any sounds.

After a couple of minutes, we just made out some stifled commotion and a rather sickening thud above the rustling of the wind in the sunflower leaves.

I was just about to voice my relief when Adam went running past us heading along the edge of the rows towards the northeast dandelion field. I wanted to move from our little scrape but Mr Rawlings put a firm hand on my shoulder and held me back. Against my urgently hissed protestations, he kept repeating; "Wait, Sir. Wait." So, taking turns to observe my house through the field glasses, we waited, interminably.

I was impatiently checking my pocket watch for the dozenth time when suddenly gunshots rang out. I was at a loss to locate them, but Mr Rawlings said they came from inside the house. That was it. I had had enough of this loitering around in the sunflowers like fearful children. I snatched up the rifle Adam had insisted I bring, and leapt forward, too fast for Mr Rawlings to stop me, and dashed for the house. It left Rawlings nothing more to do than to follow me in quick time.

Alarmingly, more shots rang out from the house, a veritable gun battle by the sound of it. In my house!

I dreaded what Minnie would say, let alone Nelly.

Rawlings and I had now thrown caution to the wind completely. We openly ran around the side of the house to the steps of the porticoed main entrance that my father had designed. The gunfire ended with a concussive boom that resounded through the building like a cannon going off. Windows rattled and even we, at the bottom of the steps, felt the reverberation.

Rawlings and I hoisted our weapons and, immediacy being the brevity of sanity, charged up the steps and through the front door.

As my eyes adjusted to the dimness of the interior I was presented with a most horrific tableau.

Adam loomed in the midst of what looked like the smoky aftermath of one of those Wild Western shootouts that one reads about in the penny dreadful magazines. He stood over the prostrate body of one man, another lay in the doorway to the Morning Room, and yet another lay crumpled at the top of the stairs.

My vestibule was peppered with holes from stray rounds. The grandfather clock that had been in my family for at least a hundred years had been shot twice, in the cabinet work. Luckily, my late mother's favourite mirror, a horrid 18th century French Rococo miscreation, was shattered beyond repair (no great loss there, I might add), and the old stuffed German animatronic monkey butler that we used for an umbrella stand had had its calling card tray and most of its face blown off. Its remaining eye, pathetically dangling on a spring from a mess of spindles and cogs that had once been enclosed inside its head, now regarded me balefully.

I was too stunned to think clearly. I picked up the little salver that lay at my feet and examined it, solid brass, embossed with a scene from Don Quixote's exploits, it was surprisingly heavy. I was thinking that if I removed the screws that held it to the remains of the monkey's paw, I could still use it as a pen tray.

Rawlings, who had gone straight over to Adam's side, suddenly exclaimed, "Bloody 'ell, Sir! It's a blooming golem!"

I shook myself out of my reverie and into the present and walked over to view the corpse. I have seen far too much death in the last few days that I fear I am becoming immune to the horror of it, but I came upon a vision so ghastly that I could only gape in disgust. It appeared to be the man from Alba Station; Knapp, or rather Lloyd, the man that had murdered the two police constables - well what was left of him.

The state of him was almost too horrific to contemplate, a gruesome, bloody mess, but what was so shocking was that underneath the flesh of his ruined face was metal. Red brass that appeared as if it was riveted in plates to the skull itself. Most of the left side of the mandible was exposed and appeared, on none too close an inspection, to be completely made of the same gunmetal. Where the crude brass eyescopic contrivance had been, there passed a huge hole through his skull and through my floorboards below.

The idiotic thought as to who would pay for the damage to my grandmother's Safavid carpet popped into my mind, almost as if to offset the shock of what I was seeing. In the cavity where the remnants of Lloyd's brain, pulped by the gunshot, remained, was also a tangle of wires and tiny glass bulb-like objects. In my time I have had to do some repairs to Karl, and I have seen such diodes inside him, but never could I ever imagine why one would want to put them inside the brain of a human being. If that is what Lloyd was? This was beyond any technology I was aware of. The marriage of man, or be it human tissue, and mechanisms, a kind of human automaton, was a truly unsettling thought.

Karl is much stronger than any three or four men, works unceasingly, and is able, by the miracle of technology, to be a splendid companion and loyal servant, but he is readily identifiable as an android. What of this? Neither machine nor man, but with the best, or worse, of both?

"Golem," Rawlings called it. Though it seems fitting, I would, through experience, hazard that it grossly underestimates the thing's capacity. This was no lumbering clay sculpture, but a man of intent and physical prowess. Enough to stand and trade blows like some bare-knuckled pugilist with Karl. I cannot say I was sorrowful to see him dead, but his death had brought me even greater anxieties.

It was then it occurred to me where I had seen before the self-same red brass gunmetal wrought into the finest articulation. A chill, like a droplet from an icicle, ran down my spine.

I looked my friend Adam in the eye. I have never seen a man move as fast, nor one as recklessly brave, nor as accurate with a gun. If anyone was a match for such a monster as Lloyd, it was he. My mysterious house guest, who had saved my life several times in the few days I have known him. The man whose arm, at least, appeared to be of the very same technology as the creature prostate before us.

When I asked, in God's good name, how we could possibly tell who was one of these things. Adam laughed at my incredulity, "No doubt it would be extremely difficult to tell."

I wished to help bury the dead, but Adam refused to allow it. There, of course, was not any time for such civilised conduct. While Adam dragged the bodies out of my house I, with Mr Rawlings' help, began to collect my belongings.

Minnie had left me a note upon my desk in the study.

27th of September 0026

Edwin, dearest,

I hope to have given you this news in person, but just in case;

I have done my best to take everything important I can think of at such short notice; including your mother's jewellery box and the Ransom Family Bible, along with the picture albums, also all the papers from your cabinet, but some things I have had to hide. (The place where your mother used to hide the best brandy from your Uncle Peter.)

I was at a loss regarding your books! I could not find your patent portfolio.

Joshua, David, Eli and Bowen are with me, as well as Neriah and the baby. We are going to stay the night at Mrs P's Guest House as you suggested before catching the train. I have paid the other's off, as best as I can (Yes, I have entered everything in the ledger!) so the money box is quite denuded.

So we will be on the first train tomorrow morning, God willing!

Your loving sister, Minnie.

P.S,

I must remind you that I do not have a key to Mr Chubb's cabinet.

At least Nelly will enjoy having Minnie's companionship and meeting Neriah's baby for the first time.

All that was left for me to do was empty the safe, find my portfolio, gather up the most indispensable books from my collection and find a few odds and sods of equipment that I might conceivably need. I also packed a portmanteau with some extra clothes. I must admit having been rotating the same three sets of apparel since I left home. As hardly anything I have at the Professor's home was suitable for adventuring in the wilderness.

So, with my possessions in a few cases and boxes, my best walking boots on and with the buffalo skin cape that Nelly brought me last Christmas over my Chesterfield, I was ready, as much as I was ever 'ready,' to leave my home for what might turn out to be the last time.

I may have sunk into quite a dull funk if it had not been for Mr Rawlings' good-humoured but continued urging.

Adam had removed the bodies from my hallway and promised he had laid them to rest in as decent a Christian manner as the situation would allow.

We gathered up my belongings and left. I could not even secure the front door, as Minnie had taken the keys with her — though on inspection Du Maurier's thugs had forced the lock and we had no time to do anything about it. I must say that, of almost all the insults heaped upon my life by Du Maurier, that single thing incensed me. How dare this obnoxious little avetrol invade my home. For the first time, I felt real cold murderous rage at the effrontery of the man.

Adam seemed to appreciate my quiet fuming and gripped my shoulder firmly, saying; "He will be made to pay a heavy price for what he has done to you, old chap. That I promise."

I had no doubt he meant what he said. How could I have suspected such a friend? Suspected of what? I can barely summon the words to my mind to compose such a bizarre notion, and if I could? What difference would it make to who he is? I met him as a stranger and welcomed him into my home and he has stood beside me through the most dangerous days of my life, in fact, I truly believe he has saved my life several times. I have never had such a friend.

Then he added chillingly; "I swear to you Edwin; you shall live to see this Du Maurier dead. If not by your hand, then by mine."

It was at that moment I grasped the thing that disquieted me most about my friend Adam; of all the terrible things that Du Maurier has ranged against me, I thank God, Adam is at my side, because, if he were not my good friend, I would, and rightly so, be far more terrified of him. I can almost pity those foolish enough to come betwixt him and Du Maurier should the time come for him to make good on his pledge to me.

Without need for further comment, I took his hand and shook it firmly, to seal our bargain.

"You shall always have my friendship, Sir. And that of my family. We are all greatly indebted to you and, though we may not have much, you shall always have a place at our table. When this nonsense is all done, I shall be honoured if you will help me rebuild my farm and my business, so I may help you rebuild your life."

I know, that as usual, it came out of my mouth with far less erudition than when formed on a page. My tongue tangled the words and my childhood stammer asserted itself, but that is what I meant to say and thankfully that is what he understood.

For a moment I saw a flash of something in his eyes, melancholy, perhaps, before he quickly looked away and began to usher us back towards the fields.

We were too loaded up to negotiate our way through the stands of sunflowers so we made our way to the track between it and the dandelion field, running like a trio of demented railway porters.

We had made it only a few hundred yards when Adam ordered us off the road into the foliage. An aircraft was approaching from the southwest. After a quick glance through Mr Rowling's glasses, I was in no doubt it was the same dirigible that had chased Miss Bryant-Drake to Alba Kirk Station.

We crouched down in the thick cover of the sunflower's greenery as it flew over our heads. I was fascinated to get a good look at it this time. It was one of the oddest looking dirigibles I have ever seen; a two-man contraption with unusual toroid engines mounted on gantries either side of the gondola, which sparked electrical expulsions. It appeared they create electrically charged vortices to provide propulsion much like a fluidal vortex can be created to move effluent through a waste system. I have never seen this ingenious but hazardous technology before. I must admit to becoming so distracted mentally computing the energy requirements required to produce such electrical charge to power such engines, that Mr Rawlings had to roughly drag me further into the leafage.

The dirigible circled the house, its two-man crew straining to survey the area for their compatriots. By their panicked behaviour, it was clear they were even more unnerved by the lack of a signal from the house.

Suddenly the machine spun on a penny and shot up into the air like a rocket. I thought they had spotted us but Adam hushed me and pointed at something far off on the horizon.

It was Sir John in his flying apparatus like some mythical brass winged Wyvern soaring over the sunflower fields to our aid.

The sight of him must have alarmed the dirigible crew because it twirled, and with a huge discharge of black smoke, it flew off at an amazing speed.

Adam waved Sir John down to where we had returned to the track. I must say I have had mixed feelings about the man over the last few days, but I could not have been gladder to have seen him. He greeted us cheerily and offered to take off after the dirigible if we so wished. I did warn him that they were awfully heavily armed, but, slapping that fearsome gun of his, he replied; "I would not be expecting a quiet chit-chat with them, old chap. Betsy here can make quite a persuasive argument on her ownsome."

In some strange way, I was reassured by his zeal while also being aware that he, like Adam, was another man that one might feel desperately grateful for being on one's side, but, in no small part, still be aware that I would not wish to ever be in opposition to him.

Adam staunched the talk of pursuing the dirigible requesting instead that Sir John return back to the ship to inform the Professor and Captain Llewellyn that there was an imminent threat from a pirate ship and its crew.

Sir John understood the pressing urgency, but it still took us several refusals of his offers of aid. And so, after imparting the news that the team had discovered and opened the tomb (I must say I was a little disappointed, at that news), Sir John flew off to return to the Seren Bore.

Once he was on his way we took no time concerning ourselves with the possibilities of ambush, we collected my luggage together and ran pell-mell for the Hornsby.

We reached it in no time, loaded up and set off at full speed back to the tomb.

Charity Bryant-Drake.
Notes to self. 33/9/26

Things are too chaotic. I shall transpose these notes into the official record when I have the time, but for now, I must get as much down on paper as possible.

Edwin guided us to the location of the burial site using the details his automaton Karl had given him. It was exactly as he had described it. My step-father Robert will be thrilled.

I set up the Maddox and took pictures of the whole process. It occurred to me that a photographic recording of the whole event was more important than a simple posed picture or two.

I was so excited that I almost knocked the Maddox over several times myself, I was all fingers and thumbs. Only after Patty made me drink one of her "coffees" did I even begin to calm down (She recommends Vodka in the morning as you cannot detect it on the breath! And a lady must not appear to be a lush! I have never known anyone to drink as purposefully as she.).

Dr Spender and the Professor spent quite a time arguing over whether or not they should open the tomb, as it seemed undamaged and thus would be in contravention of the Law on Antiquities, when Sir John Sydeian took it into his head to blast a large chunk off of one of the tomb's corners.

I thought Dr Spender was going to have another one of his seizures, but all I, Patty and Aelita could do was giggle like hysterical schoolgirls, and then he went and did it again!

At that, the decision was made. The Professor asked me to photograph the damage section. I understand they are going to claim it as proof that the tomb was damaged before we opened it. Dr Spender was so infuriated with Sir John that I thought the old man was going to punch him. Robert would have been equally furious, but it did mean they had the excuse to open the tomb.

The crew of the aerostat decanted a bewildering variety of steam-powered lifting and moving contraptions and hoists and eagerly set about raising the capstone.

To all our surprise when the cover had been lifted it proved not to be an ossuary at all but a platform leading to a staircase.

While the men stood about gaping in astonishment Patty seized a hand-lamp, leapt over the ledge and explored the inside. I did not know whether to cheer her on or cry out at her for her recklessness. She was instantly followed by a most unseemly scramble as the men rushed to join her as she peered down into the darkness.

I managed to pause them amidst all the excitement to take some pictures of the intrepid team poised at the top of the steps. It took some cajoling by Patty to encourage Aelita Fontenelli to join the team inside the tomb. We all agreed that if anyone should share in that moment it should, by rights, be Aelita Fontenelli.

The Maddox was far too cumbersome to be carried down the narrow steps. Consequently I set about taking some pictures of the richly carved bas-relief images on the underside of the capstone. Patty and her father assured me that as soon as they discovered anything they would call me to picture it first. I remained with that old windbag Jahns, but he at least did make himself useful to my task repositioning the camera and holding the flash tray for me.

I must say that the task was not as easy as I initially thought: the carvings, viewed through the lens, appeared to writhe, an optical illusion caused by the light of course, but deeply frustrating. The Colonel was remarking to me that he found the imagery rather unsettling, repugnant almost, when it struck me that the over-arching thematic of the images was an immense monstrous cephalopod, its tentacles twisted through the various tableaus.

I was just about to remark upon it when one of the Colonel's men rushed up to the tomb, jumped over the wall and ordered us, in no uncertain terms, to drop everything and return to the Seren Bore. The Colonel, seized the soldier's bicep and they had a quick exchange of words, the man then launched himself down the steps into the darkness to warn the others.

The Colonel looked me in the eye and calmly said, "My dear Miss, it would appear we are about to be beset upon by brigands." It was strange how his demeanour instantly changed; the old windbag seemed to straighten up, discarded his cigar and drew his pistol. He refused to allow me to collect my equipment, insisting I go with him immediately.

At first, all I could think of was that I could not leave the camera, at that point it dawned on me that Patty was below with the others, I tried to protest that we could not leave them but the Colonel would not hear of it. So, grabbing as much equipment as I could, I followed the orders that Mr Franklin and the Captain had drummed into us should an alarm be raised.

We had just climbed out of the tomb when the Colonel swore loudly and roughly pushed me to the ground. Over our heads flew a small dirigible heading straight for the Seren Bore with guns blazing. I am sure it was the one that chased me from Tremorfa.

Around us, attackers had appeared from the cover of the dandelion fields and the hedges. The Colonel reacted like a man possessed, cursing loudly he leapt to his feet and strode forward shaking his fist and firing wildly. I watched him with open-mouthed amazement as he rallied his men and the crew. Roaring orders like a lion he seemed absolutely indifferent to the bullets flying around him.

The dirigible suddenly banked hard to avoid crashing into the Seren Bore's envelope, but as it did I saw the steam gun turret on the aerostat's foredeck jump into motion, it swung around and burst into life. The gun thundered and the vicious little sparking dirigible all but ceased to exist.

Everyone, ourselves and the attackers, stopped as if aware some sleeping monster had been awoken. I watched, fear boiling in the pit of my stomach, as the Seren Bore rolled to its port side above us. In my panic, I thought she was going to crash down, but it was not so, as she yawed those terrible steam cannons rotated their barrels towards those on the ground.

There was a small bay tree in the thicket on the edge of the dandelion field, behind which two of our attackers had sheltered. When the steam cannons opened fire that tree instantly disintegrated. Of the fate of the men hiding behind it, I dare not dwell. The steam cannons roared on with a ferocity that terrified me to my soul.

I could do nothing braver than scramble backwards on my belly like a frenzied lizard until my boots struck the side of the tomb. Suddenly Patty was beside me. I was so relieved I just wanted to hold on to her, but instead, she swept me up and launched me over the wall back into the cover of the tomb. Ursula, Aelita's handmaid caught me and placed me on my feet.

I must admit to being so distraught that I, like a child rescued from drowning, grabbed hold of Patty once she had leapt back over the wall and did not let go.

Only Dr Spender's voice cut through my hysteria. In a low, slow manner, he murmured, "Oh... my... dear... God!"

A huge airship, in black and red livery and bristling with guns, had hoved into sight.

Interview statement taken from Prisoner 452, Henry Avery, aka "Long Harry" on the 43rd, October. 29. Tharsis Panopticon.

Convicted crew member, "rigger," of the aerostat The Wyndeyer.

Cont.

The engines were stoked to blow so much steam the boilerplate was almost melting. The Captain had us rigged so's we'd vent steam to all sides. Drifting, the Wyndeyer looked like a bloody cloud.

We were being boiled alive inside it.

The diversion on the ground had worked just as the Captain had planned and we had the drop on them.

When we'd drifted as close as we could, we opened up the engines and came screaming at them full steam ahead, then hard to starboard.

We had worked it so many times before.

The wind was with us and we wos on them like a tick on a rat.

The Wyndeyer was as fast and as manoeuvrable as a spinning-jenny in the wind.

We were turning below them, guns prepped and ready to deliver a broadside that'd rip the keel right out of their ship, when suddenly we wos attacked.

No, I never saw it.

We were hauled t' starboard and dragged back. I went flying. I got a foot tied up in the riggin' then somethin' like a bloody tree trunk knocked me for six.

I don't remember much else.

Excerpt from;
Memoirs of Aelita, Lady Sydeian.
The Athenaeum of Harendrimar Tai.
Cont.

I could not make a sound nor move. It was as if I were rooted to the very spot whereupon I stood. I have, in all my life, never seen nor imagined such things. Oh, yes, I have read, voraciously even, those adventurers yarns and tales of daring do, books smuggled into me by friends who wished me to have some amusing distraction in my life, but I have never anticipated feelings like these, I was, in the same instant terrified, horrified even, and yet, elated.

We did not tarry a moment after the Black Tellurian soldier came down into the undercroft to warn us of danger, but made our orderly way back up the stairs, with the intention of obeying Mr Franklin's instructions to return to the ship.

Patty and I were last to reach the tomb entrance, though by then there was no possible opportunity to reach the aerostat as a battle had erupted about us. The Professor instructed us to take shelter in the lee of the tomb walls, and as I joined him I looked up to witness a small airship, that had been harrying the Seren Bore, destroyed in mid-air. The sound of the gunfire was worse than anything I have ever known, no grouse shoot can compare to the deafening noise of such guns.

Colonel Jahns was standing upright in the thick of the battle like some romantic hero from one of Mr Fenimore Cooper's frontier adventures. He stood firm and resolute, even as flaming pieces of the destroyed aircraft fell about him. His brave Black soldiers had come to his aid and were back to back about him, even the one with us, asked politely if he could be excused to join his leader, though he did not wait for the Professor's approval.

I have known Giovanni to speak extraordinarily badly of such Black Tellurians, and for them to be portrayed in dreadfully unflattering. spiteful even, terms in many of the books I have read, but these men were courageous beyond any crusader knight's equerry or French musketeer.

I was so mesmerised by the chaotic spectacle I had not noticed that Charity was no longer with us. It was only when the Professor called out her name that I realised she was on the ground outside the tomb. Patty wasted no time, she leapt up and sprang over the enclosing wall of the crypt with all the grace of a cat. She snatched up Charity like a child picking up a beloved doll and passed her back into the waiting arms of Ursula. She, then, with equal effortlessness, vaulted the wall back into the safety of the tomb.

In the presence of such reckless bravery, carried through in such an offhand manner, I felt ashamedly purposeless.

THE DANDELION FARMER

What am I but a mollycoddled trophy, a pampered pet whose knowledge of everything outside the walls of her luxurious prison either comes out of the books I have been allowed to read or from the mouth of my keeper.

Confronted with what I had just experienced and with all this violent chaos about me, I found a strange bitter mixture of anger, frustration and bile rising in my breast.

Outside our little stone shelter, all Hell was breaking loose as assuredly as if those terrible gates had been flung open. The steam cannons on the Seren Bore began to fire upon the corsairs around us. The sound of the rotation guns was deafening, stupefying even, as they ripped apart the earth, plants, shrubs, trees and any unfortunates that could not flee in time. Everything outside our shelter suddenly disappeared in a tornado of debris and dandelion petals.

I found myself still standing, struck to the spot by the chaos around me, when I noticed that behind the section of wall where the Professor crouched there had appeared the head, then chest, of a man. Not a member of our ship's crew, but a rough looking brute with a mess of greasy black hair, dressed in coarse clothing, his grubby hands seized the top of the wall and he began to hoist himself over into the crypt.

I could not believe that no one else was noticing this intruder. I suddenly knew it had fallen to me to act, to do whatever it required to protect us all. I thought to scream an alarm, but in that instant, I was aware of Giovanni's heavy pistol in my hand. My palm was sweating copiously, but my fine kid leather gloves allowed my grip to remain firm. In what felt like an age, I looked from the weapon to the man and, as Sir John had taught me to, pointed it at him. In that instant, he saw me. We looked into each other's eyes; what he saw in mine caused him not even a momentary flicker of hesitation, what I saw in his eyes horrified me.

I cannot describe what it feels like to have killed another human being, because the feeling is so unutterably revolting. His eyes and mine were still locked when the odic pistol screamed and the blast struck him squarely in the chest. It evaporated a huge hole through him and propelled his body back out of the confines of the tomb. Leaving only a dusty haze of glowing cinders to shower down upon poor Professor Flammarion where he crouched.

At that moment I understood whatever fate the Moirai are weaving for me, it will never lead me back to whence I came; I can never return home. I could never again be the docile, doe-eyed, Mrs Fontenelli, sitting in her gilded cage, to be gawped at like an exotic animal in a menagerie. I also realised that I had not the merest compunctions for the life now lost to me, or what my actions might, or might not, do to the social reputation of my husband. If he could be truly described as my husband in anything other than name.

It was Dr Spender's dread-filled cry that caught my attention. The others were all gazing out at the scene unfolding in the air above us. Patty cast a vulgar oath and pointed.

Behind the Seren Bore, out of a cloud of thick smoke and steam, a huge black and red bedecked aerostat in full sail had appeared. It was as if one of the ships out of Mr Stevenson's pirate stories had suddenly burst into existence, replete with bloody red banners depicting a grinning black skull wearing a top hat. If such a thing as an airship can lend itself to the description of evil, at that moment this was the quintessence of such malevolence. Charity, Patty and I clung to each other in fear that the pirate ship was about to ram the Seren Bore out of the air above us. Then, in the last breath, it veered to bring its guns to bear upon our helpless ship.

Patty emitted an endless stream of obscenities, most of which I did not comprehend the meaning of, but it gave clear vent to all our emotions, though it would have undoubtedly made the most hardened sailor blush.

The Seren Bore seemed to flounder unable to right itself to meet the threat, and we could all do nothing other than watch its doom.

The pirate airship gave a great ear-splitting discharge of steam as its gun ports opened. There was nothing that could stop the inevitable.

All I could do was implore God himself to intercede, because all else was lost.

Even now, as I write these words, what happened seems beyond my comprehension. I have spoken of these events many times before, but writing this to bear witness to what transpired, is challenging.

It was Charity that first pointed it out to us; beyond the edge of Edwin Ransom's field boundary, there was a dune field of a darker red sand. Out of which was now rising what I can only describe in terms of the plant shoot from one of Jack Spriggins' beans. The knurled, treelike, trunk, hurtled upwards growing in girth as it did height, and then another and another. As they reached the pirate's airship, they coiled and wrapped themselves around the rigging and masts.

Suddenly it dawned upon us what we were seeing; they were not beanstalk shoots, but the tentacles of some great monstrous beast.

Even Patty fell silent as we watched in astounded disbelief.

The colossal beast wrenched the pirate ship almost out of the air, tearing masts and sails from it. Disgorging men and equipment into the air. The aerostat fought to gain height its engines screeching like an animal in terror, but, as most of its indescribably vast body revealed from the dune, the monster gave a terrible howl and heaved the ship back towards it.

Then the firing began. Not from the desperate pirate ship, but from the Seren Bore, which had now righted herself and was mercilessly pouring fire into the heart of the stricken privateer.

The monster was now winning its trial of strength against its prey. It inexorably dragged the vessel down from the sky. At that moment the aerostat's boilers must have ruptured, or the Seren Bore's gunfire reached its magazine. The ship was wracked with thunderous internal detonations. Everything stopped, even the Kraken paused its attack, as if awaiting the inescapable.

Suddenly the whole airship was engulfed in one almighty explosion.

The ground around us shuddered as the monster fell back to the sand still clutching the burning remains of its prize.

As Sir John had described in the seminar, the creature began to throw up a whirlwind of sand to rebury itself, but the Seren Bore kept firing upon it. I could not fathom out why.

I was overcome by a heart-rending sense of pain and bewilderment.

I could feel her.

Brushing away the restraining hands, I clambered over the wall and ran out into the open, waving my arms wildly and shouting up at Captain Llewellyn to stop. Did they not understand?

I screamed at the top of my voice that they must stop.

Why did they not understand?

She was protecting us.

The Diary of Eleanor Athaliah Ransom (Mrs).
Wednesday 33rd

It is still quite early, but I shall write this down now, lest something untoward should happen later in the day.

After breakfast this morning Carstairs came to me bearing the little silver card tray, we had had a caller. A "gentleman," though upon reflection, I am disinclined to use such a term, had come to the front gate and presented his calling card. By the expression upon Carstairs' face, I immediately feared the worse. I looked at the sliver of thick embossed pasteboard on the salver. Sensing my alarm, Carstairs reassured me, "He was alone, Madam, and on horseback. We ensured he left immediately."

I asked if it was definitely him. Carstairs nodded solemnly, "Most definitely, Madam. Karl confirmed it; He was a tall, gaunt gentleman, with a frontiersman's moustache, dressed head-to-toe in black, with a long duster and one of those hats they affect. Somewhat the 'cowboy,' I believe is the term."

I asked if he requested for any message to be conveyed.

"Fortunately no, Madam, for I could barely understand his accent. He merely wished to leave his calling card."

I reached towards the card apprehensively, lest by some trick it suddenly turned into a viper and strike at my hand, and lifted it from the tray.

I would never have thought that a thing as simple as a visiting card could be so perturbing. It was a simply designed thing of good quality with a thick black border around the edge. I took a long breath and examined the legend imprinted upon it in fine printer's script;

Captain Lucius A. Everheart

Frontier Battalion of Texas Rangers, Rtd.

Settler of Accounts

It was only then, as I held it, that I noticed the bottom right-hand corner was folded back. Not by accident or wear and tear in the owner's pocket, but deliberately and crisply. If it was not for

Mamma's passing I would have probably not even have noticed it, let alone understood its meaning, but now I know exactly what message it conveyed; Condolences.

Condolences upon the death of a child.

The End of First Collection

21815169R00258

Printed in Great Britain
by Amazon